OAKEN

Book One

of

The Underground Series

by Melody Robinette

This is a work of fiction. Names characters, places and incidents either are the product of my imagination or are used fictitiously and any resemblance to actual persons living or dead, business establishments, events, or locales is entirely coincidental.

Copyright © 2015 Melody Robinette
Cover illustration and jacket design by Nathalia Suellen
Editing by Todd Barselow
Interior Layout by Author's HQ

ISBN-13: 978-1507816417

ISBN-10: 1507816413

For my mom, who believed in me before I did. We've shared many firsts, so here is another one. My first book. Thanks for being the first person I call when I get a new idea, the first person to read each and every story, and the first Outsider to fall in love with The Underground.

ACKNOWLEDGEMENTS

Before you begin this story, you should know that you wouldn't even be reading it if it hadn't been for some very important people.

Eva, for giving me my first journal and pushing me to start writing.

My grandparents, for always, always rooting for me and for being some of the first readers of everything I write.

My enthusiastic beta readers/students: Michelle, Miranda, Cristian, Dalia, Kayla, and Adriana.

My dad, Jessica, Yvonne, Tara, Kason, Kynedy, Isabella, and Jack for being my cheer squad and humoring me when I talked about my book oh so long ago.

Autumn, for being my first young reader and sharing her name with my favorite character.

Janera Naron and Hettie Hicks for instilling a love of English and writing in my high school years and inspiring me to become an English teacher myself.

Vaun, for introducing me to the world of self publishing and for being my best writing buddy.

Catie, wherever you are, for being my very first reader and the reason I came up with this story in the first place. I hope Anna Libson is doing well.

All the members of Writers' Chapter for being totally awesome.

Ben, for always supporting me and loving me and being the best friend and husband in the ever.

Finally, to the people who literally made this book possible with their overwhelming generosity: Vaun Murphrey, Rick Ennis, Kathy and Chris, Mark Tower, Kate Diehl, Ashley Rea, Alec Campos, Deena Garland, Eva Harder, Ginger Sanders, Mark Williamson, Michelle Chavez, Liliana Vasquez, Dad and Jessica, Jacki Robinette, and Amy M. You guys have no idea how much you all mean to me and how eternally grateful I am to every single one of you. Thank you, thank you, thank you.

Before Everything

In retrospect, Autumn could not have chosen a worse night to get drunk for the first time.

"So, you're Luke's sister, right?" asked a senior jock with half-closed eyelids, who was much drunker than Autumn. She nodded, taking another gulp of the poison her brother had mixed up for her. "Heh. Twins. But you don't look anything like him. I mean, Luke is so tall and gangly and you are so...not," he said with a wink. "Not saying you're fat, just saying you've got curves. Good curves." Autumn downed the rest of her drink. "I don't usually go for redheads, but for you I think I can make an exception."

"Okay. Time to go, Rose," Autumn's brother Luke said from behind her, shooting the crestfallen jock a warning look.

"Rose? I thought your name was Autumn," the jock said, ignoring Luke.

"It's his nickname for me. My middle name."

"Roses are pretty," the jock said with a hiccup.

"Leaving. Now," Luke said, pulling Autumn off of the couch and out to the car.

"Are you sure you can drive right now?" Autumn asked Luke, her words slurring slightly, something she was not accustomed to. Her head swam in the alcohol and she wanted nothing more than to be in her bed. She was *never* drinking again. Ever.

"I drive better drunk than sober," Luke said, laughing as he turned the key in the ignition, his old Ford pickup roaring to life.

"I can't believe I drank so much," Autumn said, putting her face in her hands. "I was supposed to be the DD."

"Live a little, Rose!" Luke said. "Save people tomorrow."

"Hey, Oaken! Y'all leavin'?" a voice called from outside. Autumn didn't bother to look at who it was. She just cradled her head in her hands.

"Yeah, man. Our parents are early risers. They'll kill us if they find out we went to this party," Luke said.

"Lame!" the guy yelled before tripping over a beer bottle.

With that, Luke floored the gas, kicking up a wave of gravel, and sped down the dirt road leading back into their small town. A line of pink appeared on the horizon, whispering that the sun was not far behind.

"Hurry, Luke. I bet Mom and Dad are already up," Autumn said.

"Chill out. It's the weekend. They'll want to sleep in."

The tires squealed in protest as Luke turned a curve sharply, throwing Autumn against the car door.

"Slow down! You're gonna get us killed."

"You were just telling me to hurry! Make up your damn mind."

Finally, Autumn could see their small blue house in the distance. No lights shone through the windows. Their parents were still asleep. Luke flew into the circular driveway and quickly killed the loud engine to avoid waking their parents.

"Don't slam your—" Luke began as Autumn banged her door shut. "—door."

"Oops."

"Nice, Rose."

"Sorry!" she said in a harsh whisper.

Luke rolled his eyes and walked around the perimeter of the house to the window they had escaped from several hours ago. It was still cracked a few inches and Luke slowly slid the glass up, trying not to make a sound. He climbed into his bedroom, Autumn right behind him, listening for a sign that their parents were awake, but the air was thick with silence.

"I can't believe we actually got away with it," Autumn said.

"Yeah, with you slamming doors and everything," Luke said, sending her another annoyed glance. "I'm gonna go make sure they're still in bed."

Suddenly a cold chill washed over Autumn, like she had just been dunked into a tub of ice water. Her breath caught in her chest and her eyes temporarily clouded over.

"Rose? Are you okay? Maybe you should go to bed. This *is* the first time you've been drunk, after all," she heard Luke say, sounding far away.

"Something's wrong," she managed to say.

"With you?"

"No, I mean, I don't know. I just got a really bad feeling all of a sudden."

"Maybe you're about to hurl." Autumn shot Luke an annoyed look and he laughed. "I'm going to see if Mom and Dad are still sleeping. Here's a trashcan...just in case."

"Gross." Autumn groaned, collapsing onto Luke's bed as he tiptoed out of the room.

Her eyes slid shut, sleep threatening to overtake her, when she heard Luke let out a soul-shaking cry from the other room. Eyes flying open, Autumn sat upright, her heart thumping in her chest.

"Luke?" she called out.

Sporadic footsteps resounded in the hallway and Autumn waited, wide-eyed and terrified. Luke stumbled and clasped the doorway for support. The expression on his face petrified her.

"Luke, you're scaring me. What's going on?"

He opened his mouth to speak, but merely choked, letting out a sob.

"What?" Autumn cried, her voice rising. "What happened?"

He sobbed something unintelligible. The only word Autumn could make out was "dead."

Autumn and Luke stood outside, watching as their entire small town's police force—and the neighboring towns' forces as well—marked their house off with yellow crime scene tape. The first murder in nearly thirty years. The town sheriff, a man with a bulging gut and brown, water-stained teeth approached them with a morose look on his face.

"I'm afraid there was nothing we could do, kids," he said. "They're gone."

Autumn's heart dropped and her body went numb. She felt like she was falling. This couldn't be happening. It just couldn't.

"Who did this?" asked Luke in a dead voice.

"We're still investigating that, son."

"*Why?*" Autumn said, barely audible. She wanted to say more, but the words wouldn't form. Her brain didn't seem to be working correctly. It was as if the world was spinning in slow motion—or maybe the world was the same as ever and she was the one lagging behind.

"I can't say for sure, but it appears to be a random act of violence. It was simply bad luck." *Bad luck*, Autumn thought. "It's strange. There don't seem to be any signs of forced entry," the sheriff continued.

Luke's face went white and he whispered, "The window."

"What's that, son?"

"We—we snuck out through the window last night. We left it open."

The sheriff frowned, looking at the ground, but said nothing.

"We have no family now," Autumn whispered, the realization of this statement hitting her with such force that she had trouble standing upright.

"I was told that it was written in your parents' will that your next of kin lives in some town in Ireland. Arrangements are being made to get y'all over there soon after the funeral."

"*Ireland?*" the twins said in unison.

ONE YEAR LATER

ARBOR FALLS

King Olympus Oaken sat on his wooden throne wearing a dazed expression, his mind clearly somewhere else. In a different place, a different time. A year had passed since his son Alexander had been killed, but the hurt was still the same. The hole in his heart still remained. Just as fresh. Just as jagged and unfilled.

Amid the hurt lay bitter regret. Why hadn't he stopped Alexander from leaving the Underground? Why had he allowed his son to abdicate the throne? To leave the Underground? To live in the Outside? Olympus's only consolation had been that Alexander and his family were truly safe from Vyra. But that security was more than false. He should have known that she would go after them. He had been a fool.

"Sir?" a voice said. "You asked to see me?"

Olympus looked up to find his young guard, Avery Burke, standing before him looking apprehensive.

"Yes, Mr. Burke. Thank you for arriving so quickly. How is your mother?"

Avery's face fell. "She's…she's been better."

Olympus nodded gravely. "She is the last of the Dream Communicators in the kingdom. I need her to get a message to my grandchildren in Ireland. Do you think she would be able to handle that?"

A crease formed between Avery's brows. "I think so."

Olympus nodded. "Thank you, Mr. Burke. That is all."

"Sir?"

"Mm?"

"What message do you want her to get to them?"

Olympus's hazel eyes met Avery's gray ones. "That it is time for them to come home. She can send it in any way she sees fit. Just tell her to get them home."

The Dream

CHAPTER ONE

It has been said that a dream is a wish your heart makes. But, if this were true, Autumn Oaken's dreams would have been filled with comforting visions of her parents. Alive. Happy. Instead, though, she was haunted every night by the same dream...and her parents were nowhere to be found.

Tall trees towered over Autumn as if she was an ant surrounded by blades of grass. After countless nights of visiting this dream forest she was still hypnotized by the prismatic rainbow of flowers, rocks, and gargantuan trees.

Autumn followed a winding dirt path through a thick gathering of trees and under a natural arch made of twisted branches and vines. The path opened up into a clearing where a magnificent shimmering waterfall spilled into a still lake. A series of stones appeared just above the surface of the lake, creating a path to the sheet of falling water. The stones were smooth on top and Autumn skipped easily from one to the other, eventually landing on the rock directly before the waterfall, which was even more extraordinary than the surrounding forest. It did not splash or sputter. There was no breaking water at its base. It was calm. Quiet. Resembling a thick sheet of glass that glistened and moved. Autumn gazed at herself in the reflection of the water.

Someone gazed back.

A young man. Golden hair framed his angular face and his eyes were a stormy gray. The waterfall cascaded around him, yet somehow he was completely dry. A strange feeling resonated in the pit of Autumn's stomach, a sort of gravitational pull. She stretched out a hand trying to reach for him. Suddenly he was gone.

Teetering on the edge of the rock, Autumn stretched further, desperately hoping that this time she would manage to touch the veil of water. Maybe even pass through it into the realm of the gray-eyed boy. It felt as if the air around the waterfall was pushing her away like two magnets repelling against one another. It took all her energy to attempt to push through the invisible wall. Her fingertips were inches away when she heard a distant sound. Someone was calling her name.

Autumn turned to look over her shoulder, but the only thing behind her was the brightly colored forest. Darkness engulfed her as the voice calling her name grew louder...

"*Rose.* Rose! Get up!" Luke said, giving her a rough nudge. "What're you doing?"

Autumn's eyes opened blearily to see her hand stretched out in front of her as if she was trying to reach for something. She lay in the shadow of a willow tree near Blarney Castle, far away from her dream waterfall and the gray-eyed boy. Forcing herself back into reality, she glared up at her brother.

Luke looked down at her with an amused expression, his shaggy red hair falling into his hazel eyes, a mirror image of her own. "Sleeping on your lunch break? You are such a bad worker."

"I fell asleep r—r—reading," Autumn said through a yawn.

"So, you're a bad worker *and* a nerd. Come on, you have an afternoon full of fat, sweaty tourists ahead of you. Get up," he said before trudging back up the path to Blarney Castle.

Autumn ran a hand through her tangled curls. Every time she was pulled away from her dream world she felt a little disoriented, as if she was still standing on the flat rock facing the smooth sheet of water. Somehow, she found comfort in the familiar scene of her dream, frustrating as it was. For the past year everything had been so crazy and out of her control that she found herself looking forward to the predictable nightly escape.

After all, adjusting to a life without parents was never easy.

Thirteen months had passed since that unspeakable day. Autumn and Luke now lived in Blarney, Ireland, with a woman their father had known in his college years named Mrs. King. With their parents gone, she was the closest thing to family they had. Mrs. King was rather strange. At first, Autumn figured it was just an Irish thing, but the longer she lived in Ireland, the more suspicious she became of the old woman. For instance, she would enter the kitchen and nothing would be ready. Then, ten minutes later, Mrs. King would call them to dinner and an elaborate feast would be on the table. Luke didn't seem to care about this one bit. He just liked to eat and told Autumn she was paranoid every time she mentioned it.

Glancing into a small mirror she kept in her bag, Autumn smoothed down her disarrayed curls and stuffed the mirror, along with her book, back into her bag. Reading was her way of escaping when she was not in her dreamland. Luke never hesitated to make fun of her for it by saying things like, "Why don't you try reading more romance novels? They might teach you how to get a boyfriend."

Slinging her bag over her shoulder, Autumn left the shade of the willow tree and rushed up the dirt path to Blarney Castle, where she and Luke had been working all summer. Autumn ran the little merchandise shop full of Blarney Castle postcards, coffee mugs, and cheesy t-shirts that said things like "Kiss My Blarney Stone."

Luke worked at the top of the castle where the tourists kiss the stone. It was his job to hold them as they laid on their backs and were maneuvered upside down to press their lips against the supposedly magical stone that promised to give the kisser a lifetime of eloquence—a word Autumn had had to explain to her brilliant brother.

But the twins' mental lexicons were not the only things that differed between them. Physically, they looked more like distant cousins than anything. Luke was tall and thin, while Autumn was a whole head shorter and had curves that she had finally given up hiding under sweatshirts last year. Luke's hair was flaming red and Autumn's was closer to auburn. The only features they shared were their hazel eyes—a speckled mix of brown, green, and gold—and a strangely shaped birthmark on their wrists. An inherited mark. Their father had it too.

After work, Autumn and Luke decided to stop by the local pub—a popular haunt of the high school age kids—next door to the cottage in which they now lived.

The pub was dimly lit and the heavy smell of ale and spirits hung in the air along with the greasy scent of pub food. A game of hurling flashed on the television screen and the bartender laughed at a patron's joke as he expertly poured a pint of Guinness. The bartender had a head full of blonde hair, reminding Autumn of the golden-haired boy in her dreams. If only she could reach him...

"Earth to Autumn," Luke said, breaking through her reverie.

"Huh?" Autumn said, in a daze.

"I said I'm going to go get us a table."

Autumn nodded and approached the bar, ordering two sodas. When she went looking for her brother, she found him talking the ear off of an attractive brunette who looked like she would rather be undergoing a root canal than talking to him.

Not wanting to make things any more awkward for him than they clearly already were, Autumn took a seat at a different table and pulled a book out of her bag, something she rarely left the house without.

Luke liked to think of himself as a ladies' man, but girls never seemed able to get past his red hair and nervous chatter. Autumn tried to read her book, but her brother's constant rambling proved to be increasingly difficult to block out.

"So you've lived in Ireland all of your life?" he asked the girl. Autumn glanced sideways to see the brunette nod warily at him. "That's cool. I've lived in Texas most of *my* life, but I think I already said that. Then my parents were killed and my sister and I had to come live here. It's not so bad, I guess, but I do miss Texas. The people were a lot nicer there—not that Irish people aren't nice, just not as nice as Texans. Y'all have really cool accents, though. My dad was actually from Ireland, but his accent didn't really sound all that Irish. It was a little different, like a mix of Irish and English and American and...stuff."

The brunette, looking slightly overwhelmed, spoke for the first time. "Oh."

"So, do you have a boyfriend?" Luke continued, going in for the kill.

The girl's eyes widened slightly at this, as if she knew where this was going. "Er... no."

Luke lit up. "Really? That's crazy cause I don't have a girlfriend either. Weird, huh?"

"Yeah, weird. I—er—really have to be going now. See you." She stood and rushed out the door.

Luke's face fell dejectedly as he came to sit beside Autumn.

"Nice," she said, suppressing a laugh.

"Do you think it was something I said?" Luke asked, looking genuinely confused.

"Maybe you should talk a little less next time..."

"But she wasn't talking at all. I had to fill the silence."

That night Autumn returned to the familiar scene of her dream. The pure, slightly musky scent of nature filled her like smoke, evoking long-repressed memories. Memories of her father. It smelled just like him. Like he used to.

Suddenly she stopped walking. The young man had materialized behind the waterfall. A vision of gold and gray and ivory.

Autumn skipped nimbly across the flat stones, landing lightly on the last. The boy was still there, untouched by the surrounding water, his angular features distorted by the shimmering waterfall. Somehow he seemed more solid than before. More real.

His lips parted and he uttered one sentence. "Go to the castle."

Autumn's heart skipped a beat. This was the first time the gray-eyed boy had spoken to her.

"What castle?" Autumn asked in earnest. "Blarney?"

But the boy vanished before she could get an answer. As he disappeared Autumn thought she saw his head dip in a nod.

With a start, she awakened.

Blarney Castle

CHAPTER TWO

Autumn rushed through getting ready, skipping makeup and breakfast as she clomped down the stairs.

"Where are you going?" Luke asked from the living room where he was playing one of his war video games that Autumn hated so much.

"Blarney," Autumn said in passing.

"But we don't work today," he called as Autumn dashed out the door.

"Bye, Mrs. King!" Autumn called to the old woman who was pulling weeds out of the flower beds.

Mrs. King waved cheerfully at her, wearing a peculiar expression that Autumn recognized as someone who knew something they weren't letting on. *She's so strange*, Autumn thought.

She was halfway down the street when she heard Luke call, "Hey, wait up!"

Reluctantly, she slowed her pace enough for him to catch up to her.

"What're you doing?" he said.

"You don't have to be with me all the time, you know."

"Yeah, I do," Luke said in a serious tone.

He hadn't admitted it, but Autumn knew that he felt a sense of responsibility for her now that he was essentially the man of the family

"Fine," she said. "Just...walk faster."

"Why are you going to Blarney on our day off?"

Autumn opened her mouth to answer, but stopped when she thought of how crazy she would sound. "I—I just want to explore the grounds."

"Explore the grounds? We've done that thousands of times. Will you just tell me what's going on?"

She sighed in defeat. " Okay... You know that dream I've been having?"

"The waterfall one?" Luke asked. Autumn nodded. "What about it?"

"Well, he told me to go to the castle. This is the closest castle, so this is where I'm going. I know this dream has to mean something."

"Wait, *who* told you to go to the castle?"

"This guy..."

"So, first you're obsessed with the men in your books and now you're chasing guys you meet in your dreams? Come on, Autumn. This isn't healthy."

"You can leave anytime you want. I didn't exactly beg you to join me."

Luke simply shook his head in exasperation, but stayed by Autumn's side.

When they reached Blarney, Autumn headed straight for the gardens near the castle. She assumed that, if there was a waterfall that she had not seen, she would find it there. After all, there couldn't be a waterfall inside the actual castle. But after searching every tree, every path, every rock in the gardens, Autumn was forced to accept the fact that her dream waterfall was not there.

"Can we go home now?" Luke asked after an hour of following her around the grounds.

Turning in a slow circle for the hundredth time, Autumn sighed and nodded. She had been so sure that the gray-eyed boy's message had been real. Maybe Luke was right...maybe these dreams were making her crazy.

As they walked back past the castle, Autumn's eyes were drawn to a gaping hole in the crumbling stone wall. She had seen it before, but had never thought to venture into it. "I wonder where that goes," she said out loud.

"Probably nowhere," Luke grumbled.

"Let's find out," Autumn said, pulling her brother towards the dark hole.

The tunnel was located next to a dilapidated stone staircase that was blocked off by a barred iron door. They had to hunch over to enter the passage, which was pitch black. Luke pulled his cell phone out to light the way. In her hurry to get to the castle, Autumn had left hers lying on her bedside table. Sharp stones littered the ground and the farther they went, the colder the air became. They walked like this until they reached the end of the passage.

"It's a dead end," Autumn said in disappointment.

Luke frowned. "Well, this seems pointless."

Approaching the wall, Autumn pressed her hand against the rough stone, looking for a crack or fissure. Or maybe a rock jutting out of the wall that doubled as a handle. A vibration tickled her hand and she leaped back, frowning at the wall in confusion. Suddenly the rock shuddered and crumbled away, light pouring into the pitch-black passage.

Before them was a dense forest full of colossal trees and flowers of every color. And a path leading beyond Autumn's field of vision. Ireland was full of forests and flowers and other greenery, but not like this. This forest was different. Ethereal. Yet Autumn felt like she had been here before.

"Whoa…" Luke said. "Okay, what's going on? This shouldn't be here. It *can't* be."

"Come on," Autumn said, stepping forward.

"But—"

"Are you scared?"

"Of what? Some trees?" He laughed, but Autumn could hear the apprehension in her brother's voice.

"Then come on," she said.

They walked cautiously forward. Autumn glanced off to her right and stopped dead in her tracks. Luke walked into the back of her, almost knocking both of them to the ground.

"What the—?"

"Luke, I've been here before! This is where I go in my dream."

Autumn dashed off the path, weaving through a group of closely spaced trees with Luke following close behind her. "Watch, there's about to be a waterfall up ahead."

"If there was a waterfall nearby, we'd be able to hear it."

Her heart pounded in her chest when she saw the arch of vines and branches she had been searching for. She ran under this and slammed to a stop once again. This time Luke was going too fast and they both went crashing to the ground.

"Autumn, what the—?"

Before them was the very waterfall Autumn had dreamed about every night for weeks. It was all the same down to the last rock. But the gray-eyed boy was nowhere to be found. For a moment she wondered whether or not *this* was a dream...

"Autumn! What are you doing?"

Glancing down, she realized that she had started walking across the flat stones that led to the waterfall simply out of habit. She continued to skip from rock to rock ignoring her brother's attempts to coax her back to the safe ground.

"Rose!" Luke said, a note of panic in his voice.

"It's okay! I'm just going to try to touch the waterfall."

"What? Why?" Luke began edging toward the first rock.

Autumn blocked his voice out. She had to concentrate. This was it, the moment she had been obsessing over for so long. Excitement and anticipation filled her like a tide pool. She was now at the edge of the waterfall, her breathing coming in quick gasps.

Holding her breath, she slowly reached out her hand.

Revelations

CHAPTER THREE

The moment Autumn's fingertips touched the water, her world turned upside down. Quite literally, in fact. She was falling. Falling up, or down, or nowhere in particular. Colors flashed around her like a prism in the sunlight.

Just as she was beginning to fear that she would never stop falling, she landed, sprawled out on a soft bed of moss in front of the waterfall she had been standing before not seconds ago—or perhaps it had been longer. But this could not be the same waterfall because this was definitely not the same forest.

As she sat up, her breath caught in her chest. She was sitting on top of a raised hill overlooking a strange city made up of...tree houses? Surely that was the only way to describe them. But they were not average tree houses made from scrap wood with a rope ladder and a tire swing. They were actual *homes*.

It looked as though someone had hollowed out each individual tree, cut holes for the windows and doors, and moved in. Only, these trees were larger and grander than any Autumn had ever seen, dwarfing even the California Redwoods.

But more remarkable than the tree homes was what could only be described as a tree *castle*, towering over the tree town like a lone skyscraper.

"Wow," Autumn breathed, shaking her head in disbelief.

A strong breeze blew through Autumn's hair and seconds later Luke landed beside her on the bed of moss. He sat up and looked around wildly, his eyes landing on his sister.

"What the hell just happened? You just disappeared! And then I—I just started falling and—" He stopped, taking in the sight before them. "Whoa. Where...are we?"

"I don't know, but I think it's safe to say that we aren't in Ireland anymore."

"Hello?" A lilting voice emerged from the shadowy foliage. "Is everything all right?"

Autumn and Luke jumped in surprise and whipped around to see a tall, slender girl with sparkling blue eyes and flowing platinum hair. In her hands was a woven basket full of an assortment of different colored flowers. There was something odd about her. Something Autumn couldn't quite put her finger on.

As the girl moved closer, the twins scrambled up from their seated positions. "I don't think I've ever seen you two here before. Are you from Rose Valley?"

"Uh, no. I'm Autumn, and this is my brother—"

"Luke," he said, smiling smoothly.

Autumn rolled her eyes. They had just fallen through a magical waterfall, landing in the middle of some tree town and he still had it in him to flirt. Typical.

"I'm Crystal," the girl said warmly. "Where are you off to?"

"Actually, we aren't even sure where we *are*," Autumn said. "We were just in front of this waterfall and—I don't know what happened—but I touched the water and I just started falling and—"

Luke cut in. "—and then I went after her. I just thought she'd slipped or something, but now that I think about it, she looked like she just disappeared into thin air. Then I landed next to her over there." He pointed at the spongy moss in front of the waterfall.

Crystal regarded them carefully now, her eyebrows knitting together. "So...where are you from?"

"We're from Texas, originally," Luke answered.

"Then our parents were killed and we were sent to live in Ireland with this woman we didn't even know," Autumn said.

Crystal's mind seemed to be whirring as she looked from the twins, to the waterfall, and back. "If you don't mind me asking, what is your surname?"

"Oaken," Autumn and Luke said at the same time.

Crystal's eyes widened. "Seriously? Oh my goodness! I can't believe—wait," she said, sounding suddenly suspicious again. "May I see your wrist?"

"Our wrist? Why do you want to see our wrist?" Luke said, now sounding suspicious himself.

"It's okay," Autumn said, offering her right hand. "Here."

Crystal turned Autumn's hand palm up, gaping at what she saw. What before had only been a thin faded birthmark was now a dark image—as if branded into her skin like a tattoo. At first it just looked like a bunch of thick, jumbled lines. Then she realized that it was a rose.

Crystal's face broke, once again, into a wide smile. "You have the Royal Mark. That means you really are Oaken," she said, looking at them in wonder. "I can't believe it."

"How do you know who we are?" Autumn asked, reclaiming her shaking hand. Luke was examining his own wrist with a bewildered expression.

"Everyone knows who you are here, of course! No one knew you would be returning so soon. Well, the king did hint at it, but we thought surely—I'm rambling, aren't I? I'm sure you already know all of this, anyhow." Autumn and Luke shook their heads, wearing dazed expressions. "You mean your parents never told you?"

"Told us what?" Luke said.

"Oh, gosh, I don't know if I should say... Well, you deserve to know. But if no one told you—"

"Told us *what*?" Luke said more forcefully.

Crystal sighed. "That you aren't exactly human. Not full human, anyway."

Luke laughed and looked at Autumn, rolling his eyes at Crystal. Autumn wasn't as amused. "If we aren't human, what are we?"

"You're elves. *Royals.* Your grandfather is actually the king of—"

"Whoa, whoa, whoa," Luke said, holding up both hands. "Royal *what*?"

"Elves. I know it must sound crazy to you right now, but it's true. We exist. *You* exist."

An incredulous look passed between the twins.

Elves, Autumn thought in disbelief. This was ridiculous. Elves didn't exist. Autumn may have been an avid reader and a hopeless dreamer, but she had enough sense not to *believe* in the fairytales she read. As much as she wished magic could exist, she knew it couldn't—could it?

Taking a closer look at Crystal, Autumn noticed that she didn't exactly look "normal." In fact, the more Autumn looked at her, the less human she appeared. Hair as smooth as silk, teeth unnaturally white, eyelashes so thick they could be false, and skin with an ethereal glow. Then she noticed Crystal's ears. They were pointed, though not the size Autumn would have assumed an elf might have. She shook her head clear. She shouldn't be assuming anything about elves because that was crazy. As crazy as following the orders of a boy she met in her dreams.

Luke was the first to speak. "Aren't elves supposed to live in the North Pole?"

Crystal laughed, rolling her eyes. "Sure. Elves are supposed to be short people with enormous pointy ears, right? Santa's helpers? Makers of shoes, toys, cookies? Oh, and Snow White befriended seven of them in some fairy tale."

"Those were dwarves, actually," Autumn muttered.

"Yeah, but elves don't exist, though," Luke said. "Those are all fairy tales and myths and stories that people have made up over the years. They aren't actually *real*."

"Every fairy tale generally has a little bit of truth behind it. Besides, I could say the same thing about you. Down here, Outsiders are the creatures of fairy tales," Crystal said, looking slightly offended.

"Outsiders?" Autumn said.

"Oh, right. You call yourselves humans. 'The Outside' is what we call the human world and we call humans 'Outsiders'," Crystal clarified.

"Do you honestly expect us to believe any of this? Okay, so you've got pointy ears. That doesn't prove anything," Luke said.

"Watch." Crystal pointed her index finger at a nearby rosebush. With a resounding crack, the bush instantly turned into solid ice.

Autumn gasped and Luke stared at the crystal bush with a look of horror.

"You're not an elf...you're a witch!" he said, retreating hastily until his back was pressed against the trunk of a tree.

Crystal looked exasperated now. "NO. I am an *elf*. My Power is Ice."

"If our grandfather is an elf, then wouldn't our parents be elves?" Autumn asked, unable to tear her eyes away from the ice bush.

"Stop humoring her, Autumn," Luke said.

"Your father was an elf. He was next in line for the throne, but he didn't want to be king. So he traveled to the Outside, where he met your mother—"

"This is ridiculous. Come on, Autumn. Let's get out of here." Luke began tromping back towards the waterfall.

Autumn slowly turned to follow him, then hesitated, glancing again at the bush that now looked like an elaborate ice sculpture. She looked down at the mark on her inner wrist. The same as her brother's. The same as her father's. She had never thought much about it, just assumed it was a birthmark. But, then again, birthmarks weren't hereditary.

"No," Autumn said in a quiet voice.

Luke whipped around to look at his sister. "What?"

"I'm not leaving. I believe her," Autumn said louder, planting her feet.

"You can't be serious."

"I am."

Luke stared at Autumn with his mouth agape, clearly questioning her sanity.

"Are you really telling me that you believe we are elves?" he said.

"I don't know what we are," Autumn said. "All I know is that I don't want to go back there. Our parents are gone, everything we know has changed, and we are all alone. We have nothing to go back to. What if Crystal is right about all of this? And what if we really do have a grandfather here? I want to know the truth. There's a reason I've been dreaming about that waterfall for a month. It brought me here. It brought *us* here."

Luke listened to her with a contemplative frown on his face, one foot planted on a stepping-stone and one on the spongy moss.

"What was our father's name?" Luke said, turning to Crystal.

"Alexander Olympus Oaken."

This seemed to take Luke aback. Clearly he had not expected her to know this fact.

"Okay. If we are elves then why don't we look like you?" he said, still looking highly suspicious. "Why don't we have the hair and the skin and the—the ears?"

"You will soon. You've been in the Outside too long for you to transform back automatically. The longer you're in the Outside, the longer it takes to return to your elf form. You should be completely transformed in a few days."

"Oh, don't worry, we won't be staying that long," he said.

"But we *will* be staying for a little while?" Autumn asked hopefully.

"Long enough to get some answers," he said, looking like he was already regretting this decision. Autumn smiled in triumph. "But you better not turn me into a toad or something," Luke said to Crystal.

"I swear," she said with a chuckle.

"Now, where is this *supposed* grandfather of ours?" he asked.

Crystal smiled and with a wave of her hand said, "Follow me."

Arbor Falls

CHAPTER FOUR

"**W**hat do you call this place, anyway?" Luke asked as Crystal led them along a path down the steep hill.

"Arbor Falls," Crystal said. "The Elf Capitol."

"So, there are other elf towns here?" Autumn asked.

"There are several. Arbor Falls is the biggest of all the elf territories. But elves aren't the only creatures in the Underground."

"The Underground?" Autumn said, thinking that she should start writing down all of these new terms or she was bound to forget them.

"Yes. That's where we are."

"I thought we were in Arbor Falls," Autumn said, thoroughly confused.

"We are. There are many lands in the Underground, though. Arbor Falls is just one of them."

"Wait. Are you saying that we are actually underground?" Luke said. Crystal nodded. Autumn and Luke looked up at the blue, cloudless sky, the shining sun peeking through the leaves of the tall trees. "That's impossible," he said.

Crystal smiled. "Nothing's impossible."

"But the sky," Autumn said.

"The creatures here are not the only ones that have magical abilities, you know. The Underground has Powers of its own too."

"If this place was underground, people would know about it," Luke said.

"Why?" Crystal challenged. "Because Outsiders think they know everything? I believe, once upon a time, even the brightest Outsiders believed that the Earth was flat, did they not?"

Luke frowned and said, "Well yeah, but—"

"Outsiders only discover what the Undergrounders *allow* them to discover. We want to keep the Underground a secret, therefore it is impossible to detect. Outsiders don't have the ability to see the Underground because they don't have the ability to see magic. The Underground just looks like a bubbling mass of hot lava to them."

Luke shook his head, dropping the subject.

But Autumn wasn't done asking questions. "So, do you have other Powers?"

"Ice is my only Power. Each elf has just one. Some Powers are stronger and more, er, *impressive* than others, and some could hardly be considered a Power. My mother's, for example, is sewing. Other elves I know have Powers like baking or cleaning."

"Cleaning? Hey, maybe that will be your Power, Luke," Autumn said.

Luke made a face. Autumn imagined he was picturing himself in a French maid costume with a feather duster in his hand.

Crystal giggled. "I highly doubt that."

"If we stay, will we have Powers?" Autumn asked, ignoring Luke's snort.

"Of course. You're elves, after all—and royals, at that."

"How long will it take for them to appear?" asked Autumn.

"Elves discover their Power at different times. It just depends on the individual, but the Power usually shows up before they turn 13. If you were to stay—" she glanced warily at Luke, "you would probably learn your Power within a week or two, once your bodies have fully transformed and adjusted to being in the Underground."

The trio had now made their way into the heart of Arbor Falls. Autumn nearly developed a crick in her neck from attempting to view everything at once. They passed by a particularly eccentric looking tree house surrounded by strange flowers that Autumn had never seen before. The flora appeared to be stirring. Moving closer, she realized there were actually creatures inside of the petals.

"What are those?" Autumn asked, pausing. Inside the flowers were small, fairy-like creatures, all dancing, singing, or lounging around. Their skin and hair were the exact color of the flowers they inhabited.

"Those are petalsies. They're born from the flowers and live within the bud for the rest of their lives. They're vicious little creatures," Crystal said as one of the petalsies sunk its teeth into Luke's hand. He cursed under his breath and sucked on his finger, glaring at the little red petalsie who was smiling malevolently up at him.

"This is City Circle," Crystal told them as they reached the end of the dirt path. "The center of Arbor Falls."

Before them stood a grand marble fountain strategically placed in the middle of a wide circle of cobblestones surrounded by various shops with storefront windows full of displays and unique wooden signs hanging above the front doors.

They passed a bakery with a window full of delectable looking cakes, pies, cookies, strangely shaped cream puffs, and tarts filled with bright purple custard. They ambled by a bookstore, a dress shop, and a cozy looking coffee shop. Then a pet store with a display of what looked like different colored tiger cubs with wings. Two of the animals rolled around playing and a few of the others hovered near the window, looking out at the passersby with big eyes.

"What are those?" Autumn asked in awe.

"Tigerflies," Crystal said.

"They're so cute." Autumn laughed as two of the tigerflies began rolling around the display case, tugging at each other's ears.

"I'm allergic to cats," Luke said, looking at them with dislike.

As the three of them moved onward Autumn realized that she hadn't seen one vehicle, though there were tons of people—well, elves—dashing about the circle. Hardly anyone spared the twins a glance, but the few people that did notice them stopped what they were doing and stared.

"Do they know who we are too?" Autumn muttered to Crystal.

"No. You just still look like Outsiders, so you're probably freaking them out a little bit. It usually only takes us a few minutes to transform back into our elf forms, but you two show no signs of the transformation yet. Don't worry, though, they've all seen much stranger things down here. Trust me."

"Hey, Crys!" a voice called in their direction. Autumn turned to see a pale boy about their age with a head full of dark curls jogging up to them. "Have you done your Numbers proj—" He dropped off, apparently just having noticed that Crystal was not alone. "Outsiders?"

"Forrest, this is Autumn and Luke—er—Oaken."

Forrest's head snapped to Luke and then Autumn, his mouth dropping open.

"A pleasure to meet you my good sir." He shook Luke's hand and gave him a small bow before turning to Autumn. "And you my fair lady," he said kissing her hand as he bowed even lower.

Autumn pulled her hand back, perhaps a little too forcefully because Forrest looked slightly taken aback.

"Cut it out, Forrest," Crystal said, stifling a laugh. "They just found out they're royals, like, ten minutes ago." Forrest looked confused and Crystal sighed. "I'll explain later. And, yes, I've done my Numbers project and, no, you can't copy any of it."

Forrest gave her an exasperated look and turned on his heel, trudging back up the path.

"What's *his* Power?" asked Autumn, watching Forrest's retreating figure disappear up the path.

"Animal Communication."

"As in?" Autumn said.

"As in he can talk to animals and they can talk to him. Follow me," Crystal said, as if talking to animals was a normal, everyday occurrence around here. Autumn was beginning to think it probably was.

They turned onto a wide dirt road leading up to the front of the castle towering above them. A series of steps that appeared to be shaped from the wood of the tree rose up to a pair of grand oak doors. Carved into the wood on each door was a twisting knot with three points, reminding Autumn of the Celtic knots found throughout Ireland.

"Here we are, Arbor Castle," Crystal announced.

"How original." Luke snorted and then let out a grunt as Autumn elbowed him in the ribs.

Guarding the doors was a pair of burly, male elves dressed in red, standing with their arms crossed in front of their chests. They eyed the twins warily as Crystal led them up the wooden staircase.

"Hello, Miss Everly," the guard on the right said to Crystal, shooting another glance at Autumn and Luke.

"Sorry, Miss, you know there are no visitors allowed after hours," the guard on the left said.

"Boys, this is Autumn and Luke *Oaken*." She waved her hand at Autumn and Luke. "They're here to see their grandfather—the king."

The guards glanced from Autumn to Luke with suspicious looks on their faces.

"Show them your wrist," Crystal said as an aside to Autumn, who did as she was told.

The guards' mouths dropped open just as Forrest's had. One of the guards said, "Oh! Yes, of course. Welcome Prince Oaken, Princess Oaken."

They bowed and quickly stepped aside as Autumn and her brother exchanged surprised glances. As if by magic, the giant oak doors opened, permitting the three of them to enter Arbor Castle.

Arbor Castle

CHAPTER FIVE

Autumn and Luke followed Crystal into a grand room with high ceilings. If Autumn hadn't known better she would never have been able to tell that they were standing in the middle of a ginormous, hollowed out tree. She couldn't help but gaze around in awe. Every detail in the room was exquisite, from the crown moldings to the ornate furniture to the royal blue rug with golden fibers strewn throughout.

Approaching one of the light fixtures hanging on the wall, Autumn's head tilted curiously to the side as she examined it. It was a sconce filled with a strange undulating light that appeared to be neither fire nor electrical. She wondered if it was somehow lit by magic and smiled to herself at the thought.

"This is the waiting room for the subjects of Arbor Falls who have come to see the king during visiting hours. The throne room is through there," Crystal said, pointing to a pair of wooden doors as she made her way over to one of the claret-colored armchairs and plopped down, beckoning Autumn and Luke to join her. When Autumn sat down in the chair next to Crystal she sank into the cushion.

Luke folded his hands behind his head and lounged back, letting out a sigh of relaxation. "Okay, I may actually decide to stay here. Only, I'm never leaving this chair."

Crystal chuckled. "I'm sure that could be arranged. But if you think that chair is comfortable, wait until you sleep in your bed for the first time. I may only live in the roots of the castle, but the beds here are like sleeping on clouds. Maybe better."

"Well, yeah," Luke said, his eyes closed now. "Clouds are full of moisture. That would not be a pleasant sleeping experience."

"You live here?" Autumn asked Crystal, ignoring her brother.

"I'm a castle worker."

"What do you do?" Luke asked.

"I'm a couturier," she said and when she noted the vacant looks on the twins' faces she continued. "I make all the clothes for the staff and for the king. My mother is a couturier too. The best there is," she said with a proud smile. Then a look of comprehension dawned on her face. "Oh! *That's* why Olympus asked me to make all of those clothes a couple months ago. They were for you two!"

"He knew we were coming?" asked Autumn in surprise.

Crystal shrugged. "He must have."

"How?"

"The *magic* of the Underground," Luke mocked, causing Crystal to shoot him a look of annoyance that could rival the worst of Autumn's. Luckily he had not seen this due to his closed eyes.

The wooden doors leading to the throne room opened at that moment and another guard stepped inside the waiting room. "The King will see you now," he said.

Autumn, Luke, and Crystal followed the guard into a room even taller than the last and much wider. A long golden carpet led up to an empty throne that jutted out of the wall behind it, as if carved from the tree castle itself. Etched into the wood were more swirling designs that matched the stitching in the blue and gold rug.

A young man dressed in red stood next to the throne. Golden hair fell softly around his face, and his eyes were the color of steel. His gaze landed upon Autumn and she felt her breath catch in her chest. The gray-eyed boy quickly looked away, his strong jaw clenching.

It was *him*. The boy from her dreams.

Realizing her mouth was hanging open, she quickly snapped it shut.

"Who's that?" Autumn breathed.

Crystal leaned over and whispered, "That's Avery Burke. He's a guard here."

This surprised Autumn. Though his body was undoubtedly toned, his build was nothing compared to the burly men standing guard at the front doors.

"Really?" she said, unable to hide her surprise.

"His Power is Strength," Crystal said. "He's stronger than all the castle guards combined. An elf's Power doesn't necessarily define their physical appearance, it comes from within."

A door opened to the right of the throne and two more brawny guards entered the room.

"Announcing Olympus Orpheus Oaken, King of Arbor Falls," one of the guards said in a booming voice.

A tall, stout old man with long flaming red hair and a beard to match pushed through them. "Out of my way Rupert, Donald. I told you that was not necessary."

"Sorry, muh' lord," the man named Donald said, bowing.

"Where are my grandchildren? Ah!" He spotted the twins standing awkwardly beside Crystal.

Striding over, he gathered them in his arms and squeezed tightly. Just as Autumn was beginning to lose air supply he let go and held them at arm's length. "Let me look at you," he said. His hazel eyes were wet. "It's been years. Luke, you look so much like your father. I assume Mrs. King is not with you? We will send her a message, telling her you are safe."

Autumn felt a surge of guilt. She had completely forgotten about Mrs. King.

"You know her?" Luke asked.

"Indeed. She used to care for your father. She's an elf as well, but she chose to live above the Underground. Don't ask me why. I have never understood elves who would do such a thing, your father included."

"Our father never told us about any of this," Luke said, sounding slightly bitter.

Olympus nodded. "He thought he was protecting you."

"From what?" Autumn asked.

Olympus frowned. Autumn noticed a shift in the air. All of the elves seemed uncomfortable. Crystal wrapped her arms around herself and Avery tensed up.

"Perhaps we should sit…" Olympus said. "There are some things you need to know."

Vyra Vaun

CHAPTER SIX

Olympus, Autumn, and Luke sat in a corner of the throne room in a series of armchairs situated around a table set with tea and cakes. No one touched them.

"So this Vyra person—*elf*, I mean," Luke said, looking stonily at his full teacup. "She killed our parents?"

Olympus nodded solemnly.

"Why them?" Autumn asked, her voice shaking. "Why *our* parents?"

"Vyra is the leader of the Atrums—"

"What are Atrums?" Luke asked.

"Evil elves. Wickedness runs through their veins. It is in their blood."

"Okay, so they're evil," Luke said. "But that still doesn't explain why this evil elf woman would choose to kill our parents."

"Vyra desires power. Complete power. Her father was the leader of the Atrums before her, before she killed him to gain control. She killed her mother and her younger brother as well and created an army of creatures called Shadows. The only thing standing in the way of her ruling the entire elf population now...is our bloodline."

"But that means—" Luke began.

"She wants to kill us too," Autumn finished, a hollow feeling appearing in her chest.

Olympus didn't answer, which was essentially a confirmation.

"Well, we will just have to get rid of her before she tries to get rid of us," Luke said, a dark shadow passing across his face.

Autumn shot Luke a surprised look. "I thought you didn't believe any of this."

"I don't know what I believe. I just know I want to kill this Vyra person."

"I'm afraid it is not that simple. But, I would be happy if you stayed here. This is where you will be safest."

"We'll stay," Autumn said.

Olympus smiled warmly. "Magnificent. Well, enough of this morbid chatter. You're home now."

"Should we, like, sign up for elf school or something?" Luke said uncertainly.

"I've already spoken to the head of Aspen Academy, and she has set up your class schedules."

"How did you know we were coming?" Autumn asked.

"Well, I wasn't positive how long it would take, but I assume you've been receiving my dream messages?" A knowing smile spread across Olympus's aged face.

Autumn shot a quick glance towards the gray-eyed boy—Avery—who stood beside her grandfather's throne. He looked away when their eyes met and Autumn turned back to Olympus. "That was you?"

"Well not me, directly. I enlisted the help of a castle worker whose Power is Dream Communication. She was unable to give you a clearer message since you were in the Outside, but was nonetheless effective."

"I'll say," Autumn said.

Olympus laughed, reaching for a pastry. Autumn glanced down at her grandfather's right wrist. The very same outline of a rose.

"What is the significance of the rose?" Autumn asked Olympus, who glanced down at his own wrist and smiled.

"Roses symbolize many things for elves. We have one for nearly every occasion. *This* rose," he held up his wrist, "represents the royal elves. The white petals and black edges signify loyalty wrapped in strength. Two qualities we elves regard quite highly. Every Oaken before you has had the same mark. It is how we are recognized by others who may not know our faces."

"Couldn't it have been, like, a tumbleweed or something more manly than a rose," Luke grumbled.

Olympus clicked his tongue. "On the contrary, a rose is a clever little flower. Beautiful and delicate, yes, but with a strong stem and thorns for protection. Roses have a true complexity that few other magical creatures appreciate."

Just then another man dressed in the green rushed in the room. "Pardon, Your Majesty, but you are needed in Rose Valley."

"Can it wait?" Olympus said.

"A dragon was accidentally set loose by one of the Tamers. He's destroying their town…"

Olympus heaved a great sigh and turned to face Autumn and Luke again. "Got to go put out that fire, I'm afraid. We will become better acquainted later in the week. Until then, Mr. Burke will show you to your rooms, and I'm sure Miss Everly will give you a quick tour of town if you're up to it."

They stood and Olympus wrapped Autumn and Luke in another tight hug, held them at arm's length once again, and smiled before sweeping from the room.

Once the king was gone Avery approached them, accompanied by Crystal, and said, "I'm Avery Burke. If you'll follow me, I'll show you to your rooms."

He led them through yet another door into the next room. The only thing occupying this space was the enormous base of a staircase that wrapped around the perimeter of the room and meandered up past the ceiling.

"That's a lot of stairs," Luke said, tilting his head back.

Avery simply chuckled and began to climb the vast staircase. They traveled all the way up past the ceiling where the stairs continued to wrap around the next room. Autumn gazed over the railing as they continued to climb. The room below was filled with round, wooden tables, and was dimly lit by a magnificent glass chandelier, which held the same pulsating light that appeared in sconces all around the castle.

"Is this where we eat?" Luke asked.

"Er… no. This is where we eat," Crystal said indicating Avery and herself. "Castle workers. I expect you two will have a private dining room somewhere."

"Why?" Autumn asked.

"You're royals," Avery said, looking at Autumn as if this should be an obvious explanation.

"So?" Luke said.

"So, that's just how things are," Crystal said. "Royals don't eat with the rest of the castle workers."

"That's ridiculous," Autumn said. "We don't need any sort of special treatment. We can eat with everyone else." Luke nodded in agreement.

Avery raised an eyebrow at her. Autumn could tell that she was not what he'd expected, which seemed to be a good thing.

They climbed past the dining room ceiling into the next room—a sea of books. Autumn knew at once that this was the castle library. Her face broke out into a wide smile. She felt like Belle from *Beauty and the Beast*. Shelves full of books covered the walls with rolling ladders placed every so often along bookcases. Groups of heavy wooden tables congregated in the middle of the room, and oversized armchairs sat near what looked like a stone fireplace.

"Look, Autumn," Luke said. "Your dream room."

"Yeah. I'll just sleep here. No need to show me to my room anymore."

"As much fun as I think sleeping in a room full of brilliant literature sounds," Avery said, "I'd say you'll want to see your rooms before making that decision."

He likes books, Autumn thought, smiling to herself.

They continued to walk up past the library ceiling. Luke was now wheezing and Autumn's legs were beginning to feel like jelly.

"Um—how many stories up are our rooms?" Luke asked, panting.

"Your branch is just up here," Avery said, indicating one of the entryways that branched—literally—off of the staircase ahead of them. He stopped at a landing in front of a large oak door. "Luke, you'll be staying in Branch 307. Autumn yours is 308." He pointed a little ways up the stairs to another landing and oak door. "If either of you ever need anything, I live in Branch 309. Just up there." He pointed to a door a little ways up the spiral staircase and Autumn had to repress the excitement that bubbled up when she realized they were neighbors.

"Thanks, Avery," Crystal said. "I'll take it from here."

Avery nodded and started back down the staircase as Crystal pulled Autumn up the stairs to Branch 308. A shout of surprise came from Luke's branch, and Autumn turned to see that Luke had already disappeared from the landing to explore, and was apparently impressed by what it held.

Autumn turned the handle and the door swung open to reveal her new home. She gasped. She had been expecting one room, but this "branch" was more like a house than anything else. The doorway opened into a grand living area decorated in jewel tones, with downy couches and a red brick fireplace. An archway led from the living room into a study with shelves full of books, a heavy wooden desk, and yet another fireplace accompanied by two emerald green armchairs.

"It's beautiful," Crystal said from behind Autumn, who was too stunned to speak.

Autumn left the study, moving slowly back through the living room and into what appeared to be her bedroom. Here sat a golden canopy-bed covered with a bright purple comforter made out of a material that felt like flower petals. Her walls were a glimmering turquoise and her armoire was painted gold.

A dark blue curtain decorated the double glass doors leading to a balcony outside. Autumn opened them, letting in the sunlight and fresh air. She moved to the railing, looking out at her new home, breathing it in. Crystal came to stand beside her.

"This can't be real. I must still be dreaming," Autumn said.

"You aren't dreaming," Crystal said. "Trust me."

They heard the distant slam of her front door and Luke emerged on Autumn's balcony a few seconds later. "This is insane! My bathroom is bigger than my old room! No—my *bathtub* is bigger than my old room! I admit it, Crystal. This place is pretty legit."

A slow smile spread across Crystal's face. "Wait until you see the rest of the kingdom."

The Lion Girl

CHAPTER SEVEN

"**T**he castle will be serving dinner soon so I'll just take you to Arbor Lake, but we will have all day tomorrow to see everything else," Crystal said as she escorted Autumn and Luke out of the castle and down a dirt path that wound through more colossal trees and peculiar plants of varying shapes and sizes.

"So you elves just…walk everywhere?" Luke said.

"Uh huh. That is, after all, the purpose of legs and feet, is it not? Do you use them for something else in the Outside?"

"Yeah. Controlling the gas and brakes in our cars," Luke said.

Crystal made a face. "Well, we use our feet for walking. There are no *cars* down here."

"Where did you say we were going?" Autumn asked.

"Arbor Lake," Crystal said. "It's where everyone our age goes for fun. And school starts back Monday so I'm sure nearly the whole school will be there."

Luke's eyes lit up. "Will, uh, will there be girls there?"

Crystal giggled. "Of course, and I'm sure they'll all be *quite* interested to talk to the new prince."

"Who's that?" Luke asked.

"Er…*you*," Crystal said.

"Oh. Right. Then what are we waiting for?"

Arbor Lake soon appeared through the foliage. Trees and large boulders encircled the water, creating somewhat of a barrier to the forest. And, like the waterfall, the lake was eerily still and shimmered in the light as if someone had spilled glitter all over the surface of the water. Groups of elves were dispersed throughout the area. Some lounged on the grass, others sat atop boulders, or in the shade of the many trees, and a few were even sunbathing on the sandy lake shore. Autumn glanced over to find Luke gawking at all the elf girls in their bathing suits.

"Well, if it isn't the little dress maker."

Autumn turned to see a girl approaching them with two others following closely behind. Golden blonde hair spilled past her shoulders and her eyes were a piercing tawny color, reminding Autumn of a lioness on the prowl. The lion girl's mouth was turned up in a sneer. It would appear she had spotted her prey.

"Don't you have clothes to be sewing?" she said to Crystal, who shot her a look of pure loathing. The girl glanced over at Autumn and Luke for the first time and her face contorted in disgust. "*Outsiders*? Did you bring them here, Everly?"

Autumn resisted the urge to smack this girl across her perfect little lion face.

"Kyndel, this is Autumn and Luke Oaken," Crystal said. "They're staying in the castle with their grandfather. You know, the *king*."

Kyndel narrowed her eyes in suspicion, and Autumn held up her wrist to reveal her Royal Mark. Kyndel's eyebrows shot up in apparent surprise. She opened her mouth as if she was about to speak, but then quickly shut it. Flipping her hair, she trudged off with her nose in the air, her followers chasing after her.

Crystal broke into hysterical laughter. "That's the first time I've ever seen Kyndel Butler speechless. You two have no idea how perfect that was."

Luke watched Kyndel walk away with a mixture of dislike and lust on his face.

"What was her problem?" Autumn asked.

"She thinks that she's the best thing that's ever happened to Arbor Falls, and anyone who doesn't agree is automatically her enemy. So, as you just witnessed, that includes me."

Luke raised his eyebrows as another girl sauntered by in a tight-fitting dress. "Is there something in the water here that makes elf girls so freaking *hot*?"

Just then, the boy who could talk to animals jogged up to them.

He bowed dramatically and said, "Your Highnesses."

"Please don't do that, Forrest," Autumn said. "We won't have you beheaded, I promise."

"I know. I was just giving you a hard time. Are you going to school on Monday?"

"I guess so," Autumn said, her stomach dropping at the idea of going to a new school full of elves.

Her last "new kid at school" situation hadn't exactly been the most pleasant. What with her parents' deaths and the resulting survivor's guilt, added to the culture shock of moving to Ireland, Autumn hadn't made all that many friends. She had undergone several phases during that school year. For a month, she only wore black clothes, along with black eyeliner and eye shadow. Then she moved on to wearing revealing clothing to prove that she just didn't care what anyone thought. But then winter came and she had to wear a jacket all of the time, so she just didn't try at all. Didn't fix her hair, or put on makeup, or attempt to coordinate her clothing in any way. That's when Luke finally confronted her about falling apart. After that she slowly started to care again.

Autumn was pulled from her reverie when a large group of elves approached them. Kyndel, of course, was in the front, like a lioness leading her pride.

"There they are," Kyndel said, pointing towards Autumn and Luke. "The prince and princess. Told you they were here."

Rather than flash her Royal Mark, she kept her wrist pressed against her body. She didn't really want that kind of attention right now. Nor did she want to please Kyndel in any way. Luke, on the other hand, quickly obliged, raising his wrist for all of the elf girls to see. The elves let out a chorus of squeals and whoops, and a satisfied look appeared on Kyndel's face. Luke grinned from ear to ear at the sight of all the elf girls eyeing him. He waved and they giggled with delight, shooting him sultry looks. It seemed Luke was going to have an easier time fitting in here than he ever had in the "Outside." Then Autumn noticed a handful of boys staring at her and felt her cheeks flush with warmth.

"Am I missing out on the fun?" a familiar voice said.

Autumn's stomach did a small flip when she saw Avery approaching.

"Kyndel here was just being a sweetheart and introducing the entirety of the Underground to our new prince and princess," Crystal said.

"They didn't believe me," Kyndel said, gesturing to the gathering crowd. "I had to prove them wrong."

"Ah," Avery said, flashing Autumn an amused glance. "Well, *unfortunately* I was sent to fetch the new prince and princess, so I suppose everyone will just have to get their autographs some other time."

The crowd let out cries of disappointment as Avery led Autumn, Luke, and Crystal away. Kyndel was the only one who didn't seem at all upset by their departure. While Autumn was relieved to escape the staring eyes, Luke didn't seem as eager to go. He lagged behind, waving enthusiastically. This was, after all, the most attention he had ever received from females in his entire life.

"Come on, Luke," Autumn called over her shoulder. "You'll see them tomorrow."

Luke gave one last wave, evoking another round of squeals, and jogged to catch up to the others.

"*Ugh*," Luke groaned when he caught up to the others. "How many roads and paths and stairs and alleys and parks and forests are we going to have to walk through today? I've walked more today than I have in my whole life. Like, add up all the time I've ever walked and it will not equal the amount of walking I have done today."

Avery chuckled and approached one of the many oak trees lining the road. There was a knot on the bark, which he pushed in like a button.

Autumn tilted her head to the side. "What did that do?"

"It called a carriage," Avery said.

"You have carriages here?" Luke exclaimed. "Why haven't we been using those the whole time?"

"The carriages are generally for elderly elves and the injured. Young, healthy elves rarely use them," Avery said with an amused look.

Luke frowned looking embarrassed. "Oh. Well, you didn't have to call a carriage. I could've walked. I was just joking, really."

Autumn snorted.

The clomping of hooves met their ears and a large stagecoach drawn by what looked like an over-sized deer with antlers appeared.

"Is that...a reindeer?" she asked.

Crystal giggled and said, "Yes. It's a little inside joke of our ancestors."

"Elves and reindeer. Nice. Where's Santa hiding?" Luke said.

"Didn't your grandfather tell you?" Crystal stated seriously. "Olympus *is* Santa Claus." Autumn and Luke's mouths dropped open and Crystal burst out laughing. "I'm kidding! But you should really see your faces."

On the short ride home, Autumn looked out into the oversized forest, in awe of everything her eyes encountered. It was remarkable how enchanting nature could be. She had never appreciated it on the Outside. Then again, the most beautiful trees and flora on the Outside looked like weeds compared to everything here. She could feel Avery's gaze on her throughout the ride, but each time she tried to catch his eye he turned his head.

When the carriage pulled up to the castle, Avery jumped out and reached a hand up to help Autumn down. The moment their skin touched, a surge of energy coursed through her, coming to rest in her core. Autumn looked into Avery's eyes, wondering if he'd felt what she had. A confused expression appeared on his face. When his gray eyes met hers, she knew. He had felt it too.

The four of them journeyed up to the dining room, Luke grumbling something about "more stairs" as they climbed.

When they entered the dining room, a hush fell over the area. Autumn could feel hundreds of eyes trained on her as she followed Crystal to a vacant table. Clearly, word had quickly spread throughout the castle that the royal redheaded twins had finally arrived in the Underground. The castle workers watched in apparent curiosity as Autumn and Luke joined Crystal and Avery at a vacant table.

"They sure stare a lot here," Luke muttered.

Crystal surveyed the room with a stern look, giving a crisp clear of her throat, and the interested eyes turned away.

Four wooden mugs filled with a steaming amber-colored

liquid sat beside perfectly carved plates and flatware.

"What's this?" Autumn asked, peering into the mug. She was beginning to feel like Jack Skellington when he'd first discovered Christmas Town. *What's this? What's this? What's this?*

"Honeysuckle Cider," Crystal said. "Try it. It's delicious."

Aromas of honeysuckle and cinnamon wafted up from the mug. Autumn inhaled deeply before taking a tentative sip. She was pleasantly surprised when the sweet, slightly tart liquid hit her tongue. "That's amazing."

"Told you," Crystal said, taking a swig of her own.

"So, where's the food?" Luke asked.

As if he had conjured them, a line of castle workers dressed in white came streaming out of a set of swinging double doors, each carrying trays filled with food. A long table ran along the perimeter of the dining room. The workers placed the food on the tables and left the dining room in the same orderly fashion in which they had entered.

"Right there," Crystal answered.

"Why is no one getting any?" Luke asked.

"I think they are waiting for you two to get your food first," Avery said.

Autumn ducked her head, feeling embarrassed. "They don't have to wait for us."

"It's okay," Crystal said. "They'll get their food after you do. Come on. Let's check out the spread."

Carrying their plates, they approached the tables filled with food. Autumn only recognized a few things, like pasta and vegetables. The rest was a mystery. Luckily, though, there were little signs behind the food explaining what it was.

"You eat dragons here?" Autumn asked, peering at what looked like green-tinted steaks.

Avery chuckled and said, "Only the mean ones."

Autumn glanced over at Luke and stifled a laugh as his face grew more and more disgusted the longer he examined the food.

"Dandelion Stew... Blackened Piranha... Smoked Serpent... Um, ever heard of steak?"

"Cows are very rare in the Underground," said Avery. "But we do occasionally have beef at the castle. The menu changes daily.

Dragon is actually very similar to beef. If you tried it, I bet you'd like it."

Luke made a face indicating that he did not agree with this statement. "I'll just have some pasta."

Autumn loaded her plate with pasta and vegetables. Avery piled his with dragon steak.

They brought their plates back to the table and the rest of the castle workers stood and went to fill their own.

"So. Dragons," Luke said through a mouthful of pasta. "Any other sorts of fire breathing creatures here we should worry about?"

As Avery explained to Luke the different types of dragons, Autumn ate her food and watched him talk, studying his features. He had a strong face and square jaw that would clench every so often. Autumn wondered why that was. And while he was undeniably handsome there was a dark quality to his looks. Something in his eyes. Their stormy gray color was mysterious, like a violent sea full of secrets and hidden pain. Her obsessive need to help people began to kick in, and she longed to know what had caused him to become so hardened.

Suddenly he glanced up at her through his lashes, their eyes locking on to one another for a brief moment before Autumn broke the connection, looking down at her lap.

"Are you taking the Warrior Test, Avery?" Crystal asked.

"I am. Are you?"

Crystal nodded. "So far, everyone I've talked to is."

"What's that?" Luke asked.

"The Warriors protect the city from Shadows and Atrums, among other things," Crystal explained. "They're basically an army of sorts. Every five years the Warriors hold a sort of practical test in order to choose the next generation of Warriors. Only the best fighters with the best Powers are selected."

"But you're taking the Test?" Autumn said. "So elves our age can be Warriors?"

"How old are you?" Avery asked.

"Seventeen."

"We turn eighteen in March," Luke added.

"Perfect. You will be 4th quarter elves like us," Crystal said.

Autumn and Luke gave her a confused look. "I mean you'll be in the last year of elf school. The 4th quarter elves are the only elves allowed to that take the Warrior Test because we're—obviously— the most advanced of the school-age elves and we haven't started training for any other jobs. I was so excited when I found out that my class would be in 4th quarter the year of Warrior Test."

"That doesn't seem fair to the other elves," Autumn said.

Avery shrugged. "Our ancestors see it as destiny. They think the Warriors are pre-destined to be chosen. So, if they are meant to be Warriors, they will be eligible the year of the Warrior Test. Though a lot of elves will purposefully hold themselves back in school until the Warrior Test."

"Could we try out?" Autumn asked.

Crystal and Avery exchanged uncertain glances.

"I don't know... I don't think a royal has ever been a Warrior."

"Well, if we're royals, and we say we want to test, don't they have to let us?" Luke asked.

"I suppose so," Crystal said, still sounding unsure.

"Then I'm taking the Test," Autumn said, earning another surprised look from Avery.

"Me too," Luke agreed.

"So, how does it work?" Autumn asked. "You just take this Test and then you're a Warrior?"

"No, it's much more thorough than that," Avery said. "If you pass the Test, then you become an Initiate, which is sort of an in- between period. You're essentially a Warrior-in-training. After a few months of that, if you prove you are Warrior material, then you are officially initiated and you will become a Quinn Warrior."

"Quinn?" Luke said.

"There are five rotations of Warriors," Crystal began. "Each set is about five years older than the next and they all have nicknames. The first and oldest rotation is the Unum Warriors, then you have the Duos, the Triplexes, the Tetras, and finally, the Quinns. Once the Quinns are initiated, the oldest Warriors retire and each rotation moves up in rank."

"Sort of like high school," Luke said.

Autumn and Crystal shot him a confused look.

"You know," he said, "like, when the seniors graduate, the

juniors become seniors, the sophomores become juniors, the freshmen become—"

"Okay, I got it," Autumn said, holding a hand up to silence him.

"Well, I'm totally doing it," Luke said. "Killing Vyra will be a lot easier after some Warrior training."

Crystal's brow knit together. "Er...it won't be that easy..."

"Well, losing our parents wasn't that easy either," Luke said darkly. "But we managed to live through that."

The conversation had quickly taken a depressing turn, and an uncomfortable silence fell over the table—at least until the kitchen workers brought out the desserts. Luke had a sweet tooth and he immediately rushed to pile his plate with a variety of the cakes and pastries. Crystal looked relieved.

After dessert, Autumn and Luke said goodnight to Crystal and Avery before trudging up the stairs to their new rooms. Autumn couldn't help but notice Avery's eyes lingering on hers longer than would be considered necessary for a casual goodbye.

Autumn entered her branch, ambling through the dimly lit sitting room and into her bedroom. Pulling back her petal-soft comforter, she climbed in to the enormous canopy bed. The day's events ran through her head like a movie reel until she drifted off to sleep.

And for the first time in months there was no waterfall, no magical forest, no gray-eyed boy to greet her behind a sheet of water.

Her sleep was dreamless.

Zero to Hero

CHAPTER EIGHT

A beam of sunlight landed on Autumn's face, awakening her. It took several seconds for her to realize that she hadn't been dreaming and that she actually was an elf princess, sleeping in the branch of a giant tree castle.

After a bath that felt more like sitting in a giant hot tub, she pulled open the doors of her wardrobe and took in all of the clothes that were now hers. All of the clothing seemed to be made from the finest fabrics: silk, cashmere, intricate laces, and some made from the same petal-like material of her bedspread. While there were several gowns in her wardrobe, there were also skirts, pants, casual dresses, and shorts. She was thankful she wouldn't have to wear heavy gowns every day like the princesses of fairytales.

Many of the clothes looked like they could have been from the Victorian era, but with a modern twist. The word "steampunk" came to Autumn's mind, but without all of the gadgets and clocks. If she were to wear them in the Outside she would have been the envy of every girl in her school.

The common teenage girl problem of having nothing to wear wouldn't be an issue here. She had *everything* to wear, which was almost as difficult. How could she choose? After standing before the wardrobe feeling slightly overwhelmed for several minutes, Autumn reached in and pulled out a flowy, white top with butterfly sleeves. She scanned the variety of pants and decided on the navy blue ones.

As she was in the process of pulling her loose curls back away from her face with pins made from pearls, there was a knock on the door. She expected to see Luke or Crystal—she didn't let herself hope it would be Avery—but, instead, there stood a nervous looking castle worker. He wore the same green uniform Autumn had seen several other workers wearing yesterday, and she imagined that each section of the castle had a different colored uniform. Guards wore red, kitchen staff wore white, and castle servants wore green.

"Hello, Miss Autumn," he said. "The king sent me to give you this." He held out a hand and Autumn glanced down to see two leather pouches stuffed full of—

"Leaves?" Autumn said, peeking into one of the pouches.

"Gold, silver, and bronze leaves," he said. "They are elf currency, Miss. Twenty silver leaves to every gold leaf and fifty bronze leaves to every silver leaf."

Autumn pulled out a gold leaf and examined it. It was thin and pliable, about the length of her palm.

"That's incredible... Is the other one for Luke?"

"Yes, but Prince Luke would not come to the door when I knocked, Miss."

"I'll get him to answer," Autumn said with a wink as the castle worker handed over Luke's bag of currency with a relieved look upon his face.

It only took a few minutes of pounding for Luke to answer the door wearing an exasperated scowl.

"Was that really necessary?" he grumbled. "For once we don't have to get up early for work and you wake me up at the crack of dawn."

Autumn flashed him an unapologetic smile and held out his pouch full of elf money. "Here."

He opened it and peered in before shooting Autumn a bemused look. "Why are you giving me a bag of leaves?"

Autumn explained what the servant had told her and he raised his eyebrows, looking down at the contents with a different expression. Then he let out a bark of laughter.

"What's so funny?" Autumn asked.

"Money really does grow on trees here."

"Clever. Okay, go get ready," Autumn said, pushing past her brother and plopping down on the fluffy couch in his living room to wait.

"What's the r—r—rush?" Luke said through a yawn.

"No rush. I just figured you'd want to meet some more of those elf girls like the ones fawning over you last night, but if you just want to go back to sleep then—"

"I'll be ready in five minutes," Luke said, practically running into his room.

It actually took him four and a half.

Luke counted the leaves in his pouch as they traveled down the stairs into the massive dining room.

"Fifty gold leaves, a hundred silver leaves and two hundred bronze leaves. I don't know exactly how much that is compared to human money, but I'd say it's way more than I've ever had before. Including that summer I mowed all the lawns in town."

Autumn spotted Crystal and Avery sitting at a nearby table and hurriedly told Luke to put the pouch of leaves away.

"I hope you slept well because we have a busy day ahead of us," Crystal said, wearing a bright smile.

"Where all are we going?" Luke asked as he spread a generous amount of honeysuckle butter on his toast.

"Everywhere!" Crystal said. "I want you to see all of downtown: the archery range, the shopping center, more of City Circle, and then—if you want—we can go back to Arbor Lake."

"As long as there are girls there, you can take me anywhere you'd like," Luke said through a mouthful of toast.

"Do you have guard duty today, Avery?" Crystal asked.

He nodded. "Yep. All day. I'm in the throne room again."

Autumn tried not to look too disappointed that he wouldn't be joining them.

After breakfast, Crystal took the twins on a tour of downtown. It was still hard for Autumn to think of it as downtown seeing as how all of the "buildings" were trees. It felt more like a forest than a town. A rather large forest. Blisters covered Autumn's feet from the previous day of walking and hiking and stair climbing, but she knew she would have to develop tougher skin if she was going to make it in the Underground. Especially if she was going to take the

Warrior Test.

As they walked, Autumn noticed that most of the elves they passed stared at them as they walked by, and some even pointed shamelessly.

"How does everyone already know about us?" Autumn asked under her breath.

"Probably from last night at Arbor Lake. Word spreads like fire in the kingdom. Especially when Kyndel Butler is the source."

The three of them spent the majority of the day downtown shopping, walking, and eating. Luke had never been the frugal type so he spent a large portion of his silver and bronze leaves in the first hour. Autumn was so used to not having much money that she felt guilty spending more than a couple of silver leaves, especially since Crystal didn't have much money herself.

They ate lunch at a small teahouse called The Tea Tree where they filled up on delicate sandwiches, scones, pastries, and various kinds of tea. Luke started to complain about it being too girly, until a table full of attractive girls started flirting with him. That shut him up.

After lunch they went by the archery store to buy bows and arrows for Autumn and Luke. The store reminded Autumn of a library, but instead of books the shelves were filled with bows. Hundreds and hundreds of bows made from various Underground trees. And, like a library, the bows were categorized by type, arranged in order from darkest to lightest ranging from ebony to a bone white. Luke browsed the darker bows while Autumn scanned the warm, golden tones.

Luke quickly settled on a bow that was smooth and black, made from the wood of an ink tree, whose bark was as black as the ink it produced. Autumn took longer to decide but eventually chose a bow made from the golden wood of an ash tree. The finish made it so the bow would shimmer in the sunlight.

"So, you fight with these?" Luke asked as he examined a black quiver.

"Only Warriors fight with bows and arrows," Crystal said. "The rest of the elves just shoot them at the archery range for fun and some use them to hunt."

"I thought Warriors would fight with, like, swords and

machetes and stuff," Luke said in disappointment.

"I don't know about machetes, but if you become a Warrior, you'll learn how to fight with swords and knives and other weapons. Regular elves, though, hardly have any real need for weapons like that," Crystal said.

"Honestly, though, what are the chances of us making the Warriors when we've only just come here? We don't even know what our Powers are yet," Autumn said.

"You'd be surprised how much you can learn in a few months. Especially with Atticus as your Magister."

"Who's Atticus?" Autumn asked.

"He's the leader of the Initiates and the Quinns. He also teaches Powers class, which helps young elves learn how to control their Powers and, more importantly, how to use them effectively against an enemy."

They left the archery shop with arms full of their new sheaths, arrows, and bows. They had a couple of hours until dinner so they stopped by Autumn and Luke's branches to drop off their purchases before leaving again for Arbor Lake. Autumn could practically see the excitement radiating from Luke like heat waves. He was so focused on the girls he would soon meet that he managed to walk all the way to the lake without complaining once.

When they arrived, it wasn't thirty seconds before a group of adoring elf girls surrounded Luke.

"Do you think he'll be okay if we leave him alone with them?" Crystal asked.

"Are you kidding?" Autumn laughed. "He's in heaven right now. He won't even notice."

Crystal and Autumn attempted to move closer to the shore, trying to dodge all of the elves that had suddenly surrounded them, staring at Autumn with looks of interest and admiration.

"Princess Autumn?" a particularly scrawny and, by the looks of him, very young elf said. "Could you sign my book bag?"

"Uh—" is all Autumn could get out before she noticed a commotion coming up the middle of the crowd. It was Avery clearing a path through the swarming elves.

"Okay, guys, clear out," Avery commanded. "I know you've never seen a princess before, but I'm sure she's seen plenty of desperate guys in her lifetime."

He placed his hand on Autumn's back and gently moved her towards the shore, Crystal trailing behind.

"I've been looking for you everywhere," Avery said.

Autumn gazed up at him with wide eyes and said, "R-really?"

"Yeah, the king gave me a different work assignment. I'm going to be you and your brother's bodyguard from now on."

"Our bodyguard? Why would we need a bodyguard?"

"To keep you safe."

"We haven't had a bodyguard for 17 years and we've been safe enough."

"You were living in the Outside. And you weren't royalty, or at least no one knew you were. In case you didn't notice, you two have quite a few fans down here."

"How are we supposed to make the Warriors if it looks like we can't even protect ourselves sufficiently?" Autumn asked, becoming frustrated.

"I'm sure if you make the Warriors your grandfather will no longer see the need for the extra protection." His politeness seemed forced.

"Good, another reason to try out then," Autumn said with a hint of malice. She wasn't sure where this sudden resentment was coming from.

"I didn't exactly beg for this job, Autumn," he snapped, bringing her up short. She was surprised that he actually called her by her first name and in such a harsh tone. "I apologize," he said, looking guilty. "I shouldn't have spoken to you that way, Miss Oaken. I—"

"No," Autumn said. "I'm glad you did, and please, call me Autumn. I'm already tired of being treated like a princess all of the time. And you're right. You didn't sign on for this either. I was just unhappy about being assigned a permanent babysitter is all."

Avery looked at her as if he was trying to figure something out. Apparently this was not how he had expected her to respond.

Crystal cut in then, having been silently watching their interaction. "I don't know if this is a situation that needs your attention," she said, "but one of your royal elves seems to be unable to breathe properly what with that girl smothering him with her lips and all."

Autumn and Avery turned to see what Crystal was talking about and found Luke surrounded by three elf girls, one in particular was enthusiastically kissing him all over his face. Autumn shook her head wearily at her brother and Avery burst out laughing.

"I think he'll be okay without my services for now."

At dinner that night, a castle worker delivered the class schedules to all of the school age elves. Autumn opened hers and scanned the page.

Monday/Wednesday:
8:15 - 9:30 Numbers (Monroe)
9:45 - 11:15 Literature (Hart)
11:15 - 1:35 Lunch
1:45 - 3:30 Powers (Attribold)
Tuesday/Thursday:
8:15 - 9:30 Laboratory (Holt)
9:45 - 11:15 Underground History (Parkey)
11:15 - 1:35 Lunch
1:45 - 3:30 Healing (Ginger)
Friday:
8:15 - 10:15 Melodies/Art/Sports
10:15 - 11:15 Break
11:15 - 1:35 Lunch
1:45 - 3:30 Powers (Attribold)

They passed around each other's schedules, comparing them. Autumn had Healing with Luke, Literature with Avery, Numbers with Crystal, and Powers with all of them. This made her feel better. At least she would have one friendly face in most of her new classes. She was going to need that since she would to be the new kid, the new *royal* kid. With the amount of stares she knew she would be receiving from the other students...she might as well be going to school in her underwear.

New Kids on Campus

CHAPTER NINE

Autumn awoke from a restless sleep to the sound of her grandfather clock chiming a tranquil melody. Her stomach was already turning with nerves. She didn't know what to expect from her first day at a new elf school, but more importantly—she didn't know what to wear.

Sliding out of bed, she pulled open the double glass doors leading out to her balcony, taking a deep breath of the fresh air. A cluster of aromas washed over her: flowers, the sweet smell of grass, the musky scent of trees, and a smell she didn't quite recognize. Maybe it was magic, or perhaps it was actually the absence of certain smells. There were no factories in the Underground—no cars, no buildings, no piles of rotting garbage. Just nature.

Somehow this new, magical world seemed more real to Autumn than the real world. Or maybe *this* was the real world. The Underground. It sure felt more real. Since her arrival, Autumn had been more acutely aware of every one of her senses and feelings. She had appreciated the way things tasted, the sound of a breeze blowing the leaves on a branch, the electric way Avery made her feel. In the Outside, the cars and technology and gadgets all seemed to deaden those senses. People had half-hearted conversations with each other while texting away on their phones. Here, when Autumn spoke to people, she could tell they were actually listening. For the first time since she had lost her parents, Autumn felt alive.

Really alive.

Walking back into her room, Autumn passed by the full-length mirror, catching a brief glimpse of herself. She stopped in her tracks and took a few steps backwards. Turning to face the mirror, Autumn's mouth dropped at what she saw. Her reflection had changed drastically since the previous morning. Her ears were now pointed so that the tips peeked out through her auburn hair, which was now silky and smooth—a feat no anti-frizz product had ever accomplished in the Outside. She still looked like herself, but her features were naturally enhanced in a way no makeup ever could. Her eyelashes were thicker and longer, her cheeks were ever so slightly pink, her lips fuller and redder; even every blemish had disappeared. An ethereal glow shone through her skin as if there was a dim light shining from within her.

After a minute or two of staring at her new reflection, Autumn finally shook her head in disbelief and moved to her dresser, throwing open the doors in search of an outfit suitable for a princess. She searched through the entirety of her wardrobe twice and finally decided on a casual emerald-green dress that brought out the deep red in her hair. The bodice of the dress resembled a corset and the skirt was made of an airy material that swayed softly with each movement.

Stepping out of her branch, Autumn found Luke already waiting for her on the landing. He seemed to have changed as much—physically at least—as she had.

"You look different," he noted.

"So do you."

"I guess there's no more denying that we really are elves, huh?" he said, touching the top of one of his pointed ears.

Autumn laughed. "It's taken this long to convince you?"

They entered the dining room and moved to what had become their usual table where Avery and Crystal were already situated. Avery scanned Autumn's outfit and she thought she saw him blush slightly.

"Well, look at you two," Crystal said, grinning widely. "You look like actual elves now."

"I know," Autumn said, tucking her hair behind her pointed ear. "I'm trying to get used to it."

"It suits you," Avery said, looking up at her with a crooked smile.

Luke shot him a warning look and Avery lowered his gaze to his plate of scrambled dragon eggs. Autumn hardly touched any of her porridge, though what little she tasted was delectable, full of butter, brown sugar, and fall spices.

She couldn't stop thinking about how crazy everyone had been acting toward Luke and her, like they were celebrities or something. She guessed they kind of were in a way, which made her even more nervous because she had a feeling everyone was going to be paying attention to her during class instead of the teacher.

What if she was horrible at being an elf? She didn't even have a Power yet. On top of all that, royals were supposed to be the most talented and powerful of all the elves. She was sure her teachers would already have high expectations.

"Did you finish your Numbers project, Avery?" Crystal asked.

"Yeah, but I'm not sure how great it is. I hear Magister Monroe is pretty brutal, grading-wise."

"Magister?" Luke asked.

"Oh, right," Crystal said. "I think in the Outside they call them teachers or professors."

"We didn't do a Numbers project," Autumn said.

"You just found out you were elves!" Crystal said. "We've known about this all summer."

"Which is about how long it took," Avery added.

"Speaking of Numbers," Crystal said, glancing at a small wooden instrument strapped to her wrist that Autumn assumed was an elf version of a watch. "We better go soon. We have Monroe first. Better to be safe. He hates tardiness."

Autumn swallowed, feeling a new rush of anxiety.

"Don't be nervous, you'll do fine today," Crystal said.

"I'm not nervous," Autumn lied.

Luke bounced along the winding path leading toward campus. Clearly he wasn't nervous in the least. In fact, he was practically giddy. Autumn wondered if the constant adoration would ever get old for him like it already had for her. She assumed not.

Up ahead she could see students converging in clusters around the campus, talking and laughing in excitement. She tried to ignore the stares and whispers coming from the groups as they passed by. The campus was split into four sections, all meeting in the middle at a marble fountain similar to the one in City Center. Each section contained a number of trees where each class was held. The 4th quarter elves' section was located in the top left corner of campus.

Autumn and Crystal parted from Luke and Avery, traveling in the direction of the Numbers Tree.

"We better hurry," Crystal said, opening the heavy wooden door of the Numbers Tree and stepping inside.

Autumn followed, closing the door behind her. The roar of laughter and talking ceased when she turned to face the classroom. She followed Crystal to the back of the room and sat hunched over in her seat, ignoring all of the interested eyes now focused on her.

"Hey, Fall! How's it going?"

Autumn looked up to see Forrest sitting in the desk before her, swiveled around in his seat. "Fall?" she said.

"You know. Autumn and fall—same thing."

"Ha. Good one, Forrest," Autumn said as she began pulling paper out of the new satchel she bought in town the day before. "Oh, shoot, I don't have a pen."

"A what?" Crystal asked with a quirked eyebrow.

"A pen. Or a pencil, maybe?" Forrest and Crystal continued to look at her blankly. "Something to write with?" Autumn clarified.

"Oh! We write with leaf quills," Crystal said, pulling out a long black leaf with a sharp point at the base and handing it over to Autumn.

"Is this an actual leaf?"

Forrest nodded. "It comes from an ink tree. There's ink in the veins of the leaf and it comes out here when you write," he said, pointing to the tip of the leaf quill.

Autumn wrote her name with a flourish across the top of her paper, looking at the leaf quill in wonder.

A dark shadow entered her periphery then and her eyes were drawn upward, landing on a tall raven-haired boy entering the classroom. Autumn had to choke back a gasp because he was quite possibly the most attractive being she had ever laid eyes on. He would have made any Outsider male model look like a scrawny, prepubescent child.

He didn't make eye contact with anyone, just stared straight ahead and made his way to the back of the classroom. He took the open seat to Autumn's left and sat down with his eyes on his desk. She noticed that the elves seated near him leaned away as if afraid of him. She had expected every girl in here to flock to him like they did with Luke, to fight over who would get to sit next to this beautiful creature. She felt she might be missing something—a common feeling as of late.

When Magister Monroe entered the classroom everyone fell silent. A deep scowl was plastered on his face and his nose was wrinkled as if he smelled something unpleasant. His dull black hair was tied tightly back, and his sallow skin was sunken in places, giving him the appearance of a walking skeleton. If his ears hadn't been pointed Autumn would've thought he was a vampire. Apparently not all elves were attractive.

Magister Monroe moved slowly to his desk and sank into his chair, steepling his fingers as he surveyed the class. It was silent until he spoke.

"Welcome to Numbers class," he said in a monotonous voice. "I am Magister Monroe. I expect by the end of this year you will have learned the immense importance of numbers and the use of them in your daily lives. Numbers are at the base of all things. You eat, sleep, drink, and breathe numbers. So, if I hear any one of you question the relevance of this class, I will assign a ten-thousand-word essay in which you will answer that very question. Do I make myself clear?"

Everyone nodded with wide eyes.

"Now, I will call roll and then we can get started on our incalculably fascinating lesson over binomials. After which you will turn in the Numbers Project I assigned at the beginning of the summer."

Autumn saw a few people's faces go white. Clearly the summer had wiped the project from some of their minds completely. Magister Monroe called out the class list in a bored voice...until he reached the surnames ending in "O."

"Autumn O—" His eyes narrowed, leaving the paper he was

reading, and scanned the classroom. *"Oaken."*

Whispers swept like wind through the room. Out of the corner of her eye, Autumn saw the beautiful boy next to her lift his head slightly, turning his eyes on her.

Slumping down in her seat, she muttered, "Here."

Magister Monroe's gaze fixed on Autumn. "Thank you, Miss Oaken, for speaking up. Or do you prefer to be called *Your Highness?"*

His tone was mocking and Autumn swallowed all of the insults she wanted to throw at him. Gritting her teeth she said, "That won't be necessary."

A couple of chuckles echoed around the classroom.

"Ah. How very humble of you." He ran through the rest of the roll quickly before announcing, "Turn to page 247 in your books and we will begin our lesson."

After one of the most boring lectures Autumn had ever been forced to sit through, Magister Monroe separated the class into pairs to work on binomial problems out of their book. Her heart sank as Crystal was paired with Forrest. Autumn figured he would purposefully pair her with some brainless girl who could barely count to ten. Then he called her name along with Victor Lavigne, the elf-model sitting to her left.

Some of the students smirked at this pairing as if it were some sort of punishment to her. Autumn smiled tentatively at Victor as she moved her desk closer to his. He studied her with an interested look on his face, not like she was some celebrity but as if she was a puzzling problem in their Numbers book that he couldn't quite figure out.

She studied him too, but in a way that an art connoisseur would study a particularly exquisite piece of artwork. His face was perfectly symmetrical, perfectly smooth, perfectly perfect. Thick lashes framed his eyes, which were a deep green, like the color of an emerald stone. His full lips smiled at her, revealing his spectacularly white teeth.

He wore an intense look on his face and Autumn felt as if his eyes were somehow piercing into her soul. She began to feel a little exposed, so she turned her eyes to her book.

"How long have you been in the Underground?" he asked her

then.

Autumn glanced up and found that he was no longer looking at her in a puzzled way but, rather, wore a friendly smile on his face.

"Um...about three days," she said.

"How do you like it so far?"

"I love it here, but it's a little overwhelming sometimes."

"I can imagine." They were quiet for a few minutes as they worked on their Numbers problems before Victor spoke again. "Have you discovered your Power yet?"

Autumn shook her head and said, "Not yet. I'm hoping it happens soon, though. I don't know what I'll be able to do in Powers class without one." He chuckled. "What's your Power?" she asked.

"Light."

Autumn's eyebrows rose in surprise. She had been thinking it would be something a bit more threatening like Lightning, or Fire, or even Darkness—but Light?

"I know it doesn't sound all that impressive, but it's very useful. I can light a path or a room, but I can also produce a beam strong enough to blind an enemy, even burn them with the heat of it."

"Seems pretty useful to me."

For the remainder of the period the two of them mostly worked on their problems. Victor asked her a question every now and then, but otherwise kept silent. When the class bells rang they turned in their papers, and left the Numbers Tree.

"It was a pleasure meeting you, Autumn," Victor said with a small smile.

"Yeah, you too."

Autumn stared after Victor's retreating figure when Crystal came to stand beside her, wearing a sly grin. "I haven't seen Victor Lavigne talk that much in a long time. You must have had an effect on him."

"Whatever."

"Magister Monroe seems to like you," Crystal said, dropping the subject and moving on to an equally unwelcome one.

"Yeah. I think I'll be the magister's pet in that class," Autumn said. "What was his problem with me anyway?"

"I hear he's always like that. He doesn't like his students to think they're better than they are, so he tries to knock their spirits down to keep them grounded."

"Is he married?"

"Nope."

"Well that's surprising."

Crystal laughed as they turned to see Luke and Avery approaching them.

"I hope your magister liked you better than mine liked me, Luke," Autumn called when he was within hearing distance.

"Oh, he did. He loved me, in fact. I usually don't really care for History, but Underground History is actually pretty interesting. Did you know that there are all kinds of other creatures down here? Like giants and trolls and witches and leprechauns and mermaids?" Luke's face became dazed at the mention of mermaids.

"I didn't, but I figured as much," Autumn said.

"Yeah, and this really hot girl sat next to me." Luke turned to Avery. "What was her name? Alex...Alice..."

"Alyson," Avery corrected. Both of the boys laughed at this and Autumn and Crystal rolled their eyes at them.

"Autumn had a little flirting action with a guy too," Crystal added.

Luke and Avery stopped laughing and turned to face Autumn. Luke's smile had morphed into a stern frown, and Avery shot her a brief glance of consternation before quickly masking it over with indifference.

"Thanks for that," Autumn muttered to Crystal before facing Luke and Avery. "I wasn't *flirting*. I was talking. We were just Numbers partners." Autumn noticed something like relief flash across Avery's face, which quickly changed back to its indifferent stare. Crystal opened her mouth to speak and Autumn quickly interrupted her, attempting to avoid another confrontation. "What class do you have next, Luke?"

"Numbers."

"Good luck with that," Autumn said. "Apparently Magister Monroe hates royals."

"He hates authority," Avery corrected.

"I bet I can handle him," Luke said with a defiant look.

Autumn raised an eyebrow at him. "I'd like to see that.

Unfortunately, I have an Underground Literature class to get to."

"I have that class next too," Avery said. Autumn parted with Luke and Crystal, following Avery towards the Literature Tree. "So, who was your partner today?" he asked her, clearly trying to sound casual.

"Victor Lavigne," she answered, watching his expression. A shadow passed across his face, but he stayed silent. "You know him?" she asked.

"You could say that."

Autumn left the conversation at that. She had the familiar feeling that she was not getting something, but she also had a feeling that Avery wasn't the person to fill her in.

When they made it to the Literature classroom, they chose their seats and waited for the magister to arrive. Avery's mood seemed to have darkened ever since Autumn mentioned Victor's name, but she pretended not to notice.

When Magistra Hart entered the room, Autumn could tell immediately that she would like her considerably better than Magister Monroe. Hart had long, gray hair that fell down her back, deep laugh lines on her face, and blue eyes that sparkled when she smiled. When calling roll, she didn't bring Autumn's name to everyone's attention but merely winked at her and continued on.

"Welcome to 4th quarter Underground Literature, everyone. Or, better known to some as 'the last time you will be forced to read a book.' Which is the perfect segue into this semester's topic: forbidden love."

Magistra Monroe passed around the first book they would be reading. It was called *Oceans Deep*. Autumn scanned the cover. The picture was of a mermaid reaching towards the shore where a man was standing, looking longingly at her.

A boy a few chairs behind Autumn muttered, "This book looks stupid."

"All books are stupid," another boy chimed in.

Autumn tried not to roll her eyes at them. Clearly they hadn't read many books by the sound of their less than extensive vocabulary.

After class, Autumn left the Literature Tree in search of Crystal and Luke. Avery had been busy talking to the elves that hated reading, so she figured he would catch up with them later.

"Autumn wait up!" he called from behind her and she slowed her walk until he reached her. "You know, as your bodyguard, I have to keep an eye on you."

"You're Luke's bodyguard too. Keep an eye on him," Autumn said. "Besides, you're only our bodyguard when we aren't in school or on castle grounds. The campus guards are all I need here."

"I guess that's true…"

"Do we eat in a cafeteria for lunch or what?" she asked.

"We usually go downtown to eat. What do you feel like?"

"Anything but dragon."

Avery laughed. "Deal."

Crystal insisted they try the food at a small restaurant called Hummingbird Café. Autumn was convinced that there was no bad food in the Underground. Everything she had tasted so far had been nothing short of extraordinary.

After lunch, they still had an hour until their next class, so Luke suggested they go to Arbor Lake for a bit. Autumn was sure he just wanted to go where the most girls would be.

Sure enough, Luke said, "See ya," when they arrived, as he left them in favor of a giggling group of girls who were ogling him.

"The hovering hammocks are empty for once. Let's go over there," Crystal suggested, leading Autumn and Avery over to a peculiar series of hammocks that were suspended in mid-air.

"Weird," Autumn said, carefully climbing onto one. It began to sway back and forth in a rhythmic, soothing motion. Avery jumped into the one beside hers and folded his hands behind his head, letting out a sigh of relaxation.

While Autumn's body wanted to relax, her mind was still racing. She couldn't help but ask Crystal and Avery question after question about elves, Arbor Falls, and the rest of the Underground. She figured she was probably annoying them, but they answered everything patiently.

Time seeped quickly away and soon the three of them were reluctantly rolling off of their hammocks to leave for their next class.

As Autumn was smoothing out her dress, she heard Crystal

and Avery chuckling.

"What?" Autumn asked, looking up to see Crystal pointing past her and Avery nodding in the same direction. She turned to see her brother's face interlocked with a blonde elf's, occasionally coming up for air.

"He doesn't seem to have any trouble making new friends, does he?" Crystal laughed.

"Not here, anyway," Autumn said.

"Should we interrupt?" asked Crystal.

"Nah. He'll be fine."

When Autumn, Crystal, and Avery were about half a mile away from campus they realized they were going to be late if they didn't pick up the pace. The three of them began jogging towards the school. Avery glanced sideways at Autumn, wearing a challenging smirk, which she returned with a smug smile. Without warning, they simultaneously broke out into a sprint.

Autumn had always been a runner. It was the only sport she actually excelled in. Soon she pulled in front of Avery and managed to stay ahead, though she was unsure whether she was actually beating him or if he was simply letting her win. She looked back, flashing him a wide grin as she disappeared around a sharp corner before slamming into the back of a stationary figure.

"Ow!" she exclaimed as she was thrown backwards onto the ground.

A tall black-haired elf turned around angrily at first, but his face brightened when he saw that it was Autumn on the ground looking up at him, her chest heaving.

It was Victor Lavigne smiling down at her with those piercing green eyes.

Atticus Attribold

CHAPTER TEN

Victor chuckled, offering his hand to help Autumn to her feet. "Sorry about that," he said, smiling warmly down at her.

"No, I'm sorry. It was my fault. I was trying to outrun Avery and wasn't watching where I was going."

"It seems you were successful. Where are you heading so quickly?" he asked as he pulled her to her feet.

"Powers class."

"That's where I'm going. Would you care to walk with me?"

"Sure, I was just waiting for—"

Avery appeared around the corner then, slowing to a walk at the sight of Victor. Crystal jogged past Avery, coming to a stop beside Autumn.

"Victor," Crystal said. "Nice to see *you* here." She winked at Autumn, who sent her an exasperated look. Crystal's eyes focused on Victor's hand, which was resting lightly on Autumn's lower back.

Avery passed by without sparing any of them a glance and continued on towards the Powers Tree. Autumn, Victor, and Crystal fell into step a few yards behind him. Victor kept his hand on her back the entire way, something Crystal was sure to notice and comment on later. They entered the Powers Tree less than a minute before the bells rang.

Kyndel and her two "followers"—who Autumn had learned were named Ella and Dayna—were already situated in their seats, and Autumn was met with a trio of smug glares.

Avery took a seat in a desk beside Forrest at the far right of the classroom, and Victor sat in a chair to the far left. The two of them watched Autumn expectantly, both clearly waiting for her to choose. Victor or Avery.

Crystal saw Autumn's dilemma and quickly sat in the middle of the rows of desks. "Sit with me, Autumn," she said and Autumn smiled at her gratefully, joining her in the middle.

Luke jogged in just seconds before the campus bells rang, out of breath and red-faced. He took a seat next to Avery, grinning from ear to ear. The magister walked in just as Luke was sitting down. He strolled to the front of his desk and leaned casually back against it. Autumn thought he was a bit young looking for a teacher, maybe in his early thirties. He had a handsome face and scruffy facial hair that made him look like he had a bit of an edge. His light brown hair was shaggy and somewhat unkempt, but in a good way. All in all he wasn't too bad to look at...for a teacher.

"Welcome to Powers class, everyone. As you probably all know I am Magister Atticus Attribold. You can all call me Atticus, but if any of the other magisters ask, I'm Magister Attribold. All right, let's get started. Does anyone know what significant event is coming up in the next few months? No, Mr. Thomson, not your birthday, though I'm sure that's very special. Yes, Miss Everly?"

"The Warrior Test," Crystal called out.

"Correct. Now, the Warriors are a prestigious group of protectors and the Test is not something to be taken lightly. You need to think long and hard before you decide to try out. Being a Warrior is not as glamorous as it may seem. It is difficult and dangerous. If you try out you are essentially choosing your future careers. There is basically no going back. No exceptions. If you become a Warrior, you will be expected to serve until your rotation retires or if you are injured—"

"Or if you die," a boy interrupted, laughing.

Atticus frowned at the boy. Autumn recognized him as one of the boys in her Literature class that hated reading. "Unfortunately that *is* the case sometimes and is in no way humorous," Atticus said, causing the elf that laughed to shut his mouth. "For the next few months you will be practicing your Power techniques, whether you plan on taking the Warrior Test or not. As many of you know, I am the Initiates' and the Quinns' trainer. Therefore, I expect the very best out of my students. Understood?" He made eye contact with each student in the class. Autumn had a feeling his eyes lingered on her and Luke a few seconds longer than the rest. "Any questions?" A girl beside Kyndel raised her hand. "Ms. Roberts?"

"Will you, like, tell us what we're supposed to do for the Test?" she asked, smacking her gum loudly in between every word.

"The school will release the rules and expectations for the Test this Friday. So I will be able to tell you then. Any other questions?"

Another girl raised her hand and said, "Aren't Warriors really rich?"

Atticus frowned at this. "They do make a more than a sufficient amount of money, though that is no reason to take the Test." The girl didn't seem all that satisfied with this answer, but didn't speak again. "Alright, if there are no more questions, I'm going to split you into pairs and you will use your Powers to attempt to defeat your partner."

Atticus read off a list of names, pairing boys with girls, excluding Autumn and Luke. When the pairs were announced, either squeals of delight or less than thrilled grumbles echoed throughout the classroom.

"I expect by now you've learned to control the strength of your Power so as not to slay your opponent. Points will be taken off for that. Now, kindly make your way upstairs to the dueling room. Autumn and Luke Oaken, come and see me, please."

The rest of the class made their way upstairs while Autumn and Luke approached Atticus at the front of the classroom. "I'm happy to have you both in my class. I knew your father well so I'm aware of the level of talent you will be inheriting. Don't worry about not knowing your Powers yet, they'll show up within the next few weeks." Noise erupted from upstairs as the pairs began their battles. Muffled shouts of pain and laughter could be heard through the ceiling. "Let's continue upstairs. I should be supervising the mayhem."

"I have a question," Luke said as they climbed the spiral staircase. "How come you paired boys with girls?"

"Ah, because I've found that when the boys are paired together the violence can get out of hand and when the girls are paired, there's more gossiping and giggling than learning. It works out better this way. Plus, when the Warriors are chosen, they'll be put into co-ed pairs as well."

Luke nodded and grinned at a cute girl in the dueling room, who was then hit with a jet of water from across the room.

"Sorry!" a boy yelled.

"What are we going to do while we have no Powers and everyone else is dueling?" Autumn asked Atticus a little glumly.

"I'll come up with different lessons. Some days you'll learn how to fight physically. Some days, like today, I'll have you observe the others when they're fighting with their Powers."

"What's your Power?" Luke asked him.

Atticus smiled. "I can read the Powers of other elves. Comes in handy, as I always know what to expect. For instance, I'd be able to tell that Noah, there, has the Power of Water and would be able to plan accordingly."

Noah, who was very small for his age, was battling against Cera Tillman (pronounced like Sarah) who was also very small. She had short spiky blonde hair and wore all leather—or what looked like leather. Autumn noticed that Cera's petite stature didn't seem to hold her back at all because she was definitely winning the fight. Noah tried to hit Cera with a jet of water, but she easily used Gravity to change its course, usually in the direction of Kyndel or one of her followers.

Autumn discovered that Kyndel Butler's Power was Invisibility. Victor's Light couldn't help him in finding her, so she kept attacking him from behind. Autumn thought that this was a little tactless, but that did seem to be Kyndel's style.

Then there was Charlotte Locke, a curvy brunette with eyes that matched her hair color. She walked with confidence, as if she was completely sure of herself. Autumn would have immediately admired her if she hadn't seen Charlotte talking and laughing with Kyndel several times. Charlotte's Power was Fog. She was paired with Jastin Lambert, a boy with a similar stature to Avery and wavy blond hair that fell to his shoulders. His Power was Pain, emotional Pain.

"What do you mean Emotional Pain?" Luke asked, clearly dense on the subject of emotions of any kind.

"His Power can bring up the most painful memories a person might have and replay it over and over as long as he is making eye contact with them," Atticus clarified.

Autumn imagined her parents' death being replayed in her mind and shuddered. She noticed that Jastin didn't seem to be using his Power on Charlotte, though. She engulfed him in a thick gray Fog, but he only used his physical abilities to attempt an escape.

"Why isn't he using his Power on her?" Luke asked.

"Would you enjoy torturing someone you loved?" Atticus asked.

"Oh," Luke said.

Crystal was paired with Avery. Autumn thought they were a pretty even match. Ice flashed at Avery like frozen lightning and he dodged it with expert precision until he finally leaped over a jet of frost and wrapped Crystal in a hold that was impossible for her to escape.

As the class was beginning to wrap up, Autumn watched Atticus walk around the dueling room and critique each student individually, explaining what they did right and what they should have done differently. Everyone walked downstairs and took their seats.

"Very well done, guys. I want a full-page paper explaining what you think the best qualities of your Powers are and how you think you would be an asset to the Warriors. Due Friday. Autumn and Luke, you will only write the latter portion of the essay. Class dismissed."

The sound of scraping chairs and rustling bags rose up around them.

The first day of school was officially over and a large group of 4th quarter elves began to make their way to Arbor Lake. One of the boys—Drake—hurried to walk beside Autumn. Avery positioned himself a few feet behind them and, for once, Autumn was glad to have a bodyguard around.

"I'm Drake McMurtry," the dark-haired boy said, flashing her a smile.

"Autumn Oaken."

"Oh, I know."

"You were in my Lit class weren't you?" she asked, recognizing him as one of the book haters.

He rolled his eyes. "Yes. That class sucks, huh?"

Autumn shrugged. "I like it, actually."

His face fell at this. "Oh, well, yeah... It's pretty cool." Autumn sent him a confused look and he cleared his throat nervously. "So, what elective are you taking?"

"Elective?"

"Yeah. Sports, Art, or Melodies?"

Autumn frowned. She hadn't thought about electives. Well, Sports was out because running was the only physical activity at which she hadn't failed miserably. Art was no good either unless it was an art class of strictly stick figure drawing. That left Melodies.

She hadn't sung anything in a long time—not since her parents died. Autumn and her father used to write songs together. He was amazing at playing the guitar and had the most beautiful voice. Autumn could sing reasonably well, but her voice was nothing compared to his. When he died, she stopped singing and writing songs altogether. It was just too painful.

"Er...Autumn?" Drake said.

Realizing she had been silent for quite awhile, she said, "Sorry, um, I guess I'll be in Melodies."

"Oh. You don't like Sports?" He sounded disappointed.

"Not really. I just like to run." She felt like running now. Away from Drake.

Yet another boy materialized on Autumn's other side so that she was now sandwiched between the two. Drake seemed somewhat put off by this.

"You're Autumn Oaken, right? I'm Bryan Thomas."

"Hi," Autumn said, not even bothering to introduce herself.

"So you don't know your Power yet, huh?"

"Nope."

"I bet it's going to be something awesome."

"We'll see, I guess." These guys were starting to annoy her.

"I bet you make the Warriors for sure," Drake cut in.

"Why do you think that?" Autumn asked.

"Well, you're a royal," Bryan said.

"Yeah, they pretty much *have* to make you a Warrior," Drake added.

Autumn glowered, flashing Avery a "please help me" look over her shoulder and he immediately jumped in.

"Can I speak to you for a second, Autumn? It's about, er, official castle business."

"Of course. Sorry, guys, it was nice talking to you," Autumn lied. The two boys walked away looking disappointed. When they were out of earshot Autumn sighed and said, "Thanks for that."

"You seem to be as popular as your brother," he said. "Only with a different audience."

She made a disgusted face. "It sort of makes me miss being invisible."

Avery shook his head as he said, "I doubt you've ever been invisible."

When they arrived at Arbor Lake, Autumn and Avery took a seat on the sandy shore. Crystal was busy using her Power to freeze a section of the lake for the boys to play what looked like the Underground version of ice hockey and Luke was, of course, prowling around a group of girls, cornering his prey.

"I did have some official castle business to tell you, actually," Avery said.

Autumn drew patterns in the white sand with her finger and said, "More bodyguards?"

Avery laughed. "No. Olympus has arranged for you and Luke to have dinner with him tonight. He wants to personally go over the rules of Arbor Castle."

"Rules?"

"Yes. It's mostly about secrecy and behavior. Things go on in Arbor Castle that aren't to be discussed outside of the castle grounds. All of the castle workers were given a set of rules when we first came to the castle too."

"How long have you been working at the castle?" Autumn asked.

Avery stared across the vast lake, but it seemed he was seeing something that wasn't there, a memory perhaps. His gray eyes hardened as he said, "A few years." Autumn watched him expectantly, waiting for the story behind why he started working there in the first place. She was very aware of his close proximity. It felt as if some sort of magnetic force was connecting them. Suddenly the connection broke when he stood and said, "You should get back to the castle. You'll need time to get dressed for dinner. I'll go tell Luke."

Autumn watched him go with mixed feelings and wondered what she had said to make him put up his ever-present walls once again.

AVERY walked away from Autumn with a jumble of thoughts and feelings coursing through him. His skin still tingled from sitting so close, though not close enough, to her. They'd barely known each other two days and she had already managed to break through his walls more than he would like. There was a reason he didn't ever let girls in. They asked too many questions. They wanted to know everything about everything. And he didn't want anyone to know *everything*.

The difference with Autumn, though, was that he wanted to know everything about her too. It wasn't because she was a princess—it was in *spite* of that. When he'd first heard that the prince and princess of Arbor Falls would be returning, he had been expecting two bigheaded, stuck-up, spoiled brats. To his surprise, they were none of these things. Autumn especially. She was endearing and selfless, smart and beautiful, though she didn't seem to know just how beautiful she was.

Not to mention that intense feeling he had in the pit of his stomach every time she was near. What *was* that?

"Hey, Luke!" he called. Luke was entangled in a passionate embrace with yet another girl.

The redhead came up for air, giving Avery a "this better be good" look.

"You and Autumn are having dinner with Olympus tonight. You should probably start getting ready soon."

Luke looked regretfully at the girl he was kissing and said, "I guess I've gotta go, Babe. I'll see you later."

The girl watched him go with a frown on her face.

"You seem to be making friends easily," Avery said, chuckling.

"You have no idea, man. I feel like I've died and gone to heaven. I'm just glad my sister isn't making friends the same way I am."

Funny. Avery had just been thinking the same thing.

The Rules

CHAPTER ELEVEN

"**C**an't breathe," Autumn said as Crystal laced up her corset.

"Sorry."

"Tell me again why this is necessary?"

"Dinner with the king is a tremendous honor, even if he *is* your grandfather. And, as the princess, you are expected to look presentable."

This was the longest it had ever taken Autumn to get dressed in her whole life and she was not particularly thrilled about it. The gown Crystal had picked out for her was yet another masterpiece from her dresser. It was a delicate yellow with elaborate, swirling designs covering the bodice and an elegant off the shoulder neckline.

There was a knock on the door and Crystal rushed into the living room to answer it. Autumn followed as well as she could in the gown, emerging in the sitting room to see Luke and Avery standing in the doorway.

Luke looked at Autumn in surprise and said, "You clean up nice, Rose," as he walked into her branch and plopped down on her sofa. "Though, you look even more uncomfortable than I am," he added, tugging at the collar of his old-fashioned frock coat.

Autumn laughed uneasily as she glanced at Avery, who was looking her over with a conflicted expression. Their eyes met and he looked quickly away saying, "I'll take you to the king's dining quarters if you're ready."

Olympus's dining quarters branched off of the throne room. As Avery turned to leave them at the door he finally looked at Autumn. His gray eyes brightened when they met hers and Autumn's stomach flipped like she was going down a steep hill on a rollercoaster. He smiled crookedly at her and walked away.

Autumn watched him go until Luke said, "You coming?"

Olympus's dining room was even grander than the one upstairs, and also had a remarkable sparkling chandelier hanging from the high ceiling.

When they entered, Olympus's face broke out into a wide smile. "Ah, children. I see your transformations are nearly complete. Please have a seat." He waved his hand to the two chairs sitting across from him. There were only three seats, spaced equally apart so that they formed a sort of triangle around the circular table. "I apologize for my absence. I have many duties outside of this castle."

"We understand," Autumn said, taking a seat.

"I expect young Mr. Burke has informed you of the purpose of this dinner?"

Autumn nodded and Luke said, "Yes, sir."

"Very good," Olympus said as a waiter dressed in white approached the table. "I will have the dragon filet, please."

"Yes, Your Majesty." The waiter turned to the twins expectantly. Autumn hadn't even looked at the menu, so she glanced over it and ordered the first thing she saw, which was some sort of fish. Luke ordered the pasta dish.

"No dragon?" Olympus said in surprise. Autumn and Luke shook their heads trying not to look too disgusted. "Oh, you must try it! It is delectable. Bring three plates of the dragon filet, George."

The waiter nodded and left the three royals to place the order. Autumn tried not to be annoyed, even though she hated when people ordered for her. She knew Luke felt the same way, but he also kept his face impassive.

Olympus didn't seem to notice their uncomfortable silence and spoke again. "The rules of the castle are quite simple and easy to follow," he began. "However, they are of the utmost importance and I expect you to follow each and every one of them, understood?"

"Yes, sir," the twins said together.

"Very well. Rule number one: Any business or information you see or hear is forbidden to leave the castle walls. Even if it's me telling you that my favorite color is red."

"Is it?" Luke blurted.

"No, it's green actually."

Autumn smiled at this small thing she and her grandfather had in common.

"The second rule," he continued. "You must always look and act presentably. Everything you do reflects on the royal family and, as the prince and princess, you will be representing the royal elf kingdom whether you mean to or not. And, lastly, rule number three: You must not become romantically involved with any of the castle workers, for they are your subordinates. You may befriend them as you wish, but any more than that would be deemed inappropriate."

Autumn felt her face fall at this and her stomach twisted uncomfortably as Avery's face floated to the surface of her mind. Luke clearly noticed his sister's sudden mood change and shot her a quizzical look.

"There is one last thing. Not a rule, but a request from a grandfather to his grandchildren. I recommend that you do not go *looking* for trouble. If you are anything like your father then I know it is probably pointless to ask this of you. Vyra has taken your parents from you, but she has also taken my son. I assure you I am doing everything in my power to seek justice." Autumn's expression darkened to match Luke's. "However, if you become Warriors, you will be required to look for trouble. I assume you will be taking the Test?"

Autumn and Luke nodded.

The food arrived, effectively ending the rules discussion. Autumn was surprised that the dragon actually had a pleasant, smoky taste. It was similar to regular steak, but richer in flavor. Luke practically inhaled his own. Olympus spoke openly and honestly with the two of them, inquiring about their classes and magisters. Autumn almost made a comment about Magister Monroe, but decided against it as Olympus began to regale them with tales from when their father was in school.

She found that she liked her grandfather very much. He was

funny and clever, traits her father had possessed. Sitting with Olympus reminded her of the times when her father would tell a tale of his college days around the dinner table. Now she realized that he only ever told college days tales, seeing as how his childhood was spent in the Underground and, for their safety, he obviously never mentioned this fact.

At the end of the night Olympus wrapped them in one of his bone crushing hugs and ushered them through the grand oak doors. As they made the long trek up the winding staircase, Autumn stared at her feet, replaying the third castle rule over and over in her head.

"What's with you?" Luke asked, playfully punching Autumn's shoulder.

She shrugged and said, "Nothing."

"Rose—"

"I said it's nothing, Luke," she snapped. He looked taken aback. "Sorry. I'm just tired is all."

The dining room was empty when they passed by and Autumn was yet again reminded of Avery as she glanced down at their usual table. Luke bid her goodnight at his door and she climbed up the stairs to her own.

Somehow, Autumn managed to get out of the corset gown without help before running herself a bath in the great claw-footed tub. Slowly sinking into the hot water, Autumn tried and failed at vanishing that third rule from her head. It was no use lying to herself. There *was* some sort of connection between her and Avery that she couldn't explain. She'd had crushes on guys tons of times before, but this felt different somehow. Letting out a groan, she sank under the water, hoping that it would pull the unwanted thoughts out of her head.

Victor Lavigne

CHAPTER TWELVE

The next day Autumn made a real effort to avoid Avery. Luckily, she didn't have class with him on Tuesdays. Unfortunately, this meant she had to make up excuses to keep her away from him, like leaving her bag behind on purpose so she could rush back to her branch. She was the last one to arrive to her Laboratory class and found that the only empty station was the one beside Victor Lavigne, which didn't surprise her. For reasons unknown to her people were afraid of him.

He smiled warmly at her as she set her book bag down beside his.

"So, what is this class exactly?" Autumn asked.

"We learn how to make different draughts and salves and discuss how different herbs and fungi react together."

"Like witches?"

Victor chuckled. "Not really. Witches brew potions. There is no magic in what we do. What we learn here is not so different from Outsider apothecaries."

Coach Holt, the Laboratory magister, walked in then. He was a tall muscular man with a shaved head. Along with teaching Laboratory, he was also the leader of the Sports elective. It wasn't difficult to tell that teaching was a distant second to his true passion.

"Get your behinds in your seats," he said to the students who were talking to their friends or leaning on someone else's station.

After taking roll, pausing for a second on Autumn's name, he handed out a sheet of step-by-step directions with the words *How to Make a Nausea Draught* printed in bold across the top of the paper.

After barking at the class to get started without any further instructions, he proceeded to sit behind his desk, propping up his feet, and pulling out what looked like some sort of Underground sports magazine.

"Is this for *making* someone nauseated or for curing nausea?" Autumn whispered.

Victor laughed. "Curing it. We don't actually do anything that doesn't help or heal. That's the job of a warlock."

"Are there really warlocks down here?"

"There are warlocks in the Underground, but not in Arbor Falls. They live in Onyx Forest."

"How about giants or trolls or werewolves or leprechauns?" Autumn asked, remembering what Luke had said.

"Giants live in the Magnus Mountains, Trolls live in the Pravus Caves, Werewolves don't live in the Underground, and Leprechauns live in Rainbow's End."

Autumn laughed at the last one and said, "So all of the magical creatures are segregated then?"

Victor began chopping up a plant that resembled a large beet. He pushed a tray of some sort of grassy substance towards Autumn and instructed her to do the same before answering her question. "Yes, we are. We don't cohabitate."

"Why not?"

"We—er—don't really get along."

"Why?"

"Well, one reason is that we're all too different. One year the leprechauns and the trolls instigated a war against each other. The elves arrived to settle the dispute and to bring peace, but this offended both the trolls and the leprechauns—cousins of elves. So they attacked the elves as well. Then the giants and the ogres got involved because they just love a good fight. Then the warlocks, centaurs, and even the vampires joined in. That was the first Underground War. After all the magical populations began to dwindle drastically, Orpheus Oaken—the Elf king at the time—

had everyone sign a truce to agree to live separately and in peace."

"That's horrible."

Victor added the deep purple substance to the pot and the grassy piles from Autumn's chopping board, pouring in various quantities of different liquids. The directions said to stir the mixture fifty times slowly, let it come to a boil, then have it sit for fifteen minutes. Victor stirred the mixture, his muscles contracting and relaxing with every turn. He looked up at Autumn and she blushed, realizing that she had been staring. She focused her eyes on the remnants of the grassy substance on her chopping board.

Victor seemed so genuine and nice. A little shy, maybe, but that wasn't necessarily a bad thing. Autumn still couldn't figure out why everyone feared him, or why Avery and his friends hated him. She decided it couldn't hurt to ask a couple of innocent questions to figure it out.

"So..." she said. "Who do you hang out with at lunch and after school and stuff?"

Victor's expression fell. He was silent a while before saying, "No one."

"No one at all?" Autumn asked. Victor shook his head. "But why?"

"They're all afraid of me."

"Why would they be afraid of you, though?"

Victor looked surprised. He even stopped what he was working on to look at her. "You don't know?" Autumn shook her head slowly. "Oh. I figured Burke would have told you by now."

"Avery?" she said. "Tell me what?"

"He's the reason everyone's so afraid of me."

"How?"

Victor busied himself with the fire beneath the iron pot. Autumn waited.

He sighed as if he knew he would regret telling her what he was about to say. "I made the mistake of telling him what I am."

"What do you mean 'what you are'?"

Victor glanced surreptitiously around the classroom and then murmured, "I'm an *Atrum*. Or I used to be. I was born on Alder Island."

Autumn's mouth fell open. She had learned enough in the past few days to know that Atrums were evil followers of Vyra Vaun.

"But, you aren't an Atrum anymore, right?"

He shook his head. "I'll always have Atrum blood, but I don't speak with my family or any other Atrums I knew in my former life. I left the island a few years ago and came here. I didn't want to be a monster anymore. I went to the king, asking his permission to stay and he was gracious enough to let me."

"Do you live with anyone?"

"I live alone. My family was one of the wealthier Atrum families. I had my own money set aside and it's been enough to sustain me here."

Silence fell between them as they each wrote a detailed description of what their nausea draught looked like. Autumn couldn't stop thinking of Victor's heartbreaking story. He was completely and utterly alone. She couldn't imagine how it would feel to have absolutely no one to talk to, no one to help you if you needed help, or comfort you when you were upset. Her chest filling with compassion, she made a promise to herself to help him. If anything, she could be his friend and show everyone else that, if a royal elf like her could make friends with an Atrum, then so could they. Finally she could use her royal influence for some good.

When Autumn finished her paragraph she turned it in to Coach Holt and returned to her workstation to clean up. She realized she hadn't asked Victor an obvious question.

"Why would Avery tell everyone that you're an Atrum anyway?"

Victor's face darkened and the familiar end-of-class bells sounded in the distance. The room filled with noise as everyone rushed out the door.

"I'll see you later, Autumn," Victor said as he walked briskly out of the classroom.

She must have asked one question too many.

"Hey, Summer!" Forrest called when Autumn entered the History Tree.

She checked to see if there actually was someone named Summer standing around her before she realized it was just another name joke of his. Rolling her eyes playfully, she took a seat beside him. Drake, the flirty book-hater, sat in front of Autumn and turned in his seat to grin at her. She smiled politely back and focused her eyes elsewhere, though she still felt his gaze on her face.

Autumn scanned the room to keep her eyes from wandering back to Drake, busying herself with looking at the maps that were pinned up in various spaces on the wall and found herself actually studying them. There was a map of Arbor Falls and then there was one of the entire Underground. She remembered where Victor said some of the magical creatures lived and saw that each territory was spaced far apart and were clearly marked on the map. Autumn frowned at this in silent disapproval.

Magister Parkey arrived then. He looked to be in his fifties and had light brown hair with silver running through it. His soft green eyes scanned the room.

"Everyone awake?" he asked, clapping his hands together with enthusiasm. People nodded and murmured half-heartedly. "Well that's the majority." He began to call roll. "Autumn Oaken?" he said as he reached her name. "New to the Underground I assume?"

"Yes, Sir."

"Well, welcome to History of the Underground. I'm sure at least *you* will find this class to be immeasurably interesting."

Autumn nodded in agreement and Kyndel whispered something loudly to one of her cronies—Dayna—who giggled.

Magister Parkey finished calling roll and said, "Only three skips! It's going to be a good day. All right. Today we will begin our discussion of the Great Underground War of 1872. Can anyone tell me what started this war?"

Autumn looked around the room. Everyone was either looking at nothing in particular or staring at him blankly, with the exception of Drake, who was still staring at her. She turned to face the magister and tentatively raised her hand.

Magister Parkey wore a surprised yet pleased look. "Miss Oaken?"

"The war started with a dispute between the trolls and the leprechauns. The elves came to make peace, but were pulled into the war instead. Then the ogres and giants joined in, and...yeah."

Autumn glanced at Forrest who wore an impressed, open-mouthed expression. Drake and Dayna had confused looks on their faces and Kyndel was looking at her with a mixture of surprise and loathing.

"That is quite correct. You say you are new to Arbor Falls?"

"Yes, Sir. Vic—uh—my Lab partner told me about the Underground War. That's how I knew," Autumn admitted.

"Well, it's good you listened." He smiled and winked at her.

Autumn met up with Luke, Crystal, and Avery after History. In an attempt to avoid Avery engaging her in conversation, she read her Literature book all through lunch. Autumn and Luke had Healing after lunch and they parted from Crystal and Avery to travel to the Healing Tree together.

"Any new make-out sessions today?" Autumn asked.

"Two, in between classes," he said with a wide smile.

"What were their names?"

He shrugged.

Autumn laughed, though she knew she shouldn't support this kind of behavior in her brother, or any guy for that matter. But she had watched Luke strike out too many times in the Outside to not be a little happy for him now.

When they entered the Healing classroom, Autumn saw that Bryan (or Tweedle-Dum as she liked to think of him) was in this class. Luke was about to take the seat next to Bryan when Autumn pushed him to keep going.

"Good afternoon!" came a bright voice from the doorway. Autumn turned to see Magistra Ginger smiling at the class. She was an eccentric looking woman with flaming red hair that was piled on top of her head in a bun with pieces sticking out all over. Autumn thought someone with that bright of a personality would wear bright clothing, but the cheerful woman wore all black instead; maybe it was to balance things out.

"Everyone up!" Magistra Ginger said. "I don't like to stay in the classroom more than five minutes at a time. Almost a fifth of that time has gone by and this dreary atmosphere is already depressing me. Outside we go!" With this, she swept from the room. The dazed class followed her outside.

She turned around so that she was facing the class and began walking backwards. "Today we will learn about pelpy. Pelpy is a healing herb found in the shallow waters of an Underground pond or lake. It can be used to heal someone who has been poisoned by one or many poisonous water creatures. Here—" she waved her hand towards a small pond on campus near the Numbers Tree, "you will find some pelpy just below the surface of the water. So take these." She passed out a pair of long, rubber-like gloves to everyone. Some of the girls made disgusted faces as they pulled on the gloves and looked down at the dirty pond water.

Magistra Ginger plunged her hand into the water, feeling around for a few seconds and yanked up a small, purple plant that looked like a wet feather duster.

"See?" she said. "It's quite simple. Now you try. Everyone, come on! They don't bite, but the razor fish might, so it's a good thing we're surrounded by all of this pelpy."

Some of the students grumbled as they approached the water. They spent the remainder of the class pulling up pelpy while Magistra Ginger spouted off random facts about water plants and their healing powers.

One of the girls accidently slipped into the water. She screamed and splashed around before she realized the water was only about two feet deep. Luke crashed into the water eagerly and carried her to safety. The girl thanked him over and over for "saving her life" and called him her hero. Autumn sensed yet another make-out partner.

"Well done, everyone!" Magistra Ginger said. "You guys pulled a lot of pelpy today. I'll take this to the storage room for later use." The bells rang and Luke whisked the girl he "saved" away to make out.

Avery emerged from the Numbers Tree then, not far from where Autumn was standing. His eyes landed on her and he began to walk in her direction. *Uh oh*, Autumn thought. How was she supposed to avoid him this time? Although the more problematic issue was that she didn't exactly want to.

Bulls-eye

CHAPTER THIRTEEN

Autumn tried to pretend she hadn't seen Avery and turned to walk quickly in the opposite direction.

"Autumn!" he called out much too loudly for her to be able to ignore.

Taking a deep breath, she turned around, plastering on an artificial smile. "Oh, hey, Avery! I didn't see you."

"That's okay. My friend Jastin and I are going to shoot some arrows at the archery range. Want to come?"

His sparkling, gray eyes quickly made her forget everything that Victor had said in Laboratory. Autumn bit her lip. Yes, she would like to come. The real question was: should she? Then she realized she was being ridiculous. She shouldn't have to avoid Avery. He was her friend *and* her bodyguard. So, she had a tiny, miniscule, insignificant crush on him. So what? That's all it was. A crush. Surely, with time, it would pass.

"Yeah, sure," she said, unable to keep the reluctance out of her voice.

His brow furrowed. "Are you angry with me or something?"

"Why would I be angry with you?"

"I'm not sure."

"So, you said you were going with someone named Justin?" Autumn asked, trying to change the subject.

"Jastin. He's in our Powers class. The one with the long blond hair. His Power is Pain."

Autumn remembered that Jastin had also been in her History class, sitting in the very back beside Charlotte, the dark haired girl whose Power was Fog.

"Oh, yeah. I think I know who you are talking about."

"He'll probably bring Charlotte too. That's his girlfriend."

Autumn tried not to grimace at this. Now it looked less like friends casually hanging out and shooting arrows together, and more like a double date. Also, judging by how they interacted, she assumed Charlotte and Kyndel were friends, though she didn't seem to follow Kyndel around like Ella and Dayna did.

Autumn and Avery spotted Crystal near the marble fountain at the center of campus and Autumn desperately invited her to come along.

"Sorry, guys. I wish I could, but I already told my mom I would work on a few gowns with her tonight."

Stopping by Arbor Castle, Autumn and Avery retrieved their bows and arrows and made their way to the archery range. When they arrived, Jastin and Charlotte were waiting for them.

"Have you two met Autumn yet?" Avery asked them.

"Not formally," Jastin said as he shook Autumn's hand warmly.

"We have a few classes together," Charlotte said with a pleasant smile on her face—not a sarcastic sneer like Autumn had expected. But she would have to reserve her judgment.

The archery range was set up so that there were different levels. There were 10 ranges in all, each more difficult than the one before. The foursome walked onto the first range and Autumn noticed that the grass was cut close to the ground, almost resembling turf.

"This kind of looks like a golf course," she remarked, then glancing up at the others' confused faces said, "It's uh—well—never mind."

The idea of the course was to shoot three arrows as close as possible to the bulls-eye. Each target was more difficult than the last, with obstacles and trees making it nearly impossible to hit the middle circle. On the first target, Jastin and Charlotte whizzed through their arrows before Autumn had even managed to set up her first shot.

"You two go on ahead," Avery said. "I'll help Autumn."

Charlotte shot him an amused glance as she and Jastin moved on to the second range.

"Okay. Let me see you just try to shoot the arrow," he said.

Autumn shakily pulled back on the string and let go. The arrow shot a few feet ahead of where they stood and landed sadly on the ground. She sent Avery a frustrated look and he stifled a laugh.

"That was...not bad."

Autumn rolled her eyes. "It sucked. Maybe I should watch you guys shoot the arrows. I'll just be a silent observer."

He shook his head. "No. I can teach you. Besides, if you want to try out for the Warriors then you'll need to know how to shoot an arrow."

"Great."

"Now watch me and pay close attention to my form."

He pulled the string back in a fluid motion and released the arrow, which sped toward the target and fixed itself square in the middle of the bulls-eye. Autumn's mouth fell open.

"Now come stand right here," he said as if he hadn't just done something amazing. He pointed to a spot in front of him. She hesitated. "It's okay, Autumn. I won't bite."

Blushing, she took her place in front of Avery. He grasped both of her hands and her breath caught in her chest. There was a pulling sensation in the pit of her stomach like some sort of gravitational force—a magnet trying to find it's mate, which apparently resided within Avery. She felt him tremor slightly and then he cleared his throat.

"You're, uh, you're going to pull the arrow back, keeping your left arm straight and your right arm elevated at the level of your chin, like this." He moved his hand from hers and lifted her arm until her hand was level with her chin. She tried to breathe slow and deep rather than quick and shallow like her increased heart rate was telling her to. "Now," he whispered, sending a shiver through Autumn's body, almost causing her to let go of the bow, "release your right hand."

Autumn did as he said and her arrow soared through the air and landed a few rings away from the bulls-eye.

"Wow," she breathed.

"Perfect!" Avery exclaimed, giving her arm a squeeze.

"Thanks," she said, her head swimming from the rush of both Avery's closeness and successfully shooting an arrow.

They finished shooting the rest of the arrows and moved through the course with surprising ease. They even managed to catch up to Jastin and Charlotte at the sixth range.

"How've you done so far?" Charlotte asked Autumn.

"Pretty well, actually. I haven't missed a target and I've hit three bulls-eyes."

Jastin and Charlotte's eyebrows shot upwards. "Wow, beginners never do that well," Charlotte said.

"Just lucky, I guess. Avery's a good teacher."

Jastin smiled as he muttered, "I bet he is."

At the next range, Avery and Jastin decided to change up the game a little and see who could hit the most bulls-eyes in a row. Autumn and Charlotte stood back to watch.

"So, are you and Avery...?" Charlotte trailed off.

"No. We're, uh, just friends. Oh, and he's my bodyguard."

"Bodyguard? Oh right. I keep forgetting you're a royal. You act so normal."

"Thanks, I guess. You're different than I expected too."

Charlotte nodded in understanding. "Yeah. Most people think that just because I'm friends with Kyndel, I'll be as *unpleasant* as she sometimes can be."

"Why are you friends with someone like Kyndel anyway?" Autumn asked, realizing too late that her question was extremely rude.

"There's a lot to Kyndel that no one knows but me. We've been friends since we were kids, and I'm probably the only real friend she has. The way she treats people is her way of putting up a guard. It's just a defense mechanism."

"Feels more offensive than defensive to me," Autumn said.

Charlotte shrugged, indicating she didn't want to say any more on the subject.

They moved on to the next course and Jastin and Avery were now trying to invent more creative games, like seeing who could make a better design by shooting arrows at the target.

"How long have you been with Jastin?" Autumn asked Charlotte.

"Almost a year," she said with a smile. "I've liked him for much longer than that, but it took me a while to get anything out of him. He's so quiet. I think it has to do with his Power. He's a bit ashamed of it."

"Why?"

"He doesn't like to use it. Especially on people he cares about." Charlotte looked at Jastin with a mixture of sadness and fond admiration.

After archery, Autumn and Avery parted ways with the others and walked back to Arbor Castle in silence, which was surprisingly not awkward, but rather comfortable and almost familiar. The magnetic pull in Autumn's stomach grew steadily stronger as time went on. Eventually it won over and she felt her arm brush up against his. Warmth spread through her, trickling down through her arm and seeping into the rest of her body. Rather than satisfying the strange feeling, it intensified and left her wanting a bit more.

No. Remember the rules. Remember the rules, Autumn thought.

She reluctantly took a small step away from Avery so they were no longer touching.

"What's the Outside like?" Avery asked.

"You've never been?"

Avery shook his head.

Where to begin. Autumn took a deep breath and told him about her time in Texas and Ireland. About American politics and what little she had learned about the Irish government. She told him about the environment, Americans, the Irish, mankind as a whole. Avery listened intently, with a look of fascination upon his face as she told him about all of the technological advances humans had made.

Instead of going inside when they reached the castle, Avery led Autumn into the courtyard, a fairyland of blossoms and soft green grass. They sat on a marble bench among a patch of strange white flowers with buds that resembled swirling clouds.

"What are those?" Autumn asked.

"Puffinellos," Avery said as he bent to pick one and handed it to her.

Their fingers brushed and Autumn's heart fluttered. Her physical reactions were becoming a little ridiculous. She was beginning to think Avery felt them too because every time they touched or locked eyes, his square jaw clenched.

She rolled the puffinello back and forth between her fingertips. The white, cloud-like substance swirled with the motion.

"Have you always lived in Arbor Falls?" Autumn asked, still watching the flower spin and swirl.

Avery sighed. "My whole life."

"You say that like it's a bad thing."

"It's not really. I just envy people who've had the ability to travel. To see all of the Underground and even go to the Outside."

"Why weren't you able to?"

"My father. He was the Head Warrior and he felt it was his duty to protect the elves of the kingdom. So we never left."

"He *was* Head Warrior? Did he retire?"

Avery was quiet for a second. Autumn abandoned her puffinello and glanced sideways at him. His brow was furrowed and he stared unseeingly ahead.

"No," he said, not looking at her. "He died in battle."

Autumn's heart hurt for him because she knew exactly how it felt to lose a father. Forgetting her grandfather's rule for the moment, she reached over and grabbed Avery's hand.

"I'm so sorry, Avery."

He turned to face her, their eyes locking. Tingling warmth pulsed through their clasped hands. Their faces were inches apart. Her gaze moved from Avery's eyes down to his mouth and she swore her heart stopped for a moment.

Then someone burst through a jumble of bushes a few feet away from them. Autumn jumped and pulled her hand from Avery's. They turned to face the source of the commotion. The girl Luke "saved" in Healing was pulling him along through the courtyard, giggling. Luke looked their way and did a double take.

"What are you two doing out here?"

"We could ask you the same thing," Autumn said, shooting a disapproving glance at the girl trailing behind him.

Luke wore a sheepish expression as he said, "Oh, uh, Julia just wanted to see the castle."

Autumn raised a suspicious eyebrow at the girl.

"I've actually got to get home, Prince Luke," Julia said, sending

Autumn a wary glance. "Thanks again for saving me. I'll see you tomorrow?"

"Oh, uh, yeah sure," Luke said. Julia's face fell a bit as she walked off through the bushes. "Shut up, Autumn," Luke snapped when he saw his sister looking at him with a repressed smile.

"I didn't say anything, *Prince Luke*."

The Brawl

CHAPTER FOURTEEN

Autumn and Avery were silent all through breakfast the next day. She could tell Luke and Crystal sensed that something was off, but was pretty sure they were clueless otherwise. She'd had all night to think about how close she had come to breaking her grandfather's rule and felt horrible about it.

So, she made a new promise to herself to keep her distance from Avery, but in Literature he sat in the seat beside her and kept asking questions and cracking jokes when Magistra Hart wasn't paying attention. She answered his queries and laughed without hesitation at his jokes, mentally kicking herself afterwards. Aside from Luke, her grandfather was the only family she had left and she didn't want to disappoint him by disobeying one of the few things he'd asked of her. She could control herself. Really.

"Hey, do you want to go to lunch with me? Just the two of us?" Avery asked her as the bells rang in the distance.

Oh great, Autumn thought. "Um...yeah?"

His smile faltered a bit. "Is that a question?"

"Yes. I mean no, it's not a question. Yes, I want to go to lunch—with you."

Just then Luke and Crystal bounced up to them.

"Ready to go?" Luke said. "I'm feeling like pizza."

"I think Autumn and I will be having lunch alone today, actually," Avery said.

"Wha—" Luke began.

"Okay!" Crystal chimed in before Luke could finish. Though, for once, Autumn had been hoping that her brother's over-protective nature would save her from herself. "We'll just see you in Powers," Crystal said, pulling Luke with her down the path to town. Luke turned to flash Autumn a suspicious look with a hint of warning.

So bad. Not a good idea. Autumn kept telling herself this, but she couldn't help but feel a twinge of excitement as Avery led her down a path off campus.

"Where are we going? The path into town is the other way."

"We aren't going into town," Avery said slyly. "This place is really close."

He led her through a thick patch of trees and into a large clearing that held nothing but a petite tree café. Avery took a seat at one of the round, cast iron tables outside under the leafy awning.

The little tree café was actually really nice. Autumn liked the fact that it was so secluded and removed from the town. She watched as two squirrels chased each other up and down a tree.

"Ever wonder what they're fighting about?" she said.

"Huh?" Avery asked, looking away from Autumn to the two squirrels.

"I always wonder why squirrels chase each other like that. Like, maybe they're fighting over the same girl squirrel or something. Or one of them stole the other one's acorn."

"We could always ask Forrest."

"Oh, yeah! I forgot he talks to animals. I think I'd really like that Power."

"Maybe you *will* have an animal-related Power. You never know."

"Or maybe I won't have a Power at all."

"You will," Avery said. "You have royal blood. Royals are known for discovering their Powers very early, but because you and Luke have been in the Outside for so long, it will take a little while for your bodies to adjust to the Underground."

Autumn nodded, hoping he was right.

The little café offered all kinds of different sandwiches and soups, served on the freshest bread Autumn had ever tasted. And the tomato basil soup was smooth and creamy. So far, things were going pretty well. Although the pull in the pit of Autumn's stomach was working non-stop, she hadn't asked him any personal questions, she hadn't giggled like an idiot at everything he said, and she hadn't batted her eyelashes at him. Just a friendly lunch. That's all it was.

"So, did you leave a boyfriend behind in the Outside," Avery asked, trying to sound casual, but Autumn could hear the interest in his tone.

So much for a "friendly lunch."

"Nope. This soup is really good," Autumn said, trying to steer the conversation away from relationships.

"Have you ever?"

"Have I ever what?"

"Had a boyfriend."

"Um, not technically."

"Technically?"

"Well I had a couple of relationships, I guess, that lasted only a few weeks at a time. Nothing serious, though." Avery opened his mouth to speak again and Autumn quickly interrupted. "We should head back. Class starts soon."

"We still have thirty minutes," Avery said.

"Well, I want to be early for a change."

Avery frowned. "Okay..."

They paid for their food and walked back up the trail in silence. Avery opened his mouth a few times like he wanted to say something, but then quickly shut it. Finally he said, "So, are you interested in anyone here then?"

Autumn tripped over her feet, and Avery grabbed her arm before she could fall.

No. No. No. Why did he have to ask that? Lie, Autumn told herself.

"Uh, I mean, I—"

Autumn ran into the back of someone as she and Avery emerged out of the thick patch of trees onto campus. It was Victor Lavigne, once again, who she was now eternally grateful to.

"I apologize," he said, looking only at Autumn. Avery stared daggers at him. "You seem to run into me quite a lot." He smiled at her and then caught sight of Avery's expression.

"Avery," Victor said, nodding politely.

"*Victor*," Avery returned not so politely.

Autumn glanced back and forth between the two of them.

"Well, I'll see you guys in Powers then," she said, walking through the gap between them and down the path towards the Powers Tree.

Autumn heard them both turn to follow her. She couldn't make out their words, but they were definitely bickering with each other under their breath.

Crystal joined Autumn when they had reached the middle of campus. She glanced back at Avery and Victor and gave Autumn a questioning look.

"Don't ask," Autumn grumbled. Crystal raised her eyebrows and looked back at them again.

In Powers class Autumn and Luke sat out again to observe. Atticus decided to switch things up a bit and paired boys with boys and girls with girls. And, of course, Victor and Avery were partners. Autumn had a feeling this wasn't going to be good.

"Guys, you will not behave like you did last time you were paired up," Atticus warned, looking at all of the males in the classroom.

The boys nodded without hearing him as they were too busy cracking their knuckles and sneering at one another.

Atticus approached Autumn and Luke and said, "Getting tired of just watching, eh?"

They nodded glumly.

"It won't be much longer, and that's all I'm going to say."

Autumn and Luke perked up at this. Atticus could determine elves' Powers. Autumn assumed he could probably tell *when* an elf would be discovering their Power as well.

Then the battles began.

Luke watched the guys fight with extreme concentration, noting every move, probably trying to get some tips for future reference. Autumn watched Victor and Avery with apprehension.

Victor shone a particularly bright light before him, forming a shield of sorts. Avery tried to get past it without being blinded so that he could attack.

A high-pitched voice rose above the noise and Autumn turned to see Kyndel screaming at Crystal for getting ice shards in her hair. Crystal didn't seem too sorry about this, and Autumn chuckled to herself as she watched Kyndel shake her head wildly to loosen the ice crystals from her hair.

Then a loud crash sounded from the other side of the room. Avery had broken through Victor's light shield and rammed him across the room into a stack of wooden chairs that tumbled loudly to the ground as Victor smashed into them. He scrambled to his feet with a look of rage on his face, which was now bleeding profusely.

Atticus shouted at him to stop, but Victor charged at Avery, who pulled his arm back to punch him.

"Stop!" Autumn yelled. Avery turned to look at her as Victor plowed into him.

Forrest, Bryan, and Drake rushed over to pull Victor off of Avery. Atticus and a few others attempted to restrain Avery. He could've easily thrown all of them off, but he just stood there with clenched fists, fuming.

"Detention! Both of you! Victor, go to the campus healer. Autumn—" Autumn jumped as he shouted her name, "go with Victor. Avery, leave my classroom. I will be sending Olympus a message about this."

"Gross! Atrum blood," Drake shouted. "Everyone stand back. Don't want to get infected."

Autumn shot Drake a mutinous look before she led Victor down the spiral staircase and out of the tree. Avery was a few steps behind them.

Luke and Crystal watched them go with shocked looks on their faces. When they emerged from the Powers Tree, Autumn and Victor went one way and Avery went the other.

Victor was fuming. Autumn walked silently along next to him, letting him lead the way seeing as how she didn't know where the Healer's Tree was located. He clutched his arm, which had a deep gash in it, and he had a shallow cut across his cheek. He led her to a small tree behind the main office and pushed forcefully through the door.

A gray-haired woman, who Autumn assumed was the campus healer, sat behind a desk reading what looked like some kind of Underground romance novel.

She stood up quickly when she saw them enter and said, "Oh,

my."

The healer gently moved Victor over to a wooden medical table before rummaging in her medical cabinets. She pulled out a number of flasks and bottles, pouring and mixing various liquids faster than Autumn could read the labels. The healer handed Victor a glass of a milky liquid and said, "Drink."

He threw back the concoction and a blank look came over his face.

"How did this happen, dear?" the healer asked Autumn.

"Attic, uh, Magister Attribold paired the boys with the boys and—"

"Ah! I should've known. This happened the last time. Honestly, I don't know why Atticus continues to attempt pairing the boys together. It always seems to end in disaster."

She dabbed some green paste on Victor's arm and poured a blue liquid over it. Autumn watched the wound close before her eyes. The healer did the same to the cut on his cheek and then gave him a clear liquid to drink, which brought him out of his trance-like state. He seemed calmer now.

Autumn and Victor thanked the healer and left the tree.

"I'm sorry," he said after a minute of silence. "I wish you hadn't seen me like that."

"You didn't do anything wrong. Avery shouldn't have used his Power like that. It would make anyone angry." Autumn wasn't just saying that either. She was unhappy with Avery for what he did to Victor. She wished he would just get over his little issues and move on.

Rather than going home, Autumn and Victor went to Arbor Lake and stayed there for the rest of the afternoon. She noticed that he seemed to keep his guard up even more so than Avery. Everything he said was spoken with extreme caution and thought. He didn't talk freely and openly like Autumn did. She felt sort of guilty that she hadn't put more effort into being Victor's friend because she had been so consumed in Avery. Though after his behavior today she doubted that would continue to be a problem.

AVERY charged out of the Powers Tree, parting from Victor and Autumn at the base of the stairs. He chanced a glance over his shoulder at the pair of them. Victor's eyes were that charcoal black they changed to when he became angry, and Autumn was looking up at him with concern.

Avery turned back around and punched a nearby tree, causing it to crack down the middle. *Real smart,* he thought, *way to show Autumn who Victor really is. Now she thinks* I'm *the crazy one.* If only she knew what he did… Avery shook his head to rid himself of his unwanted thoughts.

He didn't understand why he even cared so much. He barely knew Autumn. He'd thought that she might have feelings for him too, but she had been acting strangely towards him lately. One minute she's holding his hand in the castle courtyard, and the next she wants nothing to do with him.

As he approached Arbor Castle a feeling of guilt and dread washed over him. Victor Lavigne was not worth losing his job at the castle. He couldn't afford to lose his job.

He walked straight to the king's living quarters and waited outside the door. Rupert and Donald, the king's main guards, looked at him in surprise.

"Everything okay, Burke?" Rupert asked. Avery just nodded.

He sat there for a long while before the door opened to reveal Olympus wearing a warm smile. *Maybe I'm not in as much trouble as I thought,* Avery hoped.

"Come on in, Mr. Burke," Olympus said. Avery did as he was told. Rupert and Donald gave him encouraging looks as he passed by.

"Have a seat," Olympus said, waving a hand at a nearby armchair. Avery sat straight-backed on the edge of his seat. "I just received word from Magister Attribold. It would appear that there was a situation in Powers class."

"Yes, sir."

"Between you and Mr. Lavigne?"

"Yes, sir."

"I know I don't have to remind you that, as a worker here, you represent this castle."

"I know, sir. I'm really sorry. I—"

"This is your first warning, Mr. Burke. If it happens again I'm afraid I will have to find somewhere else for you."

Avery's stomach dropped at this. "Yes, sir."

"Think about what your father would want, son. He wouldn't want you to lose your head over nothing, would he?"

"No, he wouldn't." Avery frowned, feeling even worse.

"All right. Well, from this point on, I don't want to hear anything but praise about you from Mr. Attribold."

"Yes, sir."

"How is your new job assignment treating you? Are my grandchildren behaving?"

"Yes, sir. They are adjusting very well."

"Excellent. Well, Mr. Burke, I believe dinner is being served soon. Try to keep your anger under control, all right?"

"I will, sir."

Avery left the king's quarters with the heavy feeling of guilt and regret resting on his shoulders. When he entered the dining room he spotted Autumn, Luke, and Crystal already seated at their usual table.

Autumn looked up, her brow creased in worry. "Did he—?"

Avery shook his head and Autumn seemed to breathe a sigh of relief. "No, but he said that if I break another rule he will be forced to let me go. I can't believe I got myself into this because of that scum."

Avery noticed Autumn's jaw clench at his words. Maybe she was still mad at him after all.

Steam Springs

CHAPTER FIFTEEN

The next day in Laboratory, Autumn and Victor spoke in hushed whispers so that they didn't bother Coach Holt, who was again reading his sports magazine. The night before, Autumn had made up her mind. She definitely had to distance herself from Avery, not only because of the castle rules, but because she did *not* want be responsible for getting Avery fired. Getting closer to Victor seemed like a good way to prevent this.

"Would you like to go to lunch with us today?" Autumn asked him.

Victor frowned. "I don't know if that's a good idea."

"Well how about just you and me then?"

He smiled at her. "Now *that* I think I can do."

Autumn found Victor waiting for her outside of the History Tree before lunch, watching her with that mysterious look he always wore, his green eyes reflecting the sunlight. She smiled in spite of herself.

They ate at a small restaurant near City Circle. Victor asked her question after question about her family, her likes and dislikes, her favorite color, her hopes and fears. She felt a little self-conscious talking about herself like this, but every time she tried to ask *him* something he seemed to redirect the question back to her. She quickly figured out that he didn't like talking about himself or his past, which was understandable given the way he grew up.

When they returned to campus they ran into Avery, Luke, and Crystal. All three of them wore looks of surprise when they spotted Victor walking beside Autumn. Avery and Luke looked mutinous. She felt a surge of guilt as she realized she had forgotten to tell them she wouldn't be joining them for lunch. This was the first time she wished Undergrounders used cell phones.

"I'll see you tomorrow," Victor murmured, obviously sensing the tension. He kissed Autumn's hand and left her side. She couldn't help but notice that she didn't feel a surge of energy or warmth at his touch, as she knew she would have if Avery had been the one kissing her hand.

Autumn stood there awkwardly for a minute before saying, "Sorry. I should have told you guys I wasn't coming."

Luke narrowed his eyes at her, Avery looked at the ground, and Crystal said, "Don't worry about it. We didn't wait that long. Charlotte told us that she saw you leave with someone."

The four of them stood in uncomfortable silence for another minute until Luke grumbled, "Come on, Autumn, we have Healing."

She walked beside her brother in silence until she said, "Look, I'm sorry you waited for me, but—"

"It's not about that," he snapped. Autumn looked up at him, confused. "You shouldn't be hanging out with that guy. Avery told me about him and, as your older brother, it's my job to keep you safe. You can't see him anymore."

"Excuse me? I *can't* see him? Why, because he has Atrum blood? Okay, one: you have no say in who I see or don't see and, two: you don't even know him. Victor and Avery hated each other long before you and I came here. You are basing this solely on hearsay. I didn't know you were this close-minded, Luke."

Luke was silent for a minute before he said, "I guess I can reserve my judgment. Avery just really seems to hate him. I figured he had a good reason. Just be careful, okay?"

Friday was Autumn's first Melodies class. Charlotte was the only person she knew by name there. Crystal was taking Art and Luke and Avery were both in Sports. Victor hadn't told her what class he was taking, of course. Magistra Halphnote immediately informed them that they would be performing a Fall Concert in two weeks, which included a group performance and a solo for each 4th quarter elf.

Autumn had a mini panic attack when she heard this. No one had said anything about a mandatory solo. Even worse, Magistra Halphnote announced that their solo piece must be an original. Meaning *they* had to write it.

Her fears temporarily abated when the whole class sang together for the first time. The sound was like nothing Autumn had ever heard before. Music floated up the Melodies Tree like bells in a tower. Now she knew why her father had been so in love with music.

Autumn continued to eat lunch with Victor, though she secretly wished she could be with Avery, Luke, and Crystal. They asked fewer personal questions and talked quite a bit more freely. But that was before. Now, Avery wasn't even speaking to Autumn and spent all of Powers talking to everyone BUT her—and Victor, of course.

Crystal approached Autumn and Luke after Powers, wiping sweat from her brow and panting. "I hate being paired with Bryan. He's so fast."

"I would hope so," Luke said, "since his Power is Speed and all."

Crystal punched Luke playfully and turned to Autumn. "Hey, I don't know if you have plans with Victor tomorrow or anything, but at lunch today we decided that we would all go up to Steam Springs for the day."

"Did you say that you're going Steam Springs?" Forrest called from behind them.

"Yeah, tomorrow," Crystal said.

"Sweet! We should all go. I'll tell everyone," he said.

"I've already invited a few people," Crystal called, but Forrest ignored her.

"Do you want to come to my workshop and meet my mom?" she asked Autumn. "You can pick out one of the swim suits I've made to wear tomorrow."

"That's okay," Luke said. "I don't think a bikini would be appropriate, although I would look damn good."

As they walked down the path toward Arbor Castle, Crystal looked over at Autumn with an anticipatory expression.

"What?" Autumn asked.

"Well? What's going on with you and Victor? I thought something was happening between you and Avery earlier in the week, but then you started hanging out with Victor."

Autumn sighed. She had been expecting this interrogation. "Well, Avery and I are just friends, except right now we aren't really talking. And Victor and I are just friends too, I guess."

Crystal grinned. "I can tell he likes you."

Autumn's heart leapt, her thoughts shifting to Avery. "Who?"

Crystal looked confused. "Er, Victor."

Autumn tried to keep her face from falling as she said, "Oh, right. Well I just felt so bad that he didn't have anyone to talk to. Everyone seems to be afraid of him just because of his Atrum background."

Crystal nodded and said, "Yeah, I've tried talking to him a few times, but he's so closed off and secretive. All of the girls think he's gorgeous, of course, but most are too scared to talk to him. You seem to have broken him out of his shell."

"I guess."

"So do you like him?"

Autumn shrugged. "He's really nice and definitely not bad to look at, but..."

"But what?" Crystal asked. Autumn stayed silent. "You can tell me, Autumn."

"All right," Autumn said with a sigh and her words began to spill out like a waterfall. "I think Victor is great. He's smart, witty, unbelievably handsome. But with Avery..." She hesitated, feeling her eyes cloud over, her mind venturing somewhere else. "With Avery it's different. When we're around each other, there's this electricity between us and all I want is to be closer to him. When he's around I don't see anyone else and when we touch—even if it's just us brushing up against one another—there's this warmth that spreads through my entire body. But I can't do anything about any of it because Olympus told Luke and me that we're forbidden to have a romantic relationship with anyone who works in the castle. Avery's already in trouble with Olympus for getting into a fight with Victor, and I would hate to be responsible for him being fired. So that's why I've been distancing myself from him and that's another reason I've been focusing on Victor, to get my mind off of Avery, but it's not working quite as well as I'd hoped."

Autumn took a deep breath and looked to see Crystal gaping at her. "Whoa," is all she managed to say at first. "Maybe you should tell King Olympus how you feel. He might understand."

"No, I can't do that. We barely know each other and I can't ask him to revoke one of his only rules just because of some crush. I'm just making a big deal of nothing, really. I don't even know if Avery feels the same way. Don't worry, I'll be over it by tomorrow and we can all go back to hanging out together."

Crystal nodded. "I hope so because Avery's going to be at Steam Springs tomorrow, and I invited Victor too."

Autumn and Crystal traveled down into the roots of Arbor Castle. It was quite a bit darker down there, seeing as how there were no windows. Sconces filled with the familiar pulsating light were placed every few feet.

"What is that?" Autumn asked.

"What?"

"That light. Where does it come from?"

"That's fay light. It comes from fay fairies."

"Oh," Autumn said, not sure what fay fairies were.

Servants greeted them as they ambled down the narrow hallways. Many bowed down to Autumn, and she tried to look gracious about it rather than uncomfortable. A large wooden door stood at the end of the passage and Crystal pushed it open.

"This is my workshop."

Autumn entered the room to see a pair of long wooden worktables taking up most of the small space. One was very neat and tidy and the other was covered in all sorts of different fabrics in every color imaginable. A wooden mechanism that looked like an antique spinning wheel of sorts stood between the two tables.

"You mean *our* workshop," a misty voice said from the corner. Autumn turned to find a woman who looked so much like Crystal that Autumn had to look behind her to make sure her friend hadn't moved. Crystal's mother had the same long, silvery blonde hair, the same dazzling blue eyes, and bright smile. "Hello, Autumn, it's so nice to finally meet you. My name is Glenda Everly." Glenda approached her and, rather than bowing, pulled Autumn into a hug. "Crystal has told me so much about you."

"Crystal's been amazing. I don't know what I'd do without her."

Glenda beamed at her daughter.

"I was just going to show Autumn some of the swimsuits I've been working on," Crystal said. "We're going up to Steam Springs tomorrow."

"That's a lovely idea," Glenda said.

"They're over here," Crystal said, moving toward the organized table. She opened one of the many drawers and pulled out an armful of swimsuits. "Pick whichever one you want," she said.

"Which one are you going to wear?" Autumn asked.

"I think this one," Crystal said, picking up a one piece made out of a silvery material, which looked like it had been spun from liquid mercury.

Autumn spotted a gold two-piece with red roses stitched into the material and red lace lining the bathing suit.

"I like this one," she said.

"That'll look good with your hair color," Crystal said.

"Yes, the gold will look lovely with your skin tone as well," Glenda said from the corner, not looking up from a dress in her hands that seemed to have appeared out of nowhere.

The next day, Autumn and Crystal were the first to arrive at Steam Springs, which was basically just several pools of hot, steaming water scattered sporadically around the top of a steep, forested hill. The two of them clambered into the largest hot springs pool. Steam rose steadily from the springs, so much so that Autumn and Crystal had trouble seeing one another.

Victor arrived soon after them. He wore green swimming trunks and a plain white shirt that he pulled off before entering the water, making Crystal's mouth drop and Autumn's face blush. His olive skin was completely flawless. She didn't think she'd ever seen a man's body that perfect in person before. This would certainly make her "getting over Avery plan" much easier.

Victor waded into the water and sat on a smooth rock beside

Autumn. She smiled shyly up at him and thought she saw him flush as he took in her gold bathing suit. She sank a little deeper into the water and Crystal giggled silently beside her.

Not long after Victor arrived, Luke, Avery, Jastin, and Forrest showed up with a dozen other people that Autumn had met in some of her classes.

Her "getting over Avery plan" slipped a little when Avery pulled off his shirt and moved into the water. His ivory skin was almost as smooth and flawless as Victor's and that persistent pulling feeling kicked in. This was going to be more difficult than Autumn thought.

Before long everyone was splashing around and laughing. Forrest made up a game that involved climbing up a nearby tree and swinging into the water, trying to splash as many people as possible. Crystal joined in while Autumn and Victor watched from the edge. Autumn kind of wanted to play too, but she didn't want to leave Victor alone.

"I'm surprised you came," she said to him.

"Why?"

"Well, you don't really get along with a lot of these guys."

"Yes, but I knew you'd be here."

"Hey, Atrum!" Drake called towards Victor, hanging from a branch.

Autumn and Victor glared up at him.

"How 'bout you join us? Atrums are used to heights, right? You did live in the Hollow Mountains on Alder Island, after all."

Victor's jaw clenched.

"Why are you even here?" Bryan chimed in as Drake splashed into the water. "Are you planning on calling a herd of Shadows to kill us all?"

Bryan and Drake burst into malicious laughter.

Victor stood to leave and Autumn grabbed his arm. He looked down at her with an expression full of pain and anger.

"Don't listen to them," Autumn said. "You know you aren't what they say."

"Maybe I am, Autumn."

"No! You aren't," she said, standing up. "There's nothing evil in you. Your blood doesn't make you who you are. I see the good in you. *I* do. If they opened their minds they would see it too."

Victor's eyes bore into her then, looking at her in a way he never had, like he was seeing her for the first time. Autumn's breathing became quick and shallow as he moved close to her, pressing his lips to hers as he ran his fingers through her hair. She was suddenly very aware of their lack of clothing and the fact that they had an audience.

Then there was a loud exclamation of anger, causing Autumn and Victor to break apart. At the same moment, something like lightning struck Victor and threw him out of the water just as heavy rain began to pour down on them and wind swirled Autumn's hair around her face.

Autumn looked wildly around at the others who had all stopped what they were doing and stood gaping, not at Autumn or Victor, but at Luke who was staring at his hands in amazement. The rain and clouds disappeared as fast as they came and Autumn's eyes widened in realization.

Luke had found his Power.

The Shadow

CHAPTER SIXTEEN

Luke wore a huge grin on his face for the rest of the day as everyone came up to congratulate him. He spent most of the day testing his Power—Weather. Making it rain, snow, hail, conjuring up wind, and then sending it all away again. No one said anything about Autumn and Victor's kiss, although Avery seemed to be in a particularly foul mood.

Since Luke's Power wasn't strong enough yet to do any real harm to Victor, Autumn decided to drop it and let her brother enjoy his newfound gift. Victor left soon after the lightning incident, kissing Autumn softly on the forehead as he did. Avery flashed them a look of disgust.

As the sun sank lower and the sky turned a soft shade of pink, people began to leave with pruny skin and dripping hair. Autumn, Crystal, Luke, and Avery traveled back to the castle together. Luke rambled on and on about his Power as they trudged down the steep hill. Autumn was happy for her brother. Really. But she couldn't help envy him just a little bit. Being the only one without a Power was beyond depressing.

"Dude! *Weather*. I can't believe it! It's so *powerful*. The girls are going to love this!" Autumn and Crystal exchanged exasperated glances. "I mean seriously, though," Luke continued. "It would've been cool if I just had lightning or something. But with Weather, it's like I have tons of Powers instead of just one. I can make thunder and lightning and rain and snow and hail and wind and—"

"Okay we got it," Autumn interrupted.

"Jeez, what's your problem?" Luke said. "You don't have to act like a jerk just because you are the only one without a Power now."

"I wasn't."

"You're lucky I didn't pulverize your little boyfriend with hail the size of baseballs."

"Shut up, Luke," Autumn said through gritted teeth.

"I'm serious. I could have conjured up a hail storm just like that," he said snapping his fingers.

"Just shut the hell up, Luke!" Autumn shouted, dashing off the path into the woods.

Autumn ran, stumbling and falling every so often. A few tears leaked from her eyes, but that was it. She was not going to let him see her cry. Yes, she was jealous and yes, she kissed Victor, but that didn't give him the right to humiliate her even more.

She stopped running after a few more minutes, collapsing onto a fallen tree branch. The giant trees were thick around her, making it seem darker than it already was. The sun had almost set and Autumn began to realize that running off the path was probably a bad idea seeing as how she was now alone in an interminably darkening forest full of unknown threats.

She sat there for a few more minutes waiting for Luke or Avery or Crystal to come after her. It didn't seem like they were. Right now would've been a great time to discover her Power. Maybe she was one of those Navigators that could find their way out of anything or maybe she would be able to change into a bird or something and fly out of there.

Suddenly there was a rustling in the distance. Finally, someone had come for her. Then she heard a strange wheezing sort of sound. Like an asthmatic trying to breathe, unable to get any air. A dark figure emerged from the trees. It wasn't an animal exactly, or an elf, or any creature Autumn had ever seen or heard of. It had the brusque body of a large man, covered in a layer of coarse black hair. It was definitely taller and wider than any man and its head was similar to that of a ram with large curling horns protruding from its skull. It also had hooves for feet and hands. Autumn couldn't make out any features otherwise. It was as if the creature was covered in a shadow. A *Shadow*.

Autumn scrambled off of the fallen branch and backed up slowly.

The Shadow took a step forward and Autumn took another step back, finding herself pressed against a tree. She reached down and picked up a heavy rock to use as a weapon if he attacked.

"I order you to stop!" Autumn said. "I am the Princess of Arbor Falls." She then held up her wrist to show the creature her Royal Mark.

The Shadow stopped for a second, his eyes on Autumn's hand, head tilting, and then continued to move slowly towards her. Suddenly he lunged. She leapt out of the way as he crashed into the tree behind her. She tried to run away when he grabbed a hold of her ankle with both hooves, pulling her to the ground. Autumn took the rock that she was still holding and smashed it into his snout.

Letting out a guttural gasp, he temporarily released her. Autumn struggled to her feet, looking around wildly for something to injure him with as he leapt on her, this time successfully knocking her to the ground. He pulled out what looked like rope and began to bind her arms, pinning them to her sides. Autumn aimed a kick to his abdomen and he bent over double. She struggled to release herself from the rope and tried to run past him, but he tripped her, jamming her to the ground once again. He quickly wrapped the rope around her entire body, like a spider capturing its prey.

This was it. She couldn't get away now. The Shadow was going to take her to Vyra and Vyra was going to kill her. Tears filled her eyes as she thought of how she left things with Luke.

Then she heard something in the distance and suddenly the Shadow was no longer on top of her. Someone had pulled him away. Autumn tried to look around, but she couldn't move her head. The Shadow had lodged it between two heavy rocks. She could hear scuffling and grunting and then a loud cracking sound... then nothing.

Someone called her name and then footsteps rushed towards her.

Avery stared down at Autumn with a panicked look on his face. "Are you okay? Did it hurt you?"

"I'm fine," she breathed, relief flooding her.

He knelt down and began untying her. "I'm so sorry I didn't get here sooner. We all split up looking for you, but you went way off the path. I started running when I heard you scream."

Autumn hadn't realized that she had screamed.

Avery finished untying her legs and pulled her gently to her feet.

"Thanks," she said.

He didn't say anything, but wrapped her in a tight hug instead. The magnetic pull was back and she gave in to it, wrapping her arms around him too.

"I'm sorry I've been a jerk. I just—"

"Me too," Autumn said.

"We should find Luke and Crystal. They're still looking for you."

They walked out of the little clearing and into the thick forest toward the path. Autumn tried to ignore the Shadow's crumpled, lifeless body as they passed by. Avery grabbed her hand and led her through the foliage. He had marked the trees every so often so he could find his way back.

"Are you sure you're okay?" Avery asked again.

"Just a few bumps and bruises is all."

"I can't believe it didn't kill you. It took me a long time to reach you once I heard you scream."

"Well I think it was planning on killing me, but then I told it that I was the princess and showed my mark. I think he decided to bring me to Vyra instead."

"That probably saved your life."

There was only a line of pink in the sky, the sun had set and the forest was rapidly darkening. The trees became sparser as they walked on. With the help of Avery's trail they made it to the path by nightfall.

"We'll never find Luke and Crystal when it's this dark," Autumn said. "What if there are other Shadows?"

"I'll call a Castle Navigator to come find them."

"Call?"

"Yeah," Avery said. "I'm sure there's one this way."

He began walking down the path toward town. Autumn had a few more questions about what the heck he was talking about, but she followed him anyway, sure he would eventually explain.

"There," Avery said, pointing to a tree just off the path.

Autumn watched in confusion as Avery jogged up to an unnaturally red tree with a large hole in its front. This tree was especially unusual because dangling from its long branches were hundreds—maybe thousands—of overgrown acorns the size of apples. Avery plucked an acorn off the tree, pulled the top off and spoke into the hollow shell.

"Navigator needed on Steam Springs Hill. Bring fay light."

He then put the top back onto the acorn, recited the castle address to the opening in the tree and popped the acorn into the hole.

Autumn stared at Avery in bewilderment.

"See? A Message Tree," he said, laughing at her expression.

Now that she thought about it, she remembered seeing a miniature tree like that one in her branch, but at the time she had just thought it was some sort of strange elf decoration.

"Now we wait," Avery said, sitting on a log just off the path. He patted the spot beside him, indicating Autumn should join him and she did. "I still don't get why it took that Shadow so long to tie you up. I wonder if it was a newborn."

"Well I wasn't going to just lay down and let it take me to Vyra without a fight."

"What did you do to it?"

"I hit it with a rock and kicked it in the stomach and played keep-away for a little while."

"That's impressive."

"It was nothing," Autumn said, flipping her hair playfully.

Avery snorted. "You may turn out to be a pretty amazing Warrior, Autumn Oaken."

"If I ever find my Power."

"You will," he said as he put his hand over hers and squeezed.

Her eyes flashed up to his, their stormy gray as inscrutable as ever. Autumn's heart fluttered. Why did it always do that around him?

Crunching leaves and snapping twigs sounded down the path, announcing the arrival of the castle Navigator. Avery greeted him and he ducked his head, looking rather uncomfortable.

"He doesn't really like to socialize," Avery murmured under his breath as the Navigator closed his eyes and began walking up the hill.

"Why is he closing his eyes? Won't he trip or something?"

"His Power is leading him."

It took him no time at all to locate Crystal and Luke, who were together and not far from the path. The Navigator retrieved them and then left for the castle once Autumn and Avery had thanked him and he had dropped his head once again.

"Autumn!" Crystal cried.

"Don't do that again!" Luke said, a mixture of relief and anger in his voice.

"Sorry," she muttered.

"I fell down like thirty times out there looking for you," Luke said.

"Well I fell down a few times myself, trying to fight off a five hundred pound Shadow," Autumn said.

Luke stopped complaining and looked at her quizzically.

"It's true," Avery said. "I barely got there in time."

Luke looked at Autumn with an open mouth. She told him and Crystal the whole story. Avery added a few details here and there. By the time they finished Crystal and Luke were looking at them with impressed and slightly horrified faces. Autumn smiled in spite of herself. Their reactions filled her with a sense of pride in herself. It would appear she actually did have a chance in a fight.

Power or no Power.

Etherelles and Dummies

CHAPTER SEVENTEEN

The following week was both easier and more difficult. It was easier because Autumn was familiar with all of her classes, and Avery seemed to have put all of the angry silences from last week behind him. He and Crystal were the only true friends she had in the Underground aside from Luke. They knew the real Oaken twins, not the *royal* Oaken twins like everyone else.

The week was harder because Autumn was forced to make time for both her friends and Victor, who was rapidly becoming a major part of her day. They went to lunch together every day, hung out during breaks and—to Luke and Avery's dismay—Victor had even started showing up on the castle's front steps to walk Autumn to school.

They had yet to kiss again, which she didn't mind because she had never planned on taking things with Victor any further than friendship. It wouldn't seem fair to him seeing as how Avery's face popped into her head every two minutes.

On top of all that, she hadn't worked on her song for the Melodies Fall Concert. Every time she thought about it, her stomach flipped uncomfortably and her palms began to sweat. So she kept telling herself that she would figure it out over the weekend.

The most difficult part of the week, though, was Powers class. Autumn was now the only elf in her class—the only elf on campus, actually—who didn't have a Power. She tried to keep her jealousy hidden when Luke announced proudly to Atticus that he'd discovered his Power. She also tried not to glower when Atticus enthusiastically congratulated her brother and put him in a group with Avery and Crystal. With a wink, Atticus told Autumn not to worry.

By Friday, though, she was beginning to think that she didn't even have a Power—or worse—that it would be something ridiculously useless like growing her hair or being an exceptionally good gardener.

When Magistra Halphnote asked Autumn about the name of her song that afternoon, though, she momentarily forgot about her Power problem. She was supposed to have already written her song so it could be entered into the program for the next weekend. Autumn swallowed and muttered that she hadn't quite worked out a title yet.

"But you *have* been working on your song, correct?" asked Magistra Halphnote with a disappointed frown.

Autumn nodded, trying not to look too guilty.

What with her lack of Power and her inability to write a song for Melodies, Autumn felt like crawling into a hole. Why did she have to choose Melodies? Even Sports would have been less embarrassing. And, even though she knew she shouldn't, she put it off for another day. Maybe her Power was, in fact, the profound ability to procrastinate.

Avery broke through Autumn's constant laments that afternoon by saying, "I know what will make you feel better. Punching things. Really hard."

"Yeah, I'm sure it would. How will that help anything, though?"

"The Warrior Test measures your physical fighting abilities too. That way, when you do find your Power, you'll only need to practice that cause you'll already know how to kick ass without one."

Autumn laughed. "I guess you've got a point."

"Training grounds, tomorrow morning, after breakfast," Avery stated. "After a full-grown Shadow, this will be nothing."

The next morning she got out of bed with a sense of excitement growing within her. She had a feeling it had less to do with punching things and more to do with the person who would be teaching her how.

Hoping some fresh air would release the butterflies in her stomach, Autumn opened the glass doors to her balcony and stepped outside. Her ears were immediately met with music. Someone was singing and playing some sort of instrument that sounded remarkably like a guitar. The sound was coming from somewhere above her.

Autumn looked up, searching for the source. It was coming from the branch directly above hers. "Avery? Hey, Avery!"

The music stopped and a few seconds later Avery was leaning over his balcony railing, looking down at her. "Autumn? What are you doing?"

"Was that you?"

"Was what me?"

"That music."

"Oh, yeah."

"I'm coming up!"

She hurried out of her branch and up the stairs, ideas running through her head. She may have found the answer to her Melodies problem, after all.

On her second knock, Avery opened the door with a mingled look of humor and confusion on his face.

"May I come in?" Autumn asked.

Avery looked over his shoulder and then nodded, waving her into his branch. It was smaller than hers, but still just as elegant. The couches had frilly pillow accents, and empty perfume bottles sat in a row on the mantle above the fireplace. Autumn had a feeling they didn't belong to Avery.

"Do you live alone?" she asked, examining a sea-glass blue perfume bottle covered in a thick layer of dust.

Avery shook his head as he led her back into his room. "My mom lives here too. She's in bed."

"Oh no, I'm sorry. I hope I didn't wake her with my knocking."

"She probably isn't asleep. She just lays there."

Autumn gave him a questioning look, but he didn't explain. She decided not to push the subject further as she followed him into his room.

"Were you playing a guitar just now?" she asked.

"A what?"

"A guitar. You know, wooden instrument, six strings, hole in the middle."

"Oh." Avery moved to his balcony and picked up what looked rather similar to a guitar, only it had eight strings and three holes in the middle. "You mean an etherelle?" He held out the instrument for Autumn to take. It was a beautiful golden color with circular designs carved into the wood.

"It's incredible." Autumn ran her fingers across the smooth wood.

"Do you play?" he asked.

"No, my dad did. Well he played the guitar, that is, but this is almost the same thing. I guess he learned it all here. He was going to teach me, but he—well, he never got around to it." Avery kept silent and Autumn remembered that she wasn't the only one who had lost a father. "So, that song you were singing earlier. Is that a song from the Underground?"

"No," he said, running his hand nervously through his golden hair. "I actually wrote that."

"*Really*," Autumn said, a sly smile spreading across her face.

"What?"

"I'm in Melodies and we have to sing an original song. Could you maybe loan me one?"

"Aren't you supposed to write that yourself," he asked, looking amused.

Autumn frowned. "Yes."

"Can you not write songs?"

"I used to with my dad. He would write the melody and I would put in the lyrics. I tried to write more songs after he died, but, without his music, they never lived up to the ones we wrote together. So I just stopped."

"What about the songs you wrote with your dad before? Could you sing one of those?"

Autumn shook her head. "I don't think I'd be able to get through it without falling apart."

"You, fall apart? The Shadow-Fighter?" Avery said with a chuckle.

Autumn rolled her eyes, but smiled in spite of herself. She sort of liked the sound of that—the Shadow-Fighter. It was a lot better than the names she'd been calling herself.

"Well, I'm not going to just give you a song, but I will compromise. I'll help you write one. That way it will be an original and you will have a part in it. I'll come up with the melody and you can write the lyrics."

"I think I can deal with that," Autumn said with a lopsided smile.

Instead of going down to the dueling grounds, Autumn and Avery worked on her song all morning. They brainstormed about song ideas and eventually decided on a powerful and inspiring ballad song about adventure and enchantment to describe Autumn's recent experience.

Avery was an exceptional etherelle player. Autumn was a little embarrassed to sing in front of him at first, but the more time they spent together, the more comfortable she felt.

By lunchtime they had completely finished writing her song and were both famished. They met up with Luke in the dining room and he told them Crystal had gone to help her mother complete a few gowns in the castle roots for the afternoon.

"Where the heck have you two been?" Luke asked.

"Avery was helping me with my Melodies assignment."

"But you're in Sports," Luke said to Avery with narrowed eyes.

"That doesn't mean *Sports* is all he's capable of," Autumn said.

Luke still looked unconvinced, but shrugged and said, "Do you guys want to go to Arbor Lake this afternoon?"

"I was going to teach Autumn how to fight," Avery said.

Luke frowned and said, "Should I be learning how to fight?"

"It wouldn't hurt. There will be a strictly physical test during the Warrior Test where you won't be allowed to use your Power," Avery said.

Luke frowned. "Damn."

After lunch, the three of them traveled down to the dueling grounds. First, Avery taught them how to get out of various different holds. He refrained from using his Strength against them so they would have somewhat of a chance. It took a while, but eventually Autumn and Luke were able to release themselves from each hold.

Next, he taught them how to attack an enemy and most effectively bring them down. They used training dummies for this exercise so they wouldn't seriously hurt one another. Once the twins had nearly mastered the art of attack, Avery paired them together to test who could use their newly found skills best. Luke attempted to pin Autumn's arms to her sides, but she slid right out of his hold. Then he wrapped an arm around her neck and stomach, and she managed to get out just as quickly.

Autumn could tell he was growing aggravated because a small storm cloud had appeared above their heads. He hadn't exactly learned how to control his power efficiently yet. Luke was able to release himself from all of Autumn's holds as well, though, so his little storm cloud soon dissipated.

As the sun sank low in the Underground sky, Autumn, Luke, and Avery traveled back up to the castle sweaty and tired. Autumn felt as though a weight had been lifted from her shoulders. But when Avery congratulated her on her newfound fighting skills by clapping a hand on her back and letting it linger there, she realized she still had a few things in her life to work out.

Melodies

CHAPTER EIGHTEEN

When Friday rolled around Autumn felt confident handing Magistra Halphnote the music for her original song. The Fall Concert was scheduled to begin at 7:00pm and Autumn's stomach had slowly filled with butterflies throughout the day. During Powers class she hardly paid the duelers any attention, and when the bells rang she rushed to the castle to get ready for the performance.

The girls' Melodies costumes were all white and made out of a lightweight, airy material. The dresses had a corset-like bodice with flowing skirts that sparkled in the light. Autumn pulled the front of her hair away from her face with pearl clips and applied a small amount of shimmering makeup before hurrying back to the campus, her nerves beginning to overtake her. She started to think of all of the things that could go wrong: she could trip and fall on her face, her voice could crack in the middle of a note, or she could forget all of the words. It didn't help that all of her friends had promised to attend the concert.

All of the Melodies students had been instructed to arrive an hour early at the outdoor amphitheater where they would be performing for dress rehearsal. Magistra Halphnote bustled about, making sure everything was running smoothly. Due to time constraints, they only practiced the group songs and went over the order of the soloists. So Autumn was only able to walk through her entrance and exit without practicing her solo.

She entered backstage to find most everyone sitting alone, nervously fidgeting or practicing their solo under their breath. Autumn found a bare spot backstage and sat focusing all of her energy on not passing out or throwing up.

"Nervous?" a voice said behind her.

She turned to see Charlotte, wearing her silky chestnut hair up in an elegant twist and a dress that was identical to Autumn's.

"A bit," Autumn said.

"Don't worry. Everyone is a little nervous—even me—and I've been doing this since I was five."

"Five?" Autumn said.

"Yeah. My mom put me in all of these elf talent competitions when I was little," she said, rolling her eyes. "She was furious when I told her I wanted to be a magistra instead of a singer. That is, if I don't make the Warriors."

Just then, somebody called for the singers to line up for the group song. Autumn and Charlotte moved to stand in line and Magistra Halphnote led everyone onstage. Autumn's stomach flipped as she glanced out at the immense audience staring up at them. Magistra Halphnote greeted the audience and then turned to conduct her choir.

Autumn scanned the crowd as they sang, looking for familiar faces. She spotted Luke, Avery, Crystal, Forrest, Jastin, and several others she knew from her classes. Victor sat alone, a few rows behind Luke, Crystal, and Avery.

When the choir finished singing, they walked silently offstage to the sound of polite applause from the audience. Magistra Halphnote stayed onstage to announce the 4th quarter soloists. Charlotte was first. Autumn listened to her sing backstage and couldn't help but envy her slightly. Her voice was powerful and smooth. Each note sounded effortless and her delivery was flawless. She could see why Charlotte's mom would force her to compete in talent shows.

Enthusiastic applause rang out as Charlotte finished her solo and she came to sit beside Autumn.

"Your voice is amazing," Autumn admitted. "I'm going to sound like a dying cat compared to that."

Charlotte laughed. "No you won't! You have a very nice voice.

And I heard you practice your solo in class. The lyrics were beautiful."

"Well, I had a little help...on the music, at least."

"Are you dating Victor Lavigne?" Charlotte asked, hitting Autumn with the unexpected question.

She blushed. "Um, no?"

"Is that a question?" Charlotte laughed.

"Well, we've been hanging out a lot lately, but we're just friends, I guess."

"I'm surprised he even talks to you," Charlotte said.

"Why wouldn't he talk to me?" Autumn asked, a little offended.

"He doesn't talk to anyone."

"I think it's more the other way around."

"I suppose that's probably true," Charlotte conceded.

"So, do you know why Avery told everyone about Victor in the first place? Weren't they friends?" Autumn asked, voicing the question Victor never answered.

"You mean you don't know?" said Charlotte, clearly surprised.

"Know what?"

Just then a stage manager called out, "Autumn Oaken! You're on next."

Autumn's stomach dropped at this and she scrambled out of her chair and over to the edge of the curtain to wait.

"Good luck!" Charlotte called.

Autumn's palms began to sweat, her mouth went dry, and her heart was beating loud enough for her to hear. Her stomach turned constantly making her grateful she had skipped dinner. As William Nash finished his song, Autumn's legs began to feel like jelly and she was unsure if she could make it on stage without collapsing.

The stage manager pushed her forward as Magistra Halphnote called out, "Autumn Oaken, singing *Once Upon a Time.*"

Autumn felt hundreds of eyes on her as she walked slowly to the center of the stage. There was no microphone because somehow the magical amphitheater could project the singer's voice out into the audience. The band began playing the music Avery had written and Autumn anxiously waited for her cue to begin.

She took a deep breath and began to sing.

An ethereal, haunting voice escaped her mouth on the first note and her eyes widened in surprise. This couldn't be her voice, yet she knew it was. It was breathtaking and otherworldly, like an echoing song of a magnificent bird. The way it sounded, however, was nothing compared to the way it made her feel. Light. Like she could fly if she tried. Calm. Happy. Powerful. Like she could do anything at all. And she knew—this was her Power. The Power of Song.

Autumn sang the whole piece and, as she neared the end, she regretted that she would have to stop because she wanted to keep feeling that way forever. The audience stared at her with open mouths and dazed expressions, as if hypnotized.

She finished the last notes of the song, her voice still echoing eerily around the amphitheater, and stood before the audience, breathing heavily and beaming down at their awe-struck faces. It took a few moments for them to shake off their trance-like states before they stood and broke out into tumultuous applause.

Autumn bowed and glided off-stage, smiling from ear to ear. Charlotte rushed up to hug her. "You found your Power!" she exclaimed.

"That was marvelous, Autumn, dear. Simply perfect," Magistra Halphnote said, smiling tearfully as she went back onstage to introduce the next two performers, who were shooting Autumn resentful looks.

When the last person performed, all of the Melodies members walked back onstage for the finale song. Autumn lip-synched the words because she didn't know how to control her Power yet and didn't want to hypnotize her fellow Melodies students. Once the finale song had ended, she barely had time to walk off stage before her friends and people she'd never met were swarming around her. Autumn tried to remain humble as everyone hugged and congratulated her, which was difficult when her face was stuck in a permanent smile.

Avery, Luke, and Crystal pushed their way to the front of the gathering crowd. Luke pulled Autumn into a tight hug, and ruffled her hair saying, "I knew you'd find your Power, Rose." Crystal hugged her, repeating over and over again how beautiful her song was.

Avery embraced Autumn too, though in a different way than Luke and Crystal had. He pulled away slowly, his face inches from hers. "I knew your Power would be something incredible," he said barely louder than a whisper. Autumn's heart stuttered as she looked into his raging gray eyes.

"I couldn't have done it without you," she said.

Luke cleared his throat loudly and Avery broke apart from her, shoving his hands into his pockets and looking at his feet.

Just then Victor appeared through the crowd and wrapped Autumn in a tight embrace. "That was exquisite," he said.

"Thanks," she said, aware of the many eyes on her.

He then pulled out a stunning red rose from inside his shirt and held it out to her. An intake of breath reverberated through the crowd around them.

"Will you accept this Rose?" he asked.

"Um, yeah," Autumn said, taking the rose from him. "Thanks, Victor. It's beautiful."

Several people in the crowd gasped at this and Autumn looked up to see Crystal's mouth hanging open, her eyes wide. Luke stared at the rose indifferently and Avery's face was difficult to read as several emotions passed across his features at once before settling into a hard, stony, detached look.

"Autumn!" Crystal said. "I just remembered that I really need to talk to you...about a dress that I'm making. For you."

Autumn wore a bewildered expression as Crystal dragged her out of the crowd and behind a hefty tree trunk.

"What's going on?" Autumn asked when they reached the silent refuge of the foliage.

"You just accepted a Red Rose from Victor Lavigne!"

"So?"

"I'm so sorry, Autumn! I should've told you about all of the elf traditions, but I didn't think to—I mean you've only been here a few—"

"What are you talking about? What do you mean elf traditions?"

Crystal took a deep breath and said quickly, "Roses are very symbolic in elf culture. Black Roses are for death, White Roses are for peace, Yellow Roses are for friendship.

"And what is a Red Rose for?" Autumn asked warily.

"A Red Rose is one of three types of roses that elves offer to one another...romantically. If an elf offers another elf a Red Rose and they accept, they are then bound together as a couple."

"WHAT?"

"I know! It's okay, though. It's not too late. You can still give the rose back, it isn't permanently binding. Not like a diamond rose."

"I can't just give it back, Crystal. He'll hate me."

Crystal stared at Autumn with wide eyes. "What are you going to do?"

"I guess I'm going to be bound to Victor."

Avabelle

CHAPTER NINETEEN

The next Monday, Autumn could hardly wait until Powers class, partly because she was excited about finally getting to use her Power and partly because she needed to get her mind off of Avery. He hadn't spoken to her all weekend and went to dinner with Jastin or Forrest every night, rather than eating at the castle.

Autumn continued to go to lunch with Victor so she wouldn't have to worry about bothering Avery with her presence. It was hard for her to think of Victor as her boyfriend because she could never get someone that attractive in the Outside to talk to her much less date her. The crazy thing was, she didn't know if she even wanted to be bound to him. Beautiful or not.

Victor was a quiet being. Normally Autumn would think someone so quiet to be shy, but Victor wasn't shy by any means. He just seemed to think quite a lot. Besides, he was probably used to not talking to anyone. When he did speak, he usually asked Autumn questions about herself and listened to her answers intently as if making a mental note on every single detail. He still wouldn't talk about himself, though, even now that they were dating. He dodged all of the questions Autumn directed at him, so she finally gave up asking.

Anticipation filled Autumn as she and Victor walked towards the Powers Tree. They were the first ones to the classroom and Autumn sat on the edge of her seat, shaking her foot anxiously. The room slowly began to fill up around them. When Avery entered the room Autumn felt a twinge of guilt, though she knew she hadn't done anything wrong. It was for Avery's own good, really, that Autumn was dating someone else. That way he wouldn't be tempted and neither would she.

When Atticus entered the classroom, Autumn nearly fell out of her chair as she rushed up to him, announcing that she had finally found her Power.

"I know," Atticus said, smiling.

"Oh, right. So, can I fight today?"

Atticus thought for a moment and said, "Yes, I think I will start you out with someone who has a Physical Power, though, and then work you up to a fellow elf with a Mental Power."

"What's the difference?" Autumn asked.

"There are two types of Powers," Atticus said. "Physical and Mental. Physical Powers are Powers that can physically harm someone like Ice, Strength, Weather, and so on. Mental Powers affect someone cognitively, like Jastin's Power, and now yours."

After Atticus assigned pairs, the class traveled up the spiral staircase to the practice room. Autumn had been paired with Noah, the fair-haired boy whose Power was Water. He was quite shy and congratulated her in a small voice before they began battling. When Atticus called for everyone to begin, Autumn let out a wordless melody. Noah instantly became still with a blank look on his face.

The note rang out and the room fell silent. Autumn chanced a quick glance around and ceased singing when she saw that the others were standing completely still with dazed expressions. Once she stopped singing everyone seemed to snap out of their stupor. Some shot her impressed looks, while others, mainly Kyndel, merely looked annoyed.

"Sorry," she said.

"Don't worry about it, Autumn—" Atticus began, but was interrupted by Forrest.

"Autumn! You can hypnotize everyone who hears you! Now we can go after Vyra and finally win!" he exclaimed as a few others emitted cheers of delight.

"Uh, not if *we* are hypnotized too, genius," Kyndel said.

The people who had cheered frowned.

Atticus cleared his throat. "Autumn cannot hypnotize all of Vyra's army. It is much too large." Atticus turned to face her. "You just need to learn how to focus your Power on one person instead of everyone who can hear you. We'll work on it after class. How about you and Noah practice your physical fighting skills."

After waiting and waiting to get a chance to fight with her Power, Autumn had to wait even longer. On the bright side, her frustration fueled her physical fighting abilities. Noah was not a very strong fighter—especially compared to Avery—so Autumn was able to escape every hold. She practiced all of the offensive techniques Avery had taught her and, by the end of class, she had Noah doubled over, panting. When the bells rang he looked more than relieved, wiping sweat from his brow.

"Autumn and Luke, stay here, please," Atticus called over the commotion of the students stomping down the stairs.

When everyone had left the practice room, Atticus addressed the twins. "All right, I don't normally do this, but in this case I will make an exception. You both have a little under a month before the Warrior Test. In this time you will have to learn how to control your Powers properly, when and how to use them, and most importantly how *not* to use them.

"Your fellow classmates have had years to slowly learn this. However, with my training you should be able to reach their level quickly. Plus, you are royals. I'm offering you both private lessons with me every day after school until the Test. Do you accept these terms?" Autumn and Luke agreed emphatically. "Excellent. Luke, I've been watching your technique. For having only learned your Power a week ago, you've already exceeded my expectations, but, like Autumn, you need to learn to focus your Power on only the person you are battling. All right, let's begin. Autumn, I want you to practice focusing your Power only on Luke. Imagine that your Song is a physical force that you are pushing into him. Go on." He waved a hand from Autumn to Luke.

She turned towards her brother and tried to direct her song only at him.

"That was much improved," said Atticus, "but I could still feel your Power's effects. Try again."

They continued like this until Atticus could hardly feel her Power's effects at all. Then it was Luke's turn and Autumn was not thrilled about being his guinea pig. When they finished, she was sopping wet, along with Atticus and everything else in the room.

"Well done, both of you," Atticus exclaimed, wringing out his shirt. "There's no doubt in my mind that you two can reach and even exceed the level of your peers. Your father would be very proud."

"You said on the first day of class that you knew our father well, right?" Autumn said.

Atticus nodded, smiling sadly.

"How did you know him?" Luke asked.

"He was a 4th quarter elf when I was in 1st quarter. He saw some kids picking on me one day and stood up for me. From that day on, he was somewhat of a mentor to me, teaching me how to fight and how to stand up for myself. Most everything I learned about fighting I learned from your dad."

Autumn and Luke exchanged a glance of surprise. Atticus didn't look like someone who would've been bullied. He was so... tough.

"Your father was a good man. Now go on home and change into some dry clothes. You both look like you went for a swim in Arbor Lake," he said, laughing at the state of their attire.

When they left the Powers Tree it was nearly five o'clock. Autumn's feet squelched around in her shoes as she walked.

"Your Power is actually pretty cool, Rose," Luke said.

"Thanks. So is yours, only I wish you wouldn't use so much rain," she said, wringing out her hair.

"Oh, sorry. Here—" He created a strong gust of wind to blow her clothes and hair dry.

Autumn chuckled and said, "Nice. That could come in handy."

As they walked down the path towards Arbor Castle, Autumn realized that this was the first time since they'd arrived that she and Luke had been alone together for more than a few minutes. She hadn't been aware of how much she had missed this. Luke had been her best and only friend back in Ireland.

They laughed and talked like they used to all the way back to the castle. To Autumn's surprise, Luke even asked her how things were going with Victor.

"Good, I guess."

"You guess?"

"Well, it kind of sucks sometimes because I feel like I can't ever be around both him and you guys at the same time because of something Victor can't help. Avery needs to get over his stupid grudge."

Luke shrugged. "Avery doesn't seem the type to hold a grudge for no reason."

"Maybe he was jealous of Victor. Before Avery told everyone his secret, they all really liked Victor," Autumn said.

"I don't think that's it."

"I just wish people would give him a chance."

"Well, bring him to lunch tomorrow. Avery and Victor can make it through lunch together I'm sure."

The following day, Autumn decided to take Luke's advice.

"So, uh, would you maybe come to lunch with me and Luke and a few others?"

Victor fell silent until they reached the Lab Tree. Autumn looked up at him with pleading eyes. Finally he said, "That's fine. I will meet you outside of the History Tree."

He was quieter than usual during Lab, apparently deep in thought. Autumn chose not to bother him and worked in silence. The assignment was identifying different types of leaves and matching them to the trees to which they belonged.

As Autumn paired a maple leaf with its tree, Victor spoke. "Do you have feelings for Avery Burke?"

She accidentally knocked her Lab book to the floor. Coach Holt glanced up from his sports magazine as she hastily picked up the fallen book and laid it on the table. Coach Holt's eyes returned to his reading. She turned back to Victor, who was watching her expectantly.

"Well?" he repeated, a hint of anger in his voice.

"No," Autumn said. "No. We're just friends, that's all."

Victor looked unconvinced and returned to his work in silence.

AVERY's face darkened when he saw Luke, Crystal, and Autumn approaching him with Victor trailing behind them. It took all his energy to make his face impassive and not spit a nasty insult Victor's way.

It was Crystal's turn to choose where they ate, and she decided on her favorite sandwich shop downtown. When everyone had ordered and found their seats, the uncomfortable silence set in. Avery and Victor both sat in the stony quiet, chewing their sandwiches slowly, avoiding each other's gaze. Avery didn't think he could keep his sandwich down if he looked at Victor anyway. Autumn kept opening her mouth as if about to speak and then closing it, clearly changing her mind. Luke and Crystal exchanged several uncomfortable glances. *Well what did Autumn expect?* Avery thought. *That we would be best buddies?*

"So, Victor," Crystal said. "What are your plans for the holidays?" Everyone jumped when she broke the crushing silence.

"I was planning on traveling," he answered shortly.

"Oh. That sounds like fun!" Crystal said a little too brightly to be considered genuine.

"Not visiting the *family*, Lavigne?" Avery muttered, unable to stop himself.

Victor narrowed his eyes at him and said, "No."

"Pity. I'm sure they miss you. Them and your pet Shadows."

"Shut it, Burke," Victor growled.

Victor and Avery sat glaring at each other unblinkingly for about a minute, Avery's blood boiling a bit more as each second passed by, before Autumn spoke.

"Well, this was fun. I'm going to go," she said. Everyone began to protest, but she whirled around, her auburn curls swirling about her angry face. "No! I care about *both* of you and if you can't even get through lunch without picking a fight then I will just have to eat alone."

She threw a couple of silver leaves on the table and stormed out the door. Victor moved to go after her, but Avery was already out of his seat rushing through the door.

AUTUMN was halfway down the path back to campus when she heard Avery calling after her. Turning on her heel, she watched as he jogged up to her.

"What do you want, Avery?" she said folding her arms across her chest.

"I want you to come back."

"No. There was no reason for you to act like that in there. Why can't you two just get along? Just...be nice."

Avery frowned and said, "I can't *be nice* to him, Autumn. I just can't. I'm sorry."

"Why? Because of something that he can't help? Because of where he comes from? The blood that runs through someone's veins has nothing to do with who they are and who they choose to be, Avery."

"I don't care about any of that."

"Then why do you hate him so much? Why did you tell everyone what he is?"

"Because it's HIS fault she died!" he shouted, catching Autumn off-guard.

Autumn started and looked up at him in confusion. "Who died?"

"Avabelle."

"Who's Avabelle?" He shook his head and ran shaking hands through his hair. "Who is she, Avery?" Autumn asked again.

"Let's just say if Avabelle was still alive, you and Luke wouldn't be the only twins around here."

"Avabelle was your twin?" Autumn said in shock.

He nodded. "She was my twin and my best friend. And, for a while, it was always just me, Avabelle...and Victor."

"Victor?"

"We were all three best friends."

"You were best friends with *Victor*?" Autumn said in disbelief.

Avery nodded. "Victor moved here during 2nd quarter and we were all in the same classes. Avabelle and I were always together and then Victor joined our little group. The three of us were inseparable until—" He broke off.

"What happened?"

"We had all three planned on meeting at our usual spot near the falls. There's a big clearing up there that we'd always go to. I couldn't go that day because I had guard duty. So, it was just Avabelle and Victor. When Avabelle didn't show up for dinner, though, I knew something wasn't right. One of our mother's rules was to be back to the castle by dinnertime and Avabelle always followed the rules. I ran up to the falls as fast as I could, but I—I was too late."

Avery stopped to take a shaky breath before continuing.

"When I came into the clearing I saw her just…just laying there. Her neck was crushed and her eyes were wide open and staring." His voice cracked at this. "Victor was wrestling with a Shadow and was in the process of breaking its neck when I walked up. I asked him what had happened and he told me they had both fallen asleep and that he was awakened by Avabelle's screams. He said he tried to save her, but he was too late. Shadows are known for sneaking up on their prey, as silent as their namesake. That's what it did to Avabelle, and then it killed her."

Avery's eyes sparkled with tears and Autumn realized her eyes were also wet. She couldn't imagine how it would feel to see something like that happen to Luke.

"But," she said, "Victor did all that he could to save her."

"I know that," he said, "but *he* is the reason the Shadow came. His blood is like a beacon calling to them. Shadows are attracted to Atrum blood. If there is one nearby they will flock to them. That's why I told everyone what he is. They needed to know for their own safety."

Autumn stood there awkwardly, wondering if she should hug him or give him space. She understood now why the two of them couldn't stand to be around one another. It was too painful for both of them, and Avery couldn't help but blame Victor for his sister's death, which was completely understandable. Of course he would rather blame Victor—an Atrum—than himself, though he probably still did.

"I'm so sorry, Avery. I didn't know," Autumn whispered.

He shrugged as he turned to wipe his eyes dry. "Now do you see why I can't be around him?"

Autumn nodded and said, "Yes. But, maybe you would feel

better if, you know, you...let it go."

Avery was already shaking his head before she could finish. "I can't let it go. Not yet at least."

"I don't want to lose you," Autumn began sadly before adding, "As a friend."

"You won't." He looked deep into her eyes then, searching. "I won't let that happen."

Unicorns and Snowball Fights

CHAPTER TWENTY

After Autumn's conversation with Avery, things went back to normal—for the most part. Half of her time was spent with Victor and the other half she spent with Luke, Crystal, and Avery. It was like she was the child of a broken family or something.

Autumn and Luke continued their daily lessons with Atticus, and every weekend they worked with Crystal and Avery on fighting and archery skills in preparation for the Warrior Test. Autumn discovered that she really loved archery, and she was actually pretty good at it. She relished the feel of a bow in one hand and an arrow in the other. It was exhilarating. Luke, on the other hand, loathed it. He quickly realized that his hand-eye coordination was not what he would like it to be. He spent most of his time grumbling and groaning as he missed each target. Every so often he would end up throwing his bow on the ground or breaking his arrow in half in frustration.

Victor always seemed to disappear off the face of the Underground when weekends rolled around. When Autumn asked him where it was that he went he said, "Everywhere."

"Everywhere?"

"I like to travel," he said simply.

"So, you just walk everywhere or what?"

Victor laughed. "No. I have a unicorn."

"A *unicorn*?" Autumn asked, trying to hide her five-year-old girl excitement bubbling up within her. She used to have a small obsession with the 80s television show *My Little Pony*.

"Yes."

"Can I see it?"

"I'm not sure that's such a good idea. He doesn't really like strangers."

Autumn's face fell and she said, "Oh, okay."

Victor sighed. "Well, if you really want to..."

The next day, after her private lesson with Atticus, Autumn ran to meet with Victor in a small clearing near campus, stopping dead in her tracks when she spotted the breathtaking beast standing beside him. Autumn had always thought of unicorns as sweet little creatures with delicate horns protruding from their heads, but this unicorn was not at all like that. His onyx fur shone in the dull sunlight leaking through the leaves above. The unicorn was twice the size of an average horse and sported a horn that was long, thin, and extremely sharp looking. His beetle-black eyes watched Autumn warily.

She started to approach him.

"Be careful," Victor warned just as Autumn stumbled on a tree root.

The colossal unicorn reared back on his hind legs and charged toward her, his horn aiming for her chest. Victor knocked her out of the way, but not before the unicorn's horn sliced a gash in her shoulder. Victor bellowed at the animal, kicking it hard in the gut.

"No!" Autumn exclaimed. "It was my fault! Don't hurt him!" Victor ignored her pleas and aimed another strike at the unicorn, which had collapsed to the ground. "Victor!"

He whipped around, his pupils dilated and his face contorted in rage. Autumn gasped at the sight of him. He looked deranged.

"Please, stop," she said, half sobbing.

He shook his head violently back and forth, closing his eyes tight, and falling to his knees. When he opened his eyes they were back to normal, his pupils retracting to reveal his green irises again.

"What happened?" he gasped. Autumn stared at him in bewilderment. "WHAT HAPPENED?" he repeated.

"The—the unicorn charged at me because I startled him. You

knocked me to the ground and started kicking him and..." She stopped because she was about to comment on how demented he looked, but decided against it.

Victor turned towards his injured unicorn lying on the ground, whose chest was rising and falling quickly, his breathing shallow.

Autumn looked sadly down at the unicorn and said, "He might have internal bleeding. Maybe we should—"

"I'll take care of it," Victor snapped.

"Do you want me to help?"

"No. Just go," he said through clenched teeth.

She didn't need telling twice. Autumn climbed painfully to her feet and hurried up the path back towards campus, pressing a hand to her bleeding shoulder. She hoped the campus healer was still there.

When Autumn ran up to the Healer Tree, she found the door to be locked. Cursing, she looked around in desperation. There was a healer at the castle, but she didn't want to risk being seen by anyone. Autumn tried to think back to all of her Healing lessons and remembered one in particular regarding a certain plant that stopped bleeding. The cauterweed plant. What did those look like again?

She moved towards the Healing Tree, squinting at the bountiful vegetation in search of something familiar while keeping steady pressure on her shoulder. She was beginning to feel slightly lightheaded. As she passed by a bush with black and red leaves, she screeched to a halt. That was it. Autumn grabbed a handful of the leaves, soaked them in the pond near the Healing Tree, and pressed them against her shoulder. The bleeding stopped almost instantly. However, it did nothing for the three-inch long gash in her arm. A wave of nausea washed over her and she had to look away.

Magistra Ginger taught them about a substance that closed wounds, but Autumn couldn't remember the name. It was white and could be found within the roots of a red cactus-like plant. She walked all the way around the Healing Tree and finally spotted the plant, which she remembered now was called a suturous plant.

Using her hands, she dug up the roots of the suturous plant, ripping them out, and squeezing the white substance onto her throbbing shoulder. Autumn breathed in sharply when it came into contact with her wound because it felt like someone was poking her with thousands of sharp needles. After a minute of biting her hand to keep from screaming, she looked down at her shoulder in amazement. Though the skin was an angry red, the wound had completely closed.

Autumn returned to Arbor Castle, dashing up the stairs, hoping to avoid being seen so as not to raise any unwanted questions about her blood-soaked blouse. Miraculously, she made it to her branch without being seen by anyone after a series of close encounters. Autumn quickly threw on another white blouse similar to the one she had been wearing. No one would know the difference.

She wasn't sure why she was going to such great lengths to hide what had happened. It had been an accident, after all. Maybe she didn't want to give Avery any more reasons to dislike Victor. She was still hoping that, by some miracle, they could stand to be around each other eventually, maybe even become friends again. Not a likely event, but still.

The atmosphere of the dining room was ebullient when Autumn arrived, plopping down in a chair next to Crystal. Luke was leaning back in his chair, talking to an attractive blonde woman at the table beside theirs.

Autumn had just sat down with her plate of food when Avery said absently, "You're wearing a different shirt."

Her eyes widened. "What? Oh. I, um, spilled something on it. I'm surprised you even noticed."

"The other one had flowers on the sleeves..." He trailed off, clearly embarrassed that he noticed such a minute detail when he was supposed to be acting indifferent.

Still leaning back in his chair, Luke raised an amused eyebrow in Avery's direction. Then suddenly, Luke's chair toppled backwards. He scrambled to his feet, his face a deep red. Most of the diners looked his way and stifled chuckles echoed around the room. Autumn, Crystal, and Avery howled with laughter.

Luke's face didn't return to its original color the rest of the night.

That weekend, nearly everyone from Aspen Academy went

to Arbor Lake. The Warrior Test loomed over them like a storm cloud—only two weeks away. Autumn could feel the nervous tension emanating from the other 4th quarter elves.

They all practiced their Power any chance they could and the Healer Tree on campus had been overflowing for the last few weeks as a result. The Head of Aspen Academy eventually sent out a notice declaring that practicing Powers in between classes was forbidden.

Victor left for the weekend once again. He and Autumn hadn't spoken about the unicorn incident, both acting as though it hadn't happened.

When they arrived at Arbor Lake, Autumn sat with Luke, Avery, and Crystal near the still, sparkling water. The sweet smell of honeysuckles and roses wafted through the air. Of course, Luke soon left the group when he noticed a petite brunette batting her eyelashes suggestively at him.

Autumn shook her head in distaste. "I hope he's not doing anything stupid."

"What do you mean?" Crystal asked.

"You know. With girls."

Avery and Crystal stared at her, clearly nonplussed.

"I'm talking about sex, guys," Autumn stated bluntly. Crystal gasped and Avery's face turned scarlet as he looked down at his hands. "What?" Autumn said, laughing at their reactions.

"Elves don't, I mean—it's not something that we…" Crystal stammered.

"You mean elves don't have—" Autumn began, her mouth falling open.

"Of course they do," Crystal whispered. "But only within the bounds of true love. Well, there are some who, er— Even so, it's not really something we talk about."

"Oh, sorry," Autumn muttered.

Avery was silent, busying himself by pulling at the grass. Crystal's face was flushed. Clearly the Underground was much more conservative than anywhere Autumn had lived in the Outside—including Texas—which surprised her, judging by the amount of elves that were willing to make out with her brother.

"Hey, Crys!" Forrest called from the edge of the lake, "Can you help?"

"'Yes! Be right there." Crystal jumped up and practically ran to freeze a patch of ice for Drake, Bryan, and Forrest, clearly glad to be granted an easy out from the sex conversation, leaving Autumn alone with Avery.

She had to repress a smile at his embarrassment. It was a little refreshing if she was being honest. That particular subject was all guys could talk about at both of her old high schools.

"Sorry," she said again.

"For what?" Avery looked up, his cheeks still flushed.

"I didn't mean to make you uncomfortable."

He smiled crookedly at her. "I've just never heard anyone talk so openly about...that. Especially not a girl."

"Yeah, well, I lived in the Outside for seventeen years. It's sort of a common subject there."

"Really?" Avery asked, looking shocked.

Autumn nodded, wearing a lopsided smile.

He cleared his throat a few times before saying, "So, have you ever—"

"No," Autumn said hastily, now blushing herself.

Once the uncomfortable silence had passed, Autumn and Avery moved on to much tamer topics, like Luke falling backwards in his chair. They were throwing their heads back in laughter when Crystal returned, looking relieved to see that they were no longer talking about sex.

"Avery, the boys are planning something and want your opinion," she said, taking a seat next to Autumn.

"What are they planning?" he asked.

"Something to do with snow."

Avery shrugged and stood to leave, flashing a small smile back at Autumn. She smiled back, her heart fluttering. Then she turned around to see Crystal watching her with a sly look.

"What?" Autumn said.

"Still getting over that crush are you?"

"I don't know what you're talking about," Autumn said, not making eye contact.

"Sure..."

"Hush, Crystal, before I hypnotize you."

"Oh yeah? Not if I freeze you first!"

Crystal playfully shot a jet of ice at Autumn as they both jumped nimbly to their feet. Autumn laughed, moving swiftly back and forth.

"Too quick for you, Everly?" Autumn laughed as Crystal shot another stream of ice in her direction. Autumn lunged to the left and the ice soared behind her, hitting something stationary—and invisible.

"Ow!" a familiar voice shrieked.

Suddenly Kyndel materialized as if from thin air. Autumn should have known it was her. Kyndel's power was Invisibility.

"Nice aim, Ice Queen," Kyndel spat at Crystal.

"I'd say I aimed pretty well that time around, wouldn't you?" Crystal said to Autumn.

Kyndel brushed the ice shards off of her black cardigan.

"What were you doing there anyway?" Autumn said. "Spying on us? You know, there are less creepy ways to practice your Power, Kyndel."

Kyndel blushed and said, "What makes you think I care about anything *you* have to say, Princess?"

"Maybe because of the way you were sneaking around us all invisible and such."

"I was just practicing my Power. I'm free to walk wherever I please, you know. Just because you're a *royal* doesn't mean you can tell me where I'm allowed to walk," she said before whipping around and stomping in the opposite direction.

Autumn rolled her eyes at Kyndel's retreating figure. "Why does everyone pretend to like her? She's such a witch."

"Her father owns almost all of the tree houses in Arbor Falls. He's basically right behind the king in terms of power. That's why she hates you so much. Before you came along, she was the richest girl in school."

"Who cares?"

Crystal shrugged. "Is it snowing over there?" she said, pointing towards the group of boys.

Apparently the guys had pulled Luke away from his new girl and convinced him to make it snow. When Autumn and Crystal approached, they were in the process of building heaping mounds of snowballs

"Are you starting a snowball fight?" Crystal asked.

"Yeah!" Forrest said.

"We want in," Autumn said.

"This is a man's game," Bryan said.

"Excuse me?" a petite girl with spiked, blonde hair said as she approached them. "A *man's* game?" Autumn realized it was Cera, the girl with the Power of Gravity. She was in Atticus's class with her.

"Yup," Drake said.

"All right, then. Let's make this interesting. Boys against girls," Cera said.

"Well, that will be a short game," Luke said and laughed.

"Oh yeah? Let's do this," Autumn said, winking at Cera and Crystal.

The three girls rounded up a few others who were willing to play on their team. With the help of Charlotte, they convinced Kyndel and her two cronies—Ella and Dayna—to join them. Pretty soon, each team had seven players.

The guys' team was: Noah, Luke, Bryan, Drake, Forrest, Jastin, and Avery.

The girls' team was: Crystal, Cera, Kyndel, Charlotte, Ella, Dayna, and Autumn.

They used the sporadic trees as blockades rather than a singular snow mound. Crystal made a wall of ice to signify the boundary between the teams.

"Okay, elves, take your places!" Cera called as if she was the director of a play.

Everyone rushed to find a boulder or a tree suitable enough to hide behind.

"Now!" Drake bellowed.

Grabbing a handful of snowballs, they commenced chucking them at the other team. The girls lost Dayna and Ella almost immediately as they got Noah out. Everyone used their Power to their advantage. Autumn had finally learned how to concentrate her power on only one person at a time and she aimed a long, piercing note at Drake, who stopped in his tracks, hypnotized by the Song. She hurled a snowball at him, effectively getting him out.

"Nice one!" Cera called.

Cera had put a shield of Gravity around herself so that she was virtually unreachable. If a snowball hit her shield, it was immediately thrown back at the other team. So, the guys mostly just avoided her snowballs.

Autumn sent a jet of song to Avery, but he threw his hands over his ears and ducked behind a tree. He jumped back out and shot a snowball at her, which narrowly missed her as she ducked. She tried to hit him with another note of song, but it seemed that he had stuffed something in his ears to make himself temporarily immune to her Power.

Charlotte lovingly called Jastin's name before hitting him with a snowball and blowing a kiss. Autumn got Bryan and Forrest out, but the girls soon lost Charlotte and Kyndel. Luke took a well-aimed shot at Crystal and got her out.

It was now just Autumn and Cera against Luke and Avery. Luke blew a gust of wind at Cera, knocking her off her feet and breaking her concentration. Her shield failed just as Avery hit her with a snowball. Avery and Luke laughed and slapped their hands together.

While Luke was distracted, Autumn managed to get a stream of song to him and hit him in the side of the face with a snowball.

Autumn and Avery were the only ones left now. Autumn darted all around her territory and ducked behind various trees when she saw something fall from Avery's left ear. Concentrating harder than ever, she aimed a jet of song at his open ear. He stopped, a dazed look crossing his face and Autumn nailed him in the chest with a snowball.

The girls' team cheered, jumping up and down and jeering at the gloomy looking boys.

"How does it feel to lose to a bunch of *girls*?" Cera called to Drake, who was grumbling something about cheating.

They were all freezing. The snow had melted through their thin garments, numbing their skin. The teams dispersed, heading in different directions. Autumn saw Luke leave with the girl he had been with earlier, and Crystal had rushed off soon after she got out of the game, claiming that she was already late for a meeting with her mom.

Autumn began to stroll towards the castle alone.

"Hey Autumn, wait up!" Avery called.

She paused and turned to wait for him. Apparently he hadn't expected her to stop so suddenly because he crashed into her and they both toppled to the ground, Avery landing on top of her.

"Ow," Autumn said breathlessly.

Their faces were inches apart.

"Sorry." His warm breath felt good on her cold face.

"S'okay," she said with difficulty.

Avery's face inched closer to Autumn's until his lips brushed hers slightly. Fighting against every urge in her body, she rolled out from under him.

"I can't," she said, climbing to her feet.

"Why not?" Avery said, his square jaw clenching.

"You know why not."

"Victor?" Avery spit the name like it tasted bad in his mouth. "Who cares about him?"

"I do," Autumn said, starting to walk away. Avery grabbed her hand and pulled her back.

"No you don't, Autumn," he said. "You just feel sorry for him."

She pulled her hand from his grasp. "You have no idea how I feel, Avery."

"Yes, I do."

"Oh yeah? How's that?"

"You feel the same way I do."

Autumn's breath caught in her chest. "And how do *you* feel?" she asked, regretting it as soon as the words left her mouth.

"I can't really put it into words."

"Try," Autumn said. Her hands were shaking, and it wasn't because of the cold.

"Every time you're near me it's like there's this *force* inside of me, pulling me towards you." Autumn stared at him with wide eyes. He had just described exactly what she'd been feeling since the moment their skin first touched. They were silent for a second before Avery said, "You feel it too. I know you do." Autumn stayed silent. "You do feel it, right?" Avery said with less conviction now.

"It doesn't matter how I feel," Autumn said, emphasizing each word.

"Yes, it does," Avery said, stepping closer so that they were only a foot apart now.

"No, it doesn't."

"Why? Because of Victor? Because you want him to believe that someone can care about an Atrum?"

"I *do* care about him."

"Not the way you care about me."

Autumn sighed. "It's not just about Victor. It's everything, Avery. This—us—just can't happen."

"Says who?"

"Olympus," Autumn stated, daring him to disagree.

"Olympus?" Avery said. Autumn nodded. "He says you can't be with me?"

"Not *you* specifically. He said Luke and I aren't allowed to be with any of the workers in the castle. It's a rule."

Avery took a step back from her, an expression of intense resentment and disgust on his face. "You don't want to be with me because I'm a castle worker? Because I'm beneath your *social status*?"

"No! That's not what I said. You're twisting my words."

He began backing away from her saying, "No, I got it. If you'll excuse me, *Your Highness*, I must be getting back to my duties at the *castle*."

He stormed off in the direction of the path that led to the castle, leaving Autumn to decipher whether the sting from the cold or the look in his eyes was more painful.

AVERY trudged up the path to the castle, fuming. The last thing he saw was Autumn staring after him with a hurt look on her face. What did she have to feel hurt about? *Royals*, he thought with distaste. He had thought she was different, but she wasn't. *She deserves Victor.* He mentally kicked himself for thinking that. No one deserved that. No one.

He charged into Arbor Castle and up the winding staircase to his branch. He didn't feel like eating tonight. Opening the door to his branch, he stepped quietly inside in case his mother was asleep.

As he passed her room she called out, "John?"

Avery sighed and backtracked, opening his mother's door slowly. She was lying on top of her comforter in her thin nightgown, making her frail body look even more emaciated than it already was. Her eyes were hollow, underlined with dark shadows, and her mousy brown hair was splayed out on her pillow. "John?"

"No, Mom. It's me, Avery."

"Where've you been, John? Have you found Avabelle? Have you found our baby?"

Avery stared sadly down at his mother. He didn't feel like correcting her tonight. "Yes. I found her."

"Good," she sighed, closing her eyes. "Good."

"You should eat your dinner," he said, frowning at the bowl of cold soup on her nightstand. The castle nurse must have already made her daily visit.

"Mmm," was all his mother said. He waited, but she stayed silent. He backed out of her room, shutting the door behind him.

"Goodnight, John," he heard her say.

He was used to being called by his father's name. Ever since Avabelle died, his mother hadn't been normal. She talked to people who weren't around anymore: his father, his sister, even his grandmother. But she never talked to *him*. Not in person that was. She was still able to contact him through his dreams. He was relieved that she still had some control of her Power, if nothing else. She must have retained her sanity in her sleep.

Their dream connections were not always pleasant, though. Sometimes she shared her own dreams with him. Sometimes he couldn't tell the difference between his mother's messages and his own nightmares.

Warrior Test

CHAPTER TWENTY-ONE

The way Avery was behaving now made Autumn almost miss his old silent treatments. He shot her numerous glares throughout the school day and occasionally broke the hostile silence to say something dripping with sarcasm like, "Good morning, *Your Highness*," and, "I sincerely hope you slept well last night, Princess. I made sure all of the peas were removed from under your mattress."

Autumn tried to ignore him, and when that didn't work, she merely shot him a look of annoyance. Their friends had obviously noted the change in their behavior, but no one commented on it.

To put it mildly, Victor was quite pleased with the new development and hardly had trouble showing it. Every time Autumn gave Avery one of her loathsome looks, Victor smiled to himself.

Atticus had been pushing his Powers students harder than ever in a last-ditch attempt to prepare them for the upcoming Test. As the days went by, Autumn became more and more nervous. It was like the Melodies concert all over again, but with much higher stakes. She continued her daily practices on the dueling grounds at the castle along with Luke, Crystal, and to her annoyance, Avery. She made sure to steer clear of him during this time. With her nerves already on edge, any comment from him might have caused her to snap.

She wondered if anyone else was practicing as much as the

four of them. Autumn secretly hoped that they'd all come down with a terrible case of procrastination. The day before the Warrior Test, Atticus sat the entire class down and surveyed them with a serious expression.

"As you are all aware, the Warrior Test is tomorrow. I'm sure you've all been practicing very hard, or at least I hope. We counted up the numbers yesterday and have found that more than half of the 4th quarter elves will be taking the Test, nearly 100. Out of these only ten will be chosen to become Warriors."

Autumn's face fell, along with many of her classmates. These weren't the best odds. She had been fairly confident about her chances...until now.

"There will be three components on which you will be tested," Atticus continued. "One: archery skills. Two: fighting skills, without the use of your Power. And three is, of course, your Power. Once everyone has performed these three tasks, we will dismiss you until the results are posted at 9pm tomorrow night. Any questions?"

Everyone stared up at him with wide eyes. No one spoke.

Atticus chuckled and said, "Don't worry, guys. I've taught you well. Remember that I'm on the judging panel and know your potential."

"Who are the other judges?" Forrest asked tentatively.

"The current Head Warrior, Gregorius Dodge, and the Head of Aspen Academy, Alphreda Hopkins." Everyone in the class looked slightly sick to their stomachs as they registered all of this information. "All right, that's it for the day. I suggest that you eat a nice dinner and go to bed early. I do not advise practicing tonight. You'll need your energy tomorrow. I will see you all in the morning at 9am sharp on the school dueling grounds."

That evening, Autumn joined Luke, Crystal, and Avery at their usual table and ate without tasting anything, too absorbed in her incessant thoughts.

A female castle worker sitting at the table next to theirs stood to leave, brushing up against Luke's back and smiling demurely at him as she apologized. Luke gazed longingly after her. "Man," he said. "Stupid castle rules. I would so hook up with her if Olympus wouldn't have me beheaded."

Avery looked up from his plate. "What?" he said with a look of disbelief.

"Oh, are you related to her or something? Sorry," Luke said sheepishly.

"No. What did you say about castle rules?"

Autumn raised an eyebrow at him and pursed her lips.

"Oh," Luke said, looking relieved. "Autumn and I aren't allowed to date castle workers because we're considered their 'superiors' and it would be inappropriate or something. It's one of Olympus's rules. But I think it's lame. I mean, look at the classic story of the princess and the stable boy, only it would be the prince and the hot castle worker girl."

Avery glanced up at Autumn as she gave him a smug "I told you so" look.

"That wasn't a rule before," Crystal noted thoughtfully. "But, then again, there weren't any young royals at the castle."

"Yeah, but Olympus was the only royal elf around here for a while and he wasn't about to hook up with one of the maids or something, was he?" Luke snorted.

Autumn burst out laughing as the ridiculous mental picture of their grandfather wooing a maid popped into her head. "Well, I'm going to head off to bed," she said once her laughter had subsided. "Want to be well rested before I embarrass myself in front of 100 elves. Plus the judges. Night, guys."

She walked up the stairs to her branch looking down over the enormous library, which she had yet to take advantage of. Now that she thought of it, she hadn't read one book since she'd arrived. Evidently her real life was now more exciting than a novel.

"Autumn?"

She turned to see Avery standing on the steps below her, hands shoved in his pockets and head hanging. If he were a dog, his tail would have been between his legs.

"Yes?" Autumn said, folding her arms across her chest. "Come to turn down my bed for me, sir? I think you may have missed a couple of peas as well. I've been sleeping horribly lately."

Avery ran his hand nervously through his hair as he said, "I know. I've been a jerk. You tried to tell me."

"Yup."

"I guess this makes everything pretty clear. Do you think he'll change his mind?"

"Olympus?" Autumn asked and Avery nodded. Autumn had spent enough time with her grandfather to know that he was a very laid back man, but when it came to rules, he was exceptionally strict. "I don't think so."

Avery frowned and said, "Well I suppose we can just...be friends."

"I'd like that," Autumn said with a smile. "But no more calling me 'princess' and whatnot. I hate that."

"Yes, Your Highness," he said. Autumn glared at him. "Kidding!"

After a restless night and an early morning, Autumn moved slowly downstairs to the dining room. She sat at their table and poured herself a mug of honeysuckle cider. Her stomach was too uneasy to eat much of anything so she nibbled on a piece of dry toast. Luke soon joined her looking as nervous as she felt. He piled his plate with food, but instead of inhaling it as usual, he pushed it around his plate while studying the swirling wood-grain of the table.

When Avery arrived a few minutes later, Luke began shoveling his cold food into his mouth, probably not wanting Avery to suspect that he was nervous, though Avery seemed to be just as anxious. He kept running his hand through his hair until it was sticking up every which way. As he moved to do it once more, Autumn absentmindedly grabbed his wrist.

"If you do that one more time, your hair will be permanently stuck that way," she said with a nervous laugh.

He chuckled and flattened his hair back down. "Well, if you bite your nails any more you won't have any left," he said, pulling Autumn's hand from her mouth. She hadn't even realized she'd been doing it.

Autumn was glad they were finally on the same page, which was that they both wanted the same thing—each other, and they both knew that it wasn't an option. She couldn't help but notice that the magnetic pull, a constant presence whenever she was near Avery, grew stronger each time they touched. It would go away, she hoped. Surely.

Once Crystal showed up, announcing she was too nervous to eat, the four of them left for the campus dueling grounds. When they arrived, Autumn was relieved to see that they weren't the only ones who had shown up early. At least 50 people were nervously pacing back and forth, sitting on the grass with their heads in their hands, or practicing their dueling techniques.

Forrest, Jastin, and Charlotte came bounding up to the four of them.

"I saw Atticus talking to a group of Warriors in the Powers Tree. Do you think they're going to help judge?" Forrest said.

"Probably," Avery nodded, running his fingers through his hair for the thousandth time that morning.

The dueling grounds filled steadily until almost all of the Warrior hopefuls were standing around, anxiously awaiting the start of the Test. Victor arrived a few minutes before 9:00 and came to stand silently beside Autumn.

Atticus emerged from one of the Training Trees and breezed onto the field before them. "Good morning everyone," he called to the now packed field, which had fallen silent at the first sight of him. A few elves muttered a greeting, but most just nodded in acknowledgment.

Atticus smiled and continued, "We will begin the Warrior Test with archery. You will be given a bow and five arrows. Your task is to hit as many bulls-eyes as possible. We will be starting with the elves whose last names begin with the letters A-H. The rest of you will wait in one of the three Training Trees. Last names starting with I-P will be in the middle Training Tree and Q-Z will be in the final Training Tree. When it's your group's turn, a Warrior will come retrieve you."

At this time a tall, burly man accompanied by a petite, fragile looking woman walked onto the field, followed by ten elves dressed in a dark leather-like material. They were rather intimidating.

"Who're they?" Autumn whispered to Crystal.

"Those are the Quinn Warriors. That's what we will be if we become Initiates and live through the Warrior Trial."

"Oh. Wait, there's a Warrior *Trial* too?"

Crystal shushed her as the burly man, who Autumn assumed

was Gregorius Dodge, and the woman, who must have been Alphreda Hopkins, settled themselves down in two high backed chairs behind a heavy wooden table. The judges' table, which Autumn hadn't noticed until just then, was situated to the side of the field. There were stands set up behind them where the rest of the Warriors would sit to observe the Test. A single archery range stood in the center of the field.

Autumn wished Avery and Crystal good luck and walked with Luke, Victor, and the rest of the I-P group to the middle Training Tree, which was only a few yards from the dueling field. The Training Tree had two levels. The upper level had a small window, so everyone hurried to the top. Drake and Luke fought their way through to the window and called Jastin, Charlotte and Autumn over. Victor took a seat in the back of the room, not bothering to join them.

"I wonder what those Quinns are doing with Dodge," Luke said as he craned his neck to see out of the window. "Shouldn't they be sitting in the stands with the rest of the Warriors?"

"Maybe they're going to do a demonstration or something. Like a passing of the torch sort of thing," Charlotte said.

"Maybe Dodge always has some Warriors with him in case he gets attacked," Drake said.

Autumn rolled her eyes.

"Don't be an idiot, McMurtry," Jastin muttered.

"Well, what's your brilliant idea then? Why are they just standing there behind the judges?"

"I think they're just for show," Jastin said. "To demonstrate to us what being a Quinn looks like and to intimidate us a bit. We *are* taking their places, after all."

"Only as Quinns," Drake said. "They're going to be Tetras anyway, which are the coolest level of Warrior in my opinion."

"Luckily no one cares about your opinion," Jastin said, receiving a punch to the shoulder from Drake.

"Maybe we have to fight them," Autumn said.

Jastin, Drake, and Luke went silent. Autumn took her eyes off of the field and turned her gaze on them. A look of terrified comprehension had dawned upon all of their faces.

Drake cursed.

"Makes sense," Jastin said. "Who better to test our fighting skills than an actual Warrior?"

"Look, they're starting!" Charlotte exclaimed, pointing out the window.

A large group of elves gathered around them, trying to see out the small window. Their Training Tree was situated a little to the left of the archery range so they could see the arrows that were being shot, but not the elves shooting them. Autumn wondered which ones were Avery's. She watched as arrow after arrow soared through the air and hit or missed the bulls-eye. Few people hit five bulls-eyes in a row.

Some of the elves grew tired of watching countless arrows fly through the air, so the crowd behind the window began to disperse. Soon it was just Luke, Jastin, Drake, Charlotte, and Autumn.

"Not very good, are they?" Charlotte noted.

Autumn stifled a laugh. "Not particularly," she said, trying not to be too critical. However, she had to admit that her confidence had been boosted a bit by watching the arrows fly past the range, or land on the outermost ring. The last few times Autumn had visited the archery range, she had been able to hit the bulls-eye every time, thanks to Avery's coaching.

Just then, a Warrior appeared in the doorway and said, "Elves with last names beginning with I-P are up next. Please exit the Training Tree and make your way to the right side of the field."

He reminded Autumn of a worker on a theme park ride.

Jastin, Drake, Luke, Charlotte, and Autumn followed suit behind the others who were hurrying out of the tree. Victor moved to stand beside her. Autumn's nerves seemed to have doubled.

The A-H group was nowhere to be seen, apparently already situated in the first Training Tree. Another Warrior met the I-P group at the base of the field.

"You are to wait here until your name is called. Once they call your name, you are to stand to the left of Boone over there." He pointed over his shoulder at an enormous onyx-skinned Warrior who was standing next to a basket full of arrows. "Boone will hand you your five arrows. Once you finish, you are to exit the field and wait in the Training Tree until your next test." He then left to join the rest of the Quinns, who were standing behind the judges' table.

"Tyler Ike," Atticus called from the judges' table.

Tyler, a particularly scrawny boy, emerged from the group and ambled nervously up to Boone, who held five arrows in his oversized hands. The boy was so nervous his entire bow was shaking uncontrollably, and when he finally let go of the arrow, it shot several feet to the left of the bulls-eye. Sadly, his aim became progressively worse. The last arrow landed within a foot of the judges' table. He walked off the field with his head hung low.

Autumn's confidence steadily grew as she watched each elf go before her. Apparently archery wasn't many elves' forte. This surprised her because in many of the legends she'd read as a child, elves were experts at archery. Autumn voiced this to Victor and he said, "Archery isn't something all elves know how to do well. It's a lost art. The Warriors and retired Warriors continue to push it on their children and grandchildren, which is why some of your *friends* enjoy going to the archery range."

Autumn assumed by *friends* he meant Avery, whose late father was once the Head of the Warriors.

Jastin, Victor, and Charlotte had no reason to be nervous because each of them hit almost every bulls-eye. Victor seemed immensely relieved as he walked off the field. Autumn had actually been surprised that he did so well because she'd never once seen him shoot an arrow.

Drake, on the other hand, only hit the bulls-eye once. The other four arrows were all over the place. A wave of curse words escaped his mouth as he tromped off the field.

Then Atticus called, "Autumn Oaken."

She jumped slightly when Atticus called out her name. Luke gave her a nervous grimace, which she assumed was supposed to be a look of encouragement. She strode quickly onto the field, surprised she wasn't more nervous. Before the Melodies concert, she'd been almost paralyzed with fear, but she had been unsure of herself then. Now she was confident. She had been to the archery range with Avery, Luke, and Crystal countless times and had perfected her technique. Luke had improved greatly and he'd even stopped breaking his arrows in half out of frustration.

The Warrior named Boone nodded curtly at Autumn and handed her the first arrow. She tried her best to ignore the whispers of her peers behind her and the unblinking stares of the judges. Taking a deep breath, she pulled the string steadily back and released the arrow. It cut through the air like a bullet and landed with a thud in the middle of the bulls-eye. She let out the breath she'd been holding as Boone handed her another arrow. The remaining four arrows left her bow as smoothly as the first, coming to rest in almost exactly the same place each time.

Autumn tried not to look too excited as she left the field. She wanted the judges to think that she had expected to make all five bulls-eyes. No big deal. When she entered the Training Tree, Victor jumped up from his seat looking anxious.

"Well? How did you do?"

Autumn's face broke into a wide grin as she said, "Good."

"How good?"

"Five bulls-eyes."

His face relaxed and he pulled her into a tight hug. "Good."

Luke walked in a few minutes later, frowning slightly.

"How'd it go?" Autumn asked as he plopped down beside her.

"I made four bulls-eyes and one on the outer ring. Someone freaking sneezed behind me just as I was letting go of the arrow!"

"But that's great!" Autumn said. "Four out of five is really good, and I'm sure they'll take the sneeze into account."

He shook his head. "Not if more than ten people make five. They're not going to pick me when I just made four."

"That's not the only thing we're being judged on," Jastin said from behind them.

"Easy for you to say," Luke muttered, "You made all five."

Jastin shrugged and said, "I'd be more worried about the fighting test than anything. If you can't fight, you have no business being a Warrior."

"Oh, trust me, he can fight," Autumn grumbled. Charlotte laughed.

Bobby Parker was the last of their group. When he entered the Training Tree, he announced that group Q-Z was beginning. A long table was set up at the back of the Training Tree full of sandwiches and drinks. Few people were eating even though it was lunchtime. Autumn nibbled on a piece of fruit just to have something to do.

"How do you think Crystal and Avery did?" Luke asked her as

he pulled off a piece of bread from his sandwich and rolled it into a sphere before popping it mechanically in his mouth.

"I don't know. They always do well when we practice," Autumn said.

Victor glanced sideways at her, but said nothing. Although she noticed him fidget a little as he always did when Avery's name was mentioned.

"They're starting the next test!" a girl squealed from in front of the small window. Everyone in the tree went silent, listening intently to the single voice coming from the field. Autumn couldn't hear a word Atticus was saying and looked around to see if anyone else could. Most everyone wore a look of intense concentration, but no one seemed to know which test was coming next.

"It's the fighting test!" the girl squeaked, her face pressed up against the window like a starfish on a fish tank.

The tree filled with noise as people discussed the news with one another. Autumn began chewing her nails again. If she was right about having to fight the Warriors, then this was not going to be easy. Sure, she could fight her fellow classmates and succeed, but the current Quinns had been fighting Atrums and Shadows for five years.

The girl who was pressed against the window gasped. She turned her head, her face white, and said, "We have to fight a Warrior."

Autumn hated being right sometimes.

And the Warrior Is...

CHAPTER TWENTY-TWO

A long time passed before the I-P group was called out of their Training Tree to begin the next portion of the Test. When the Warrior finally came to retrieve them, they exited the tree and assembled at the base of the field. Atticus approached the group.

"We will begin the fighting portion shortly. When I call your name, you will walk to the center of the field, as will one Quinn Warrior. When I blow this," he held up a reed that resembled a miniature flute, "your task will be to free yourself completely from your Warrior's hold within one minute. If you haven't accomplished this within the allotted time, you will simply move on to the next task. In the second task, you will attack your opponent in any way possible until you bring them to the ground. Questions?"

They stared at him, wide-eyed and silent. If anyone did have a question, they were either too scared to ask or afraid they might vomit if they opened their mouths. Drake seemed to be part of the latter group because his skin was a light shade of green and his mouth was squeezed shut.

"Tyler Ike," Atticus called once he'd re-joined the other judges.

The small boy was shaking even more violently than before. Autumn saw Atticus murmur something to the group of Quinns. The smallest male Quinn, Jack, who still towered over Tyler, nodded and entered the field, stopping in front of the trembling boy.

The reed let out a high-pitched whistle and the battle began.

It was a bit sad watching Tyler struggle to release himself. He kicked and jumped, trying to get out of Jack's hold, but by the time Atticus blew the whistle again, Tyler hadn't so much as moved an inch out of the Warrior's strong grip. The whistle blew again and Jack waited for Tyler to attack him. Tyler kicked and pushed and pulled and even bit, but Jack didn't budge. Atticus's whistle sounded again, and Tyler walked off the field looking exhausted and disheartened.

Jastin managed to escape his Warrior's hold and brought his opponent to the ground in less than a minute each round.

Victor walked onto the field as confident and silent as before, managing to both release himself from his Warrior's hold, and force him down in under thirty seconds each time. Luke and Drake looked impressed with this, though Drake was still a delicate shade of green.

Charlotte was paired with a Warrior named Nyx, who looked pretty intimidating, but Charlotte was able to release herself from Nyx's hold and slammed her violently to the ground even quicker.

Drake turned chalk white when it was his turn and just barely released himself from his Warrior's hold when the time was up, but was unable to bring his Warrior to the ground in the allotted time.

After Thomas Norris left the field Atticus called out, "Autumn Oaken."

She gulped and stepped forward.

"Good luck," Luke whispered as she left his side.

To Autumn's disappointment, she was paired with Candi, the most menacing looking female Quinn. Quite a deceiving name this was because Candi didn't look at all sweet, unless she was the kind of candy that was so sour it made people's eyes water. She had yet to be defeated and was clearly aware of her intimidation as she sneered down at Autumn with a look that clearly said, "Yeah, like *you* can beat me."

Autumn flashed her a defiant look as she stood before her, waiting to be restrained. Candi wrapped her arms tightly across Autumn's sternum and locked her hands into place. Autumn ran through a list of strategies in her mind and settled on one that hadn't failed her yet.

When the whistle sounded, she threw her head forcefully back onto Candi's nose, hearing it crack. Candi let out a yelp, but didn't release her hold. Autumn then stomped on her instep, causing Candi's leg to buckle. She managed to release one of her arms and elbowed the Warrior hard in the ribs. Candi released Autumn's other arm and she was free.

"Thirteen seconds," Atticus announced, smiling proudly at Autumn.

Candi looked murderous. Blood streamed down her face in a torrent and she clutched her ribs with claw-like hands. When Atticus blew the second whistle, Candi charged. Autumn rolled out of the way just in time as Candi stumbled to the ground. Before she could stand up straight, Autumn leapt on top of her, pinning her to the ground.

"Nine seconds," Atticus called loudly so that everyone could hear.

Murmuring erupted from the crowd of waiting elves and the two other judges whispered behind Atticus. Autumn held out her hand for Candi to shake, but the Warrior pretended she didn't see her as she trudged off the field. Autumn smiled confidently as she entered the Training Tree.

"Wow, that was fast," Jastin said, "Tom just came in a minute ago."

Victor looked up from the bench on which he was seated with an eyebrow raised. "You're already finished?"

"No need to sound so surprised," Autumn said as she sat next to him.

Victor didn't say anything. He seemed lost in thought.

"How long did it take you?" Charlotte asked.

"Twenty-two seconds."

"For which part?" she asked.

"Both," Autumn stated. "Thirteen for the first part and nine for the second."

Charlotte's mouth dropped open, along with everyone else within earshot.

Just then Luke walked in beaming. "Fifty-seven seconds in all," he announced. "Not as fast as you, Rose, but good enough." He took a seat across from her.

"That's great!" Autumn exclaimed.

"Man, I can't believe you pinned that stripper in just nine seconds," he said, shaking his head in awe.

"Stripper?" Autumn laughed.

"Come on. Her name is Candi. She has to be a stripper."

Autumn burst out laughing as the others stared at the twins in confusion.

Another few hours passed before a different Warrior came to retrieve them for the final test. After this test they would be dismissed and the hardest part of the day would begin—waiting for the results.

Their group followed the Quinn Warrior onto the field for the third time that day, awaiting Atticus's instructions.

"The last test is quite simple. You must demonstrate your Power for the judges. Tyler Ike, you may remain on the field, everyone else, clear off."

Tyler had the Power of Reading. He could read an entire book by placing his hand on its cover, immediately acquiring the information. Autumn doubted very much that he would make the Warriors.

It was difficult to watch Jastin demonstrate his Power. Atticus had him use it on each of the Quinn Warriors and every one of them collapsed into shouts of misery and despair, even the men.

Luckily, the sky had darkened enough for Victor to demonstrate his Power of Light. He let his light start out small and made it grow steadily brighter until it was so blinding Autumn could no longer keep her eyes open. The warmth of his Power pulsed from the field. Then the light went away and Victor left the field.

Charlotte was up next and immediately filled the field with a dense fog so thick no one could see two feet in front of them and, just as quickly, she pulled the fog back in, leaving the area as clear as it was when she arrived. Smiling, she pranced off the field.

Drake showed the judges his Power of Speed, running as fast as he could up and down the entire field in a matter of seconds. He then made the mistake of running around the judges' table, causing their papers to swirl around them. They shot him disapproving looks as he walked off the field.

Autumn entered the field after Thomas Norris had shown the

judges his Power of Bubbles, which were still floating around in the air above her head. Atticus gave her an encouraging smile as she opened her mouth to sing, first aiming her Song at the remainder of the 4th quarter elves waiting off the field. Every one of them went still and silent, their eyes glazing over and their mouths falling slightly ajar. Then demonstrating her ability to concentrate her Power on one person, she focused her Song on each judge individually. She finished by hypnotizing the entire field: judges, Warriors, and the waiting elves alike.

When Autumn finished, she turned and exited the field, breathing a sigh of relief. It was over. Now all there was left to do was wait.

Autumn met up with Victor, Charlotte and Jastin near the path that led to Arbor Lake, where everyone had planned to wait for the Warrior results. She was pleased to see that Charlotte and Jastin were actually speaking to Victor. Jastin complimented him on his fighting abilities and Charlotte nodded in agreement. Victor looked unsure of them, but thanked them quietly.

Luke soon joined them, soaking wet, but beaming.

"It went well, then?" Jastin asked, grinning.

"Yeah, my thunderstorm got a bit out of hand and the judges got a little damp, but they looked impressed, especially when I conjured up a nice-sized tornado *and* a blizzard."

They walked down the path towards Arbor Lake together. Autumn spotted Crystal and Avery near the water, their backs to the path. When Autumn said, "Hey guys." Crystal jumped about a foot off the ground.

"Oh, Autumn!" she said. "How'd you do?"

"All right, I guess."

"All right?" Luke interrupted, sitting down next to Crystal. "She had the fastest time during the second round."

"That's amazing!" Crystal said as she pulled Autumn to the ground, hugging her.

"I could've beat her time, but I wanted to make her look good," Luke said with a haughty smile.

"Right," Charlotte said from behind them.

Autumn looked around for Victor, but he had disappeared. No

one else seemed to notice his absence, so she turned to join in the conversation.

Within an hour, the grounds around the lake were packed with people from the Test. One of the Warriors brought all the waiting students more sandwiches and fruit, which they wolfed down because hardly anyone had eaten more than a handful of food all day. The more time went by, the quieter the elves around the lake became. At half past eight the grounds began to empty as elves returned to the field to await the announcement of the Initiates. At fifteen till nine, Crystal suggested that they head towards the training grounds.

The field was dead silent as they waited in anticipation for the three judges, who had been deliberating for two hours, to emerge from the Training Tree. Floating torches filled with fay light were suspended above them.

A few minutes before nine, Victor came to stand by Autumn's side in silence. She gave him a questioning look, but his eyes were focused on the Training Tree. While they were away, someone had erected a platform at the base of the field where Autumn was sure Atticus would proclaim the names of the ten Initiates.

When the campus bells began to chime, Autumn felt the anxiety of the elves around her increase. On the ninth chime, Atticus emerged from the middle Training Tree, followed by Gregorius Dodge and Alphreda Hopkins. The nervous tension was palpable as the three judges made their way onto the platform. Atticus turned to face the crowd of elves and Luke grabbed Autumn's hand, squeezing so tight she had to stop herself from yelping in pain.

"After long deliberation, we have made our final decision," Atticus stated. "We will begin with the four alternates, who will take the Initiate's place if they are unable to continue on. The four alternates are: Ember Burns, Edric Ogden, Catherine Heath, and Griffin Vance."

There was polite applause at this.

"Now for the Initiates," Atticus continued. It felt as if everyone around Autumn was holding their breath. Luke still had a death-grip on her hand. "When I call your name, please come onto the platform and stand in a line to my left." Everyone stood still, in nervous anticipation. *"Cera Tillman.* Power: Gravity."

Cera, the pixie-like blonde and Autumn's fellow snowball fight winner, let out a shout of joy and pranced onto the platform. Atticus shook her hand as she came to stand to his left.

"Forrest Akerley. Power: Animal Communication."

Forrest whooped and flashed his friends an ear-to-ear smile as they patted him on the back and congratulated him. Avery gave him a quick "guy hug" before Forrest jogged onto the platform.

"Charlotte Locke. Power: Fog."

Charlotte squealed and received a tight hug and a kiss from Jastin. She smiled widely as she skipped onto the platform.

"Jastin Lambert. Power: Psychological Pain."

The crowd cheered as Jastin bounded onto the platform to join his girlfriend.

"Kyndel Butler. Power: Invisibility."

Autumn frowned as Kyndel pushed past her to take her place on the platform. Not only was Autumn disappointed that Kyndel made it, but now five Initiates were on the stage...and neither hers, nor Luke's name had been called.

"Victor Lavigne. Power: Light."

Victor's eyes blazed with light as he glanced down at Autumn. This would definitely help in Autumn's cause to help Victor find friends. Who wouldn't want to be friends with a Warrior? Even if he was an Atrum. He kissed her lightly on the forehead before walking briskly onto the platform.

"Crystal Everly. Power: Ice."

Crystal half sobbed, half laughed, as Autumn wrapped her in a hug. If anyone deserved this, it was her. Avery and Luke gave her a quick hug as well before she ran up onto the platform.

"Avery Burke. Power: Strength."

Avery let out a sigh of relief and turned to face Autumn, giving her one of his intense looks as he wrapped her in a tight embrace. For a second she thought she might pass out from the forceful pull her body felt towards him. It almost hurt when they broke apart.

Luke's hand was damp with sweat as they exchanged worried looks. Two more.

"Luke Oaken. Power: Weather."

Luke let out a choked sound. Autumn's hand went limp as

she looked into his face. She wanted to be happy for her brother, but she couldn't quite make her expression translate this. "Congratulations," she whispered, unable to speak any louder.

"You're going to make it too, Rose," he said, squeezing her tightly before turning to join Avery and the others onstage.

She felt a dark weight fall on her shoulders. All of her friends were going to become Warriors and she would spend her days stuck in the library at the castle while they spent their time training and making a difference in the Underground. It wouldn't be so horrible, would it? After all, she did enjoy reading. Though she hadn't done much reading lately. But this was because everything else was so much more exciting. Without her friends and Luke, though, life would be as it was before, only lonelier.

Atticus broke through her reverie then. "And the last Initiate is..."

Autumn's heart was racing. She could hear it in her ears.

"*Autumn Oaken*. Power: Song."

Warrior Duties

CHAPTER TWENTY-THREE

Autumn let out a cry of relief before bounding onto the stage. Tears of happiness welled up in her eyes as she and the other nine Initiates stood tall above their peers, who were looking up at them with a mixture of resentment, admiration, and awe. She could now completely relax. She was a Warrior. Well, almost.

The following week was somewhat of a blur. School was even more overwhelming than usual what with all of the staring eyes and autograph requests. The Initiates had a number of new duties on top of school. Every day was something new. Right after school let out they would meet on the training field and have a grueling two-hour practice with Atticus. Then at some point in the afternoon/evening they would have some sort of public appearance or Warrior duty.

Monday they saw a professional designer who had been appointed to fashion their Warrior uniforms. The material was made from a deep green dragon hide so it was nearly indestructible. During her fitting, Autumn found that the supple material was surprisingly comfortable and breathable, as were the high-top boots to match. Once the uniforms were finished, the Initiates would wear them to each public event.

On Tuesday, they had the Initiate "Meet and Greet" in City Circle, giving the residents of Arbor Falls a chance to meet their new Warriors. Elves streamed into the center of City Circle, chatting excitedly. Young elves craned their necks and climbed onto their parents' shoulders to get a good look at the new local celebrities. The ten Initiates stood on a raised platform surrounded by the sea of elves. Autumn felt strangely like an actor on a Q&A panel.

After Atticus had introduced the new Initiates and spouted off a short bio about each individual, they then demonstrated their Powers for the crowd. Each Power elicited thunderous cheers and applause from the steadily growing crowd. Once the Initiates had all done a little showing off, they sat in a row of high-backed chairs as the crowd formed a line to walk across the stage, shaking hands with the Initiates and congratulating them.

Autumn and Luke seemed to be the most intriguing to the elves of Arbor Falls because of their royal status. Autumn figured Kyndel was quite piqued by this because she kept shooting her glares full of resentment and loathing.

Many of the women seemed rather infatuated with Victor. The fact that he was an Atrum had less of an effect on them now that he was a Warrior Initiate, apparently. They giggled and batted their eyelashes as they shook his hand, and one girl in particular seemed reluctant to let go. Autumn snorted with laughter when she overheard the girl ask him if he was single. Victor glanced in Autumn's direction as he said, "No, I'm afraid I'm not."

Autumn winked at him and his face lit into a smile. Luke made a gagging noise beside her.

On Wednesday the Warriors had dinner with King Olympus, which was clearly a great honor to most of the Initiates. Autumn and Luke had dinner with him every few weeks, but they were happy for the extra time with their grandfather.

Autumn was surprised to find that a few of the Initiates had never even set foot inside the castle before. Forrest had been to visit Avery, Victor met with Olympus when he first came to Arbor Falls, and Kyndel had come with her father a few times, but this was a first for Charlotte, Jastin, and Cera. Autumn noticed the look of awe on their faces as they took in the grand interior of the castle and imagined that was how she had looked when she first arrived.

Dinner with the king was extravagant. A large, twelve-person table was set up in Olympus's private dining quarters, and was covered with a feast of every food an elf could ever imagine. There were rolls, various forms of potatoes, several vegetables, meats—

including a plate full of dragon meat—creamy soups and thick stews. After dinner the waiters brought out a tray full of delicate and rich desserts. The Initiates ate and laughed until they left, sleepy and full, to pass out in their beds before they had to wake up and do everything all over again.

Thursday was an autograph signing in City Circle and, by the end, Autumn could barely open her hand from holding her leaf quill for so long.

Friday was their group picture. Autumn watched in amazement as the photographer pulled out a large, gray paper that shimmered slightly. He arranged everyone in a group pose and shined a pulsing light through the paper. He did this several times and each time the gray paper turned a brilliant white before an actual picture formed on the page.

"What is that?" Autumn asked in amazement.

"Memory paper made from a memory tree. If you shine a light through the page, it will record whatever image is before it," Crystal said.

Autumn shook her head in disbelief. The Underground never ceased to amaze her.

It was now Saturday and the Initiates were told that, in seven days, the traditional Warrior Initiation Ball was to be held in the Arbor Castle grand ballroom to formally initiate them as Quinns, to acknowledge the Unum Warriors who would soon be retiring, and to graduate the other Warriors up to the next level. It was rumored to be an elaborate event with dancing, music, and ball gowns.

Later that night, Crystal came to Autumn's branch to take her measurements to make sure that the ball gown she would be making her would be absolutely perfect in every way.

"Will you be able to make a ball gown in a week?" Autumn asked doubtfully.

"I already have all the material, design, and details made up. I just have to sew it."

"What about yours?"

"Oh, I already made it."

"When?" asked Autumn, surprised.

Crystal blushed. "Well, it took me about a month to make it

perfect. I know it sounds presumptuous, but I knew there would be a ball for the Warriors and I wanted to have the perfect gown in case I did make it."

"Is that what you were really doing all those times you said you were helping your mom?" Crystal nodded and Autumn laughed. "I think we all hoped we'd make it. Don't worry, I'm not judging."

"I have to go get started on your dress!" Crystal said, dashing out of the room.

Autumn was shaking her head in amusement at Crystal's hasty departure when she heard a loud *thump* resound from her balcony, where the double glass doors were standing open to let in the cool, fall breeze.

She whirled around to see Avery casually leaning against the railing as if it was completely normal for him to suddenly appear on her balcony. Autumn raised her eyebrows as she walked towards him.

"How did you get up here?" she asked.

He smiled mischievously and said, "Wouldn't you like to know."

Autumn crossed her arms, waiting.

Avery chuckled. "I climbed down from my balcony. It's right above yours, remember?"

Autumn looked up to see his balcony, which was slightly to the left, but still above her own. She examined the bark of the tree castle. It was similar to the bark of an ash tree, smooth and bone white. "How did you climb down? There's nothing to hold on to."

"Did I say climbed? I meant jumped."

She shook her head at him. "You're crazy, Burke."

Avery let out a barking laugh and said, "Probably."

"So, we've established how you got here—" Autumn began.

"And that I'm crazy," Avery cut in.

"And that you're crazy," she agreed. "But we haven't covered *why* you're here."

Autumn joined Avery near the railing, facing the courtyard and forest beyond. He leaned back against the railing with his elbows propped up next to him. There was a slight breeze outside and Avery watched as it blew a strand of Autumn's auburn hair across her face. She looked into his steely gray eyes, searching for something within their depths. What she was looking for, she wasn't sure.

"So, why are you here?" Autumn said.

Avery's eyes narrowed as he looked past her into the distance. "Good question," he said quietly and then added, "Actually, I was going to tell you that you don't have to worry about having me as a bodyguard anymore."

"Really?" Autumn said, though she'd become so used to Avery being around, she hadn't even thought about it much. "So, you're a castle guard again?"

"Yeah, but Olympus cut my hours so I won't have to work as much what with my new Warrior duties and all."

"Why don't you just quit?" Autumn asked, trying not to sound hopeful. "Warriors make plenty of money."

"We don't start getting paid until we pass the Warrior Trial in January. Initiates have to spend a few months in training first. Besides, it's the only way my mother and I can live here. I don't want to take her away from her home," he said.

Autumn nodded in understanding, not pushing the topic any further. She knew he didn't like talking about his family.

"Is Victor happy to be a Warrior?" Avery asked, with a hint of resentment.

Autumn looked at him questioningly, trying to figure out where this was going. "I assume he's happy, seeing as how he tried out and everything."

"You assume? Haven't you two talked about it?"

Autumn frowned, looking back at the forest. "He doesn't talk about much of anything, really."

"Well I could've told you that."

This particular subject had been bothering Autumn lately. The time she spent with Victor had become unbearably silent. He seemed perfectly content to just sit in the quiet with her, not saying anything. She would try to start a conversation, but he would simply give her the shortest answer possible before returning to his daydreams—or whatever it was he was thinking.

"Do you think you and Victor will be partners?" Avery asked.

"Partners?"

"Yeah. Warrior partners, remember? Atticus told you about it your first day at school."

"Oh, right. When do we find that out?"

"Atticus will announce them at the Warrior Initiation Ball."

"How are they chosen?"

"By Lady Carys."

"Who?"

"Lady Carys. She's been using her Power to determine the Initiates partners for years now," he said.

"What's her Power?"

"She can sense chemistry between elves. She can tell who would work best with each other...which elves are most compatible."

Autumn's heart sank and lifted at the same time, a strange sensation. Their eyes locked on to one another's now.

"I see."

"Are you afraid?"

"Why would I be afraid?"

Avery moved closer so that he was inches from her face. "Because now Victor will know how you really feel." Autumn's breathing ceased temporarily. "And so will I." Her eyes widened, but she said nothing. Avery backed slowly away. "I have to go. See you later...partner."

Avery smirked as he crouched down and sprang up to the branch above them. He caught a hold of the balcony railing and swung lithely over.

Autumn let out a slow, shaky breath.

The Warrior Initiation Ball

CHAPTER TWENTY-FOUR

The whole castle was talking about the upcoming ball. Preparations were already being made in the castle's ballroom. Autumn and Crystal tried to sneak a peak, but were caught by Luke and Avery. Autumn hadn't talked to Avery much since their little conversation on her balcony.

One afternoon, Autumn asked Crystal about Lady Carys and the extent of her Power.

"Well, this is just something she does every five years when the Initiates are chosen. She is usually in her little psychic shop downtown. Couples go to her to see if they're compatible and if their connection is strong."

Autumn gulped. "So, how exactly does she evaluate the Warriors' connections?"

"She'll evaluate us while we're dancing. Each girl will dance with each guy at least once and Lady Carys will be watching the whole time."

This was even worse than Autumn thought. She knew how strong her and Avery's connection was. She could definitely feel it and knew he could too—he'd told her as much. What would Victor think if Lady Carys announced that she and Avery were partners? What would Olympus think? Autumn shook her head to clear the unwelcome thoughts. It wasn't like her to worry so much about what other people thought. Then again, she'd never been a princess or a Warrior before.

The next day, the Initiates found that they would be taking dancing lessons with the castle dance instructor all week to prepare for the ball. Since the main ballroom was occupied by castle decorators they had to use the second, smaller ballroom in the castle for lessons, which still could have held the entirety of Aspen Academy.

Kyndel and Charlotte were the only Initiates who had previously taken dance lessons, and Victor and Avery were clearly naturals. However, during practice time, the rest of the group moved clumsily around the dance floor. The dance instructor made the mistake of pairing Luke and Cera together—the two most uncoordinated of all—and Autumn had to stifle a laugh when Cera attempted to twirl into him, but instead ended up knocking him to the ground.

"Oops," Cera said, chuckling.

Luke glared up at her from the ballroom floor.

Autumn tried not to be jealous of the ease with which Kyndel and Avery danced together. They spun gracefully around the dance floor, although Avery didn't seem too happy with his partner. As they twirled by, Autumn overheard Kyndel bragging about her ball gown, which was the most expensive one in the store, of course.

Victor had somehow made certain that he was Autumn's dance partner. He moved well on the dance floor and made it easy for her to follow his lead. She was happy to find that she was not the most uncoordinated one of the group. Luke and Cera definitely topped all of them. Near the end, the two of them seemed to have given up on ballroom dancing and Luke ended up teaching Cera the "robot."

Rigorous dance lessons took place every day up until the ball and Autumn found herself too tired to worry about Lady Carys and the Warrior partners. She felt particularly sorry for Avery and Crystal, who both had work on top of everything else. Crystal worked tirelessly on Autumn's gown when she wasn't in dance lessons or school or Warrior training. Autumn had repeatedly told her not to worry about it, but Crystal insisted.

The morning of the ball, Autumn was reading in her little library when there was a loud knock at the front door. Autumn opened it to find Crystal hiding behind a heap of gold fabric.

"Finished!" she announced, breezing through the branch to Autumn's room, laying the gown across the bed. Autumn's mouth dropped open as she took in the golden gown that was now hers.

"Crys, it's gorgeous. How did you do this so fast? I've never seen anything like it."

Crystal beamed. "I'll bring mine up here after lunch so we can get ready together. What time is your hairdresser going to be here?"

"One o'clock. She's doing your hair too, you know."

Crystal's eyes widened. "She is?"

Autumn nodded, smiling. "I told her that she would be styling us both."

Crystal wrapped her in a hug, thanking her repeatedly.

They had lunch brought up to Autumn's branch and talked about what the other girls might be wearing.

"I know Kyndel is wearing a hot pink ball gown. I heard her telling Avery," Autumn said, laughing through a mouthful of soup.

"She *would* wear hot pink to a ball," Crystal said, rolling her eyes. "So, who do you think your partner will be?"

Autumn looked at her lap. "Uh, I'm not sure. It could be anyone, I suppose."

"I bet you're with Victor, Avery, or Luke," Crystal said.

"Luke?" Autumn said in disgust. "Gross."

Crystal laughed. "It's not a romantic thing, Autumn. It's about compatibility and connection. Luke is your twin. I'll bet you two have a strong connection simply because of that."

Autumn breathed a sigh of relief. Avery had made it seem like whoever she would be paired with was who she was meant to be with romantically. Now she realized that was probably a stupid thing to think.

"What if Victor isn't your partner?" Crystal asked. "Do you think he'll be mad?"

"Um, I'm going to say yes."

"He's very protective of you."

"Yeah, well he needs to realize that I don't need to be protected," Autumn said a little too hotly. "I mean, I'm a Warrior too."

Crystal shook her head. "Boys. They think they are the rulers of the Underground."

"Trust me, they think they are the rulers wherever they are."

When the hairdresser arrived, the girls ceased their talk of boys and got back on the topic of the ball and their desired looks. Crystal wore her hair in a sleek bun with small crystals pinned throughout. She looked like a ballerina.

Autumn's hair was pulled elegantly back in a low chignon with loose curls framing her face. The hairdresser did their makeup as well, which was very light since elves hardly had the need for it.

It took Autumn quite a long time to get into her gown as it was a corset and had to be laced up the back. Crystal beamed when Autumn emerged from the bathroom in her gown. "You look beautiful!"

Autumn approached the full-length mirror, staring in wonder at her reflection. The golden gown was made of a smooth, supple material with a thin overlay of sparkling gold gossamer. The bodice was encrusted with golden jewels and diamonds. The warm color brought out the gold in her hazel eyes and auburn hair.

There was a knock at the door and Autumn went to open it, expecting Luke needing help with some oddment on his coat, but instead she found Olympus standing before her wearing magnificent robes of emerald. She retreated into her branch to let him enter, his sudden appearance striking her speechless.

He smiled warmly down at her and said, "Autumn, you look positively stunning."

"Thank you. I like your, um, robes."

He chuckled. "Why, thank you. I like them quite a lot myself. They're incredibly comfortable. I know you're busy getting ready so I will be quick. I've brought you something that I should have given you sooner. I am happy to see that it will match your ensemble nicely."

He pulled out a thin square box that looked like a jewelry case belonging to an oversized necklace. But when he opened it there was not a necklace but a dainty, golden tiara covered in miniscule diamonds.

Autumn's eyes widened as she looked up at her grandfather in question.

"It belonged to your grandmother long, long ago. Now, it's

yours." He lifted it out of the box and gently placed it on Autumn's head. "Perfect," he said, smiling.

"Thank you," she whispered, unable to speak any louder for fear of her voice wavering.

His hazel eyes crinkled in a smile. They were the same color as her father's, the same as her own.

When Olympus left, Autumn turned to see Crystal gaping at her from the doorway. "You look like a princess," she whispered, taking in the tiara. "I mean, I know you *are* a princess, but now you really look like one. Not that you didn't look like one before, I mean—"

Autumn laughed and said, "I know what you mean. You look like a princess too, Crys."

Crystal's worried frown turned up in a smile. Her dress was not quite as extravagant as Autumn's, but was still just as beautiful and elegant. It was a soft, periwinkle blue and the overlay was a sheer, sparkling material that looked as if she had weaved it out of the water in Arbor Lake. The sparkles made her blonde hair shine brighter than the actual crystals running through her hair.

Once Autumn and Crystal had put the finishing touches on their gowns, they traveled down to the base of the staircase, where Luke and Avery had promised to wait for them. Music floated up from the ballroom as they walked down the winding stairs.

When Luke and Avery came into view, Autumn saw that Luke was also wearing a small crown like a halo around his head. The boys were facing away from them, chatting and joking with a nervous undertone in their voices.

Crystal cleared her throat and they turned around. Both of their mouths fell slightly open at the sight of them. Avery's eyes were trained on Autumn and Luke was looking back and forth from Crystal, to Autumn, then back to Crystal.

The four of them stood at the base of the staircase for an awkward second, taking each other in until Crystal said, "Shall we?"

Autumn and Avery walked side by side and she noticed him glancing sideways every few steps. Luke and Crystal walked in front of them and Autumn overheard Luke say, "You, uh, you look really, um, really beautiful."

Autumn bit her lip to hold back her giggle.

"You're making this 'friend' thing exceptionally difficult tonight," Avery said barely louder than a whisper.

Autumn frowned as she said, "What 'friend' thing?"

"The thing that we do where we pretend we only care for each other as friends, when we both know we're just fooling ourselves," Avery said under his breath so only Autumn could hear.

"I—I don't know what you're talking about."

Avery raised an eyebrow. "Right. Well, you're better at it than me."

Victor was waiting for her just outside the ballroom and Avery moved swiftly past him, leaving Autumn with a jumble of emotions at the door.

"You look exquisite," Victor said.

She managed a "thank you" as they passed across the threshold, Avery's words still echoing hauntingly in her head. The grand ballroom was filled with hundreds of round tables covered in a silky, red material. A band dressed all in white played a light, cheerful melody to welcome the guests to the ball. An oversized throne resided on a raised platform overlooking the ballroom. Upon the throne sat Olympus, looking like a king from a fairytale.

Two elves sat on either side of Olympus in slightly smaller chairs. One of the elves was Gregorius Dodge and the other was an older woman with crazy, flyaway, gray hair and a hunched back. Autumn assumed she must be Lady Carys, quickly looking away when the woman's cloudy blue eyes locked on her. Autumn wondered if Lady Carys was examining the connection between her and Victor—or the lack thereof.

Atticus and the rest of the Warriors were positioned at tables near the platform on which the king sat. All of the Initiates were situated at a table together. As Autumn and Victor took the two seats between Crystal and Cera, Autumn scanned the other girls' dresses. Kyndel's gown was just as she had described it, bright pink and over the top. She wore flashy diamond jewelry and her strawberry-blonde hair was pinned back with chunky diamond clips.

Charlotte looked elegant in a sleek, red corset with her chestnut hair pulled back in an intricate French twist, and Cera wore a mint green gown. Her normally spiky hair was slicked down with old-fashioned waves running through it.

During dinner, the girls all complimented each other on how beautiful the others looked, gushing over dresses, hair, and jewelry while the guys complained about how uncomfortable they were and how dumb they looked. After dinner, Olympus stood and welcomed everyone to Arbor Castle.

There was a drawn out ceremony which honored the retiring Warriors and welcomed the Initiates. The old Unum Warriors said their goodbyes and thanked their fellow Warriors, families, and friends for their support and remembered the Warriors they had lost in battle. Then there was a final ceremony to acknowledge the graduation of the five groups of Warriors to the next rotation. Duos became Unum, Tetras became Duos, Quinns became Tetras and, finally, the Initiates became Quinns, though this wouldn't be final until they passed the Warrior Trial. Until then they were still considered Initiates.

After the ceremony Atticus announced that it was time for the Initiates to dance with one another so that Lady Carys could choose their partners. Autumn was more worried about the partner selection than the dancing, which she'd become much better at thanks to their rigorous lessons all week.

Each male Initiate stood in a circle and the females stood before one of them. When the chime sounded, the guys were to move clockwise to the next girl.

Autumn danced with Jastin first. His long, wavy blond hair was pulled back from his nerve-stricken face and he kept craning his neck to look at Charlotte. Autumn definitely felt no connection with him.

Forrest was next. He hated being serious so he goofed around the entire time, making her laugh. Autumn didn't feel anything with him either.

Then it was Luke's turn.

"You really do look beautiful, Rose," he said as the music started back up.

"Thanks, Luke. You look pretty dashing yourself."

He rolled his eyes. "I look like a penguin, but at least I'm not wearing ruffles. I was kind of worried about that."

"I like your crown," Autumn said.

"I know, right?" Luke grinned. "It makes me feel even more like a prince. I kind of want to wear it all the time, but then I think people would think I'm just full of myself."

"Well it isn't mandatory for us to wear crowns, so probably," Autumn said with a laugh. "But I do see what you are talking about. It makes me feel more like a princess too."

"Now that I think about it, though, it would probably get in the way when I'm making out with all those girls."

Autumn laughed again, rolling her eyes as they parted and Victor cut in. She could feel Avery's eyes bearing into her, looking for some sign of a connection.

"You will be my partner. I know it," Victor said.

"We'll see, I guess."

"You don't think so?" he said, his voice turning dark.

"No—it's not that. I just don't want you to be upset if we aren't, that's all."

"Why wouldn't we be? You chose to be with me. You chose to accept my rose."

"I know, but—"

"Are you having regrets?" His eyes narrowed and his hands tightened on her waist and hand.

"N—No. Calm down," Autumn said, looking around. Avery and Luke were watching them with narrowed eyes.

"I am calm," he growled. His pupils slowly dilated as they had before in the meadow with the unicorn. There was hardly any green showing. The chime sounded just in time. Autumn stepped back from him and he shook his head. When he looked at her again, his eyes were back to normal and he seemed slightly confused.

When it was Avery's turn to dance with her, she could already feel the familiar pulling sensation in the pit of her stomach. As he rested his right hand on her waist and grasped her hand in his left, Autumn felt the magnetic pull move from her stomach into the region of her chest, as if her heart was trying to move closer to his. Her breathing became shallow, and she noticed his had too. Their eyes locked and she had to tell herself to keep dancing.

"You feel it too, don't you?" Avery murmured.

Autumn gazed into the gray depths of his shining eyes. She

needn't say anything for him to know that she felt what he did.

Glancing away from him, Autumn turned her eyes on Lady Carys. The gray-haired woman was literally on the edge of her seat, watching them with her head tilted slightly to the side. She wore a look of intense interest and wonder. Autumn was curious to know what exactly it was that she could see.

Autumn turned back to Avery to see that he'd been looking at Lady Carys as well. He had a satisfied smile on his face as he whispered, "Looks like I was right."

The music ceased and Autumn walked to stand beside Crystal who wore an interested look on her face. "Did you see the way Lady Carys was looking at you two?"

"Yeah," muttered Autumn.

"She looked like she had never seen anything like that before."

Autumn shushed her when she saw that Victor was glaring at the two of them.

Lady Carys, Atticus, and Dodge spent half an hour discussing what Lady Carys had seen when, finally, Atticus stood and held his hand up for silence. The room went quiet.

"With the help of Lady Carys, we have come to a decision. Initiates, when you and your partner's names are called, please make your way to the middle of the dance floor and stand by one another so that we may all witness the traditional Warrior Partner Initiation Dance."

The Initiates all anxiously nodded their assent.

"Jastin Lambert and Charlotte Locke."

The unsurprising pair looked relieved as they made their way to the middle of the dance floor, Jastin grasping Charlotte's hand.

"Forrest Akerley and Cera Tillman."

Forrest and Cera looked at each other with amused expressions. They were definitely the clowns of the group and would work well together. When they were in position a few feet from Jastin and Charlotte, Atticus spoke again.

"Luke Oaken and Crystal Everly."

Luke and Crystal looked at one another in surprise, but seemed content with this. They high-fived as they joined the others on the dance floor.

Autumn's heart was racing. Her partner was either Victor or

Avery and she was fairly certain which one it would be.

"Avery Burke and Autumn Oaken."

She was right.

Autumn didn't know which emotion to feel first: excitement, guilt, relief, regret, or happiness. Avery wore a sly grin as he offered her his arm. She rolled her eyes at him, but smiled in spite of herself. When she turned to see Victor's reaction, her smile faltered. He looked murderous with his black eyes and fists clenched by his side. As Autumn and Avery moved to stand by Crystal and Luke, Atticus said, "And finally, Victor Lavigne and Kyndel Butler."

Victor was fuming. He kept shooting Avery looks of pure loathing and, worse, he was looking at Autumn as if she had committed some great betrayal. It was bad enough for him that she'd been matched with someone other than him, but the fact that it was Avery, his ex-best friend and current enemy, was obviously too much for him.

Autumn felt slightly ashamed of herself because she had been a bit relieved when she found out that Victor would not be her partner. She felt like she was abandoning him. On the other hand, though, it wasn't her fault that she and Avery had this strange connection. And it wasn't like it was her decision to choose him as a partner. Though, if she *had* been given the choice, she probably would have anyway.

"Autumn," Avery said, interrupting her thoughts.

She shook her head clear and said, "Hmm?"

"We're supposed to be dancing."

She looked around to see the other partners twirling around the dance floor.

"Oh—right," she said, taking his hand as they joined in the dance.

"What're you thinking about?" asked Avery.

"I just never wanted things to get so complicated."

"What's complicated?"

"Everything."

"They don't have to be," Avery said.

Victor and Kyndel nearly knocked into them as the two of them came spinning by. Victor's face was contorted into a death glare.

"Victor's angry," Avery noted with a small smirk.

Autumn sighed. "I know."

"So, are you still saying that you care about him?" he asked, his voice full of doubt.

"I do. I just—I want to help him. He needs a friend."

"A friend, maybe, but not a girlfriend."

"Well, I, uh—didn't exactly know what I was doing when I accepted his rose," she admitted under her breath.

Avery raised his eyebrows and said, "Seriously?"

"I just thought he was giving me a rose for the concert. That's what Outsiders do, at least. I didn't realize the significance of it until Crystal told me."

"Well, whatever you do, don't accept a golden rose."

"Yeah, I know. Crystal told me that too."

"You know you can still get out of it," he said twirling her in a circle and pulling her back to him. "A red rose isn't binding."

"It's not so simple, Avery."

"Sure it is." He smiled crookedly.

The partner dance ended and, subsequently, so did the ball.

Autumn saw Victor storm out without saying a word to anyone.

Olympus told Autumn and Luke how proud he was of them and that they could not have found better partners. Crystal left looking exhausted, yet pleased with how many compliments she had received for the gowns she'd made. She even got a few requests from some wealthy women in need of new gowns. Luke left with a girl Autumn had seen at school before, but was unsure of her name.

"Well, I guess this is goodnight," Avery said, taking Autumn's hand and brushing it with his lips. He winked at her as he walked away.

Autumn's eyebrows knit together as she opened her hand to find a small piece of paper. Avery must have slipped it there without her noticing. She opened it slowly, making sure no one was around. It read:

Meet me on your balcony at midnight.

Pegasus Ride

CHAPTER TWENTY-FIVE

Autumn's stomach fluttered as she read the words and, ignoring her protesting conscience, moved as fast as her ball gown would allow up to her branch to change. It took her several minutes to wiggle out of the restrictive material. Once she was free, she pulled on some dark-blue pants and an ivory blouse. Curls spilled to her shoulders as she pulled her hair down from its chignon.

For how tired she'd been before, she was wide awake now. Autumn knew this was wrong on several different levels, but she was becoming bored of doing everything she was told. For once, she wanted to do what *she* wanted to do and forget about the consequences. She had been trying so hard to please everyone else that she'd completely ignored her feelings and the things that she wanted to do.

Autumn watched the grandfather clock in her room restlessly. Time seemed to slow down the longer she kept her eyes locked on it, so she turned her gaze away. Forty-five minutes until she was supposed to meet Avery. She paced back and forth through her branch, thoughts flowing like a restless river through her head. Finally, she decided to bring a book into her room and read. For once, the words on the pages weren't enough to distract her and she found herself creating her own story in her head about what Avery might be planning.

The clock struck midnight just as a number of loud thumps sounded from her balcony. Scrambling off her bed, she moved cautiously forward, pulling open the double doors. Her mouth fell open at the sight before her.

Avery was there, a dark silhouette in the shining moonlight, standing beside a gray horse, or at least that's what Autumn thought it was until she saw a pair of long, feathered wings protruding from its back. Her face lit up, but then she remembered the unicorn incident with Victor and backed swiftly away.

"Is that—?"

"A pegasus," Avery said. "You don't have to be afraid. They're gentle creatures. He was my father's."

"What's his name?"

"My father?"

Autumn laughed. "No, the pegasus."

"Oh. This is Knight."

Autumn gazed wonderstruck up at the magnificent creature. He was thinner and sleeker than a horse, but much larger in proportion. Definitely not as intimidating as Victor's unicorn. Knight's feathery wings waved as if he was anxious to get back into the air.

"Hey, Knight," Autumn said, rubbing his snout. The animal turned his head her way, his electric blue eyes peering at her with a calm and trusting look.

Avery smiled as he said, "So are you ready?"

"Ready?"

"To fly," he said. "You should probably wear a coat, though. It's going to get pretty cold up there."

Autumn put on a brave face as she left the balcony to retrieve her coat. It wasn't the animal that was making her heart pound violently against her sternum. It was more of a combination of being so close to Avery—and the height. She'd nearly had a panic attack on the flight to Ireland. Her favorite part about that plane ride was the landing part simply because that meant they were back on solid ground.

"Ready," she said, pulling on her thick, green coat.

"Need a lift?" Avery asked, offering his hand.

"Nope," Autumn said, climbing effortlessly onto Knight's back. "I'm from Texas."

Avery raised his eyebrows and shrugged, not appearing

to understand how that explained anything. He climbed onto Knight's back, sitting in front of her.

"Why do you get to drive?" Autumn said.

"Because I know where I'm going."

"And where's that?"

"It's a surprise. You're going to want to hold on," Avery said as he lightly patted Knight's side. Autumn gasped as Knight shot into the air. She wrapped her arms tightly around Avery to keep from falling backwards, his laughter ringing out over the wind that was whistling in her ears. Once they'd reached a certain height Avery touched Knight's side again and the pegasus leveled out.

"Whoa," she breathed, looking down below.

They flew higher than even the top of Arbor Castle. Most of the tree houses below were dark, their inhabitants fast asleep. Avery touched Knight's right side with two fingers and the pegasus changed his direction, moving to the right over the forest.

Autumn sighed contentedly as they glided over the treetops. Everything was so peaceful and quiet. She definitely preferred travelling by pegasus compared to airplanes. Absentmindedly, she began humming *A Whole New World*.

"You're hypnotizing me, Autumn," Avery said drowsily.

"Oops." Autumn ceased her humming.

"You don't have to stop. I like how it feels."

"You insisted on being the driver, so no hypnotizing. I can't imagine that would be very safe."

"You're probably right."

"It's so beautiful," Autumn said. "I could stay up here forever."

"Fine by me."

He placed his hand over hers and, though she knew she probably shouldn't, she let him.

"I'm sort of surprised you agreed to come," Avery said.

"Me too."

The crisp night air stung her nose and cheeks so she buried her face in his back. He had a musky smell about him that was slightly intoxicating, and she only pulled away when Knight began to descend.

"Close your eyes," Avery said.

Smiling, Autumn let her eyes close. Knight landed and Avery

climbed off, grasping her hand and pulling her into his arms before setting her feet gently on the ground. She could feel warm light on her face and had to force herself to keep her eyes closed until told otherwise.

Avery grasped Autumn's hands and pulled her a little farther forward.

"Open your eyes."

Autumn's eyes slid open, blinking in the dazzling light, and she gazed at her surroundings in awe, revolving in a slow circle. They stood in the middle of a clearing that Autumn assumed was in some sort of forest. Thousands of small twinkling lights filled the air, moving here and there from flower to tree to bush. The lights bounced off the leaves and petals, making everything glow. A literal fairyland.

"What are they?"

"Fay fairies. This is where we get the fay light for the Kingdom."

One of the fay fairies flew close by Autumn's face and she saw that they looked like miniature elves with wings, only their ears were larger in proportion to their bodies, and they put off a glowing light that pulsed with energy. They smiled and waved at Autumn. Apparently they were friendlier than Petalsies.

"They're beautiful," Autumn said, smiling back at Avery who was watching her with an unreadable expression.

He moved to a nearby tree and leaned against it, watching her. Slowly, she approached him, mimicking his stance. Their shoulders touched and Autumn realized that, once again, the magnetic sensation they shared had moved from her stomach to her chest. Perhaps it was a permanent change. She'd grown so used to it now that it no longer bothered her. It had not only become tolerable, but welcome. Its presence meant that Avery was near.

The fay fairies put off warmth and Autumn found that she wasn't so cold anymore. Avery's close proximity didn't hurt either.

Two fairies flew in front of them, twirling through the air together as if they were dancing. "I've never seen anything so beautiful before," Autumn said in wonder.

"Me either," he said, but rather than watching the fairies, his eyes were on her.

Autumn turned to face him and he fixed her with an intense

gaze.

"What's wrong?" she asked.

He paused, apparently thinking something through and then took a deep breath and spoke.

"I'm not used to...*feeling*. For the past few years I've just kind of been numb. But then you come along and I'm feeling things that I can't explain and it sort of terrifies me. But it also makes me feel like I'm actually alive."

Autumn listened with wide eyes, her heart pounding erratically in her chest.

"I know we're forbidden to be together, and I know you're with Victor, but I just can't ignore this anymore. I know I have nothing to offer you. No gold leaves, no diamonds or jewels and I'm in a completely different class of elf than you, but I know you feel the same way. I see the way you look at me. I see the way your breathing changes when I'm near you.

"You're afraid. So am I. And I don't know about the Outside, but down here we call this fate. When two people are as drawn to one another as we are. It isn't just chance or an accident, it's destined to be. Written in the stars. And if you tell me you don't feel the same way, I'll take you home right now and never speak of this again."

He stopped and took a slow, shaky breath, waiting for her answer with a tortured expression.

Autumn tried to collect her thoughts and say something somewhat logical when she did the last thing she should do. She grabbed his face with both hands and pulled him fervently towards her. Their lips met and the feeling in her chest spread like a current throughout her entire body making her skin tingle with electricity. She pushed him up against the tree and ran her fingers through his golden hair as he wrapped his strong arms around her, pulling her closer. She could feel his heart beating against her chest, as if it was searching for her own. And, in that moment, nothing else mattered but Avery. He kissed her hungrily at first and then a little more softly until they slowly pulled apart, their breathing shallow.

Avery leaned his forehead against hers and closed his eyes, his chest heaving. They stayed like this for some time until Autumn pulled back and slid down the tree, resting her head in her hands.

Avery sat beside her, his hand on her back. "What is it?"

"I don't know if I can do this."

"Because of Victor?" His tone was dark.

"Yes, because of Victor. And because of you. I don't want to hurt *anyone*, Avery."

"It's a little too late for that, Autumn. Besides, you don't want to be with him. I can see it in your eyes."

"I know," she said, finally admitting to him what she'd been trying not to admit to herself for so long.

"Then return his rose. Just—just give it back to him. We can keep us a secret until we graduate and I'm not a castle worker anymore. Just leave him. Not for me, for you."

"I can't," Autumn said, lifting her face to look at him with a tormented expression.

"Why?" he asked, his eyes darkening.

"*Because.* Because then he'll be alone again and it'll be all my fault. I promised myself a long time ago that I would help him. I just thought that if others could see that if the *princess* could accept him for who he is, despite where he comes from, then maybe they could too. I've been making progress, not a lot, but enough. People aren't as afraid of him. Some even talk to him now, or try to anyway. I know how it feels to be alone and I even had Luke. Victor has no one. No family. No friends. No one. Everyone needs *someone*, Avery, even an Atrum."

Avery was silent for a few minutes before he finally said, "Okay."

Autumn turned to him with wide eyes. "Okay?"

"If that's what you promised yourself then you should do it. Help him. I don't want you breaking any promises to yourself on account of me."

"You're really okay with this?"

"Not particularly, but I understand why you're doing it and I," He hesitated for a moment, frowning. "I can help you."

"Really? You would do that?" she said. "But I thought you hated Victor. Why would you want to help him?"

"It's the only way you and I can be together. I'll do whatever it takes."

"Avery, I—" Autumn searched for the right words, but all she could say was, "Thank you."

"But once he's made some friends..."

"Then he won't need me anymore."

"We aren't going to pretend anymore now are we?" Avery said after a while. "At least not with each other?"

"No. No more pretending." Autumn leaned against him and he wrapped his arms around her, pulling her closer to him. Closing her eyes, she smiled, feeling perfectly content for the first time in a while.

The pegasus ride back to the castle was a silent one. The Underground sun began to rise in the distance, filling the sky with orange, pink, and yellow. Autumn tried to take in everything that had just transpired. It felt like it had all been a dream.

The realization that things were about to become especially difficult came crashing over her. She couldn't stand hurting people in any way, and she knew every time she let Victor kiss her or hold her hand or even hug her, she'd be hurting Avery. And how was she supposed to act natural with Victor, or act like there was nothing between her and Avery? She'd never been known for her acting skills.

Avery laughed when she voiced these fears to him as Knight began to descend slowly towards the castle. "You're a plenty good actress, Autumn."

"Why do you say that?"

"Because it took me a long time to decide whether you had feelings for me or not. I'm usually really good at reading people, but I just couldn't figure you out."

Knight landed lightly on Autumn's balcony and Avery jumped down, offering Autumn his hand. They looked intently into each other's eyes. Things seemed much more real now that they were back at the castle. Back to reality.

"I'm scared," whispered Autumn.

"So am I," Avery said, leaning his forehead against hers. They stayed like this for a while before Avery pulled back and said, "We should really get some sleep. We have Warrior training this afternoon, after lunch."

Autumn looked at the brightening sky behind him and nodded.

"Everything's going to work out. I promise." He leaned in,

kissing her softly on the lips, causing her heart to skip a beat before climbing onto Knight's back.

Autumn watched him for a second as he flew Knight back to the stables before walking sleepily into her room. Though she was dead tired, she found it increasingly difficult to fall asleep. She kept replaying the night's events over and over in her head. She was terrified that she wouldn't be able to act naturally at Warrior training. What if Victor suspected something?

She shook her head to rid herself of these incessant thoughts, forcing herself to focus on something else. After counting sheep, counting backwards from 100 in her head, and trying to empty her mind completely, she decided to just sing to herself. She hummed a soft lullaby that her dad used to sing to her and Luke at night when they were little. Her Power immediately began to take effect: her nerves began to ease, her body relaxed, and her mind went blissfully blank. Finally, Autumn drifted off into a restless doze full of dreams of Avery and Victor—and herself, singing the echoing song of her betrayal.

Truce

CHAPTER TWENTY-SIX

It felt as though Autumn had just gone to sleep when she was awakened by the sound of knocking on her door. She groaned and quite literally rolled out of bed to answer it.

Opening the door, she found Luke, raising an eyebrow at her appearance. "Did you just now wake up?" he asked. She nodded, yawning. "Why are you wearing clothes?"

Autumn looked down, realizing that she'd never changed out of her outfit from last night. "What time is it?" she said, hoping Luke wouldn't realize that she'd dodged his question.

"A quarter after eleven. We have practice at one."

"Oh, right. I'll get ready and then I'll meet y'all down in the dining room."

Autumn hurriedly took a shower and dressed in her Warrior training clothes. She pulled her damp hair into a ponytail, exposing her pointed ears—which she was still not completely used to—and left her branch.

Luke, Crystal and a tired looking Avery waited for her at their usual table. Autumn and Avery exchanged a shy smile as she sat beside her brother and poured herself a glass of orange juice.

"I knew you two would be together," Luke said, looking from Autumn to Avery.

Autumn choked on her orange juice. "W—what?" she said after a short coughing fit.

"I said I knew you and Avery would be partners," Luke said,

looking at her with a quizzical expression.

"Oh—right. Wait, why?" Autumn said.

"Lady Carys was looking at you guys really weird. Like she hadn't seen anything like that before."

"That's what I said," Crystal added.

Autumn shrugged, not making eye contact with anyone. "Hmm. Well did y'all not think you would be together?" she said, attempting to move the subject away from Avery and herself.

Crystal and Luke both shook their heads, smirking at one another.

"I thought I would be with Forrest," Crystal said.

"I figured I would be with you," he said to Autumn, "Or maybe Cera," Luke added thoughtfully.

"Why Cera?" Autumn asked.

"She's the only one I wouldn't get with out of the other four girls," he said. "It made the most sense to me."

Crystal blushed because this meant that Luke was saying that he *would* get with her.

"Why wouldn't you get with Cera?" asked Autumn.

"She scares me a little bit," he said seriously.

Autumn, Crystal, and Avery burst out laughing.

They met up with the rest of the Initiates on the dueling grounds. Everyone seemed pleased with his or her partners, except for Kyndel and Victor. Autumn could tell that Kyndel's pleasure at having the most attractive partner had quickly worn off because of Victor's stormy mood and overwhelming silence. He continuously glared at Autumn and Avery, so she kept her eyes trained on the ground, feeling extremely guilty.

Atticus wanted to build the trust between the partners, so he had them go through an obstacle course of sorts, which would've been no problem if they weren't going to be blindfolded, guided only by their partner's voice. The course was a trek across the entire campus. It began with the pond outside of the Healing tree, which they had to cross by stepping on a number of small, slippery stones.

Autumn and Avery both did well during their turn, a real feat given their lack of sleep. All of the others accomplished the task fairly quickly, except for Victor and Kyndel. Victor gave Kyndel short and vague directions and she screamed at him to be more specific before stepping the wrong way and falling backwards into the pond. She emerged, fuming, sopping wet, and pulling pelpy out of her hair. Victor didn't seem to care all that much.

The next portion of the course involved climbing up one of the many massive oak trees on campus, blindfolds still intact. Nearly everyone had a little trouble on this part because it required a great amount of upper body strength. Autumn slipped a few times, dangling ten feet above the ground, but managed to complete the task without falling.

When Victor's turn came to climb the tree, a soaked Kyndel purposefully gave him the wrong directions, telling him to step up with his left foot when there was nothing there but air. Somehow, though, Victor was able to complete the task without listening to her. This impressed the other Initiates and Autumn was pleased to see that Forrest even gave Victor a quiet compliment as he jumped down from the lowest branch. Atticus looked at Kyndel with a disapproving frown.

The final portion of the course included sprinting across a particularly uneven stretch of ground full of dips, holes, hanging branches and tree roots. Autumn and Avery both finished in under a minute, pulling their blindfolds off and panting when they reached the end of the course. Victor and Kyndel were the last to go. They were now so angry with one another that neither spoke one word of direction, and literally ran blindly through the course, Kyndel tripping frequently and Victor, somehow managing to miss every obstacle. Atticus glared at them both as they crossed the finish point.

"Well done, everyone. Great partner work. As long as you are Warriors, your partner is your rock and you have to learn to trust one another. At the end of January you will be participating in the traditional Warrior Trial, which is the final step before you begin officially training and working with the rest of the Warriors. You will be completing the trial with your partner and your partner alone. It will be difficult and extremely dangerous. I need you to take your training with me very seriously," Atticus looked at Victor and Kyndel as he said this. "That is all for today. Victor, Kyndel, I need a word with you."

The two brooding partners shuffled towards Atticus as everyone else left the field. Autumn and Avery lagged behind.

"I think I should talk to Victor," Autumn muttered.

"Not about...?"

"No! Not about that. He just seems really mad and I can't help him if he won't even talk to me."

"I think I should talk to him too," Avery said.

"Are you sure that's a good—"

Just then Victor passed by, ignoring both of them. Autumn made an indignant noise in the back of her throat and called, "Victor!" He kept walking. "Victor! Seriously? Victor Lavigne, stop walking before I give you back your rose!"

He stopped and turned slowly towards her, a glare on his face and green eyes narrowed. Autumn's guilt from earlier was gone and now she was just as mad as he appeared to be.

"What is your problem?" she said, catching up to him.

"What do you think?" He glanced back at Avery, who was standing awkwardly nearby.

"Oh, because I was partnered with someone other than you? Something I had absolutely no say in? I'm sorry, I didn't think that could be it because that would be a completely ridiculous reason to be mad at someone."

His glare flickered. "It's not ridiculous. You two obviously share something that you and I apparently do not."

Autumn kept her face blank, even though he was quite correct.

"Partners aren't chosen because of anything romantic, Victor. You should know that. You and I probably wouldn't have been good partners *because* we care so much about each other and our judgment would be tainted."

Autumn hated lying.

Victor was silent for a second. Then he said, "Maybe you're right."

"I am."

"I apologize," he said after a moment.

"You're forgiven."

"Victor?" Avery said from behind them. Autumn jumped at the sound of his voice.

Victor glanced up at Avery, his glare back in place. "Yes?"

"Could I speak with you?"

Victor raised an eyebrow and looked at Autumn. She shrugged her shoulders, pretending she had no idea what Avery could possibly want.

"I suppose so," Victor said. "I'll see you later, okay?" he said to Autumn, kissing her on the forehead. She had to tell herself not to flinch or flash Avery a guilty look.

Autumn walked down the winding path until she was out of sight of Victor, but still within hearing distance. She hid behind a nearby oak tree, listening intently.

"Listen, Victor," Avery began, "I know things haven't been great between us since...well, you know."

There was silence from Victor.

Avery cleared his throat. "Anyway. Since Autumn and I are partners now, I figure you and I should at least be civil to one another for her sake. It will just make everything easier. We've been acting childish."

Silence.

"Er, what I guess I'm trying to say is that I'm sorry...for blaming you. I know it wasn't your fault Avabelle died. I just needed to blame someone other than myself to make it easier."

"I see," Victor said.

"So, I'll, er, see you later then?" Avery said.

Victor said nothing so Autumn assumed that he had just nodded. She peeked around the trunk of the oak tree to see him walking away in the opposite direction as Avery started down the path towards the castle.

When Autumn thought Victor was a safe distance away, she jogged after Avery.

"Wait up," she called ahead. Avery stopped and turned. His eyes seemed clearer and he wore a smile on his face. "Thank you for doing that," she said. "I know it must have been really hard."

Avery shrugged. "It wasn't as bad as I thought. It actually felt sort of good to let it go."

Autumn smiled slyly at him and said, "Oh *really*? I think *I* may have told you that."

He laughed and said, "I don't think I recall that." He grabbed her hand and brought it to his mouth, kissing it softly. When his lips parted from her skin, he held her hand for a few seconds before reluctantly letting go. Luckily he let go when he did, though, because, when they rounded the corner, they met Crystal and Luke, who had been waiting for them.

"What took you guys so long?" Luke asked.

"We were, uh, talking to Victor," Autumn said.

"We?" Luke raised an eyebrow at Avery.

Avery nodded. "I figured that Victor and I should be civil with each other if Autumn and I are going to be partners."

"Yeah. They called a truce," Autumn said.

"Good for you!" Crystal said as the four of them traveled back to the castle for dinner. "That will make training easier. We need to be as prepared as possible for the Warrior Trial."

"So, what do you two know about the Warrior Trial?" Luke asked Crystal and Avery as they climbed the stairs into the castle.

"Well, Atticus wasn't lying when he said that it is dangerous. A lot of Initiates have died during the trial," Avery said.

"*Died?*" Autumn said.

Crystal nodded. "They put the Initiates in war-like situations, to prove that they can handle it with the rest of the Warriors. One year they had to make it through a mountain pass occupied by giants. They lost half of their Initiates that year."

"Half?" Luke said. "But there are only four alternates."

Avery shook his head as they entered the dining room, "There are more than four. They just announce the four alternates that are next in line, but Atticus and the other judges will have chosen at least twenty alternates."

"Holy crap," Luke said, making Crystal laugh.

"But the alternates don't train with us and they don't go through the Warrior Trial. How can they just take a Warrior's place?" Autumn said.

"They don't train with us, but they do train. The other Powers magister is their trainer, Magister Thorn. He's the first and second quarter elves' Powers magister. In the case of the loss of a Warrior, the alternate taking their place will go through a month of intensive training where they practice all day, every day and will have to go through a Warrior Trial of their own," Avery said.

"Bet it isn't as hard as *our* trial," Luke said.

"When do we find out what we'll be doing for our test?" asked Autumn.

"We won't know anything until the day of," Avery said.

Autumn gulped. "So...there's actually a chance that one of us could die?"

Avery and Crystal exchanged glances before both giving a grave nod.

Back to the Outside

CHAPTER TWENTY-SEVEN

Ever since their names were called, the Initiates had become a fairly close-knit group. Given that all of the other elves at their school were either jealous of or intimidated by their newfound fame, they had sort of ganged together. Kyndel had even dumped her little "followers" who she less-than-lightly told that they weren't good enough to hang out with a Warrior.

This new development made Autumn and Avery's job of helping Victor make friends significantly easier. The only problem was that Victor had become increasingly introverted. When he did come to lunch with the others, he usually sat quietly, appearing to be deep in thought and no one—not even Autumn—could bring him out of his reverie.

"This is going to be impossible," Avery said to Autumn one afternoon. "How can he make any friends if he won't even talk to anybody?"

"He'll come around. He's just not used to being around all of these people without being ridiculed and whatnot. Just have to be patient is all."

One Sunday in October all of the Initiates met up at Arbor Lake. Sunday was their only day off of Warrior training so they chose to do nothing but lounge in the hovering hammocks all day.

"I'm so glad we have Sundays off. I don't know what I'd do if I had to go to Warrior training *every* day of the week," Forrest said.

"Hey! Next Sunday is Halloween," Autumn said.

Luke's face brightened. "Oh yeah!"

The others, however, made disgusted faces.

"*Halloween*," Kyndel scoffed.

Autumn was taken aback. "What's wrong with Halloween?"

"Everything," Charlotte said with a frown.

"Outsiders think it's entertaining to mock all of the magical creatures every year," Kyndel said. "Dressing up like us and prancing around like idiots, but I can see why *you* would like something like that, Princess."

Autumn rolled her eyes and Luke said, "Halloween isn't about mocking magical creatures."

"Then why do they dress up like us?" Forrest asked.

"Because it's fun for them," Autumn said. "For just one day they can pretend to be whatever they want to be. Little girls can be princesses and fairies. Little boys can be wizards and superheroes. They aren't doing it to mock you. They're doing it because they want to *be* you."

"Yeah," Luke said. "And they don't even know that magical creatures exist. They just think it's a bunch of fairy tale nonsense, like Autumn and I did before."

The others frowned, taking in this apparently new information.

"So it's just the Outsider children that do this you said?" Jastin asked.

"Well, no. The kids dress up and go trick-or-treating," Autumn said. Then at the look of confusion on everyone's face she added, "Trick-or-treating is where the kids go door to door and ask for candy."

"What about Outsiders our age?" Cera asked.

Luke laughed. "They dress up too, but their costumes show a bit more skin. I love Halloween." He sighed, staring into space with a dazed smile.

"People our age dress up and go to parties," Autumn clarified. "In the bigger cities they have tons of celebrations in all of the clubs and pubs and stuff. It's pretty fun, actually."

"We should have a Halloween party," Charlotte said, apparently having changed her mind about the Outsider holiday.

There was a murmur of agreement from everyone, except

Victor, of course, who sat in distracted silence beside Autumn.

"Or we could do something better," Luke said with a sly smile.

Avery chuckled. "Like what?"

"We could go up into the Outside."

The group went silent, everyone exchanging nervous glances. Even Autumn looked at Luke in surprise.

"But most of us have never even been to the Outside before," Charlotte said. "We aren't allowed without a chaperone."

"There's a first time for everything," Luke said. "Besides, we're Warriors now. We can take care of ourselves."

"But our ears...our skin," Crystal said. "We won't start to look like Outsiders for at least a day. We've all been in the Underground so long. Remember how long it took you and Autumn to transform completely into elves?"

"I know! It's perfect!" Luke said.

Everyone shot him a confused look.

"How is that perfect?" Cera asked.

"It's Halloween," Luke said. "We can just say that we have really good costumes. We can go as elves!" Luke looked to Autumn then. "You'll go, won't you, Rose?"

Autumn thought for a second before nodding silently, a smile forming across her face.

"I'm in," Avery said, smirking at Autumn.

"Me too," said Forrest.

Charlotte and Jastin exchanged glances before agreeing too.

"Sounds pretty cool to me," Cera said.

"I'll make the costumes!" Crystal chimed in.

Everyone looked expectantly at Kyndel, who sat with crossed arms and a disapproving look upon her face. Eventually, she sighed, rolling her eyes. "Fine."

"How about you, Victor," Jastin asked. "Are you coming?"

Victor started at the sound of his name and looked up, confused. "What?" he said.

"Are you coming with us to the Outside on Halloween?" Forrest asked again.

Victor grimaced. "Why would I do that?"

"It will be fun," Charlotte said.

"I'm not going to the Outside," he stated.

Autumn sighed and Avery shook his head slightly in exasperation.

"Okay," Luke said, "So, Crystal, how fast do you think you can make ten, I mean nine costumes?"

"We'll have them by Halloween."

By sundown, everyone dispersed, talking excitedly about the next weekend. Victor began to walk away in silence.

"Victor?" Autumn called after him. "Are you okay?"

He turned, looking surprised to see her there. "Yes. Why?"

"You just seem a little...out of it."

He shrugged. "I'm just tired from all of the training, that's all."

"Are you sure you don't want to go with us on Halloween? It will be really fun."

He shook his head. "No. I don't go to the Outside."

"Why not?"

"I don't like it there."

"What don't you like about it?"

"Outsiders."

Autumn frowned. "What's so bad about Outsiders?"

"Outsiders think they rule the world. They don't care about any other living creature except themselves. They are the reason we had to come down here, to escape them. Outsiders are destroying the Earth."

"Not *all* Outsiders are like that, you know."

"Perhaps not, but majority are. Listen, I'm really tired. I'm going to go home. I'll see you tomorrow, Autumn." He kissed her forehead and left down the path toward his empty tree house.

Autumn walked slowly towards Arbor Castle. Avery was waiting for her around one of the curves and moved to walk beside her.

"This is going to be harder than I thought," Autumn said.

"Maybe we should just—"

"No. I can do this. I just need more time."

Avery looked as though he wanted to say more, but simply nodded in response.

"You have to be prepared! I'm not going to lose any of my Initiates this year," Atticus shouted after Friday's practice as half of the Initiates grumbled about how tired they were and the other half were about to collapse from exhaustion.

"We still have three months until the Warrior Trial. Why is he working us so hard?" Luke complained as they left the field.

"You heard him," Crystal said. "He doesn't want any of us to die. Avery and I weren't exaggerating when we told you about all of those deaths that happened during the Warrior Trials."

"I'm just ready for a break," Luke grumbled. "I can't wait until Sunday. How are the costumes coming?"

"I have one more to go!"

After Saturday's practice, everyone walked to Arbor Lake together to go over the Halloween plan. Everyone, that was, but Victor, who had already left the practice field.

"Okay," Luke began, having taken over the leadership position of this adventure. "We're meeting in front of the waterfall boundary at 7:00pm. Make sure none of your parents suspect anything." Everyone nodded. "Crystal, you'll bring all of the costumes with you. We can't leave our houses wearing them. It would also be smart if we all left separately. It would look too suspicious if we walked up there in a group. Any questions?"

"Are we done here?" Kyndel yawned.

"We are now. I'll see y'all tomorrow at seven. Get ready for some fun, elves!"

Sunday went by quickly and soon Autumn was rushing out of the castle alone. Luke and Avery had left about five minutes before her and Crystal would follow once Autumn was out of sight. Hurrying down the path from the castle, Autumn dashed down another that wound up to the waterfall.

When she arrived, Luke, Avery, Forrest, and Charlotte were already there. Crystal showed up soon after carrying a large sack full of the costumes, followed by Jastin, Cera, and finally Kyndel. The Underground sun began to set in the distance.

Crystal passed out the costumes to everyone and they all changed out of their normal clothes behind the vast trees. The girls' costumes were a soft green color resembling ballerina apparel with long sleeves made of a sheer material and skirts flowing around them like the branches of a willow tree. Charlotte had the brilliant idea to cover the girls in a shimmering powder to make them look even more ethereal than they already did.

The guys were a little less thrilled with their costumes. They wore white, Renaissance-style shirts with tightly fitted green pants to match the girl's costumes.

"Are you sure Outsiders think elves wear these, Crys?" Forrest said, pulling awkwardly at the pants.

"I did some research on elf Halloween costumes and this style was the most popular. All the others were for Christmas elves," Crystal said apologetically.

"I think they're great," Charlotte said, looking Jastin up and down with a wry smile on her face.

"Nice," Cera said and chuckled, glancing over Luke, who blushed.

Avery stepped out from behind his tree, raising his eyebrows at Autumn's costume. She repressed a coy smile.

"Shall we?" Jastin said, waving his hand towards the waterfall.

Autumn and Luke were elected to go first seeing as how they were the only ones who had gone through the boundary alone before. Luke went before Autumn, disappearing at the first touch of the waterfall. She stepped up after him, holding her breath. The memory of the last time she had touched this waterfall surfaced in her mind before she plunged her hand into the water to return to the Outside.

Outsider Halloween

CHAPTER TWENTY-EIGHT

Returning to the Outside took much less time than leaving it, and before she knew it, Autumn had landed on the expanse of flat rock in front of the waterfall boundary. She stood, peering back at her reflection, a much different one than she'd seen there a few months ago, which felt like years.

"Welcome back to Crap World!" Luke exclaimed as Autumn stepped away from the waterfall.

"Crap World?" Autumn said with a laugh. "The Underground really has changed you, hasn't it."

"Uh, yeah. I'm a prince and a badass Warrior in the Underground. *And* I get to make out with hot elf girls every day. You can't really beat that, can you?"

They moved together across the flat stones on the still water so that the others had room to land. Autumn immediately felt different—heavier—like there was more gravity in the Outside. Everything looked so much smaller than she remembered it. Sort of like an adult returning to their childhood home and realizing the ceilings were much lower than they had originally thought.

The trees were miniscule compared to the sequoia-sized ones in the Underground. The colors were duller than she remembered and the air no longer smelled of flowers, but instead, was permeated by a strange, unpleasant smell that she couldn't recognize.

One by one the other Initiates landed on the flat rock in front of the waterfall.

"Ugh! What is that disgusting smell?" Kyndel said, gagging.

Autumn noticed that the others were all making similar faces. Then she was struck with a realization.

"I think it might be the pollution," she said.

"Pollution?" Cera said. "What is that, some sort of disease?"

Luke snorted and rolled his eyes. "We've been in the Outside two seconds and you are already talking about pollution. Come on, Autumn."

"Seriously, Luke, I think that's what it is. They're used to pure air in the Underground. There aren't any factories or cars there or piles of trash that'll take hundreds of years to decompose. *I* even think it smells different here too, don't you?"

He frowned and sniffed the air. "I guess. Who cares? We don't live here anymore."

Autumn glared at him. "We are half Outsider, Luke. Don't you care about your old home?"

Luke shrugged in dismissal. "Okay, so I guess now we just go through the tunnel and into town and catch a—crap!" he said, smacking himself in the forehead.

"Catch a crap? I hope that means something else here," Cera said.

"What's wrong?" Autumn asked.

"I forgot about money!"

"I have some," Charlotte said, pulling a wad of silver leaves out of her costume.

"*Outsider* money," Luke said.

"Should we just go back, then?" Kyndel said, sounding hopeful.

"No," Luke said. "I left all of my savings from this summer in my old room. We'll just have to stop by there first. Hopefully Mrs. King hasn't found it."

They followed Luke out of the forest and into the tunnel that opened up in Blarney Castle. Nine elves trying to maneuver through a narrow tunnel was not the easiest thing. Every few steps Autumn heard someone trip or hit their head on the low rocky ceiling. To everyone's relief they soon emerged on the grounds of Blarney Castle.

Autumn looked back to see everyone walking together in a tight group, apparently afraid of what they might encounter in this strange, unknown world. Most of them wore looks of excitement, with the exception of Kyndel, whose nose was turned haughtily up in the air.

"Your trees are very small," she noted.

"Well Outsiders don't live in them, so they don't really have to be all that big do they?" Autumn said, slightly defensive.

"Now girls. Let's try to get along," Cera said with a chuckle, winking at Autumn.

Kyndel rolled her eyes, flipping her strawberry blonde hair back and Autumn smirked back at Cera, who was watching Kyndel with an amused expression.

Avery came to walk beside Autumn.

"I like your costume," he said.

She raised an eyebrow at him, looking around to make sure no one was listening. "I like yours too. You should consider wearing tights more often."

"I'm considering it. Once I got past the initial embarrassment, I realized they're really quite comfortable."

Autumn laughed a little louder than she had expected to and Luke turned to look at the two of them. He seemed to note their close proximity to one another and his eyes narrowed slightly. Autumn's face fell and she moved a few feet away from Avery.

They continued to travel down the rocky path to their old cottage. Finally, after what felt like half an hour, Autumn spotted it in the distance. The pub beside it was already packed full of people in costumes. The lights were all off in the cottage so she assumed Mrs. King was out.

"You *lived* in that?" Kyndel said. "No wonder you don't act like royalty. You were used to living like servants."

Crystal and Avery glared at her, since that was precisely what *they* were. Autumn gritted her teeth and resisted the urge to backhand her.

"When you say we don't act like royalty, I'm guessing you mean we don't act like we're better than everyone?" Autumn said. "You know, you don't have to be royalty to act like that. You seem to accomplish it pretty well."

Kyndel shot her a look of loathing and muttered something under her breath.

They ambled up the walkway and Luke located the spare key underneath a rock near the front porch, unlocking the door and stepping into the house. Autumn followed him into the entryway. It looked exactly the way it had a few months ago—the umbrellas in their holder, the coat rack covered in Mrs. King's many colored coats of various sizes, the spotless floor. Autumn wondered how Mrs. King had kept it so clean without their help. Then again, their absence had probably led to a tidier house in general.

The rest of the group entered cautiously behind them, mesmerized by all the strange Outsider objects situated around the house. Forrest picked up an umbrella, examining it closely with a look of amazement and shouting when it accidentally popped open. Crystal ran her fingers over Mrs. King's coats, marveling at the different fabrics. Autumn moved blindly down the dark hallway towards her old room.

"Will you turn the light on, Luke?" she called over her shoulder.

Luke flipped on the light-switch and there was a collective intake of breath in the cramped entryway. Autumn halted her progress down the hall and turned to see everyone except Luke looking up at the light fixture in amazement.

"Can you do that again?" Charlotte asked Luke, looking awestruck.

He chuckled, flipping the light switch down, then back up again. Everyone looked significantly impressed by this small bit of Outsider "magic." Charlotte beamed and said, "That is *so* cool."

"You can try it if you want," Luke offered, standing aside for Charlotte to have a chance to turn the lights on and off.

"Do you mind if we look around a bit?" Jastin asked.

"Not at all," Autumn answered.

The elves dispersed through the house, opening the refrigerator doors, turning on the television, and picking up the phone to listen to the dial tone. Luke found Autumn's old cell phone, which had been dead for quite some time, and handed it to Crystal. Her eyes widened as she pressed a few buttons.

Autumn laughed to herself as she resumed her progress down the hall to her old room. Turning on the lights, she frowned slightly. Everything was the same as she'd left it. All of her books were on the shelves, her bed was made, and her clothes were put up, but for some reason she felt an overwhelming sense of despair. Thinking back on her time spent there, she realized how sad she had been. Her parents had just died and she hadn't made any friends in Ireland. She had cried many tears in this room. Now that she was back, all of those old feelings were creeping back into her memory.

Shuddering, she hastened to empty the contents of her "sheep" bank onto her bed. She had saved up almost six hundred Euros while working at Blarney Castle. She grabbed a handful of the Outsider money, stashed it in her costume and turned to leave. She let out a small gasp when she saw Avery standing in her doorway with his arms folded across his chest, fixing her with a penetrating gaze.

"You scared me," she said, breathless. Avery was silent. He looked as if he was contemplating something. "What's wrong?"

"You're different here," Avery said.

"How do you mean?"

"Your light is gone."

"My light?"

Avery nodded. "In the Underground you sort of...shine. Like you have a light inside of you. I can almost see it when you smile or laugh. I can feel it when I'm around you, the warmth of it, but here it's nearly gone."

She gave him a small smile. "It's probably just an effect of the Outside. Let's get out of here," she said, moving a little closer to the doorway.

"You don't like this room, do you?"

Autumn shook her head, glancing over her shoulder at her small room. "I associate it with a bad time in my life, I guess."

"Maybe this will help you associate it with something good," he said in a low voice, approaching her slowly. She smiled coyly up at him and he kissed her lips softly, running his fingers through her hair. A shudder moved through her like before, but for a much different reason this time.

Autumn heard footsteps in the hallway and took a quick step back from Avery, who moved swiftly to a corner of the room, pretending to examine her old computer just as Luke entered the doorway.

Luke glanced at Avery, but fortunately seemed unconcerned by his presence in Autumn's room. "You ready to go?"

"If they're finished turning the lights on and off," Autumn answered with a forced laugh.

"They've actually moved on to the—"

Luke was interrupted by the sound of a vacuum cleaner being turned on and a high-pitched scream emitting from the living room.

The three of them hurried out of Autumn's room to find Kyndel standing on the couch and Cera laughing hysterically, vacuum cleaner in hand.

"What kind of creature is that?" Kyndel shrieked at them.

Luke looked at the vacuum and a sly smile spread across his face. "That is the notorious cleaning monster—the *vacuum*. It eats people's toes and anything else it can get its mouth on."

Kyndel's eyes widened and she climbed even higher up the couch, away from the vacuum monster. Autumn shook her head at Luke, laughing. "Calm down, Kyndel. It's just a machine that cleans the floor and it's about as dangerous as a petalsie. Get a hold of yourself. Aren't you supposed to be a Warrior?"

"We can't use our Powers up here, Princess," she spit. "How am I supposed to know how to kill a vacloom monster?"

Autumn had to leave the room before she exploded with laughter.

"Hey, Elves!" Luke called throughout the house. "Are we going to party or what? Let's go!"

Once all the lights had been turned off and the vacuum put up, the nine of them filed out of the cottage. Luke locked the door and hid the spare key back under the rock.

"Are we going there?" Charlotte asked, pointing to the pub next door.

"No," Luke said. "They don't like me there. We will take a cab to Cork."

They were able to fit into two cabs by squeezing five people in one car and four in the other. Autumn rode sandwiched between Crystal and Avery. Luke sat on Crystal's left side and Cera rode in the front seat.

"Nice costumes," the cabdriver said, looking Cera over.

"Thanks," Cera said.

"What're you supposed to be?" he asked.

"*Elves*," Cera stated as if this should be quite obvious.

"Elves, eh? Your ears are a bit small for elves, though, aren't they? Elves' ears are 'spose to be really massive."

"No. They aren't," Cera said, "They—" Autumn cleared her throat loudly and Cera stopped talking, crossing her arms and leaning back against her seat in moody silence. The cabdriver looked confused as he pulled onto the main road to Cork.

Cera, Crystal, and Avery seemed impressed by the car and the fact that it could move without being pulled by a magical creature. It felt strange to be back in the Outside. Autumn had become so used to traveling by foot...and sometimes pegasus.

Once Cera had taken in enough of the Outside scenery, she turned around in her seat to face the others. "Did you see Kyndel's face when I turned that vacstoom thing on?" The cabdriver glanced at Cera with a bemused look on his face. Cera, however, didn't notice this and continued on. "I don't think I'll ever forget the vision of her squealing and jumping onto the couch. I'm going to store that in my memory for the next time I need a good laugh," she said. "I need to bring one of those vacrooms back to—"

Luke faked a hacking cough to cover up the last of Cera's sentence. Cera raised an eyebrow at Luke, who nodded his head towards the cabdriver. A look of understanding crossed her face and she turned back around and went silent again.

"Where did yeh say yeh were from?" the cabdriver inquired.

They all exchanged panicked looks before Autumn said quickly, "We're from all over, actually. We're part of a foreign exchange program."

"Yeah," Luke added. "My sister and I are from Texas. Texas is a state in America, you know. Although some Texans think that it should be its own country. It's definitely big enough to be a country, like much, much bigger than countries over here. Can you tell we're from Texas because of our accents?" The cabdriver opened his mouth to answer, but Luke prattled on. "I don't think I have that strong of an accent, but then again, I bet you don't think you have an accent either because you're used to it and all.

"You know, lots of people think that Texans ride horses

everywhere, but we don't. We drive cars too. We drive on the other side of the road, though, and our steering wheels are on the other side of the car. You know how you have all those sheep everywhere? Well, in Texas we have cows everywhere, but they don't walk across the streets like the sheep do here. Y'all should really consider fencing them in. It could be considered a driving hazard."

Luke continued on like this the rest of the way to Cork. The look on the cabdriver's face made it clear that he was extremely sorry that he had asked where they were from.

"Well played," Autumn told Luke once they arrived downtown and had paid the weary looking cabdriver.

"What was well played?" Cera asked.

"Luke did his Texas rambling bit," Autumn said. "He used to do that with girls he was trying to hit on. Only, it actually worked to his advantage this time."

"Oh! That's why you kept talking about Texas," Cera said. "I was about to tell you to shut it, but I didn't want the cabdriver to ask me more questions."

"I thought it was actually pretty interesting," Crystal said.

Avery, Cera, and Autumn raised their eyebrows at her and Luke puffed out his chest. "Why thank you, Crystal. I knew I had the smartest partner of all the Warriors," he said ruffling her blonde hair. Crystal blushed as she smoothed her hair back down.

The other cab pulled up then. Charlotte, Jastin, and Forrest climbed out of the car with exasperated expressions. Kyndel emerged with pursed lips. "What happened?" Autumn muttered to Charlotte as Luke paid their cab fare.

"Kyndel kept criticizing 'Outsiders' and their world and we kept shushing her. Needless to say, the man driving looked pretty confused by the end of the ride."

Autumn shook her head wearily and said, "Cera slipped up too, but luckily Luke has a gift of incessant rambling."

"Luckily?" Cera said.

"Hey, I saved your—" Luke began.

"Okay," Autumn interrupted. "Let's go already."

"I'm down with that," Luke said, forgetting what he was about to say to Cera.

As they made their way downtown they could hear the uproar of people celebrating. Halloween had always been somewhat of an extravagant celebration in Cork. All of the pubs and clubs filled up with locals and tourists alike, wearing crazy and creative costumes and drinking until early in the morning. Autumn and Luke had gone the previous year. They didn't drink, of course, though Luke probably would have if Autumn hadn't stopped him.

The others' heads whipped back and forth as they tried to take in everything around them. Charlotte had a firm clasp on Jastin's hand due to the staring eyes of the Irishmen they passed. Kyndel walked beside Charlotte, keeping her eyes on the ground. Autumn noticed that Crystal was walking particularly close to Luke, who was talking animatedly to Forrest about the Halloween costumes that Outsider girls their age typically wore. Forrest listened intently, with wide eyes. Cera looked unconcerned about her safety in this new world and studied the architecture of the buildings surrounding them with a look of interest upon her face. She looked more like a pixie than an elf in her costume with her spiked, glitter-covered, blonde hair.

Autumn and Avery walked side by side at the back of the group. She wished she could reach over and grab his hand, but she had to restrain herself. She suspected Avery was thinking the same thing because his left hand kept twitching slightly towards hers. She folded her arms across her chest so as not to temp either of them. She'd thought that admitting their feelings to one another, and sharing secret, stolen kisses, would lessen the physical tension between them, but, on the contrary, it seemed to have grown in intensity.

The street became gradually more crowded as they neared the strip of pubs and clubs. The elves unconsciously squeezed more tightly together so as not to lose anyone.

"Autumn," Luke called over his shoulder. "How 'bout that one place we went last Halloween? The one with the bar in the middle and you can go downstairs into that dance area. Pretty sure they don't ask for ID."

"Yeah, they'll probably just let us in," Autumn agreed.

Autumn heard Luke tell Forrest that they had cheap drinks. She narrowed her eyes at him, but chose not to say anything. He was a big boy. He could make his own decisions. She hadn't had another drink since that night...

"Do elves drink much alcohol?" Autumn asked Avery.

"Wine, mostly, but not usually in excess. Though there are some who do."

"But no one in our group has?"

"I doubt it," Avery said.

Autumn frowned. If anyone did drink tonight, they were sure to become intoxicated far more quickly than the average seventeen-year-old Outsider since their bodies had not been exposed to alcohol. She hadn't really thought of this when she agreed to come.

They approached the door of the bar and were immediately let in without having to show any form of identification. The place was completely packed full of people in various Halloween costumes. As Luke had promised Forrest, most of the girls wore costumes that left little to the imagination. One wore what could only be described as lingerie with a pair of rabbit ears on her head.

"I love Halloween," Luke sighed as they traveled down a staircase to the lower level of the bar to find an empty space to stand.

Autumn chuckled at the expressions on the others' faces. The males in the group stared, wide-eyed at the Outsider girls' costumes—or lack thereof. The girls were both looking disapprovingly at the girls' costumes and blushing as they glanced fleetingly at the many Outsider men who were wearing rather lewd costumes themselves.

"Alright!" Luke said, clapping his hands together. "Who all is having a drink?"

Autumn gave Luke an exasperated look, which he ignored.

"I'll try something," Forrest said, not taking his eyes off of the girl in lingerie and bunny ears.

"Me too," Cera said.

Jastin and Charlotte exchanged glances and then nodded at Luke. Seeing this, Kyndel agreed too.

"Crystal, Avery?" Luke asked.

They both glanced at Autumn before turning to Luke, shaking their heads. He rolled his eyes, but didn't push them.

"It's okay," Autumn said to them. "I don't mind."

"I really don't want anything," Crystal assured her.

Luke went to the bar and ordered the drinks, soon returning with his arms full of pints.

"I got you three some Bulmers 'cause I didn't think you'd like Guinness very much," he said to Cera, Charlotte, and Kyndel. Cera glowered at this, obviously offended that he didn't think she could handle what the guys could.

Everyone took tentative sips of their drinks, the majority of them making disgusted faces. Cera downed hers and smiled widely. "Still think I can't handle a Guinness?" she said to Luke, whose eyebrows rose in surprise.

The more sips the elves took, the more they seemed to lighten up and actually start enjoying themselves. The DJ began to play a fast, upbeat song and Cera pulled Charlotte onto the dance floor, leaving their empty pints on a nearby table. A guy dressed as a vampire approached Kyndel and began talking loudly over the blaring music.

"I like your costume," he said, half shouting.

"Thanks," Kyndel said.

"Would ya' like to dance?" he asked.

She glanced towards Cera and Charlotte who were dancing and laughing before turning back to the vampire guy and nodding demurely. He took her hand and pulled her onto the dance floor. Luke left soon after Kyndel to try dance with the lingerie girl, but his prince status was left behind with the Underground and she soon shook him off.

"Want to dance with me, Crystal?" Forrest asked.

Crystal nodded and followed him onto the dance floor. It was humorous watching them dance together because Crystal was about three inches taller than him. None of the elves were accustomed to Outsider music and looked a little out of place trying to dance to it. They didn't really seem to know how to move with the beat. Autumn noticed a few people shooting them funny looks.

Autumn laughed out loud and shook her head at them. "I'm going to go help them," she told Avery, leaving him with Jastin, who was nursing his Guinness as he kept his eyes trained on Charlotte.

Autumn approached the others with a look of suppressed

humor on her face.

"We look ridiculous," Crystal grumbled as she glanced at the Outsiders dancing around them.

"No you don't," Autumn said. "You're just dancing a little offbeat. I'll show you."

Autumn swayed her hips to the pulsating beat and raised her arms letting her inhibitions go. Being musically inclined had its perks on the dance floor as well. She had no trouble moving fluidly to the music, waving her hand at the others, telling them to join her. They looked a little uncomfortable at first, but eventually let loose and began mimicking Autumn's moves.

"That's it!" she said, laughing.

Luke, Jastin, and Avery exchanged glances before joining the girls on the dance floor.

Unconsciously, the Initiate partners paired up just as a base-heavy song with a fast beat came on. Autumn looked over to see that most of them had really caught on. Crystal, being so tall, was still having trouble and Luke offered to help her, putting his hands on her hips and moving them with the beat. He clearly didn't notice that Crystal's face was bright red.

"I sort of wish *you* were a bad dancer so I'd have an excuse to put my arms around you," Avery murmured in her ear, sending a chill coursing across her skin.

Then a popular hip hop "line dance" song came on that everyone knew the moves to—everyone, but the Undergrounders, that was. Luke and Autumn coached the others through it, laughing hysterically at Forrest, who was too frustrated to follow along, so he just started doing what Outsiders would call a poor attempt at break-dancing.

The song ended and they walked off the dance floor wiping at their foreheads and fanning their faces.

"That was actually fun! Lucky everybody was here so we had our partners to dance with," Charlotte said, winking at Jastin.

"Victor's not here," Autumn noted.

"Oh yeah," Charlotte said, giving her a sheepish look.

"Victor is Kyndel's partner, though," Cera said. "But where *is* Kyndel?"

Everyone looked around, craning their necks to see over the

horde of dancers. But it was no use. Kyndel had disappeared...and she wasn't Invisible either.

Fight Like a Girl

CHAPTER TWENTY-NINE

Panic began to set in as they searched the club for Kyndel.

"She wasn't dancing with us," Crystal noted. "She must have disappeared before that."

"We have to find her," Cera said.

"Let's split up and look for her and meet back here in a few minutes if we haven't found her," Luke said.

They dispersed throughout the club in search of Kyndel. Autumn may not have liked her all that much, but that didn't mean she wanted anything bad to happen to her. She went into the girl's restroom and called out her name, earning a few annoyed looks from the girls reapplying their makeup. Leaving the bathroom, she climbed the stairs into the rest of the bar and walked past a doorway that led outside. Its doors were propped open to let some fresh air into the stuffy, packed club.

She peeked out the doorway, looking right, then left. And that's when she heard Kyndel's panicked voice from around the corner of the building in a deserted alleyway.

"No! Stop! I have to go find my friends!" Kyndel shouted, followed by a quickly muffled scream.

Autumn's stomach dropped and she burst into the alley, looking wildly around. She spotted Kyndel being pressed up against the grimy wall of the club by the man dressed as a vampire. He had his hand pressed over her mouth and was in the process of pulling her skirt up.

Running at a dead sprint, Autumn kicked him hard in his side. He let out a grunt of pain, stumbled, and released Kyndel, who was trembling and sobbing uncontrollably. The guy bent over holding his side. Autumn took this opportunity to kick him again, but this time where it really hurt. He let out a yelp and fell to his knees. She then proceeded to punch him, hard, in the jaw.

"Don't you EVER touch a girl like that again!" she yelled, kicking him in the side again, causing him to collapse onto the ground. She grabbed a handful of his hair, yanking his head back. *"You are scum,"* she growled. He glared painfully up at her, but didn't say anything. His lip bled freely. Autumn punched him in his Adam's apple causing him to take a loud, rasping breath. One of his fake vampire teeth came loose, falling onto the cobblestones. "And if you do touch a girl like that again, it will be the *last* thing you do. Trust me. I know people much more dangerous than vampires," she said darkly before pushing him to the ground and kicking him once again for good measure.

Kyndel stared wide-eyed at her with tears streaming down her face. "Let's get out of here," Autumn said to her, grasping her trembling arm and guiding her back towards the club's open doors. Kyndel let Autumn lead her without saying a word. Instead of taking her straight to the group, though, Autumn led her into the girls' bathroom.

Two girls dressed as a devil and an angel stood touching up their makeup in front of the mirror. "Get out," Autumn said.

"Excuse me?" one of them said indignantly.

Autumn glared at them and they glanced over at Kyndel, taking in her blotchy, tearstained face and smeared makeup. The girls put their makeup back into their purses and left, shooting Kyndel a pitying look. Autumn grabbed a handful of paper towels and ran some cold water on them. Kyndel stood there in silence, tears still leaking from her eyes.

"Here," Autumn said, handing her the damp paper towels. "Fix your makeup."

Kyndel took a deep breath as she gingerly accepted the towels and dabbed at her face with shaking hands, looking absently into the mirror. Autumn began rearranging Kyndel's disarrayed hair back to the way it was before.

"Why are you being so nice to me," Kyndel asked, her voice wavering.

"I don't know," Autumn said through a mouthful of hairpins. "I figure you don't need someone acting like a jerk to you right now."

"Thanks," Kyndel muttered. She pulled out a jar of the shimmer powder that Charlotte had earlier and applied it again to her face, which covered the blotches nicely. She took a deep, shaky breath and made eye contact with Autumn. "How do I look?" she asked.

"You look fine," Autumn said, opening the door for her.

"Just fine?" she said, sounding slightly put off.

"Sorry. You look positively stunning, Kyndel."

"That's better," she said.

They made their way back to the others who were looking around worriedly. Avery and Luke, in particular, appeared slightly panicked. Autumn assumed this was because she had been gone for a good fifteen minutes.

"Rose!" Luke said in relief when he spotted Kyndel and her approaching them. He pulled his sister into a bone-crushing hug. "Why do you always disappear like that?" he said with a mixture of anger and relief.

"Sorry," she said, her voice muffled against Luke's chest.

Avery looked as though he wanted to wrap her in a hug too, but knew that wouldn't quite look right. She gave him a reassuring smile, which seemed to calm him slightly.

"Where have you been?" Charlotte asked Kyndel in concern.

"Er..." Kyndel began, glancing at Autumn.

"She was outside," Autumn said, causing Kyndel's eyes to widen in horror. "She was just cooling off," Autumn added hastily. "Cause it's so hot in here."

Charlotte looked at Kyndel for confirmation, and she nodded. "It's disgusting in here," she said with a look of revulsion.

"Well, do you guys want to go to the next place?" Luke asked.

Autumn saw a look of panic and fear flash across Kyndel's face.

"It's getting late, Luke," Autumn said. "Maybe we should just go back."

"What?" Luke said, looking incredulous.

"She's right," Avery added, looking at Autumn in concern.

"Yeah. I'm pretty tired," Crystal said.

The others nodded in agreement.

"Don't you want another drink?" Luke directed desperately at Forrest and Jastin.

Jastin frowned and looked back at his now warm Guinness that he'd abandoned. Forrest shook his head, looking a little queasy. Cera looked as though she could go for another one, but didn't speak up.

"Fine," Luke said. "Let's go back."

They traveled out of the pub and down the street to where the cabs lined up waiting for fares. As they walked, Luke told Forrest about the lingerie girl and how she wasn't quite as into him as the elf girls were. Jastin had his arm slung around Charlotte, who was leaning tiredly up against him. Crystal and Cera were giggling about the Outsider men's costumes. Kyndel had her arms folded tightly across her chest. Her eyes were staring, unfocused, at the ground. Autumn frowned at her in concern, her urge to help people more overpowering than her dislike of Kyndel.

"What *really* happened?" Avery asked Autumn under his breath.

She looked up at him with raised eyebrows.

"What do you mean?" Autumn asked.

He took her right hand in his, palm-side down and pointed to her bloody knuckles. She pulled her hand back, tucking both hands under her arms.

"Nothing," she muttered.

"Autumn."

She glanced up at Kyndel who appeared to be lost in her own thoughts. Autumn sighed and said, "That guy Kyndel was dancing with took her into the alley and was..." she hesitated. "Well, he was about to make her do something that she didn't want to do. Luckily, I stopped him before he could go through with anything."

Avery made a disgusted face, which quickly turned to anger. "Did he touch you?"

She resisted the urge to laugh. "Not quite. I didn't exactly give him time to touch me."

Avery shook his head looking impressed and a little exasperated. "You really know how to handle yourself, don't you?"

"I suppose I do."

They took two cabs again like before. Luke paid the drivers and trudged back up the path the Blarney Castle. It took twice as long to get up to the castle and through the tunnel because everyone was so exhausted. Luke admitted that it had been a good idea to leave when they had because, by the time they reached the waterfall, it was already almost 3am and they had school early the next morning. Luke, Avery, Crystal, and Autumn stepped through the boundary at the same time.

They landed on the spongy moss in front of the waterfall and climbed wearily to their feet.

"Nice of you to return," a voice said from the shadows. They all jumped and turned to see Atticus step out of a thick clump of trees, looking livid.

Making Friends and Drinking Cocoa

CHAPTER THIRTY

Atticus's arms were folded tightly across his chest, his eyebrows knit together. Autumn, Luke, Avery, and Crystal looked guiltily up at him, not speaking. Suddenly the rest of the group burst through the waterfall, knocking them to the ground.

"What the—? Why didn't you guys move?" Cera groaned, pushing Forrest off of her.

There was a collective gasp from the others as they took in Atticus, who was standing ominously before them.

"Oh crap," Forrest muttered.

"My thoughts exactly, Mr. Akerley," Atticus said. "Would someone like to inform me as to why you found it necessary to venture into the Outside with no adult present?"

At this, everyone focused their attention on Luke. He raised his eyebrows, looking around at the group.

"Mr. Oaken?" Atticus inquired.

Luke gulped. "Um... Well, you see, today is Halloween and everyone thought that it was about mocking magical creatures. So, Autumn and I wanted to show them that it wasn't really like that in the Outside. You know, so they didn't have the wrong idea about Outsiders. Really, it was a valuable learning experience for everyone."

Atticus raised an eyebrow, looking amused. "Even so, Mr. Oaken. It was an extremely risky learning experience. If I hadn't known that you and Ms. Oaken were familiar with the Outside, I would have been forced to go up there after you."

"We just figured that since we're Warriors and everything—" Luke began.

"*Because* you are Warriors, it is crucial that you abide by the rules. You are future protectors of the elves of Arbor Falls and, as such, you should be setting an example for those who look to you as leaders."

The Initiates looked guiltily down at the ground, muttering apologies.

"As punishment," Atticus began, everyone's heads snapping upwards, "you will be training for an extra hour every day this week. Including Sunday."

Groans resounded around the group.

"Where is Mr. Lavigne?" Atticus asked, scanning the group.

"He didn't come," Autumn said.

"Ah. Well, I suppose you all will have to explain to him why he will be working an extra hour every day as well."

"What?" Autumn protested. "Victor has to work extra too? But he didn't do anything wrong."

"The sooner you all realize that the Warriors are a team, the better. You're in this together."

Autumn frowned, not seeing how this was fair. Victor was going to be furious.

But she was wrong. When Atticus informed Victor that he would be completing an extra hour of training that week because of the others' choices, he simply nodded, saying nothing. The other Initiates raised their eyebrows in surprise at this and, without any effort from Avery or Autumn, the rest of the group seemed to respect Victor quite a bit more, shooting him an apologetic look as they began training. Victor worked the hardest out of everyone. Though that was partly because he was the only one who had actually received a decent night's sleep.

To everyone's surprise, Atticus had not informed any of their parents or guardians about their Halloween adventure. When Forrest asked him why, Atticus simply shrugged with a crooked smile on his face as he asked, "Would you like for me to inform them?"

Everyone shook their heads.

After practice, Autumn walked with Victor to the point where the path split. Luke, Crystal, and Avery weren't far behind. She could see Avery watching her intently out of the corner of her eye.

"Are you angry with us?" she asked Victor. He shook his head. "Really?"

"Really," he gave her a small smile. "Besides, this extra practice will benefit us in the long run. We need to be prepared for the Warrior Trial."

Autumn raised her eyebrows. She hadn't thought of the benefits of this extra practice. Her only focus had been how tired she was and how all she wanted to do was crawl back into bed.

"You surprise me sometimes," she said.

He frowned at this. "How?"

"I don't know... I'm just impressed that you can be so positive when you don't even deserve to be punished."

He shrugged. "Well, technically I should have stopped you guys from going, but I didn't really think it was my place."

They reached the split in the path where Autumn went left and Victor went right. He kissed her softly on the forehead and she tried not to flinch, knowing that Avery was right behind them, looking stonily at the ground.

The following week was nothing short of torture. End of semester tests were coming up, so all of Autumn's magisters had nearly doubled their workload. Magister Monroe's class, in particular, had become unbearably difficult. Autumn didn't like math much to begin with, but now they worked from the time they entered the room to the time they left, their satchels full to bursting with even more homework.

After days full of studying, reading, writing, and lab work, the Initiates had three hours of Warrior training to endure. This amount of work would have been difficult any day, but the Underground was becoming colder as winter approached, which made all of the training that much harder. Any free time they had was spent sleeping or eating.

The only positive thing about the week—at least to Autumn and Avery—was the fact that everyone was being exceptionally friendly to Victor. His acceptance of the extra practice without complaint had impressed all of the Initiates.

After finishing their last day of training punishment on Sunday, all of the Initiates decided to meet up at the hot chocolate shop downtown called Cup O' Co after dinner. Victor, however, refused. Autumn frowned, frustrated at his lack of interest in making any friends. He was making her efforts to help him extremely difficult, if not impossible.

"Um, Victor?" Autumn asked, when the others had dispersed.

"Yes?"

"Can I talk to you for a second?"

"Of course."

"Do you..." Autumn hesitated, trying to find the right words. "Do you even want any friends?"

He frowned at her for a minute before speaking slowly. "Why wouldn't I want friends?"

Autumn shrugged. "Well, you never talk to anyone but me, and on the rare occasions that you *do* hang out with the rest of the Initiates, you just sit there quietly without acknowledging anyone."

Victor's brow furrowed. Autumn bit her lip, hoping she hadn't upset him. "You're right," he said. "I'm just not used to being treated kindly by these elves. I still have my guard up, but I will make more of an effort."

"Really?" Autumn said with a hopeful smile. Victor nodded. "That's great!"

"Just curious," he said, "but why do you want me to make friends so badly?"

She felt her cheeks flush as she thought of the main reason she wanted this. Then she cleared her throat quickly and said, "I care about you, Victor. I just want you to be happy."

"You do?" he asked, studying her face.

"Of course I do," Autumn said sincerely.

Victor's face brightened and he pulled her into a deep kiss. She felt herself tense slightly, and couldn't help but feel that she was betraying Avery, when in all actuality it was the other way around. Victor was the one being betrayed here.

Their lips parted and he smiled warmly down at Autumn. "*You* make me happy."

She looked up at him with wide eyes. "I'm glad," was all she could get out because her immense guilt threatened to take over. "So, would you like to meet us at Cup O' Co later?"

Victor was silent for a minute before he said, "I'd love to."

When Victor and Autumn entered the hot chocolate shop, the others did a double-take.

"Victor? I thought you weren't coming," Jastin said, seeming pleased by his appearance.

"I decided that I would...if that's alright."

"That's great!" Charlotte said. The rest of the group smiled at him in welcome.

Autumn and Avery shared a small, celebratory high five unseen by anyone else. They all ordered their favorite flavored hot chocolate and sat in a group at the back of the cocoa shop. They had a variety of flavors ranging from vanilla all the way to chili. Autumn ordered the peppermint.

They sat in their corner talking happily about the end of their drawn out punishment and sipping their cocoa. To Autumn's surprise and jubilation, Victor actually joined in the conversations. He even got into a deep discussion with Jastin and Forrest about unicorns and whether or not they were too dangerous to own as a pet. Victor spoke animatedly about his unicorn and the others listened intently, with obvious fascination.

Autumn and Avery exchanged satisfied looks as they watched. Finally, Victor was beginning to open up to the others. This was the first step to him making friends and not needing her anymore. But Autumn had a bad feeling that this wouldn't exactly work after what he had said earlier—that *she* made him happy. What if she was getting in too deep? What if, once she returned his rose, he went back to being introverted and alone? She glanced up to see Avery looking at her in concern. She shook her head slightly as if to say, "it's nothing."

He frowned, but turned away to continue listening to the conversation between Victor and the others. They stayed at the cocoa shop until closing time at 10:00pm. Everyone left, chatting happily with Victor and waving goodbye as he walked back to his secluded tree house.

"Victor is pretty cool," Forrest said.

"I can't believe he has a unicorn," Charlotte said in awe.

"I can't remember why we never really talked to him before," Cera added.

Autumn smiled inwardly at their comments. Everyone seemed to have forgotten why they were ever afraid of Victor in the first place. They all parted ways at City Circle, Luke, Crystal, Avery, and Autumn traveling towards Arbor Castle.

"Victor seemed much more talkative than usual," Crystal noted.

"Yeah," Luke agreed. "I think that's the most he's talked the whole time I've known him."

When they reached Arbor Castle, Crystal headed down to the roots to her room and Luke, Avery, and Autumn trudged up the stairs. Luke said goodnight to them when he reached his branch.

Autumn was about to enter her own branch when Avery said, "Can I come in?"

Her mouth fell open slightly in surprise and she looked around to check for any onlookers before opening the door to admit him. She moved to sit in the armchair that was situated beside the fireplace. Avery took a seat in the chair opposite her.

"I still don't get how you can have an open fire in the middle of a tree," Autumn said, not wanting to talk about Victor.

"All of the trees in the Underground are fireproof," Avery stated simply. "What was wrong earlier?"

She sighed, already knowing what he was talking about. "It's just Victor."

"But he did so well tonight. He talked to everyone and they all seemed to get along with him."

"It's not that. He did do well tonight. It's just...when he and I were talking earlier, he said that *I* make him happy. What if this doesn't work, Avery? What if he goes back to the way he was after I return his rose?"

"So, do you want to stop trying to help him?" he asked with a small hint of hope in his voice.

Autumn shook her head vehemently. "No. I'm just worried, is all. I still want to help him, and I'm still going to return his rose once he's made some friends. There's nothing I can do if he goes back to the way he was."

"But you'll feel guilty," Avery said and Autumn nodded. "Just know that we're doing all that we can to help him, Autumn. After that, it's up to him. It's not your job to keep him happy."

"I know."

"You know, you're going to make a really great queen."

She laughed. "What?"

"I'm serious. You care about people. You have empathy. Not many elves, especially royals, can say that."

Autumn felt herself blush. Avery smiled crookedly at her then and the magnetic pull within her suddenly kicked in to high gear. Her skin tingled in anticipation. Though, what she was anticipating, she wasn't sure.

"I should go to bed," he said.

"Okay," Autumn breathed.

They stood at the same time, putting them inches from one another.

"Well, goodnight," Autumn said, looking bright-eyed up at him.

"Goodnight."

His pupils dilated, alerting her to what was about to happen. Without warning Autumn reached out and pulled him forcefully to her. His lips met hers and the magnetic sensation intensified. He wrapped both arms around her and pulled her closer to him so that they were pressed right up against each other. Her hands moved up and she ran her fingers through his soft, golden hair. His arms tightened around her. They stayed like this for some time before they broke apart, chests heaving. Autumn looked into his torrential gray eyes, the flickering firelight reflected in them.

His breathing was shallow and she leaned forward, resting her head in the crook of his neck. He held her like this until his breathing slowed.

"You should probably go to sleep now. You have guard duty tomorrow," Autumn whispered.

"Probably," he said. She could feel his vocal chords vibrate as he spoke.

"But?"

"But I don't want to."

"Me either," she said. "But we need to."

"I know," Avery sighed, kissing her softly on the lips, lingering there for a moment. "Goodnight, Autumn," he whispered.

"Goodnight."

He left her branch slowly with the shadow of a smile on his face. Autumn watched as the door closed behind him and sank back into her armchair. "Goodnight," she repeated to the empty room.

The Rules Are... There Are No Rules

CHAPTER THIRTY-ONE

The next couple of weeks, Victor made a clear effort to hang out with the rest of the Initiates. He talked to everyone during Warrior training and went with them to Arbor Lake and City Circle. His stormy mood seemed to have disappeared along with his introverted tendencies and everyone seemed to think he was the coolest elf they'd ever met.

As the days passed, though, the Initiates had less and less free time with the finals coming up. They still found time to spend together by forming a study group, which met every day after Warrior training. One afternoon they met in a coffee house called Sugar Brown's in City Circle because it was too cold to meet at Arbor Lake. Today they were studying Laboratory, which was Victor's best subject and most everyone else's worst, except maybe Luke, who'd always loved and excelled at Science.

Notes were spread out all over three tables that they had pushed together. Sugar Brown's felt more like a cozy living room than an actual shop, and Autumn's steaming cup of honeysuckle cider warmed her from the inside out. The comforting atmosphere wasn't enough, though, to soothe her pre-exam nerves.

Forrest threw his leaf quill forcefully onto the table. "I'm never going to get this!" he exclaimed in frustration.

"If Coach Holt would *teach* instead of read sports magazines all period maybe we would actually learn something," Autumn grumbled.

"It's really very simple," Victor said patiently. "You just have to mix a precise dose of uquarium with the rose extract before adding it to the mixture." He wrote out the formula for the Hydrating Salve they were studying, which was a substance elves put on dry skin or lips for hydration. Autumn thought of it as a sort of cross between lotion and lip balm.

"Obviously. Jeez. Y'all are acting like this is rocket science or something," Luke stated.

Autumn scowled at him.

The next day they met at Sugar Brown's again to go over Literature, which was Luke's *worst* subject. Now it was Autumn's turn to be slightly smug about her extensive knowledge on the written word. Luke glared moodily at her as she explained all of the detailed theories they'd gone over in class. She discussed the common theme of "forbidden love" in the three novels they'd read that semester.

Everyone seemed to understand Autumn's explanations and took copious amounts of notes. She even noticed Luke grudgingly pick up his leaf quill and scratch out a few pages. She read a few excerpts from each of the books and, as she read, her voice took on a sort of dreamy, rhythmic quality as it usually did when she read anything out loud. When she looked up, Avery was watching her read with a lopsided smile. As was Victor.

Autumn wrapped up her discussion and everyone began stuffing their notes and leaf quills into their satchels.

"We should do something this weekend since our finals are next week and we won't have any free time then," Charlotte suggested. "I think we've studied enough to deserve a little fun."

"How about ice skating on Arbor Lake?" Crystal said.

"Ice skating is boring," Cera complained. "We should play that Outsider ice game we learned in Sports."

"Hockey?" Luke clarified.

"Yeah, that," Cera said.

"How do elves know about hockey?" Autumn asked.

"Lots of adult elves go up to the Outside just to learn new things that they can bring down here," Jastin explained. "One of our coaches went up there specifically to learn some new sports. He learned that one for us to play during the winter months."

"They go up there to learn from Outsiders?" asked Autumn in surprise.

"Yeah," Crystal said. "My mom goes up there every couple of years to study all the clothing fashions that the Outsider's wear."

"How did we get from Sports to fashion?" Cera asked. "So hockey Saturday, then?"

They met up at Arbor Lake, which had completely frozen over, a few days later. Just to be on the safe side, though, Crystal reinforced the ice with another smooth layer on top.

"Good thinking, Crys," Luke said, pulling on a pair of ice skates that he'd borrowed from the Sports supplies closet. Forrest had originally asked to borrow them and was instantly refused. That's when they sent in "the prince" to ask again. Coach Holt had no problem with Luke taking ten pairs of ice skates for the weekend.

"I can't get away with things like that," Autumn had said when Luke was boasting about this.

"You don't have my natural persuasion skills and charisma," Luke had laughed.

After they all pulled on their ice skates, they split into two teams of five. Cera and Luke were appointed team captains.

"We need team names," Luke said.

"I call Petalsies!" Cera exclaimed.

"Petalsies?" Luke laughed.

"They are the meanest creatures in the Underground," Cera said seriously.

"Okay. We are the Dragon Slayers," Luke said in a growling voice.

"Pretentious much?" Cera muttered.

Luke picked Avery first, and Autumn glared at him for not picking her, his twin sister. Cera got Victor. Luke then picked Autumn, lucky for him. Cera picked Jastin. Luke chose Crystal. Cera picked Charlotte and then, of course, Luke's team was left with Kyndel, who did not seem at all pleased to be picked last.

Since Crystal was the quickest of the Dragon Slayers, she was appointed the goalie. Jastin was the goalie for the other team.

Luke had also managed to borrow ten hockey sticks and a puck from the Sports supplies. He passed a stick to everyone and they all moved onto the ice. As Autumn stepped onto the frozen lake, she tripped over a small rock on the edge of the lake and Avery caught her just before she hit the ice. She laughed as he pulled her smoothly to her feet, but quickly stopped when she spotted the look on Victor's face. The goalies took their places and the rest spaced out around the lake.

"Don't we need a referee?" Autumn asked.

"What's that?" Cera said.

"Someone who calls penalties on people who break the rules," answered Autumn.

"There are no rules today," Forrest said, grinning.

"Oh good," Autumn said sarcastically. The others laughed.

"Are we allowed to use Powers?" Crystal called from her goal, which was made up of two large rocks spaced evenly apart behind her.

"No, but we will anyway," Luke said with a laugh.

Autumn felt they were in for an interesting game seeing as how no one really knew all of the rules and there was no one to enforce them even if they did. It was basically a group of elves using their Powers and whatever means they had to get their puck into the goal.

As the game began, Autumn was immediately proven correct. Cera didn't even use her stick, but threw out her hand, using gravity to push the puck to Forrest. He passed it quickly to Charlotte who attempted to shoot it into the Dragon Slayers' goal. Crystal shot a jet of ice at the puck, knocking it away.

Charlotte scowled at the ice as the Dragon Slayers took possession of the puck. Luke shot a gust of wind at the puck, aiming it towards Avery, who lifted his hockey stick to shoot the puck into the other goal. Autumn aimed a stream of song at Jastin, a dazed look crossing his face as the puck shot right past him. The Dragon Slayers let out a cheer and Autumn and Luke high fived as Jastin shook his head, looking confused as to what had just happened.

"Keep your ears covered!" Cera shouted at Jastin.

"So I'm supposed to protect the goal with just my legs?" Jastin asked, irritated.

"Here." Victor tossed Jastin his earmuffs.

"Thanks," Jastin called, stuffing them quickly on his head.

The Petalsies were now in possession of the puck. Forrest

skated quickly towards the Dragon Slayers' goal, passing it to Cera who shot the puck forcefully at the goal. Crystal sent another jet of ice, but this time Victor melted the ice with a hot beam of light, allowing the puck to sail straight into the goal. The Petalsies let out a round of cheers and the Dragon Slayers were back in possession.

Autumn had never witnessed such a fast paced hockey game. It made Outsider hockey look like tee-ball, which was technically related to baseball, but she didn't know what little kid hockey was called. Tee-puck?

Autumn played more defense than offense, sending streams of song at random players on the other team. Though, she did manage to score one goal. It was an accident, but no one needed to know that.

Kyndel had proven Autumn wrong by scoring four goals on her own, skating expertly around the lake, even pulling off a double-helix or two.

After about another hour of playing, the Dragon Slayers and the Petalsies were tied 14-14. Before the game started, they had agreed to play to 15, so the next team to score would win it all.

Things were getting ugly. Cera tripped Kyndel, Luke rammed Forrest, and Charlotte surrounded Autumn in a thick column of fog so she couldn't see anything. Autumn attempted to skate out of it, but the fog moved with her.

She listened intently to the game around her, trying to decipher the sounds of people's voices and the scraping of the skates on the ice. Suddenly she heard a groan from Crystal and a resounding cheer. The fog around Autumn dissipated and she saw the Petalsies surrounding Victor, clapping him on the back and ruffling his perfect hair. He wore a wide grin on his face and Autumn assumed it was safe to say that he had just scored the winning goal.

Autumn and Avery couldn't help but exchange triumphant glances because this was another small step in the right direction with Victor. The rest of the Dragon Slayers, however, were not too pleased about their loss. Crystal and Luke grumbled to each other under their breath and Kyndel rolled her eyes at the other team, hands hitched up on her hips.

Everyone's faces were red and Autumn couldn't feel her fingers or toes. Victor told everyone to close their eyes and he shone a warming light over all of them. As everyone got ready to leave, Autumn heard Jastin and Forrest make arrangements with Victor to study Laboratory some more the next day. She smiled to herself.

Victor approached Autumn and pulled her into a warm hug.

"Congratulations on the win," she said happily.

Victor beamed and pressed his lips against Autumn's, taking her by surprise. She had to force herself not to pull away because she knew Avery was watching from five feet away. She was not just surprised by the suddenness of the kiss, but by the fact that Victor didn't usually kiss her in public. Even in private they rarely kissed.

They broke apart and Autumn tried her best to smile up at him, but she wasn't sure the smile reached her eyes. Whether Victor noticed this or not, he didn't comment and left soon after, talking with Jastin and Forrest on the way.

Taking a deep breath, Autumn turned to face Avery and the others. Avery's face was strangely blank, but his eyes were hard and trained on the ground. Luke and Crystal didn't seem to notice anything out of the ordinary and waited for her, looking glum about losing the hockey game.

Autumn, Crystal, and Avery helped Luke carry the hockey sticks and skates back up to the castle to keep until he could bring them back to the Sports coaches. Autumn and Avery kept silent the whole way there. Luke and Crystal complained about the obvious unfairness of their loss, though they had only lost by one point.

Autumn didn't even bother asking Avery what was wrong because she knew very well what was bothering him. It was bothering her too. They couldn't keep this up much longer or both of them were going to fall apart. Sometimes she wished she wasn't so empathetic towards people and that she could just focus on her own happiness, but helping people did make her happy. She couldn't explain the elation she had felt seeing everyone cheering for Victor and his big, goofy grin, when not long ago he was completely alone and rarely smiled.

When they reached the castle, Autumn frowned slightly as Avery simply said goodnight to her and continued to climb the stairs to his branch. She supposed she didn't blame him.

Dragging her feet all the way to her room, she pulled her Numbers notes out of her satchel. She knew that she was going to have the most trouble on this particular exam and Magister Monroe would show her no mercy. She worked and re-worked the equations until her eyes refused to focus on the numbers any more. She rested her head in her hands and then nearly fell off the bed when a loud THUMP resonated from her balcony followed by three knocks on her balcony door.

"Come in," she called.

Avery opened the door slowly then leaned back against it, looking somber.

"Avery, I—"

"No. You don't have to say anything. I knew what I was getting myself into when I told you how I felt."

She frowned up at him. He came to lie back on the bed beside her so that he was looking up at her, and she down at him.

"I'd rather have half of your heart than none at all," he said.

Autumn gave him a half smile. "You have more than half of my heart, Avery."

"You have all of mine," he replied.

Leaning down, she kissed him gently at first and then more deeply until they broke slowly apart. She laid her head on his chest and smiled to herself. She knew she should probably get back to studying her Numbers notes that were now strewn all over her floor, but the gentle rising and falling of Avery's chest was too peaceful for her to resist. So she stayed like this. At some point their breathing synced. They said nothing. Just lay there. Breathing in time with one another.

Jumping on the Bed

CHAPTER THIRTY-TWO

December is the best month, really, because it both wraps up the end of a year and introduces a new one. Plus, it has snow, hot chocolate, fire in the fireplace, and candy cane flavored everything. Well, the Underground didn't have candy canes, but it had peppermint. Not that they had time to enjoy any of that due to semester exams. Though, they were not as difficult as Autumn had expected. This was partly due to the fact that she and the rest of the Initiates had studied at least 80% more than the other students, and partly because the magisters had made them seem more difficult than they actually were.

The magisters look as relieved as Autumn felt when the exams were all over and done with, which was understandable. Autumn wouldn't want to deal with a bunch of unruly teenagers day in and day out either. She thought magisters probably had more challenging jobs than Warriors sometimes.

The Initiates said goodbye to Atticus, who'd given them most of the break off. They would start training again December 27th.

"I still expect you to train on your own," he called as they ran off of the practice field.

"Sure thing, Mr. A!" Forrest called back.

"Let's go to Sugar Brown's," Charlotte said cheerfully.

Everyone ordered a coffee or cider and took a seat in their normal corner talking excitedly about their plans for the break.

"We go visit my grandparents in Windy Meadows every

holiday," Forrest said, sounding less than enthusiastic.

"Is that another elf town?" asked Autumn.

The others nodded. "It's very small," Forrest said. "Like, you wouldn't even see it if you flew a pegasus right over it. And there is approximately nothing to do there."

"We never travel," Charlotte said glumly.

"My mom told me that she'd take me up to the Outside this Christmas to see their clothing styles. She's making a huge deal of it because it will be my first time in the Outside—well, that *she* is aware of," Crystal said, looking guilty.

Everyone laughed.

"So you have Christmas here?" Luke asked.

The others looked at him with raised eyebrows.

"What?" he said.

"Why wouldn't we have Christmas here?" Kyndel said.

"We assumed it was a Outsider holiday," Autumn said.

"You're forgetting that elves lived among Outsiders for many years before their disgusting actions forced us to relocate," Kyndel scoffed. "We've celebrated Christmas just as long as they have.

"When did the magical creatures come down here, anyway?" Luke asked.

"In the mid 1600s," Victor spoke up. "Elves had long since hidden their identities by using their magic to hide their pointed ears. They were tired of hiding their Powers just because Outsiders were too intimidated by them. The elves were the first to suggest the creation of the Underground to the warlocks and the witches. They agreed and, using their combined powers, created the Underground together with the help of the rest of the magical creatures. Some stayed behind, but most moved to the Underground for good."

"What do elves do on Christmas?" Autumn asked.

"Everyone has different traditions, just like in the Outside, but Arbor Falls has a big celebration on Christmas day with performers and food. Even the king attends," Crystal said.

"Except we don't call it a Christmas celebration because the king refuses to force any singular religious tradition on his kingdom," Jastin said. "We call it the Winter Festival."

"Undergrounders are religious?" Luke asked in surprise.

"Some are *very* religious," Charlotte answered. "The Underground has more religions than the Outside does."

"I'm Jewish!" Forrest exclaimed proudly, making everyone laugh.

"So, do we get presents during the Winter Festival?" Luke asked. Autumn shot him an exasperated look.

Crystal laughed. "Usually a gift is exchanged between family members. The king actually sends gifts to every family in Arbor Falls."

Autumn beamed at this, proud of her grandfather. Luke smiled too.

When everyone left Sugar Brown's, Victor walked with Autumn towards Arbor Castle. He told Luke, Crystal, and Avery to go ahead without them. Avery didn't seem all that happy with this, but followed Luke and Crystal anyway. Autumn looked questioningly up at Victor.

"I won't be seeing you for a little while, so I wanted to say goodbye."

"Why won't you be seeing me?" Autumn asked.

"I'm traveling for the holidays."

"Traveling? Alone?"

He nodded.

"Why don't you stay here? You can hang out with all of the Warriors. We're your family now."

Victor's expression became unreadable. "Yes, well, I have already made plans to travel," he stated, letting Autumn know that this was not up for debate.

Autumn frowned. She'd hoped that he would become even closer to the other Warriors during the break, but now he wouldn't even see them at all for a few weeks. She wondered why he was just now telling her this. Victor stopped walking.

"I'll see you on the first day of Warrior training," he said cupping her face in his hands and kissing her tenderly. "Goodbye, my Autumn."

She watched as he trudged off down the path, away from Arbor Castle.

"What was that about?" Luke asked as she joined them at the dinner table.

"He wanted to say goodbye to me," Autumn said, glancing at Avery, his eyebrows furrowing.

"Goodbye? Where's he going?" Crystal asked.

"He said that he is travelling for the holidays."

"Alone?" Luke said.

Autumn nodded. "He doesn't have any family or anything. I assume the holidays are pretty lonely for him."

"But he has the Warriors now," Avery said.

"I know, but he seems to have already made up his mind."

Avery frowned at the table. Autumn expected he was thinking the same thing she was. The more time Victor was away, the longer it would be until she could return his rose.

The next day Autumn and Luke were stunned to discover all of the tree houses in Arbor Falls covered in twinkling lights.

"They're fay fairies," Avery said, winking at Autumn, who blushed, remembering the last time she'd seen fay fairies.

"What are fay fairies?" Luke asked, raising an eyebrow at his sister's flushed cheeks.

Crystal explained fay fairies to Luke as Autumn glared playfully at Avery. He simply flashed her an amused grin.

"When have *you* seen fay fairies?" Luke asked Autumn when Crystal finished describing the glowing creatures.

Autumn looked at him with innocent eyes. "I haven't." He narrowed his eyes and she continued. "Avery told me that the lights in the castle are lit with fay light, which comes from fay fairies."

"Oh," Luke said, seeming satisfied with this answer.

"Well if Luke didn't suspect something before, he does now," Autumn said to Avery later that evening. He had brought his etherelle down to her branch so he could help her write a song to sing at the Winter Festival. The city council leaders had heard about her Power and asked her to perform. She had agreed, though reluctantly. Autumn had never been one to flaunt her talents, not that she had many before she came to the Underground. Atticus had taught her how to direct her singing at an inanimate object so her Power wouldn't hypnotize anyone too heavily. They would still feel some calming effects, but they wouldn't be paralyzed.

"Stop worrying about it, Autumn," Avery said as he experimented with a couple of melodies. He sat cross-legged on the floor with the etherelle in his lap and Autumn was perched on the foot of her bed watching him.

"Fine," she said with a sigh. "I like the way that one sounds," she said, indicating the melody he had just played.

He played it again and built on to it. Autumn grabbed a piece of paper and a leaf quill and started scribbling down the song that suddenly washed over her. They worked on the song until the sun started to fall and the sky filled with a warm, orange glow. Once it was all written, they played through it once, impressed with their work. Autumn made sure to incorporate the fay fairies into the song.

Avery didn't even look at his etherelle, keeping his eyes trained on Autumn as she sang. She had been aiming her song at the full-length mirror in the corner so as not to hypnotize Avery, but then decided to direct the notes straight at him. His hands slowly ceased playing the etherelle, his eyes glazing over. Autumn finished and laughed as he shook his head to clear it, smiling crookedly up at her.

"That feels sort of amazing."

"I know."

He set his etherelle aside and moved to the base of the bed, coming to stand in front of her.

"I think that's enough practicing," he said.

Autumn looked up at him, a coy smile dancing on her lips.

He put both hands on either side of her face and pulled her gently to him, their lips meeting and the gravitational pull taking over. She leaned back onto the bed and Avery moved with her so that he was hovering over her. His lips moved from her mouth to trail softly down her neck. Autumn let out a small gasp and felt Avery's lips curl up into a smile.

He moved back to her lips, kissing her tenderly, which was bliss, but left her wanting more. Wrapping her arms around him, she pulled him forcefully to her. He caught on and kissed her more hungrily, their breathing quickening. Her hands clawed into his back as she pulled him even closer so that they were pressed right up against each other.

Suddenly they heard a knock on the front door and the creak of it opening. Autumn and Avery froze.

"Rose?" Luke called from the living room.

She cursed under her breath and slid quickly out from under Avery.

"Get under the bed," she whispered.

"What?" Avery said.

"Under the bed!" she urged.

Avery chuckled, kissing her quickly on the lips and slipping under the bed. Right as she saw Avery's foot disappear, Luke ambled into her room. He paused, scanning the disarrayed room, Avery's etherelle on the floor, and the lyric papers that had spilled off the bed and were now littering the ground. Luke raised an eyebrow at her.

"What were you just doing?" he asked.

"What do you mean?" Autumn said, though her quick, shallow breathing gave her away.

"Your face is all red and you're breathing hard..."

She glanced at the reflection in her full-length mirror and saw her flushed cheeks and tangled hair.

"I was, uh, jumping on the bed," she said, forcing an embarrassed laugh.

"Why?"

She shrugged. "I was bored."

Luke scanned her messy floor, looking confused. "Why is Avery's guitar here?"

"He let me borrow it. I was writing a song."

"You can't play guitar."

"It's an etherelle."

"You can't play that either."

"I'm learning." She wished he would stop asking questions. "So, what's up? Did you need something?"

"I was going to tell you that Crystal and I are going to City Circle to eat and was going to see if you wanted to come."

"Oh, yeah, sure. I'll meet y'all downstairs in ten minutes," she said.

"Okay, well, I'm going to go ask Avery if he wants to come," he said, still looking suspicious.

"Sounds good," she said, smiling.

Autumn listened as Luke left her branch, closing the door behind him.

"You have to go up to your branch!" she said as Avery crawled out from under his hiding spot.

"Jumping on the bed?" Avery said with a sly grin.

"It was the first thing that came to my mind. Now go. Hurry!"

Avery laughed and kissed her once again before he bounded onto her balcony, springing up to his own. She took a deep breath and let it out slowly. That was close. Way too close.

An Underground Christmas

CHAPTER THIRTY-THREE

The next week was blissfully lazy. The Warriors who were still in town met up at Sugar Brown's or Cup O' Co every day and just hung out, talking about nothing in particular. They hadn't had this long of a break from training since they'd become Initiates and were taking full advantage of their free time.

On Monday, Crystal and her mom traveled up to the Outside for a few days to study Outsider clothing styles. Autumn gave Crystal a large portion of her remaining Outsider money for her to buy some things. She refused at first, but Autumn shoved it in her hand until she reluctantly accepted. Autumn also asked her to stop by Mrs. King's house to retrieve something for Olympus for Christmas.

On the day before Christmas Eve, it snowed a couple feet and the seven Initiates still remaining in Arbor Falls decided to go sledding, or what elves called "leafing." They picked the oversized leaves off of an elephant ear plant and rode them down the steep hills that surrounded the city.

"Aren't these tropical plants?" Autumn asked.

"In the Outside, maybe," Cera said.

"All plants are able to grow anywhere here," Jastin clarified.

They spent the day leafing and rolling snowballs down the hills. Kyndel even managed to go the whole day without insulting Autumn, a real Christmas miracle.

Olympus had arranged to spend Christmas Eve with Autumn

and Luke. They met him in his dining quarters for dinner, which was a spread unlike any she'd ever seen. Every dish imaginable was on the table before them. He'd even asked the chefs to prepare Outsider recipes from Texas like sweet potatoes with marshmallows on top, cornbread stuffing, and green bean casserole. The three of them talked and laughed as they ate their way through the feast.

"So, my young Warriors," Olympus said, "how is training coming?"

"Really well," Autumn said.

"Yeah, we're getting pretty strong," Luke boasted, showing off his growing biceps.

Olympus chuckled. "Are you prepared for the Warrior Trial in January?"

They frowned. "I think so," Autumn said, unsure.

"We'll be okay," Luke assured her.

"I'm sure you will." Olympus smiled. "I always thought your father would have made an exceptional Warrior."

"Was the Test not during his senior year?" Luke asked.

"No, it was, actually. He simply thought he was not meant to be a Warrior—or king for that matter. He wanted to explore the Outside, where he went to college and met your mother," Olympus said, eyes sparkling.

"Why didn't they ever tell us about The Underground?" Autumn asked. She had wanted to ask Olympus this question for a long time now.

"I believe your father knew how dangerous this world can be for a royal elf. He wanted to protect you."

"By lying to us?" Luke said.

"By...omitting information," Olympus said.

"Same thing," Luke muttered.

"Luke, I know you are angry with your father for hiding your heritage from you, but everything he did was because he loved you."

"Yeah, look what happened to him and mom," Autumn said. "He knew Vyra would try to come after us if we ever came here."

"She came after us anyway!" Luke exclaimed. "And now they're dead. At least here, they would've had protection. Warriors and

Powers."

"Luke," Olympus said, "you need to let go of your anger. It is only hurting you."

"You sound like Autumn," Luke grumbled.

Olympus laughed at this. "Autumn is right."

Luke rolled his eyes. That wasn't going to cheer him up.

"How about I give you your gifts now," Olympus suggested.

Luke perked up at this. "Gifts?"

"It *is* Christmas, after all."

He stood and beckoned for them to follow him to his private library. He moved to the balcony doors at the rear of the grand library and pulled them open. Standing there, regally still, were two pegasus ponies. One a brilliant white and the other a sleek ebony. Oversized feathered wings protruded from their backs. Autumn was unable to repress her squeal of excitement.

"Are they ours?" she asked.

Olympus nodded, smiling widely.

She rushed over to the white pegasus and ran her hand across its smooth body. Luke was beside her, scratching the black one behind its ear.

"What are they?" Luke asked Olympus. "I mean boys or girls?"

"The black pegasus is male, and the white, female."

"Excellent." Luke grinned, apparently forgetting his anger about their father.

Autumn's pegasus rubbed fondly against her leg and Luke's nipped playfully at his fingers. "Whose is whose?" she asked.

"It would appear they've already chosen their owners," Olympus said. "What will you be calling them?"

"Thunder," Luke said. "You know, cause of my Power, and he's all dark like thunder."

Autumn laughed. "Thunder doesn't look like anything, it's a sound."

"Yes, but the storm clouds are dark," Luke retorted. "What're you naming yours then?"

Autumn frowned, thinking and then remembered flying with Avery as the sunrise broke over the horizon. "Sundance," she said decidedly. Luke snorted. "What's wrong with Sundance?"

"Nothing," he said innocently.

Autumn glared at him and said, "At least I didn't name her *Lightning* or something."

"You're just jealous that your pegasus doesn't have an awesome, intimidating name."

"I find both of them quite fitting," Olympus stepped in and said.

"Oh! I forgot to give you your present," Autumn said.

Olympus smiled. "Surely your presence is present enough."

"It's nothing big," she replied, leaving the room and retrieving Olympus's gift from the dining room. She hurried back into the library and handed him the package.

"It's from Luke too," Autumn said.

Olympus looked as if he was about to well up, but simply cleared his throat roughly and slowly unwrapped the package to reveal a leather bound photo album. He opened it gingerly and flipped through the pages. It was a photo album Autumn had of them from when they were kids all the way up to a few years prior.

"You cannot know how special this is to me," Olympus said, smiling. He wrapped them into a tight hug. She pulled back, wiping her eyes quickly. Luke even looked like he was trying to hold himself together. "Thank you," Olympus said gruffly.

"Thanks for our gifts too," Autumn said.

"Yeah, they're amazing," Luke agreed.

"Speaking of your gifts, I think it is time that they got back to their stables. They are too small to ride, but they will meet you there if you call them."

Autumn and Luke thanked Olympus again, hugging him once more. They hurried out of the castle and around to the stables. They both called out their names and were pleasantly surprised with how quickly the little pegasi arrived at the stables.

"They seem to fly pretty well," Luke said, ruffling Thunder's mane. "Wonder when we'll be able to ride them."

"I'll ask Avery," Autumn said.

"Why him?" Luke said.

"He has a pegasus too. Right there," Autumn said, pointing to Knight's stall.

"How did you know that?" Luke asked.

"He told me."

"How did you know that one was his?"

Autumn frowned. She supposed she wouldn't know that if he'd simply told her. "He told me he had a gray pegasus."

"That one is gray too," he pointed at another pegasus a few stalls away from Knight.

"Well that one is a light gray, Avery told me that Knight is dark gray. Let's put them up now, they look hungry." She couldn't say she cared for how many questions Luke had been asking about her and Avery lately.

They moved Thunder and Sundance into the same stall since they were so small that they would still have plenty of room. They made sure they had enough hay and promised to come visit them tomorrow. Then the winged ponies curled up next to each other and fell instantly asleep.

After they returned to the castle and Autumn had left Luke at his branch, she walked into her own with a wistful smile on her face. She hadn't had such a happy Christmas in a long time. As she entered her room she saw Avery's etherelle propped up against the wall. He had yet to retrieve it since their close call with Luke. She picked it up, leaving her branch and climbing the short way up to Avery's. She was sure he and his mother wouldn't mind if she just dropped it off really quickly and then she would have the chance to tell Avery about Sundance.

Autumn knocked a few times on the front door and waited. She was about to leave when she heard yelling coming from inside. Leaning a little closer to the door, she listened intently. Suddenly, a loud crash met her ears and Autumn hastily opened the door.

She froze, her mouth dropping open at the scene before her.

Avery was restraining his frail mother, who was thrashing about, trying to release herself from his grasp. Glass glittered on the floor. His mother's foot was bleeding profusely, but she didn't seem to care.

"Avabelle? Avabelle! Come back! John, help her! John! Please someone help my baby! Avery, why aren't you helping her? Avabelle!" she sobbed.

Avery's face was contorted in misery.

"Mom, stop. You're stepping on the glass," he said in a dead voice.

Autumn could tell that he was trying not to hold too tight. She looked so emaciated that she could easily break in half with too much pressure.

"My baby! It's hurting her, please! Help her! Help her, John! Avery!" his mother continued sobbing.

Autumn stood paralyzed in the doorway, the etherelle still clutched tightly in her hands. Suddenly Avery's mother thrashed towards the door. Avery's eyes widened as he took in her frozen stance and his expression turned angry.

His mother reached for Autumn. "Please help my baby—my baby, Avabelle, please."

Autumn moved back a few steps in shock. "I—I..."

"Get out, Autumn!" Avery shouted.

"I'm sorry, I didn't—"

"Get out!"

She stumbled backwards, stung by his angry tone, pulling the door shut behind her and moving quickly down the stairs back to her branch. She walked numbly through the living room and dropped the etherelle onto her bed, where she sat in silence, eyes staring into space as she attempted to process everything that just happened.

Avery had always been quiet about his family, but Autumn had just figured it was because it was too painful to talk about his father and sister's deaths. She never even really thought about his mother. Now that she thought back, he *had* said that she was always in bed.

A familiar THUMP coming from her balcony pulled her from her thoughts. Autumn faced her balcony doors. The curtains were open, but all she could see was her reflection as she sat, wide-eyed, on the edge of her bed. The balcony doors slammed open to reveal Avery standing hunched over like his chest was too heavy to hold upright. His face was twisted with despair and his eyes looked empty. Autumn left her bed and approached him cautiously.

He looked up at her with a tortured expression and she could see all the pain he'd been hiding for so long in his stormy, gray eyes. She wrapped her arms tightly around him, and he collapsed to the floor sobbing, taking her with him. His shoulders shook and his tight hold around her was almost bone crushing. The frigid air from outside poured into the room, but Autumn didn't care. In that moment, she didn't care about anything except the boy in her arms.

She'd been so busy trying to help Victor that she hadn't realized the one who really needed her help and support...was Avery. She held him as tightly as she could, letting him break down. Warm tears spilled over her cheeks as she embraced him and, for once, the magnetic pull between them didn't feel pleasant, but painful. Autumn literally hurt with him.

AVERY's breathing evened out after a while and he wasn't sobbing anymore, just trembling. Autumn didn't let go until he leaned slowly back from her. He was surprised that he didn't feel more embarrassed for breaking down like that. If anything, he felt a calming sense of relief. He stood to shut the balcony doors and moved to Autumn's bed. She watched him from the floor and he patted the bed beside him.

Autumn moved to the bed, keeping her eyes trained on his face. He gave her a small smile, taking her hand with both of his and trailing his fingers across her palm. She was the most solid thing in his life. The most real thing. But also the most unreal. He had never thought of himself as lucky before, not with everything that had happened. But, with her, all of that disappeared and all he saw was her. So, he took a deep breath and told the story he swore he never would.

"After my father died, Avabelle and I were all my mom had," Avery said. "She leaned on us for support and we let her. She's a very caring woman, but she's not very strong. My father was the strong one, and she leaned on him until he passed away. She was terrified of losing us, so she kept us close. We always had a curfew and we had to tell her where we were going before we went anywhere. We told her that she was being paranoid, but then Avabelle was killed." Autumn squeezed his hand.

"When Avabelle died, my mom sort of...went away. She didn't talk to me or anyone else. She wouldn't eat and she lay in bed all day. I was afraid I was going to lose her too, but she eventually began eating again. She started talking to me too, but always in a monotonous voice. She still lies in bed all day, but she does eat enough to survive. Sometimes she has fits like the one you just witnessed. I don't know what triggers it, but she will just start screaming and crying and calling for my sister. She will yell for me to help her or for my dad."

"John?" Autumn asked.

Avery nodded. "I can't stand when she gets like that. Sometimes I think maybe I'm the one who triggers it because I'm always around when it happens. Maybe it's because I'm Avabelle's twin. I don't know. So I try to stay away as much as I can. I don't want her to be in more pain than she already is."

"I don't think your presence causes her pain, Avery," Autumn said. "Maybe she only breaks down when you're around because she knows you'll be there to help put her back together."

Avery quirked a small smile at this and kissed Autumn's hand, which was still clasped in his.

"What's your mom's Power?" Autumn asked.

"She's a Dream Communicator. That's how she talks to me sometimes."

"A Dream Communicator?" Autumn said looking deep in thought.

"Yes, why?"

Avery watched as realization lit Autumn's face and her lips turned up into a small smile. "That's why..." she trailed off.

"Why what?"

She looked at Avery with her bright hazel eyes. "That's why you were in my dreams before—in the Outside. Your mother must have been thinking about you while she was trying to communicate with me."

"You dreamt about me before you came here?" Avery asked with a wry smile.

Autumn laughed. "It would appear that I did, but don't be getting a big head or anything."

Avery chuckled. He felt light. The weight on his chest was gone. He lay back on the pillows that covered the bed and closed his eyes in exhaustion. He felt Autumn lay silently beside him and he pulled her to him so that she was nestled against his chest. He tried not to hold onto her too tight, but he couldn't help but worry that somehow...she would disappear too.

Back to Square One

CHAPTER THIRTY-FOUR

A bright ray of sunshine fell across Autumn's face and she opened her eyes groggily and looked up to see Avery smiling crookedly at her. She sat up and looked around.

"Is it morning?" Autumn asked. Avery nodded. "Did you sleep here?" He nodded again. "We have the Winter Festival today. I'm supposed to sing," she realized, glancing at the grandfather clock. It was eight in the morning. The celebration started at nine. "Oh man." Autumn jumped out of bed and headed to her bathroom to take a shower, and then looked back at Avery who was still lounging on her bed.

"I'll go," he said reluctantly. "I'll see you at the celebration. Better take this," he said, grabbing his etherelle, which was still at the foot of the bed where Autumn had left it last night. He kissed her on the cheek and left through her balcony doors. She watched him go with a lopsided smile, and a jolt of realization coursed through her. She was starting to fall for this boy...if she hadn't already.

Luckily, she made it to the Winter Festival on time. It certainly wouldn't have looked good for the Princess of Arbor Falls to arrive late. She was the last performer and sang her newly written song to the crowd that had gathered around City Circle. Avery played his etherelle beside her as she sang. They didn't speak of what she'd witnessed the previous night or of anything he told her. She figured that talking about it, though, had helped him in some way. He seemed much lighter, his gray eyes clearer.

After hours of dancing, eating, and laughing till tears were rolling down their cheeks, Luke, Avery, Crystal and Autumn walked back to Arbor Castle.

"Oh, I need to check on Sundance," Autumn said.

"Who's Sundance?" Avery asked.

"Her pegasus, dude. Where have you been?" Luke said.

Avery grinned at Autumn and she blushed, looking at the ground. She wondered what Luke would think if he knew exactly *where* Avery had been.

"I don't know. Autumn never tells me anything," Avery said.

"I know the feeling," Luke said, shooting a weary look in her direction.

"Did you get a pegasus too?" Avery asked Luke.

"Yeah! He's all shiny and black. He's going to be a beast."

"Bet he can't beat Knight in a race," Avery taunted.

"You wish, dude! Wait till Thunder grows up. He's definitely going to live up to his name."

"Like he has a choice," Autumn muttered.

Crystal giggled.

Autumn and Luke let Thunder and Sundance out of their stall so they could stretch their legs. The ponies ran clumsily around the stables, their frail wings flapping in the wind. Autumn laughed as she watched them, and Avery let Knight out of his stall.

"Man, I can't wait until Thunder's this big. I want to fly already," Luke said, running a hand along Knight's smooth coat.

"You can fly Knight if you want," Avery offered. "He knows where to go. You won't have to lead him or anything."

An excited smile spread across Luke's face. "Really?"

Avery nodded, chuckling.

Luke swung onto Knight's back like Autumn had the night Avery took her to Fay Fairy Forest.

"I'm from Texas," Luke stated, an answer to Crystal's questioning gaze.

Autumn and Avery burst out laughing, causing Crystal and Luke to shoot them bemused looks.

"Why don't you go with him, Crys?" suggested Autumn.

"I hate heights," Crystal said.

"There's nothing scary about heights. Just come with me, Crys," Luke encouraged. "I'm your partner. Don't you trust me?"

Crystal looked a little pale, but she eventually agreed. Luke pulled her easily onto Knight's back and she clung to Luke tightly, looking even paler than she had before.

"Be gentle with them," Avery said, patting Knight's snout fondly. Knight blinked his intelligent eyes and took off into the air. Crystal let out a small squeal. Autumn laughed, watching them soar higher.

She and Avery leaned against the stable wall as they watched Knight soar slowly around Arbor Castle, and the two pegasus ponies chasing each other around the grounds. Autumn smiled happily as she watched them play. She felt Avery's eyes on her and she gave him a sidelong glance.

"What?" she asked.

He sighed and shook his head.

Autumn turned back to watch Thunder and Sundance prance playfully around.

"I haven't thanked you for last night," Avery said. "I needed that, I think."

"I think you did too," Autumn said. "And there's no need to thank me. I'm here whenever you need me, Avery. Day or night."

"I know," he said, gazing unseeingly at Thunder and Sundance.

Avery moved a few inches to the right so that he was pressed up against Autumn's left side, satisfying the magnetic pull for the moment. They both jumped when Knight landed a few feet away.

Luke let out a whoop as he jumped off of Knight's back. "That was insane," he exclaimed and then turned to Thunder calling, "You better do some growing up, boy!" Crystal was still clinging to Knight with shaking hands. "Oh. Sorry, Crys," Luke said as he lifted her from Knight's back.

"Are you considering investing in a pegasus, Crystal?" Autumn jested.

Crystal stumbled a little as Luke set her on solid ground. Her face was still a chalky white and she simply shook her head from side to side in answer to Autumn's question. The others laughed at this. Luke herded Thunder and Sundance back into their stalls and the four of them left for the castle.

"Better sleep in late tomorrow. It's our last day before Warrior training starts again," Avery said wearily. Luke, Crystal, and Autumn groaned.

Monday morning Autumn, Luke, Crystal, and Avery left for the Warrior training field on campus. Forrest, Cera, Jastin, and Charlotte were already there, and Kyndel arrived shortly after. Atticus showed up a few minutes before they were scheduled to start.

"Have a good break, everyone?" he said cheerfully. They nodded in unison, too tired to reply with any enthusiasm. "Did you get some practice in?" he asked, arching an eyebrow.

Everyone exchanged uncomfortable glances, saying nothing.

"Ah, well, today should prove to be exceptionally difficult, then," Atticus said, still sounding cheerful.

Autumn spotted Victor approaching the group from a distance. There was something different about him; his shoulders hunched forward and he wore a scowl on his face. The others turned to welcome him, shouting greetings.

"Hey, Victor!" Forrest said.

"How've you been, man?" Jastin called.

Victor said nothing, but gave a small nod of his head in acknowledgement. Forrest and Jastin's faces fell slightly at this. Autumn and Avery exchanged worried looks.

"Well, now that everyone's here, we'll get started," Atticus said.

Victor glanced at Autumn and she gave him a questioning look. He immediately turned away. Her stomach sank as she was immediately and painfully reminded of the old Victor. His eyes were closed off and his stance was defensive, more so than ever before. Any progress she and Avery had made before the break had apparently disappeared. Avery seemed to be thinking along the same lines because he wore a weary look. Autumn shook her head sadly as they followed Atticus to the center of the field.

With the Warrior Trial looming over them, the Initiates were pushed to the limit. Atticus insisted the harder they worked, the easier the Trial would be. This was by far the most difficult training session they'd had yet, and Autumn had a feeling they were only going to get worse.

Atticus set a number of obstacle courses throughout the campus. The finale of the day was Shadows. Somehow Atticus had convinced the Tetra Warriors to capture five Shadows for the Initiate's training session.

"What do we do with them?" Charlotte asked, eyeing the rope-bound Shadows warily.

"Kill them," Atticus stated.

Everyone's eyes widened, except for Victor, who looked stonily at the ground.

"What?" Kyndel said, an edge of hysteria in her voice.

"You heard me," Atticus said.

"Can we use bow and arrows?" Forrest asked.

Atticus shook his head. "Too easy."

The ten Initiates stared at the struggling Shadows in horror. They'd done a lot of training over the past few months and had been taught countless techniques to aid them in killing a Shadow, but never had they had to fight a real one. Autumn's encounter with the Shadow near Steam Springs was still fresh in her mind. At least she knew she could handle herself—and she hadn't even had her Power then. Avery looked ready as well. He glared at the Shadows with narrow eyes, full of hate. They were, after all, the creatures that killed Avabelle.

Atticus spaced the Initiates out so that they had room to fight. He asked Autumn to paralyze all five Shadows with Song. She obeyed and Atticus went around removing each of the ropes that had been binding them. None of the creatures moved. The others stared up at the Shadows with expressions of fear and determination.

Atticus made eye contact with Autumn and made a short, slashing motion through the air, indicating that she should stop singing. She did and all five Shadows silently zoned in on the Initiates.

Autumn immediately focused on her and Avery's Shadow, which was pawing at the ground with his hooves, horned head tilted downward as if about to charge.

Autumn shot a blast of song in the Shadow's face as Avery sprinted forward, leaping onto its chest. Taking a hold of its ram-like horns, he jerked the Shadow's head quickly to the right, effectively breaking its neck as easy as if it were a small twig. The Shadow crumpled to the ground. Autumn stared at it with wide eyes, impressed with the ease they'd had at destroying it—and also a little horrified.

"Well done," Atticus said as he passed by. Autumn looked down at the body of the Shadow, a small frown on her face.

"What's wrong?" Avery asked as Atticus moved on to observe the other partners who were still fighting their Shadows.

"I've never killed anything before," she said.

"Technically I did the killing. You just made it possible for me to approach it without getting rammed." Avery chuckled. Autumn didn't smile at this, but flinched slightly. "They don't have souls, Autumn. They shouldn't even be alive," he said, more serious now.

She raised her eyebrows at this. "How can you know that?"

"They were created by Vyra, made from her own blood. No creature created by an Atrum like Vyra is going to have a soul. And, if it did, it wouldn't be a soul worth saving."

"How did she do that?" Autumn asked in disgust.

"No one really knows. Some say that she's enlisted the help of a warlock, but we can't be sure."

A whoop of celebration resounded to their right and Autumn turned to see that Luke and Crystal had successfully brought their Shadow down as well.

Autumn's eyes moved to Cera as she pressed her Shadow down with Gravity and Forrest managed to stab the creature in the heart. Charlotte and Jastin had a little more trouble with keeping the Shadow in one place. Charlotte covered it in a thick fog and Jastin closed his eyes in concentration as he tried to mentally reach the Shadow so he could cause it pain. The Shadow seemed to be resisting this pain, but finally it stayed still long enough for Charlotte to kill it.

Kyndel and Victor were the only partners left. Victor covered the Shadow in a blinding light and Autumn assumed Kyndel was trying to find a way to bring the Shadow down, without being blinded herself. After another couple of minutes, the Shadow crashed to the ground.

Atticus clapped his hands. "Well done, everyone, well done! I must say that I'm quite impressed with your performances. You'll be allowed a bow and arrow during the Warrior Trial, making it much easier to fight them, though I think it's safe to say that you won't be dealing with just one. Now, go get something to eat and get some rest. I'll see you all tomorrow."

Autumn saw Victor exiting the field in the direction of the path towards his tree house. She sighed in exasperation and hurried to catch up to him, calling his name a few times before he stopped, looking wary.

"Hey," she said, sounding awkward even to herself.

"Hi."

"How was your break?" she asked, trying to sound cheerful.

"Fine."

"Nothing bad happened or anything?"

"No."

"You seem upset," she said. Victor said nothing so Autumn continued, "Well, I think all of us are going to grab a bite to eat in City Circle if you want to—"

"No, thanks," Victor interrupted.

She looked up at him, taken aback. "Okay..."

"I'll see you tomorrow, Autumn," he said, not even bothering to kiss her on the forehead like he usually did. He turned and stalked down the path towards his lonely tree house.

"Ugh!" Autumn exclaimed in frustration.

"Really now?" Luke said from behind her.

Crystal and Avery flanked either side of him. Avery wore a concerned expression. Autumn turned and began walking, brows furrowed. They informed her that they were meeting the others at Pasta Café in City Circle. She grunted in acknowledgement.

"What's wrong, Autumn?" Crystal asked.

"Nothing," she muttered.

Crystal and Luke decided to drop the subject and began talking enthusiastically about their quick defeat of the Shadow. Autumn and Avery slowed a little so that they were walking a few feet behind the others.

"What's wrong with Victor?" Avery asked under his breath.

"Who knows," she said angrily. "He won't tell me anything. I invited him to come eat with us and he said 'no' before I even finished my sentence."

"Obviously something made him act like this. I wonder what happened during the break," Avery said.

"I don't know, but I'm starting to get really frustrated."

"Well, maybe we should—" Avery began, but then stopped when he saw Autumn glaring at him. "Never mind."

Rose Returned

CHAPTER THIRTY-FIVE

As the days went by, Autumn and Avery weren't the only ones who noticed Victor's altered personality. One day after Warrior training Forrest and Jastin approached Autumn, looking concerned.

"Hey, Fall, what's up with your boyfriend?" Forrest asked. "We just asked him to come shoot some arrows with us and he blew us off."

"He seems troubled," Jastin added.

Autumn shrugged helplessly. "I really don't know, guys. He's been like this since the break. Maybe he'll go back to normal when school starts again."

On the first day back to school, though, Victor looked moodier than ever. He continued to walk Autumn to classes, but stayed silent the whole time and only grunted in response to her desperate attempts to start a conversation.

In Coach Holt's class, he completed the entire assignment without speaking to Autumn once. When Victor refused to hang out with the rest of the Initiates on Saturday, Autumn decided she'd stayed quiet for too long.

She waited under a gray, cloud-covered sky for the rest of the Initiates to leave the training field before confronting him.

"What's your problem, Victor?" she called after him before he could disappear again.

"What?" he said, turning around slowly.

"You leave for winter break and come back a completely

different person. You won't say more than two words to me at a time, you constantly have a scowl on your face, and you refuse to hang out with any of your friends!"

"They aren't my friends."

Autumn gaped up at him, thunderstruck. "What?"

"*They are not my friends,*" Victor said again, enunciating each syllable.

"They were before you left."

Victor said nothing, but looked at her with black eyes, only a thin ring of green visible in them. Autumn took a step back from him.

"I am no different from the elf you first met," Victor said.

"True, but you're different from the elf you had become...and I liked him much more," Autumn said, turning on her heel and leaving Victor to stare after her.

She walked straight back to Arbor Castle, not feeling like meeting up with the others at that moment. Halfway to the castle it started to rain. Big drops fell on her head in splashes and she ran the rest of the way to avoid getting soaked. She made it through the large, double oak doors just as it began to pour. The rain was freezing and Autumn hurried up to her branch to light a fire in the hearth.

Sighing, she sat back moodily in her oversized armchair near the fire. She couldn't take much more of this with Victor after putting everything she had into helping him and it hadn't made any sort of a difference whatsoever. Then a THUMP resounded from her balcony and she grudgingly traveled to her room.

Avery opened her balcony doors, dripping wet from the deluge. He moved towards Autumn and grabbed her face in his hands, pressing his lips greedily to hers. He pulled away slowly, leaving her gasping for breath.

"Hi," she breathed.

"Hi," he said as he smiled warmly down at her. When he saw her downcast expression, his face fell. "What's wrong?"

Autumn looked at the ground and said, "Nothing."

Placing two fingers under her chin, he lifted her face until she met his gaze. "What is it?"

"Victor."

Avery shook his head. "Of course it is."

"I just don't know what to do anymore," she said.

"Why do you even have to do *anything*?" Avery stated, closing her balcony doors.

She shot him an irritated glare. "I've already told you—"

"Yes, I know. You want to help him because he's all alone," he said. "But have you ever thought that maybe he *wants* to be alone? That maybe he doesn't want any friends?"

"Why would anyone want that?"

"It's in his blood, Autumn. Atrums don't keep friends. They like being alone."

Autumn shook her head at him in exasperation. "I don't care if he's an Atrum. No one deserves to be alone."

Avery raised his hands in surrender. "I can't do this right now." He threw the balcony doors open again and stormed back out into the rain.

Autumn followed him, the rain immediately soaking her. "So, you're just going to give up?"

"Yes! I can't help someone who doesn't want to be helped. You can't help everyone."

"I can try," Autumn said.

"You drive me crazy sometimes!" Avery proclaimed.

"If I drive you so crazy then why the hell are you with me? Why don't you just give up on me too?" demanded Autumn.

"Because I love you too damn much!" he shouted over the rain.

She froze and stared at him open mouthed. He looked at the ground.

"What did you just say?"

"I said I love you too much," Avery repeated looking up at her through his wet lashes.

Autumn took a deep, shaky breath and strode up to him, grasping his face in her hands and pulling his lips to hers. They were warm compared to the freezing rain that was still pouring relentlessly down. He kissed her hungrily, not seeming to care about the fact that they were both shaking from the cold. As Avery caressed Autumn's lips with his she had a revelation. *This* was what she wanted. All that she wanted. How could she stay with Victor when Avery was the one who loved her. The one *she* loved.

She couldn't. She couldn't stay with Victor.

Autumn pulled back slowly. "I can't do this anymore," she said. Avery stepped back, with a hurt look on his face. "I mean with Victor," Autumn said, causing Avery to sigh in relief. "I can't be with him, not when I'm in love with someone else."

"I hope you're talking about me," Avery said, smiling that crooked smile that made Autumn's heart skip a beat.

"I just wanted to help him," she said, feeling warm tears fill her eyes and spill hotly down her frozen cheeks. Avery pulled her back inside, closing the balcony doors behind him.

"Some people are beyond help," he said, wiping her tears away with his thumbs. Autumn nodded, knowing he was right. "We're soaking your floor," he noted, looking at the rug on which they were standing, now covered in water. Autumn retrieved a couple of towels from her bathroom and moved to her living room to dry in front of the fire. She stared blankly at the flickering flames with feelings of elation and failure battling against one another.

"What're you going to do?" Avery asked.

"I'm going to return his rose."

Autumn woke the next morning with a light feeling in her chest. Avery had told her he loved her last night. She smiled widely as she rolled out of bed and then her face fell as her eyes landed on the vanity sitting against the wall. Approaching it slowly, she carefully pulled one of the drawers open. Autumn lifted Victor's red rose from its hiding place and rolled it between her index finger and thumb, spinning the bud slowly. Somehow it was still perfectly fresh and whole. She supposed binding roses had some sort of magic within them that kept them whole as long as the relationship was intact. She wondered what would happen once she handed it back to him and shuddered at the idea.

She couldn't help but think that she was going to be hurting Victor, then she thought back on the previous week. Maybe she wouldn't be hurting him. He didn't seem all that concerned with talking to her. Perhaps he would even be relieved to be rid of her so he could climb back into his comfortable hole of solitude.

Approaching the miniature red Message Tree in her living room, Autumn picked up one of the acorns from its branches.

With shaking hands, she opened the top of the acorn and spoke into the empty shell.

"Victor, it's Autumn. Meet me in the clearing in the woods, east of Arbor Castle at 5:00pm today." She then recited his address and popped the acorn into the hollow tree. She took a deep breath and let it out slowly, hoping he got the message.

When she met the others in the dining room for breakfast they immediately sensed that something was wrong, casting worried looks her way.

"What is it, Rose?" Luke asked gently, something extremely out of character for him.

Autumn raised an eyebrow at him. "Do I really look that bad?"

"You're very pale," Crystal noted, looking concerned.

Autumn hesitated and glanced over at Avery, wondering if she should tell them about Victor. They would find out eventually, so she figured she might as well.

"I'm, um, returning Victor's rose today," Autumn said, looking at her lap.

Crystal's eyes widened and Luke's brow furrowed.

"Why?" Luke asked, glancing suspiciously at Avery, who was pretending to be hearing this for the first time as well.

"Have you not seen how he's been acting lately?" Autumn said.

"Yeah." Crystal nodded. "He's back to how he was before, all quiet and everything, but now he also looks angry all of the time too."

"I haven't noticed," Luke admitted.

"That's because you only notice female elves. Victor isn't in that category," Autumn said.

Luke chuckled, saying, "I guess you aren't too upset if you still have it in you to scold me for being the ladies' man I am."

Autumn snorted at this, rolling her eyes.

"How do you think he's going to take it?" Crystal asked.

"I doubt he'll be too crushed or anything. He's barely spoken to me all week."

"He should be happy to be a free man," Luke said through a mouthful of eggs. "What kind of a Warrior would want to be tied down to just one girl when he has the chance to be with a new one every day?"

Avery laughed at this, winking at Autumn when the other two weren't looking.

Autumn stood on her balcony, leaning against the railing as she waited for 5:00pm to arrive. Looking out at the thick green forest she was reminded of Victor's perfect, emerald eyes. Many would call her crazy to break up with someone so unbelievably beautiful, but Victor was the prime example of the phrase "looks aren't everything."

Without warning, Avery leapt over his balcony railing, landing loudly behind Autumn, causing her to jump. She punched him on the arm in frustration and he laughed heartily.

"You have to warn me before you do that," she scolded. He wrapped his arms around her waist.

"Sorry," he said, kissing her softly. She breathed him in, smelling that familiar woodsy smell that she associated with him.

"You're forgiven," Autumn said as she turned back to face the forest.

"Are you nervous?" he asked.

"Sort of."

"Do you want me to wait for you here?" he asked.

"If you want to," Autumn said, not wanting him to think that she couldn't handle something like this.

"You don't have to be so strong all of the time, Autumn," he whispered in her ear.

"I know, but I don't know how else to be," Autumn said. Ever since her parents' deaths, she'd had her guard up towards everyone, feigning strength. The alternative was to simply fall apart.

Avery wrapped her in a tight hug and she sank into him.

"I don't want to hurt him," Autumn muttered into his chest.

"I know," he said soothingly. "But you've done everything you could for him. It's time for *you* to be happy. Think about yourself for once."

"Can I just think about you?" Autumn said with a small smile.

Avery chuckled. "That works too. As long as it makes you happy."

"It does." She smiled, leaning up and kissing him deeply. "I better go." Avery sighed, but released her. "I'll be back soon."

He followed her through her room and into the living area.

"Aren't you forgetting something?" he said. Autumn turned to him, arching an eyebrow in question. "The rose…"

"Oh!" she exclaimed, smacking herself in the forehead before traveling back into her room, snatching the rose out of the vanity.

"Good luck," Avery said.

She blew him a quick kiss and hurried out the door, nerves beginning to overtake her as she rushed down the spiral staircase of the castle and out the double oak doors. She placed the rose in the inside pocket of her coat so that it wasn't the first thing Victor would see. Autumn wanted him to hear her out first. As she approached the designated clearing in the forest, she shoved her hands into her pockets to keep them from shaking.

She ran through her rehearsed speech in her head again as she ambled through the thick trees and jumped when she saw that Victor was already waiting for her. It was clear he was upset about something as he paced back and forth, muttering under his breath, hands clenched in fists by his side.

"Um, Victor?" Autumn said.

He stopped pacing abruptly and looked at her with black eyes. She'd never seen him look so angry before. He was practically shaking with rage.

Victor said nothing as Autumn cleared her throat to begin speaking. She walked past him so that they weren't face to face. She knew it was cowardly, but she didn't want to see his expression. "Well, first of all I just wanted to say that—"

"You're cheating on me," Victor spat out from behind her.

Autumn stopped mid-sentence, her eyes wide and mouth agape. She gave herself time to regain composure before turning around slowly to face him.

"What?"

"You heard me," he growled.

"Why would you think that?"

"Are you cheating on me with Avery Burke or not?" Victor asked with a dark expression.

"Avery?" Autumn said, trying to keep her expression clear.

"Yes."

"We—we're just friends," she said.

"Do *not* lie to me, Autumn," Victor said through clenched teeth.

"I'm not lying," she said. Victor snorted in disgust. "Listen, Victor, I—"

"Don't even try to defend yourself. Of all the elves you could've picked, you choose Avery Burke."

"I didn't *choose* anyone."

"I saw you on your balcony!" Victor bellowed. Autumn's mouth dropped open slightly and her pulse quickened. She tried to speak, but nothing came out. "Are you telling me that you weren't just kissing him? That you weren't just pressing yourself tightly against him, looking into his eyes, in a way that you've *never* looked at me."

Autumn swallowed and attempted to speak again. "My balcony is very high up. Perhaps you were seeing things."

"Oh, I assure you I saw everything quite clearly," he said and then added, "How long?"

"What do you mean?"

"How long have you been seeing him?" he said each word slowly.

"I haven't—"

"Liar!" Victor shouted, causing Autumn to stumble backwards. She felt the red rose slip from her coat pocket and fall to the ground.

Victor stared at the fallen rose.

"What is that," Victor said quietly.

Autumn looked up at him through narrowed eyes and said, "Your rose."

"And *why* did you bring it here?"

"I'm returning it to you."

"Why?" His narrowed eyes looked from Autumn, to the rose, and back to her.

"Because I don't want it anymore," she answered in a whisper.

His eyes were now completely black. No trace of green was visible.

"So you can be bound to Avery," Victor growled.

"No," Autumn said, regaining her voice. "So I no longer have to be bound to you." Victor's eyes narrowed to thin slits as she continued. "You don't talk, you don't smile, you don't laugh, you don't cry, you don't do anything. You have no feelings, no emotions, no compassion. I tried to help you. I tried to show you that just because you have Atrum blood doesn't mean you have to act like one, but maybe I was wrong."

"Stop," Victor warned.

"Maybe all you'll ever be—"

"Silence!"

"—is an Atrum."

Victor's chest heaved and he shook with rage. Shudders ran through his body like vibrations on water. Suddenly he sprang at her, arms outstretched, and wrapped his hands tightly around her neck, blocking her windpipe. She clawed at his hands, attempting to free herself, but his grip was too strong. Her vision began to fade, her eyes blacking out.

The last thing Autumn did was look into Victor's coal-black eyes. His pupils were dilating and constricting rapidly and he had a dead, unaware look in his eyes. Just when Autumn felt she was about to pass out from lack of oxygen, she saw Victor's pupils constrict to a small dot, his green irises clearly visible. Awareness washed over his features. He took a deep, rasping breath and released his hold on her. She collapsed to the ground, clutching her throat, her head swimming.

She squeezed her eyes shut, then opened them, looking up at Victor to see him staring at his hands in horror. His expression changed to a look of triumph, but Autumn figured she must be too disoriented to be seeing clearly. He glanced down at her and his face contorted in agony.

"Autumn—"

She threw her hand out, warning him not to come closer.

"Don't come near me," she said, her voice hoarse.

"But—"

"Just leave!"

Victor's eyes widened and he stumbled backwards.

"Take the rose," she whispered.

His face fell as he crouched down and grasped the rose gently. It wilted on contact, the petals floating morosely to the ground. Victor stared down at the petals, a haunted look in his eyes.

"Leave, Victor."

He blinked and turned slowly, exiting the clearing with a

tortured expression on his flawless face.

Autumn sat on the cold, hard ground, staring at the fallen rose petals. She couldn't exactly wrap her head around what had just happened. After some time, unsure of how long precisely, she stood and made her way back to Arbor Castle, moving in a zombie-like state up to her branch.

Avery was waiting for her on the couch and stood up hastily when she entered the room. He registered the empty look in her eyes and rushed over to her, pulling her gently towards the couch and onto his lap. He held her as if she were a small child in need of comforting. Autumn breathed in the smell of him, and felt herself relax in his strong hold, her head resting against his chest.

"It's over now," he soothed.

Nodding, Autumn tried not to wince from the pain. Luckily she was wearing a turtleneck so Avery wouldn't be able to see that she'd traded Victor's rose for the necklace of bruises decorating her throat.

M.I.A.

CHAPTER THIRTY-SIX

Monday morning, Autumn woke up to find her neck covered in deep red markings. Gingerly, she touched the tender skin as she stood before her full-length mirror, tracing the shape of Victor's fingers imprinted on her skin. A turtleneck or scarf would be a mandatory clothing item for a while. She knew she should probably tell someone what Victor did, but she couldn't bring herself to do so.

With only two weeks left until the Warrior Trial, she didn't have the time or the energy to deal with people fussing over her or having to deal with the guilt of what might happen to Victor if anyone found out. So, she decided to keep yet another secret to herself.

Autumn was still a little shaken up, but she thought she was doing pretty well for someone who had almost been strangled the night before. Throwing on a silver turtleneck and black pants, she traipsed down the stairs to meet up with Luke, Avery, and Crystal in the dining room.

"Hey, single lady," Luke said with a chuckle.

Autumn rolled her eyes at him, but smiled nonetheless.

Luke then began dancing and singing the song *Single Ladies* by Beyonce. Avery and Crystal looked at him strangely and Autumn let out a loud laugh. "Stop that. You're just embarrassing yourself."

"I'm not embarrassed," Luke said.

"I think I'm missing something," Crystal said.

"Same here," Avery replied.

"So it went well then?" Luke asked.

Autumn nodded, not wanting to talk about it.

"Did he take it okay?" Crystal asked.

Frowning, Autumn took a bite of toast and chewed slowly so she could think of what to say. They watched her expectantly as she finally swallowed and said, "Um, he was a little upset, but I'm sure he'll be fine today. Guys usually get over break ups after a couple of minutes."

"That is not true," Luke protested.

Autumn, Crystal, and Avery raised their eyebrows at him in surprise.

"It only takes me about thirty seconds," Luke stated.

Dread filled Autumn as the four of them approached campus. She was not looking forward to seeing Victor, especially since she had first period with him and he was usually her partner. But Victor never showed up to Numbers class and Autumn started to get a little worried. She tried to tell herself that he was sick or something, but she knew that elves never skipped school because of sickness. The school healer had a remedy for just about every virus in the Underground and elves rarely got sick anyway.

Autumn didn't see Victor anywhere on campus all day, nor did he show up to Powers class either. She hoped that he would at least come to Warrior training that afternoon.

During the thirty-minute break between Powers and Warrior training, her eyes kept flitting to the path that led to Victor's tree house. When Atticus arrived on the training field, Victor still hadn't shown up, so Kyndel had to group up with Charlotte and Jastin for the day.

"Maybe he took it a little harder than you thought," Luke muttered to Autumn.

Her brow furrowed as she thought this through. Maybe he thought that she was going to tell everyone about what he did so he decided to stay home.

Avery hadn't missed Victor's absence either. "Where do you think Victor was today?" he asked after practice.

Autumn shrugged, trying to appear indifferent, but not quite succeeding. "No idea."

"You don't think he's still upset about you returning his rose do you?"

"I doubt it."

On their way back to Arbor Castle, Autumn tried to convince herself that Victor was just pouting because he thought he was too handsome for anyone to return a rose to him, or maybe he felt rebellious and wanted to skip for the fun of it, or perhaps he had simply forgotten he had school. Of course each excuse was more unlikely than the next. She was sure the real reason was that he figured she would tell everyone what he had done to her, proving that he really didn't know her at all.

Even as a child Autumn never told on Luke because she didn't want him to get in to trouble because of her, even if he had deserved it. Of course, this situation was far more serious than Luke pulling off one of her Barbie's heads. Autumn began to analyze why Victor would even do what he did. It was rather strange that his pupils always dilated when he was angry. She wondered if he had a psychological problem that caused him to black out when he was angry or something. She was pretty sure she'd heard of that before. Though, that was in the Outside. Surely elves were not immune to psychological diseases.

Autumn was sure that must be it. Well, then it really wasn't his fault if he couldn't control it. Of course he would be angry after seeing her with Avery. It was natural to become upset when being yelled at, as she was yelling at him. Autumn vigorously shook her head to clear these thoughts. She was *not* going to blame herself for this.

"Rose?" Luke said.

She looked up to see Luke, Crystal, and Avery staring at her in concern. "What?"

"Are you alright?" Crystal said.

"Yeah, I'm fine. I was just thinking." She mentally kicked herself for saying this because, of course, she knew what was coming next.

"What're you thinking about?" Avery asked. Yes, that's what she was expecting.

"Nothing in particular. The Warrior Trial, school...you know, stuff."

The three of them looked at her suspiciously, but she pretended not to notice.

Autumn managed to go the whole night without any further questioning and she realized that Avery was right about what he had said before—she was a better actress than she thought she was. She laughed at Luke's jokes and talked animatedly with Crystal about a new gown she was creating for a woman she had met at the Warrior Initiation Ball. Avery continued to cast her concerned glances, which she ignored. Okay so maybe Avery wasn't quite buying her act, but she was pretty sure she at least had Luke and Crystal fooled.

Autumn could tell Avery was about to question her as she moved to enter her branch. So, she did the most logical thing she could do to clear his mind. She pulled his face firmly to hers and kissed him long and deep. He pulled away gasping a little.

"What was that for?" he said, breathless.

"I just wanted to kiss you. Is that a bad thing?" Autumn asked innocently.

He shook his head slowly. It would seem that she had achieved her goal. She smiled wryly and murmured, "Goodnight, Avery."

"Night," he said as she left him staring dazedly after her on the landing.

On Tuesday, Autumn walked into her Lab class to find that Victor hadn't shown up again. *Seriously? What is he thinking?* Autumn thought. They had less than two weeks until the Warrior Trial and he was skipping because of a stupid breakup and an attempted strangulation? Autumn frowned at this thought and realized that she may be taking this situation too lightly.

When Victor didn't show up to Warrior training that afternoon the other Initiates became anxious as well.

"What if something happened to him?" Charlotte said after practice. "Doesn't he live alone?"

"He probably got lost on the way back from getting his heart broken." Luke started laughing then stopped abruptly when he saw the death glare Autumn was shooting his way.

"What?" Cera said with raised eyebrows. The others turned to face Autumn as well, with similar expressions.

She gave them a sheepish look before saying, "I, uh, returned his rose Sunday evening."

Everyone began talking at once.

"Why would you do that?" Forrest asked, incredulous.

"Aw, how come?" Charlotte exclaimed.

"Is that why he hasn't shown up to practice?" Jastin said.

"Well, he was sort of depressing to be around sometimes," Cera admitted.

"Does that mean he's free then?" Kyndel asked, though she didn't seem remotely interested.

Autumn didn't know who to answer first, but found herself cracking a smile at Kyndel's comment.

"He's all yours," Autumn told her with a smirk.

Kyndel raised her eyebrows, obviously not expecting that answer.

"You don't seem all that upset about it," Forrest said.

Autumn shrugged. "It just didn't work out."

When Victor didn't show up to Numbers class Wednesday morning, Crystal and Forrest turned to Autumn, looking concerned.

"Maybe we should go look for him after school," Forrest suggested.

"Or during lunch," Crystal said.

Autumn nodded in agreement. Maybe something bad really had happened to him.

So during lunch all of the Initiates left in search of Victor's tree house.

"Hey, that's Victor's unicorn," Autumn said, spotting the horned beast grazing in a passing clearing.

The others took a few steps back, looking wary, but Forrest approached the beast slowly, speaking to him in his Animal Language. He returned quickly, telling the others that Victor's tree house was not far down the path.

They immediately knew when they had found it because it was the only tree house around in the remote area. It was made of a very dark, almost black bark and the branches were completely bare. It was much larger than Autumn originally pictured and she wondered absently why Victor had never invited her here and then realized she was glad he hadn't.

The house looked empty and desolate. Cera approached one of the windows and peered in. "It's completely dark inside. I can barely see anything. He isn't home," she determined bleakly, pushing away from the window. They all exchanged worried glances. Kyndel narrowed her eyes at Autumn in accusation. Of course she would think this was entirely Autumn's fault.

Forrest spotted a doe watching them from behind a nearby tree and approached it, speaking once again in his strange language. He turned back to the others with a grave look upon his face. "She says Victor left a few days ago and hasn't been back since."

Everyone exchanged a nervous glance at this.

"It would've been nice if you would have waited to return your little rose *after* the Warrior Trial, Princess," Kyndel hissed. "I don't have a partner now thanks to you."

"Shut it, Kyndel," Avery growled. "You're just mad because you actually have to try now that you don't have Victor doing all of the work."

Everyone looked at Avery in surprise. Autumn doubted they'd ever heard him talk like that to anyone other than Victor, especially not to a girl. Kyndel glared at him, but said nothing.

They made their way back to the campus in nervous silence, everyone at a loss.

"Should we tell Atticus?" Charlotte spoke up.

"Probably. I'm sure he'll be concerned too when Victor doesn't show up to training again," Forrest said.

"Maybe we should send a Navigator out to look for him," Luke suggested.

The others nodded in agreement. They decided not to discuss it with Atticus until after Powers class so the students who weren't Warriors wouldn't overhear. They all met up on the training field, waiting for Atticus to show up when they saw a silhouette approaching in the distance, bracing themselves to give him the bad news.

Autumn narrowed her eyes at the approaching figure. "Victor!" she exclaimed in surprise. The others gasped as they registered what she was seeing as well.

"Where have you been?" Kyndel called in a stern voice.

"You had us worried, man," Forrest said.

As Victor came into the light there was a collective intake of breath. He looked horrible. His skin was pale, he had dark circles under his eyes, and he wore a dead expression upon his face. Autumn swallowed thickly at the sight of him and couldn't stop herself from brushing her fingers softly across her bruised neck.

"Are you alright?" Jastin asked him.

Victor didn't answer.

"Okay!" Atticus shouted from behind them, causing everyone to jump, "Everybody ready to get started? Ah, Victor, nice to see you back. You been sick?"

Victor nodded absently. Atticus did not question this due to Victor's appearance. Autumn's brow furrowed as she continued to take him in.

Practice was just as grueling as ever. The Tetras had captured ten Shadows this time, two for each Warrior pair. Victor seemed to come back to life as training went on. He didn't speak to anyone, but managed to kill both of his Shadows before anyone else had killed one. He left Kyndel staring at him with a mixture of indignation and awe.

When Atticus announced that practice was over, Victor immediately left the training field, avoiding a bombardment of questions. They all stared after him blankly.

"He looks bad," Jastin said.

"Well at least he's back," Kyndel said.

"Yeah, you didn't have to do anything at all today." Forrest laughed, jumping out of the way as Kyndel moved to slug him angrily on the arm.

Victor's reappearance did nothing to soothe Autumn's unease. If anything, she felt even worse.

Scarves and Roses

CHAPTER THIRTY-SEVEN

The rest of the week passed semi-normally. Autumn went to classes, Warrior training, and went home exhausted. Autumn and Luke were able to squeeze in some time to visit Thunder and Sundance, who had both grown quite a lot since Christmas. Avery said that they would be able to fly in a few months.

Victor kept up his silent treatment, which really wasn't all that different from how he had been acting before. The only difference was that he didn't say one word to Autumn whatsoever. He wouldn't even look at her. She was sure he was ashamed of what he did and that he had noticed the fact that she wore a turtleneck or a scarf every day to cover her bruise-striped neck.

On Saturday, the Initiates had the most challenging practice to date. Atticus even allowed them Sunday off so they could recuperate, even though the Warrior Trial was the next weekend.

After dinner, Luke, Avery and Autumn walked tiredly up to their branches and Crystal left for the roots. As Autumn began to enter her branch, she felt Avery grab her hand. She turned to him in question and he simply bent to kiss her hand, keeping eye contact. She felt him slip a piece of paper into her palm. She raised an eyebrow at him, but he simply gave her a crooked smile and continued up the stairs.

Autumn walked into her branch and opened the paper to read it.

Meet me on your balcony at midnight.

AVERY climbed astride Knight with a feeling of nervous anticipation in the pit of his stomach. He wanted tonight to be perfect. Autumn deserved nothing less. Knight leapt into the air and glided to Autumn's balcony. He heard stirring within her branch and seconds later she was throwing the balcony doors open. Her auburn curls framed her soft, heart-shaped face, upon which rested a coy smile, her hazel eyes shining brightly in the moonlight.

He felt that gravitational pull somewhere within the region of his chest.

"I think I'm experiencing déjà vu," she said.

"Oh, you just wait," Avery said and laughed as Autumn swung easily onto Knight's back, something that still impressed him.

It was much colder this time around than it had been the last time he took her to Fay Fairy Forest. Avery felt Autumn bury her face in his warm back and wrap her arms tightly around him to keep from shivering too badly. He smiled to himself.

They soon landed roughly on the ground, immediately engulfed in warmth of the hundreds of thousands of fay fairies surrounding them.

"I had a feeling this is where you were taking me," Autumn said as Avery pulled her off of Knight's back. He knew she could have managed to get down herself, of course, but he didn't want to miss the chance of wrapping her in his arms. He watched as she closed her eyes and smiled as the fay light kissed her porcelain face.

Avery pressed his lips to hers and she kissed him softly back, the ghost of her smile still lingering. Pulling slowly away, he looked into her hazel eyes, piercing them with his gaze. His lips turned up at the corners as he pulled a flawless red rose from out of his jacket. He could feel his fingers shaking and hoped she wouldn't notice. Autumn's eyes widened as she focused on the perfect flower and then flashed up to his. He took a breath and said the words he had been reciting over and over in his head for the past few days.

"Autumn, I am so in love with you. I've never felt this way about anyone in my life, nor did I think that I ever could. You're everything to me and I can't imagine a world—Underground or otherwise—without you in it. Will you accept my rose?"

AUTUMN looked at the rose in Avery's hand, which was shaking slightly. Not long ago she had returned a rose to Victor, but this one seemed different. It had a warm glow about it. Its petals were a beautiful ruby red and its stem an emerald green, but this gift was far more precious than either of those stones. Reaching out, Autumn took the rose gently from him and pulled it to her chest, pressing it against her heart.

"Of course," she whispered, looking up at him through her lashes. His eyes sparkled at her words and he pulled her into a tight embrace. Autumn moved the rose so as not to crush it, though she knew that nothing could or would ever be able to damage this.

They returned to Arbor Castle as the sun broke over the horizon. Everything about this night would forever be etched into her mind: the fay fairies dancing around them as she and Avery lay under the same tree where they'd shared their first kiss, the way he held her so tightly, as if he never wanted to let her go, the smell of the forest, the look in Avery's eyes as she inhaled the sweet aroma of their rose. Their rose.

Knight landed lightly on Autumn's balcony and Avery turned to look at her over his shoulder. Leaning forward, she kissed him deeply before sliding off of Knight's back.

"Goodnight, Autumn."

"Good *morning*," she corrected him. He turned to look at the orange and pink sky and laughed.

"Good morning, then," he said as Knight leapt off of her balcony and glided to the castle stables. Autumn sighed contentedly as she slipped into her room and turned to close her balcony doors.

"Good *morning*, Autumn."

Autumn froze where she stood and slowly turned to see Luke and Crystal standing in her bedroom with their arms folded across their chests. Autumn's mouth fell open at the sight of them.

"Wh—what are you guys doing in here?" she said.

Luke glanced at the rose in Autumn's hand and raised an eyebrow at her. Crystal frowned at the rose. "I believe the question is: What were *you* doing out *there*?"

"I was just—" Autumn began, but then stopped, not knowing what to say.

"Nice rose you got there," Luke spoke up.

Autumn held it tightly in her hand, the thorns cutting into her skin.

"I thought you said you returned Victor's rose," Crystal said.

"I did," Autumn muttered.

"Then what are you doing with a new one? How else would you be in possession of a red rose?" Luke asked, feigning stupidity. Autumn glared at him and he continued speaking. "It couldn't possibly be from a certain elf who you've been forbidden to see by your one and only grandfather, could it?"

Autumn looked at him through narrowed eyes. "What if it is?"

"Then we will be forced to tell Olympus," Luke stated.

Crystal nodded in agreement.

"What?" Autumn exclaimed, her mouth dropping open.

Then Luke and Crystal exchanged a glance and doubled over in hysterical laughter. Autumn stared at them, dumbstruck.

"What the hell, you guys," she said.

"You should have seen your face," Luke said, gasping for breath. Crystal wiped away tears of laughter.

"I hate both of you," Autumn grumbled.

"No you don't," Crystal said, sitting on the canopy bed.

"How did you find out?" Autumn asked.

"I heard you two from my balcony earlier. I couldn't sleep and I was just sitting out there when I heard Knight land on your balcony. Then I watched you two fly off," Luke said.

"Luke came and woke me up to tell me what he'd heard. So, we decided to wait for you here," Crystal said smiling innocently.

"So, you're not mad?" Autumn asked Luke.

"Nah. If anything, I'm proud," Luke said. "It's about time you started breaking the rules a bit."

"I don't see why you didn't tell us, though," Crystal added.

Autumn gave her a sheepish look. "Sorry. I just figured it would be easier to keep secret if it was just between Avery and me."

"Well, we both kind of suspected that something was going on between you two," Luke said and Crystal nodded.

"I thought you might," Autumn admitted. "But I just wanted to wait until the right time to tell you."

"You mean now that you're seeing only Avery and not Avery *and* Victor?" Luke smirked.

Autumn sighed as she climbed onto her bed to explain in detail the whole story behind her little love triangle situation. Luke rolled his eyes as she told him why she'd stayed with Victor for so long.

"So you could *help* him?" Luke said. "Come on, Rose. You need to stop with the 'I must help everyone whether they ask for it or not' mentality. Some people are just beyond help."

"That's what Avery said about Victor," Autumn said with a frown.

"Avery's right," Crystal agreed.

"I know," Autumn said.

"Don't worry. You did what you could," Luke said, taking in her downcast expression.

"I know that too," she said with a small smile. "Thanks, guys. I'm glad you know about everything now. I hate keeping secrets." Her fingers absentmindedly grazed her neck.

"Do you want to go down to breakfast?" Crystal asked.

"I want to go to sl—sl—sleep," Autumn said through a yawn.

Luke and Crystal laughed and moved to leave.

"Oh, don't tell Avery that we know," Luke said from her bedroom doorway. "We want to mess with him too."

Autumn smiled slyly and said, "I think I know how to accomplish that."

She met Luke and Crystal in the dining room for lunch and Avery joined them, looking quite tired. Crystal smiled into her napkin and Luke cleared his throat as Avery sat beside Autumn.

"We missed you two at breakfast," Luke said.

Autumn pretended to look embarrassed, not making eye contact with Luke. "I was really tired from Warrior training yesterday," she said.

"Yeah, me too," Avery said.

Luke winked at her as Avery took a big gulp of cider. Autumn had to repress a laugh.

"Oh, Autumn," Luke said. "I forgot to tell you that Olympus wants to talk to us tonight."

"About what?" she asked, sounding serious.

"I'm not sure. The servant elf that told me said something about reviewing the castle rules or something," he said, taking a bite of toast.

Avery's eyes widened as he shot her a sidelong glance. She gave him a nervous look.

"Did you guys hear something weird last night?" Luke asked them.

"Like what?" Avery said.

"Like loud thumping noises," Luke said.

Avery coughed and Autumn said, "No, I didn't hear anything like that."

"That's weird," Luke said, stroking his chin in apparent thought. "It was around midnight or so. I could've sworn I heard voices too."

"Voices?" Autumn said.

"Yeah," Luke said. "I think we should talk to Olympus about increasing security outside our branches. Anyone could get to them if they wanted to."

Avery frowned down at his plate and Autumn and Crystal exchanged humorous glances. Luke may have been an even better actor than Autumn.

"You still have guard duty three times a week, right Avery?" Luke asked.

"Yeah, why?"

"I overheard Olympus talking with some elves about having to hire a new guard as soon as possible."

Avery swallowed heavily and stared with wide eyes at Luke. "Really?" he said.

As a look of fear passed across Avery's face, Autumn decided she had to stop this. Leaning over, she kissed him gently on the cheek. His eyes widened in surprise and his mouth dropped as he looked from Luke to Crystal, who were both wearing sly smirks.

"What the—" he began and then his eyes narrowed as he took in Luke's wide grin. "When did you find out," Avery said dully. Luke, Crystal and Autumn burst out laughing.

"Last night," Crystal said.

Avery turned to Autumn in question. "I didn't tell them," she said, raising her hands in defense.

"I heard you two love birds last night on Autumn's balcony," Luke said.

"I hate you guys," Avery said, evoking another round of hysterical laughter.

The Pact

CHAPTER THIRTY-EIGHT

"**G**et up, Oaken! Five days until the Warrior Trial! This is no time to give in to weakness!" Atticus shouted at Autumn after she had collapsed for the third time while attempting to fight off Jastin's Power. Atticus had broken up the partners and paired each of them off with their biggest threats in the group. Jastin was the only other Initiate with a mental Power and was the only one who could easily defeat Autumn.

"Again, Lambert!" Atticus commanded Jastin, who was clenching his jaw in irritation. He hated using his Power against anyone who didn't deserve it. While Autumn couldn't physically feel any pain, the emotional pain that his Power brought about was far more scarring.

Jastin took a deep breath and Autumn braced herself for the wave of intense emotions that was about to hit her.

Suddenly her vision blacked out again and she was standing outside of her house in Texas and seeing it surrounded by yellow crime scene tape, hearing the sound of police sirens, seeing the EMTs rolling the bodies of her parents out of her house, hearing her screams as the weight of what had happened crashed over her, being told to calm down by the unfeeling police woman.

The vision changed, flashing to Autumn rocking back and forth in her bedroom in Ireland, a hollow feeling in her chest as she pressed a picture of her mom and dad against her heart, trying desperately to heal it.

Flash to Luke breaking down in her arms on the anniversary of their parents' deaths and Autumn had had enough.

Opening her mouth, she shot a jet of angry Song at Jastin, causing the images to stop flashing through her mind. She collapsed onto the ground, chest heaving and hot tears falling down her face. She wiped them away, angrily.

"Better," Atticus said. "Now once more, but faster this time."

"No," Luke said from a few feet away, glaring at Atticus.

"It's fine, Luke," Autumn said in a tone of warning.

"He's right," Avery said, approaching them looking furious and tortured all at once. "That's enough."

Atticus looked wearily from Luke to Avery, thinking this through. "Very well. Autumn, pair up with Kyndel. Jastin, with Luke."

Luke frowned at this, but said nothing. "No, not Luke," Autumn protested, knowing he would see the same horrible images that she had. Jastin looked miserably at the ground.

"It's okay, Rose. I can handle it," Luke said.

Autumn stared at him with a troubled expression and he looked resolutely back at her before she submitted and stalked over to Kyndel, who surprisingly didn't make a rude comment about having to partner up with Autumn.

"Let's just get started," Autumn said.

Kyndel nodded silently, but didn't disappear. Autumn waved a hand for Kyndel to go ahead, but she simply looked at her with an interested expression.

"What are you doing?" Autumn asked, frustrated.

"What do you see?" Kyndel asked quietly.

Autumn frowned at this. "What?"

"What do you see when Jastin uses his Power on you," Kyndel clarified. Autumn took a deep breath and sighed before telling her exactly what she saw in a dull, monotonous tone. When she finished, Kyndel was looking at Autumn with wide eyes. "Oh," she said.

They stood there in silence for a bit before Autumn said, "What do *you* see?" Kyndel's wide eyes turned angry.

"Let's just get started," she hissed, as if Autumn was the one who started all of this talk. Autumn raised her eyebrows at this, but decided to comply. She didn't even think she wanted to know what Kyndel saw anyway. Probably a bad hair day or something.

Atticus trained the Initiates harder than ever this week in preparation for the Warrior Trial. They all knew that he was trying to help them and that he didn't want to lose any of them in this dangerous task, but they couldn't help but feel a bit overworked.

Luke had fared much better than Autumn when Jastin used his Power on him, but he was uncharacteristically silent all Monday evening.

On Thursday Atticus brought in the new Tetra Warriors for the Initiates to fight against. A few of them were extremely intimidating and unsympathetic, though some were down to earth and friendly. They'd been in this exact position five years ago, and they had made it through their Warrior Trial alive. Autumn knew there was no way they were going to go easy on them today.

For some reason Autumn always thought of the rest of the Warriors as much older, but she kept forgetting that the Tetra Warriors were only five years older than them, all around the age of 22 or 23. They looked at the Initiates as if they were a bunch of immature children, which some of them were.

As Atticus introduced them, Autumn recognized Candi, the Warrior that she'd gone up against during the Warrior Test. She shot Autumn a malicious look, like she wanted to get even with her for breaking her nose. Well, Autumn beat her once. She could do it again.

Lucky for Candi, though, Autumn was paired with someone else, a slender elf with platinum blonde hair named Eden. She sort of reminded Autumn of an older Crystal with her slight frame and long blonde hair, but Eden's eyes were a mint green color and she was not quite as tall. Her power was Silence, which proved to be quite a problem for Autumn. As she opened her mouth to shoot a jet of Song at her, Eden immediately raised her hand and Autumn was unable to produce any sound.

After being silenced for the fifth time, Autumn decided to give up on using her Power against the Warrior and charged forward to attack. Eden was not expecting this and tumbled to the ground as Autumn pounced on her, pinning her to the ground in a matter of seconds. Atticus gave her an approving nod and Autumn smiled in satisfaction as she let Eden go.

"You're quite a fighter," Eden said, dusting herself off but looking impressed.

Autumn smiled in recognition, attempting to look as if this wasn't news to her, but secretly feeling quite pleased. They fought again, and Autumn managed to pin her three out of five times. Their chests heaving, Autumn and Eden took a short break from attacking one another to watch the others.

Avery was paired up with a big hulking Warrior with chocolate colored skin named Boone. He had a loud, jolly laugh and was a lot kinder than he looked. His Power was Earthquakes. Avery managed to reach him across the trembling ground and pinned him in seconds using his Strength.

Luke was paired with Jack, who had the power of a Tornado, leaving a path of destruction everywhere he went. Luke was able to conjure a tornado as well, but it was not quite as powerful or destructive as Jack's, so Luke struggled to overpower him.

Crystal fought against Willow, a brunette with colorless eyes whose Power was the ability to morph into animals. Right now she was in the form of a penguin, wearing an expression that looked suspiciously like a sly grin. Crystal's ice had no effect on Willow in this form. The Willow penguin slid lazily around on the random patches of ice.

Kyndel was paired with Thaddeus, whose Power was the ability to slice through solid objects like a knife. Kyndel used her Power of Invisibility to avoid being hit. There were a number of slashes in the surrounding trees and rocks, where Thaddeus had missed her.

Autumn watched with interest as Victor battled against a female Tetra called Nyx, whose power was Darkness. They were each trying to overpower the other, Darkness against Light. Autumn secretly hoped Victor would win simply because she thought light should always conquer darkness.

Forrest was becoming increasingly frustrated with his pairing. Killian, a red headed Tetra, had the power of Persuasion and was confusing the many animals that Forrest had called to his aid. While Killian could not understand the animals, he was able to persuade them not to attack him. Forrest was not used to his animals listening to someone other than him and glared at Killian in frustration.

Cera was smiling proudly as she pressed her Warrior, Olivia, into the ground with her Gravity. Olivia's Power was Healing, which was extremely useful to others, but it was definitely a defensive power, rather than offensive. Cera seemed to be toying with Olivia, easing off of her Power long enough for Olivia to charge at her, then pushing her to the ground again. She didn't allow the Tetra to get close enough for her to attack.

Charlotte, on the other hand, was having trouble with her Tetra, Lucian, who had the Power of Hypnosis. She was able to hold him off with her thick fog at first, but he managed to reach her and look her right in the eyes, hypnotizing her. Her fog began to dissipate, remnants of it still floating lazily on the ground. Lucian's Power was not unlike Autumn's, but he had to make eye contact for it to be effective.

The most interesting pair to watch was Jastin and Candi. Autumn didn't even find out what Candi's Power was during Warrior Test because they weren't allowed to use them in the fighting portion. Now she was glad she'd never had to find out because her Power looked slightly ominous to say the least.

"Her power is Fear," Eden informed Autumn. "She's able to fill her opponent with an intense terror that isn't easy to ignore, but this Initiate seems to be handling himself rather well considering. Though, he's not as quick as you. If I'm not mistaken, I believe you were the one who broke her nose in the Warrior Test?"

Autumn gave her a small smirk and nod.

"She can stand to be taken down a notch or two," Eden said.

Apparently Autumn was not the only one who disliked Candi.

Autumn and Eden stopped watching the others and managed a few more duels before Atticus called for the Initiates to group up. They said goodbye to the Tetras, respectfully shaking hands with one another.

"Good luck on the Warrior Trial," Eden said to Autumn.

Her stomach flipped as she thought of the nearness of that day. Avery approached her and said, "You two seemed to get along well."

"Yeah, she's nice. Especially compared to that Candi girl. She's not so pleasant."

"Well you're going to have to get used to her," Avery said.

"Why?" Autumn frowned.

"The Tetra and Quinn Warriors work together often because we're the youngest. We're also the strongest physically and do most of the fighting while the older Warriors do more guard work and station themselves higher in the trees to attack with arrows from above."

"Oh."

"Good work today, guys," Atticus said. "There will be no training tomorrow so you have time to recuperate and rest before the Warrior Trial. On Saturday morning you will all be informed as to what your task will be and its location. You will then be transported to that location in pairs. It will just be you and your partner starting out, though it's not unlikely that you'll run into another pair along the way. It'll be up to you whether you continue on alone or if you decide to group up. I'll say no more. Make sure and eat a good breakfast Saturday morning. You'll need the strength. Until tomorrow, Warriors."

During Powers class the next day, the Initiates were made to sit out of practice. The rest of the class shot them looks of envy and admiration. None of the Initiates seemed to pay much attention to this, though, because they were all so nervous about the Trial.

"We should all meet at Sugar Brown's after dinner tonight. You know, just in case," Charlotte began.

"Don't say that," Cera said. "Nothing's going to happen to any of us."

Charlotte swallowed and nodded mechanically as Jastin wrapped a comforting arm around her.

"We should still go," Autumn said. "To celebrate our last night as Initiates. After tomorrow, we will officially be Quinns."

The others nodded in agreement, except for Victor, who was gazing at the floor with a dead look in his eyes.

"You going to come, Victor?" Forrest asked doubtfully. Victor blinked and looked at him in confusion. "To Sugar Brown's," Forrest clarified. Victor shook his head before Forrest finished his sentence.

When Powers class let out, Autumn decided to swallow her pride and talk to Victor.

"Victor?" Autumn called as she exited the Powers Tree. He turned to her, his face etched with surprise. "Can I talk to you?" He studied her for a moment, but eventually nodded. They walked a little ways away from the Powers Tree and came to stand awkwardly beside an old willow tree. "I don't hate you, you know, for...what you did."

His eyebrows shot up at her bluntness, his eyes flicking down to her scarf-covered neck, which was almost unnecessary because there was only a shadow of a bruise left now. When his eyes met hers again she continued, "I know what I did with Avery was wrong and I hope you'll forgive me for any pain I've caused you. I'm sorry things ended the way they did and no matter what happened between us, I know there's good in you even if you can't see it yourself." He continued to study her, saying nothing, an unreadable expression in his eyes. "Well, that's all I have to say, I guess. I'll, uh, see you later, Victor."

Autumn turned to leave and he said, "Stay safe tomorrow," in a quiet voice. She turned slightly and gave him a small smile, nodding and left him standing behind her, a dark silhouette in the setting sun.

After Autumn and Luke had dinner with Olympus, they left with Crystal and Avery for Sugar Brown's. The rest of the Initiates were already waiting for them. They sat in silence, drinking their coffee or cider, and staring blankly into space.

"What do you think it will be?" Forrest spoke up.

A few people started at the sound of his voice.

"Maybe we will have to fight warlocks or something. They would be our biggest threats right?" Luke said.

"Their magic isn't as powerful as our powers, but they do have a larger variety of it," Jastin said.

"I'm thinking we'll have to deal with Shadows since Atticus has had us train with them so much," Autumn said.

"Shadows live on Alder Island with Vyra and all her followers," Kyndel sneered. "They aren't going to put us in that much danger.

We'd all die."

"Shadows aren't just on Alder Island," Crystal spoke up in Autumn's defense. "There are Shadows all around Arbor Falls. Why else do you think we need Warriors to protect the elves?"

"Oh, what a thrilling Trial *that* would be. Running around Arbor Falls, trying to kill stray Shadows," Kyndel said, her voice dripping with sarcasm.

Autumn rolled her eyes.

"We should just drop the subject," Cera said. "We'll find out soon enough. Let's just enjoy our last night as little Initiates."

"Agreed," Luke said, raising his mug in mock celebration and splashing it all over himself. Everyone burst out laughing as he cursed under his breath.

"Let's make a pact," Charlotte said.

"What sort of pact?" Kyndel asked, looking wary.

"A pact that we will all make it through tomorrow no matter what," Charlotte stated.

Everyone exchanged amused glances. Autumn put her hand in the middle of their circle, palm down. The elves raised eyebrows at this, not knowing the significance of this gesture. Luke grinned and placed his hand on top of hers. Crystal smiled in understanding and laid hers on top of Luke's. The rest of the elves mimicked them until everyone's hands were stacked in the middle.

The Warrior Trial

CHAPTER THIRTY-NINE

When the Initiates met in the Powers Tree the morning of the trial they were surprised to see Gregorius Dodge, the leader of the Warriors, there as well.

"Welcome, young Warriors," he said cheerfully. Atticus watched them enter with a proud look upon his face. They were dressed in their official Warriors uniforms with their bow and quiver full of arrows slung across their backs and knives in their holsters. "I expect you are all eagerly anticipating your final Trial?" Everyone nodded in unison, too nervous to speak. Dodge laughed at this. "Very well. The components of this test are quite simple, yet equally dangerous. This year's Warrior Trial will take place on Alder Island."

Autumn's eyes widened, her mouth hanging slightly ajar at this news. Glancing sideways she saw her expression mirrored in the others.

"As I am sure you all know," Dodge continued, "Alder Island is the home of Vyra Vaun, her many Atrum followers, and hordes of Shadow creatures. Your task will be to cross the Opacious Sea to reach Alder Island. Once you've made it to the island, you will travel to the center where you will find five silver roses, one for each pair of Warriors. You must retrieve a silver rose and return to the shore, where we will be waiting to greet you. There are many dangers lurking on Alder Island. You will have to keep your senses sharp and your eyes open. Never let your guards down. In the unfortunate event that your partner should perish, you must continue on."

At this point their faces twisted into matching looks of terror as they looked from one to the other, wondering if they would all make it through this alive. Avery and Luke simultaneously grasped either of Autumn's hands tightly, and she squeezed back just as hard. Luke took hold of Crystal's hand as well, her crystal blue eyes full of fear. Autumn didn't know what she would do if she lost any one of them. She glanced around the room at the others. These elves had all become so important to her. They were more than her friends. They were her family.

"You and your partner will be transported to the shore of the Opacious Sea. Once you arrive, your Trial will begin. Tetra Warriors will be stationed along the shore to await each of your return. There will also be Navigators informing Atticus and myself of each of your locations and informing us in the event any of you perish."

The casual nature with which Dodge said the word "perish" was unsettling. Autumn was sure that, as head of the Warriors, he'd had to use that word a multitude of times.

The reality of the extreme danger of this test was clearly beginning to seep into everyone's minds. Charlotte and Jastin clasped each other's hands tightly, while Kyndel squeezed Charlotte's other hand. Autumn's eyebrows rose when she saw Kyndel's other hand occupied by Cera's. Apparently in the face of danger, all known grudges were temporarily forgotten. Cera and Forrest's fingers were locked together as well. Victor was the only one without any physical contact, an empty look in his eyes. Autumn supposed their talk the day before had little effect on him.

"At this time we will be taking you to your designated positions. If you would all follow me," Dodge said.

They exited the Powers Tree and he lead the Initiates to the training field where several pegasi were waiting, along with five Tetra Warriors: Lucian, Thad, Eden, Willow, and Jack. Autumn heard Crystal groan slightly at the sight of the winged horses and had to suppress a laugh. Each Initiate pair was to share one pegasus and would have one Tetra as a guide. Before they parted, Luke wrapped Autumn in a tight hug.

"Don't die, okay?" he said. She laughed and nodded, feeling a lump form in her throat at the thought of the dangers they were both about to face.

Crystal gave Autumn a quick hug as well and left with Luke to meet their Tetra guide.

Willow, the brunette who could change into animals, approached Autumn and Avery. She greeted them warmly, her colorless eyes shining. "Nervous?" she asked.

Avery shrugged, but Autumn nodded truthfully.

"You'll do well," she said before transforming into a pegasus herself, her mane the same chestnut color her hair had been seconds before. The black and white spotted pegasus Autumn and Avery were riding followed Willow obediently into the air. The weather was pleasantly warm for January. Regardless of the warmth, Autumn began to shake slightly in nervous anticipation. Avery laced his fingers through hers.

"You *will* make it through this," he stated without question. "I'm not letting anything happen to you."

"I'm not worried about me," she said.

Avery shook his head in exasperation. "Of course you're not."

They flew for what felt like at least an hour before they began to descend. Autumn could smell the salt water and had to stop herself from asking how the heck there was a subterranean ocean. She was sure the answer would be, "It's the magic of the Underground," anyway. There was an Underground sun and Underground stars—why not an Underground ocean? It was truly a world within a world.

Willow landed softly on the black sand of the shore and transformed back into her elf form. Autumn and Avery's pegasus landed beside Willow and they climbed off slowly, taking in the sight before them.

The violent sea was a stormy gray—a reflection of Avery's eyes—surrounded by a black-sand beach. In the distance was a large mass of land, too ominous to be called an island, covered in thick, dark Alder trees, true to island's name, with mountainous rocks jutting up on the right side.

"I'm not technically supposed to be saying this, but that's Vyra's Lair," Willow said, pointing to the large, menacing rocks. "I would try to avoid that if at all possible."

Autumn and Avery nodded their thanks.

"I'm supposed to remind you again that your silver rose is in the center of the island. Your task is to retrieve the rose and bring it back to the shore where a Warrior will be waiting for you. Be safe," she said, smiling supportively at the two of them.

Willow retreated then, leaving Autumn and Avery to discuss their plan of action.

"The island is basically half rocks and half forest. I figure if we're able to walk a little to the left of the rocks, we will be pretty close to the middle of the island," Avery said.

"Okay, but first we have to figure out how we're going to cross the ocean to the island. It looks closer than it actually is. We should avoid swimming the whole way because we're going to need our energy once we get there," Autumn said.

"You can hold on to my back and I'll swim the whole way," Avery stated.

Autumn was shaking her head before he had finished speaking. "Your Power is Strength, Avery, not endurance. It may help with how fast you swim and how quickly, but it won't keep you from becoming fatigued." She glanced at the water and wondered if there were some sort of helpful creatures in there, and—if there were—would her Power work on them? She approached the shore with caution.

"What're you doing?" Avery asked.

"I'm going to Sing underwater."

Avery raised an eyebrow at her, but didn't argue.

Autumn waded a little ways into the freezing water until she was about waist deep. Plunging her head underwater, she opened her mouth to sing. Though she couldn't see in the salty water, her Song came out as clear and loud as it did in air. The image of her lyric-less melody traveling through the waves floated across her mind. Her air supply soon ran out and she pulled her face out of the water, inhaling deeply and wiping her frozen face dry.

Then they waited. After several minutes had gone by, Autumn turned to frown at Avery. "I guess it didn't work. It was worth a try, though."

Suddenly there was a loud splashing sound and Autumn

turned to see three of the strangest looking creatures she'd ever laid eyes on. They looked like a mix between a giant sea horse and a baby dragon. They were peering up at her with their heads tilted to the side in curiosity, and she was strongly reminded of a puppy eagerly waiting for a treat.

"That's a sea dog," Avery said in wonder. "How'd you do that?"

Autumn shrugged. "Animals like my Song." Sundance listened to her sing all of the time.

Turning back to the sea dogs, Autumn sang a couple of notes to them. Their round eyes glazed over for a moment before becoming focused again as she stopped. Their long, green tongues lolled out of their mouths and their backsides moved back and forth in the water as if they were wagging their long tails.

"I think they like you," Avery noted in amusement.

"Do you think they'll let us ride them?" she said.

"Worth a try."

Autumn held her hand out cautiously and two of the sea dogs moved backwards in the water, eyeing her hand and quiver full of arrows warily, but the third one moved closer, allowing her to pat it gently on its rubbery nose.

"Sort of feels like a dolphin," she noted. The sea dog's backside moved even more quickly as she rubbed its nose. "Can you take us to the island?" Autumn asked the sea dog, feeling slightly foolish for talking seriously to a sea animal. The sea dog, however, seemed to understand what she was saying and glanced at Alder Island. He swam closer, allowing Autumn to climb onto his smooth back. "Call the others," she said to Avery.

"Here...doggie," he said, holding his hand out. The other two sea dogs seemed more trusting after watching Autumn's interaction with the first one. The larger sea dog moved towards Avery, allowing him to scratch the animal behind the ear and climb onto its back.

"To the island, please," Autumn said to the sea dogs and gasped a little as they jetted off towards the ominous rocks in the distance. The third sea dog swam playfully next to the others. Autumn found herself temporarily forgetting her worries and simply enjoying the strange, yet thrilling ride. As the sea dogs neared Alder Island, they slowed their progress. The waves became larger as the rocky shore neared. At a certain point, the sea dogs stopped swimming, and Autumn realized they didn't want to go any closer to the dangerous island.

She patted her sea dog gently and slid off into the dark, cold water, trying not to think of what might be waiting beneath her. "Thanks, Buddy," she said, absentmindedly naming him. She sang a short note to send them off and Autumn and Avery made their way to shore, the powerful waves throwing them mercilessly around in the water.

"Climb on my back," Avery insisted. "The shore's not far."

Autumn did as he said, wrapping her arms under his, securing them tightly around his torso. When the water became shallow enough to walk, she released her hold on Avery and began making her way clumsily to shore. The water slowed them significantly, pulling at their legs as if they were walking through thick tar. Autumn looked at the dense foliage before them with a wary expression.

Glancing reluctantly to her right, she saw the steep, rocky cliffs in the distance that contained Vyra's Lair. Her expression became dark and suddenly she felt much more prepared to kill as many Shadows as it took to get to their silver rose, the sweet and bitter taste of revenge resting on her tongue.

It took Autumn a moment to remember why they were here. As much as she wanted to make Vyra pay for what she'd done to the Oaken family, she recognized that now was not the time to do so.

Autumn and Avery finally made their way onto the rocky shore.

"Hey," she said, looking down at herself. "My boots and uniform are completely dry."

"They're water proof," he said. She supposed she could have worked that out given a few more seconds.

Her hair, however, was not waterproof and she pulled it off of her neck to wring it out.

"What's that?" Avery asked.

She turned to him in question. "What is what?"

He approached Autumn with narrowed eyes and she jumped slightly as he trailed his fingers across her neck, right along the shadow of her faded bruises. She looked at him with wide eyes.

How had he seen that? She could only barely notice the traces of Victor's fingers that morning in her mirror and she even knew where to look. Maybe they were more pronounced in the sunlight.

He tilted his head, looking at the marks in confusion and then looked down at his own hands. He came to stand in front of her so that they were face to face and placed his fingers along each bruise. Almost a perfect fit, Autumn was sure. His eyes widened in horror and she took a step back, letting her wet hair fall to partially cover her neck.

"The turtlenecks and the scarves," he said, realization dawning across his face.

"Avery—" Autumn began.

"*Victor*," he growled.

Autumn's mouth dropped open, staring in horror as he punched a nearby tree letting out an angry shout. The tree split easily down the middle and collapsed into itself.

"WHEN DID HE DO THAT TO YOU?" he demanded.

Autumn flinched at his angry tone. She opened her mouth to answer, but nothing happened. He narrowed his eyes at the ground in concentration, obviously thinking something through.

"The night you returned his rose. You were all upset. I thought it was because you felt guilty—but it wasn't, was it? You were upset because he nearly *killed* you," he said in a tortured voice.

"He didn't mean—" she began, finding her voice.

"STOP defending him, Autumn!"

"I'm not!"

"He's exactly what I always thought he was. A *monster*."

"Avery, please, just stop. You were right, okay? Just stop. This isn't the time to go losing your head. We're on Alder Island for goodness sake. We can deal with this later, all right?"

Avery stopped shouting, his chest heaving. He looked over his shoulder at the immense forest, full of Shadows and Atrums and countless other horrors. "All right," he said in defeat. "But if we happen to run into him, I can't promise I won't treat him like the Atrum he is."

Autumn gulped at this, but said nothing, hoping very much that they did *not* run into Victor. "Now, let's go," she said. Avery nodded.

They traveled into the thick woods, keeping an eye on the rocky land to their right, so that they were able to figure where they were in relation to the middle of the island.

"The farther we go, the thicker the trees will be," Avery stated. Autumn already knew this, but she nodded anyway.

Avery sliced marks in the trees they passed so they could find their way back to the shore, even though they had the boundary between the rocks and forest to guide them. She followed him silently, placing her steps where he did. They came across their first Shadow about five minutes in. Autumn immediately stunned it with her Song and Avery just as quickly snapped its neck.

"That was easy," Autumn said.

"Don't get too comfortable," Avery warned. "The farther in we go, the more Shadows there will be. It's the Atrums we have to worry about, though."

After another ten minutes, Autumn heard a twig snap and immediately shot an arrow in its direction. Avery disappeared into the foliage to see what she'd hit and came back holding a rabbit with Autumn's arrow jutting out of its chest. She slapped a hand over her mouth in horror as he dropped the dead rabbit to the ground, pulling the arrow out of its carcass.

"You might want to wait to shoot your arrow next time. That could've been another Warrior," Avery said. Autumn's eyes widened as she took this in. She could've just killed one of her friends. She shook her head at her own stupidity. "That was a good shot, though," he said as he chuckled.

"I can't believe I killed a rabbit," Autumn said, frowning sadly.

"Big picture, Autumn," Avery said as he casually sent an arrow through the skull of a Shadow behind her.

Autumn shook her head clear. "Right."

After walking for half an hour and taking down another eight Shadows, Autumn realized why this forest looked so different from Arbor Falls. "Do Atrums not live in trees?" she asked.

Avery shook his head. "They live in the rocks," he said, nodding to their right. "Those are the Hollow Mountains."

"Oh. I thought that was just where Vyra—" Avery slapped a hand over Autumn's mouth, silencing her.

Voices. Shadows didn't speak, but Atrums did. Autumn and

Avery both stopped in their tracks, pulling out an arrow and aiming it at the spot where the hushed voices were growing steadily louder, leaves and twigs crunching beneath the owners' feet.

Suddenly Cera and Forrest entered through the trees and both let out loud curses as they ducked. Autumn and Avery's arrows shot through the trees overhead as they realized at the last second who the voices belonged to.

"Holy petalsies, you guys!" Cera exclaimed. "You just scared the hell out of us."

"Sorry," Autumn muttered, threading her arm back through her bow.

"Holy petalsies?" Forrest laughed, looking at his partner.

Cera shrugged dismissively and turned back to Autumn and Avery. "Why are you guys so close to the Hollow Mountains?"

"The rocks run down the middle of the island. We figured they would lead us right to the silver roses," Avery answered.

"Good idea," Forrest said.

"Yeah," Cera frowned. "Except for Vyra lives somewhere in those mountains."

The four of them stood there awkwardly for a minute.

"So, should we carry on together, then?" Forrest asked.

The other three nodded. Autumn sighed in relief, immediately feeling safer with the increased number. She noticed that there was a bird resting on Forrest's shoulder.

"Is he your guide?" she asked.

Forrest nodded. "He flies up for a bit and then comes and tells us which way to go. We're nearly to the silver roses, I think."

"Good," Autumn said in relief.

"How many Shadows have you come across?" Cera asked as they began walking again.

"Only about ten," Avery said.

"Really?" said Forrest, sounding surprised. "We've killed over twenty of them. Maybe there are more in the forest part than this rocky part."

"Any Atrums?" Autumn asked.

"None," Cera said.

Autumn wondered if she was the only one a little unnerved by their lack of opposition.

They heard someone running quickly in their direction and all four of them raised their bows in preparation to shoot. Suddenly Kyndel burst through the trees and then let out a piercing scream when she saw four arrows pointed at her chest, immediately disappearing. Autumn sighed in exasperation as they lowered their bows.

"Kyndel, it's just us," Forrest said, suppressing a laugh.

Kyndel reappeared, looking both relieved and terrified, her chest was heaving and sweat poured in rivulets down her face.

"What happened?" Autumn asked with a frown. "Where's Victor?"

"They took him!" she said, slightly hysterical.

"Who took him?" Forrest asked.

"The Atrums!" she said, gasping for breath. "About ten of them showed up and then they all disappeared into thin air! Including Victor."

"All of them disappeared?" Autumn asked in disbelief. "How? Elves can't do that unless it's their actual Power."

"I don't know, Princess, I was busy getting the hell out of there," she snapped.

"Okay, okay, calm down, Kyn," Forrest said. "Summer here was only wondering how all ten of those Atrums could just disappear, taking Victor with them, without any outside magic."

"Well obviously they had outside magic," Avery said. "The question is, from where. I'm guessing Vyra has recruited a couple of warlocks to do her bidding."

"Now we have warlocks to worry about too?" Kyndel whined. "How am I supposed to fight off a warlock on my own?"

"You won't be on your own. You'll be with us. Right, Cera?" Forrest said, looking to his right, then realizing Cera wasn't there.

"Cera?" Autumn said, looking around.

Her eyes landed on three Shadows holding Cera's broken body, her eyes hauntingly blank. Autumn breathed in a shuddering gasp. Avery yelled at her to stun them and she had to force herself to breathe so she could let out a piercing jet of Song at the three Shadows. Their eyes rolled back, and Cera's body slipped from their hooves, dropping with a sickening thump as it hit the ground.

Ambush

CHAPTER FORTY

Avery and Forrest pounced on the three Shadows, Forrest stabbing one through the heart with his knife and Avery snapping the other two Shadows' necks. The creatures slumped to the ground, forming a semi-circle around Cera's body. A sob escaped Forrest's lips and Avery's strong arms caught Autumn as she lost the ability to stand upright. Silent tears rolled down her face as Avery pulled her close to his body. She couldn't help but stare at Cera's vacant expression, which had been full of life and laughter not long before.

Taking a deep breath, Autumn stepped away from Avery, managing to stand on her own. Forrest knelt over Cera with his eyes squeezed tightly shut, tears streaming down his long nose and falling heavily to the ground. Avery moved to close Cera's staring eyes. Autumn turned to see Kyndel staring at Cera's body in apparent shock, her face a delicate shade of green and her tawny eyes sparkling with tears.

"We can't just leave her like this," Autumn choked out.

"We'll have to bury her here," Avery said.

"Here?" Forrest asked in disgust.

"What else can we do?" Avery said.

"Carry her," Forrest stated. Avery examined Forrest's grief-stricken face and nodded, bending to pick up Cera's limp body.

"No," Forrest stated. "I'll do it."

"But, Forrest," Autumn began, about to state that Avery's

Power would easily allow him to carry her.

"It's okay, Autumn," Avery said softly. "Let him carry her."

Autumn looked at him with wide, searching eyes and understood that Forrest probably felt that it was his duty to carry his partner through until the end.

"That's two," Kyndel said in a dead voice. Autumn looked at her questioningly and then realized that she was talking about Victor and Cera. Two less Warriors. Autumn refused to think they'd lost anyone else or examine her feelings about the fact that Victor might not be alive.

"We should keep going," Autumn said in a dull voice. "The silver roses aren't far from here."

Forrest bent to pick Cera up into his arms, carrying her as if she were a small child, and with her petite frame, it wasn't difficult to picture her as one. Cera's big personality always overshadowed her small stature, but now that it was gone—Autumn shook her head to rid herself of these unwanted thoughts and trudged forward through the forest, the other three walking soundlessly behind her, the shock of losing Cera still hanging thick in the air.

As they neared the middle of the island, the Shadows came more frequently, though the Atrums were still noticeably absent. Autumn and Avery did most of the killing. Kyndel walked clumsily behind them in silence, stumbling over the sporadic tree roots. Forrest followed, cradling Cera's body tightly in his arms.

Forrest sent the bird that had been silently perched on his shoulder up to see how close they were to the silver roses. When the bird returned, he tweeted softly into Forrest's ear. "They're just ahead of us," Forrest said, the strain of carrying Cera's body evident in his voice.

The four of them quickened their pace slightly as they saw a circular clearing up ahead with a large, flat stone in the middle where five silver roses lay untouched. They broke into the clearing, looking at the roses in awe. Autumn's heart rose and fell just as quickly. They were the first ones to make it there.

Suddenly malevolent laughter filled the clearing followed by, "Why, hello there, Princess." There was a flash of light and Autumn's world went black.

AVERY's heart dropped to his stomach as he yelled out, "Autumn!"

But it was too late. She was already gone, disappeared to some unknown location.

Avery, Forrest, and Kyndel stood back-to-back in the middle of the clearing where the five silver roses lay forgotten on their flat, marble stone. Atrums and Shadows alike surrounded the clearing. The three Warriors stood in the eye of the storm.

Avery heard Forrest whisper urgently and the bird on his shoulder flew quickly away.

"Disappear," Avery murmured to Kyndel. "Go get help."

"But—"

"Go," he urged.

The Atrums were busy laughing and boasting about capturing the princess that they weren't paying any attention to the three remaining Warriors. Kyndel took a shuddering breath before vanishing. Avery hoped she could find a place to escape in the tightening circle of Shadows and Atrums.

"What do we do with those two?" a scratchy voice said.

"I thought there was a girl too," another remarked.

"Nah, just that dead one right there." The first one laughed, sending a wave of hatred and disgust through Avery. He felt Forrest stiffen beside him.

"Miss Vyra said to get rid of 'em."

"Excellent," another Atrum said, cracking his knuckles and sneering at Forrest and Avery.

"Get 'em, Shadows," the other commanded. "I have to save my energy for when the prince arrives."

Dozens of Shadows moved slowly towards the two Warriors, their hoofed feet pawing the ground menacingly. The Atrums, however, had made the critical mistake of leaving Avery and Forrest with their bows and arrows.

Avery pulled out a handful of arrows and took down a line of Shadows in a matter of seconds. Forrest followed his lead. Avery emptied his quiver of arrows as Shadow after Shadow collapsed to the ground.

"Oi! You were supposed to take their bow and arrows away, you idiot!" an Atrum exclaimed angrily.

"Don't blame it on—" The Atrum was cut off by an arrow through his heart.

Avery and Forrest looked wildly around for the source of the arrow, seeing as both of their quivers had been emptied.

Suddenly a thick fog rolled through the clearing, hiding the two boys from view, just as dark clouds appeared overhead. A ring of lightning struck the ground with a loud CRACK followed by shouts of pain from the Atrums.

Avery ran forward to help the others. The fog was too thick for him to differentiate the Atrums from the Warriors so he stuck to the Shadows, snapping their necks as easily as if they were small twigs. He leapt over a Shadow's body and landed on one of Crystal's patches of ice. It seemed as though everyone else had made it this far through the Warrior Trial.

Charlotte pulled her fog back in, revealing a clearing littered with the bodies of Atrums and Shadows.

Avery's stomach dropped as he scanned the trees lining the clearing. More Shadows. Moving towards the clearing as slow and steady as Charlotte's fog.

"There's too many of them!" Crystal shouted.

Luke kept up a constant stream of lightning and wind, creating a barrier between the Warriors and the Shadows. His face was twisted in concentration and sweat streamed down his forehead. His legs were beginning to shake from the effort.

Suddenly the clearing was filled with the sound of beating wings. Avery's hair was blown back as he looked up at five pegasi hovering above them. Forrest's messenger bird was flitting around their heads. The relief emanating from the Warriors was palpable as the pegasi landed beside them.

"Jastin, Charlotte—take your rose and go tell Atticus what's happened!" Avery ordered. "Kyndel and Crystal—go with them. Forrest—take Cera's body back."

"Where's Autumn?" Crystal asked in a slightly hysterical voice.

"The Atrums took her to Vyra's lair."

At this statement Luke's Power failed, allowing the Shadows to break into the clearing.

"Go!" Avery shouted.

Forrest grabbed his silver rose before lifting Cera's body onto a nearby pegasus, climbing on as the winged horse shot into the air. Jastin and Charlotte followed his lead. Kyndel and Crystal swiped their roses from the marble stone and jumped onto their own pegasus.

Avery grabbed a rose and climbed onto Luke's pegasus just as a Shadow leapt at him. The pegasus sprung into the air, leaving behind the Shadows and their echoing growls.

"Where are we going?" Luke exclaimed.

"To save your sister," Avery stated as he turned the pegasus towards the Hollow Mountains.

Vyra's Lair

CHAPTER FORTY-ONE

Autumn blinked dazedly as her eyes came in and out of focus. When things finally stopped spinning, she found that she was no longer in the forest, but sitting in a dark, damp room made of stone. Immediately she was reminded of the time she visited Kilmainham Gaol in Dublin, an ancient, supposedly haunted, prison. At the time, it had been one of the creepiest places she'd ever visited. Now she would gladly live there after seeing this place.

She took in the small window with the steel bars, the dirty floor, and the moss-covered wall. How anything grew here, she wasn't sure. Autumn shuddered from cold and fear. It was at least fifteen degrees colder in here than it had been outside.

She moved to stand, but soon realized that she was chained to the floor by thick, steel manacles. *That's just excellent*, she thought, looking over her shoulder to see that someone had removed her bow and quiver full of arrows. She pulled at the chains desperately, accomplishing nothing before sighing in defeat and looking around the floor for something to aid her in breaking free.

"You won't be getting out of those anytime soon," a cold voice said, followed by a mirthless laugh.

Autumn's head spun to the doorway to see a woman with gray-tinged skin standing there wearing an amused expression. Her long, black hair and haunting, violet eyes told Autumn precisely who she was.

"*Vyra*," Autumn spat before belting a jet of angry Song at her.

Vyra smirked, folding her arms across her chest, waiting for her song to finish. Autumn stopped singing abruptly, her face full of confusion.

"While I would love to listen to your disgustingly beautiful, little voice, I don't particularly have the time."

"How—?"

"This room has been enchanted to keep only its prisoners Powerless. Nice try, though." She laughed again and Autumn shuddered at the sound.

"So, you *are* working with warlocks," Autumn said.

Vyra arched a brow and smirked. "More or less."

Autumn shot her a glare, hatred overpowering fear. "You destroyed my family. You took my parents away from my brother and me. They had done nothing to you! They didn't even live in the Underground and you still killed them. You're a monster."

Vyra pointed at Autumn and something purple shot from her finger. Suddenly every nerve in Autumn's body was on fire, her limbs shaking and convulsing involuntarily. Just as quickly as it came, the feeling was gone. She looked weakly up at Vyra, too stunned to speak.

"Electricity," Vyra stated simply. "Hurts, doesn't it? Your parents are lucky I killed them the way I did. In their sleep. Very humane of me, really."

"Or very cowardly," Autumn said in disgust. "You took everything from me that night. *Everything.*"

"No. I *would* have taken everything had you and your brother been home. Unfortunately, by the time I did away with your parents, the potion I'd taken to repel all physical attacks had nearly worn off."

"Afraid you couldn't take on two little teenage kids?" Autumn spat.

Vyra ignored her. "It's no matter. Now I can finish the job."

"What do you want with the Oaken family anyway? You have your Atrums and your Shadows and the fear of the creatures of the Underground."

A malicious smile spread across Vyra's face. "Yes, well. It's nothing personal, *Sweetheart.* Your family is simply in my way. Do you actually think I feel any remorse for killing your precious parents when I killed *my own*? Somehow they expected me to allow them to tell me what to do." She laughed. "The Oaken family has been my main focus for years now. They're the only thing standing in the way of me taking over the entire kingdom. Two Oaken down, three to go. Soon to be two."

Scooting back against the grimy wall, Autumn attempted to put as much distance between Vyra and herself as possible. "You can do what you want with me, but you will not touch my brother."

Vyra laughed heartily at this as she sauntered closer. "Your brother is on my island at this very minute, Love. It's only a matter of time before one of my Atrums captures him as well. Your little Warrior Trial made this exceptionally easy for me. Disappointing, really. I was hoping for more of a challenge."

"How did you even know about the Warrior Trial?"

Vyra strolled slowly through the small, frigid room, keeping her cold, violet eyes trained on her royal prisoner. Autumn's own narrowed eyes followed Vyra as she made her way around the room.

"Oh, I know everything about you and your little friends. Let's see..." She steepled her hands and placed them under her chin in a thoughtful manner. "*You* have a sickening need to help people, whether you get anything out of it or not. You hate killing living things, but have no problem killing my precious Shadows. You're an excellent fighter, and a skilled archer, but you're much too trusting for your own good. You have a handsome little boyfriend, a castle guard I believe, which you've managed to keep secret from your beloved grandfather. Your twin brother is your best friend, and he's rather protective of you. He'd be so terribly upset if he knew where you were at this very moment."

Autumn's mouth hung open as Vyra spouted out so many personal and extremely accurate details that few people could possibly know about her. She narrowed her eyes in suspicion.

"How did you—?"

Vyra laughed again, clearly enjoying this. "I have a reliable source."

"You mean someone's been spying on me?" Autumn asked in disbelief.

"I suppose that would be an accurate statement. This particular elf has been rather beneficial to me. Capturing you would not have been possible without their help."

"Who?"

"You will meet soon enough, let's not be hasty," she said, wagging her finger at Autumn. "Though, you've met before."

"We've met?"

Vyra nodded and then laughed, saying, "Oh, this is fun."

Autumn glared at her in disgust.

There was a noise from somewhere outside of the doorway. Vyra turned to look, and then faced Autumn, smirking. "Ah, here they are now. I believe it's time you were re-introduced to my informant," Vyra said, waving a hand at the doorway. "Autumn Oaken meet my brother, Victor Vaun."

Victor stepped inside the doorway and Autumn stared, wide-eyed, up at him.

"Victor...*Vaun* ?"

Victor looked narrowly down at Autumn and came to stand beside Vyra—his sister.

"Yes, this is my adorable little brother," Vyra said, clearly pleased with Autumn's reaction.

"Your brother," Autumn said in disbelief. "I thought—I thought you killed your brother."

Vyra nodded. "Yes, that's what I told everyone. You see, I realized that my dear baby brother was much more valuable to me alive than dead. So, I decided to keep him around."

Autumn glanced at Victor, who didn't seem fazed by this in the least. Looking at him made her even more nauseated than she already was, so she turned back to Vyra, who continued on.

"So, after I did away with our parents, I sent Victor to live in Arbor Falls to gain the trust of the residents of the kingdom. His main goal, though, was to become a Warrior. But he went and killed that little elf girl and screwed things up quite a bit."

Victor stirred slightly at this, but said nothing.

"Killed...?" Autumn said trailing off and then realization struck her, causing her head to spin and stomach to churn. "*Avabelle*? Avery's sister?"

"Yes, her!" Vyra said, smacking herself dramatically in the head. "I always forget her name."

"You killed Avabelle?" Autumn said to Victor in disbelief. He didn't make eye contact, but nodded unfeelingly.

Autumn absentmindedly moved her hand to touch her own neck, but her hand was stopped by the manacles. "But Avery said the Shadow killed her."

"You silly girl," Vyra said. "The Shadow was just a cover up. Victor strangled the poor girl and then called a Shadow to batter her body up a bit so the elves wouldn't suspect him. Victor can control the Shadows. They were made with *his* blood, you know. And, as long as Victor is alive, they will continue to multiply, which is why he is so very special to me," she said, gazing lovingly up at her brother.

Autumn felt like she was going to be sick, but she swallowed the bile that rose in her throat to speak again. "Why would you kill Avabelle?"

"Victor has a bit of an anger problem," Vyra said, patting Victor fondly on the arm. "I believe you already know that, though," she said, nodding at Autumn's neck. "So nice of you not to tattle on him, by the way. Foolish perhaps, but still nice."

Autumn silently had to agree with her on this, trying not to think about how different things might have turned out if she *had* told someone about what Victor had done.

"Yes, that little choking incident put a bit of a damper on our original plan," Vyra said absently before turning to speak to Victor. "Though you weren't actually supposed to *date* her, you idiot. I said to befriend her and her brother, not woo her."

"It was the only way," Victor said through gritted teeth, as though it was a frequently repeated phrase.

"Doubtful, but no matter. She's here now and her brother will soon join her."

"What about the others," Autumn said. "Where are they?"

"My Atrums were instructed to kill the others. I've no use for them," she said waving a hand dismissively.

Autumn felt her heart sink.

No. They couldn't be dead. They got out of it somehow. They had to.

"You were right, Victor, she does value the wellbeing of others above her own. Foolish girl," Vyra said, shaking her head in disapproval.

Suddenly a short, husky Atrum came panting into the room. "Your Highness, the Oaken boy has made it to the roses, but we are unable to approach him. He came, knowing we were waiting for him and opened attack. There are others as well. I barely managed to get away." His voice shook in fear.

Vyra let out a frustrated shout and pointed her index finger at the quivering man. The purple streak of light hit him in the chest and he fell to the floor, convulsing. Autumn almost felt sorry for him. Almost.

"Fools!" Vyra bellowed and then sighed heavily in frustration. "Must I do *everything* around here?" She turned abruptly to look at Autumn and then to Victor. "Victor, Darling, watch her for me. It would appear that my servants are incapable of even the simplest of tasks. Looks like you won't be the first of the twins to die, Princess. Oh, goodie! I can bring your brother's body here for you to get a little taste of what you have coming!" she said joyfully, clapping her hands together.

Autumn's heart temporarily stopped.

AVERY and Luke pushed their pegasus to the limit towards the towering mass of rocks that was Vyra's Lair.

"Where do you think she is?" Luke asked.

Avery hadn't thought that far. "She could be anywhere," he admitted, trying not to feel too hopeless.

"Look for the tallest room in the highest tower, or the highest room in the tallest tower. Either one," Luke called out over the wind howling in their ears.

"What? Why?"

"It's what all the people in the fairytale books do!"

Avery shrugged. It was worth a shot.

"*Not so fast,*" a cackling voice called from below just before a jet of purple light struck their pegasus, immobilizing her wings, her body going rigid. They plummeted from the sky, crashing against a slope of rock, and rolling down amidst a landslide of rubble until they reached the bottom. Avery and Luke groaned as they sat up to see Vyra Vaun approaching them with an amused smile dancing on her cracked lips.

"Fancy meeting you boys here," she said with a sickening laugh. "So nice of you not to make me travel all that way to get you."

Luke cursed at her as he lunged forward. Vyra lazily held out single finger and a beam of purple streaked through the air, hitting Luke in the chest. He let out a strangled cry and collapsed to the ground, trembling and shuddering until Vyra released her Electricity.

"You're just as foolish as your sister," she said, shaking her head sadly back and forth.

Luke lay motionless on the ground and for a moment Avery was afraid he was no longer alive until he saw the dark storm cloud forming just behind Vyra.

Avery had to stall.

"What have you done to Autumn?" he shouted at her.

Vyra moved her gaze from Luke and flashed Avery an amused grin. "Let me guess, you're Autumn's little lover boy. Victor's arch-nemesis."

Avery temporarily forgot that he was supposed to be distracting Vyra because now *he* was the distracted one. "Victor? How do you—?"

"Oh, right. I forgot your girlfriend is the only one who knows," she said, tapping at her chin. "What the heck, I'll be killing you soon anyway, right? But I've little reason to tell you this. You've always known what my brother truly is."

"Your brother..." Avery frowned before he understood what she was saying. "Victor's your *brother*?"

Vyra laughed madly, slapping her hands together like a mentally unwell person who'd been stuck in a white room for too long. "It's even more fun the second time around!"

The cogs in Avery's mind kicked into high gear as everything started clicking into place. "He's been spying on all of us, hasn't he? That's why you knew we would be here and why all of those Atrums and Shadows were waiting to ambush us."

"Aren't you a little smarty!" Vyra said with a cackle. "It took your girlfriend much longer to—"

Vyra's words were cut off by a bolt of lightning shooting out of the full-blown storm cloud Luke had clandestinely conjured.

"*Bitch*," Luke growled.

Vyra lay motionless, but Avery had a feeling she was still very much alive. He didn't have time to worry about that, though, because a wave of Shadows and Atrums were now charging towards them.

AUTUMN stared daggers at Victor, who kept his eyes averted.

"You're pathetic," she spat at him. Victor's jaw clenched as he continued to look away from her, his emerald eyes slowly growing black. "You're a disgusting, pathetic, murderer. Avery trusted you!" He continued to glare at the floor. "Look at me you coward!"

Victor's eyes flashed to hers then, full of anger and something else she couldn't identify. "I am many things, Autumn, but a coward is not one of them."

"You are the very definition of a coward, Victor Vaun."

"Do not presume you know me. I have done things that you could never even dream of. Things a coward could never do," he said, looking away again.

"Things *only* a coward could do," she snarled.

"You know nothing."

"I know enough," she retorted, which was true. She knew enough about the boy before her, simply from what she'd witnessed and from what Vyra—his *sister*—had said to know that he was exactly what everyone said he was.

An Atrum.

That was all he would ever be, and she had been naïve enough to think otherwise.

"Everyone was right about you," Autumn said, voicing her thoughts. Victor remained silent. "Everyone but me."

Victor's eyes narrowed as he glanced towards her, on the verge of lunging at her throat.

His mouth opened to speak just as an arrow soared through the barred window, piercing through his chest, and spraying blood across the grimy floor.

Aftermath

CHAPTER FORTY-TWO

Autumn gasped, looking wildly around. She spotted Avery and Luke *hovering* outside of the barred window looking like they'd been through a lot more than she had. Their faces were bruised, eyes blackened, lips swollen.

"Luke! Avery!" Autumn said in disbelief, watching Avery effortlessly pull out the steel bars of the window and squeeze through. He rushed over to her and ripped the manacles off her wrists, pulling her into a tight hug. "How—What—?"

"Later," he said, pulling her to the small window. She looked out to see Luke sitting on a tired-looking pegasus waiting for them in midair. His face filled with relief when he saw her.

Just then, the door to the cell slammed open and Avery pushed Autumn out of the small window onto the pegasus, simultaneously shooting an arrow over his shoulder. Autumn heard a screech and saw a flash of purple, which narrowly missed Avery as he jumped out of the window, landing on the pegasus behind Autumn.

"Go!" Avery shouted.

The winged horse immediately obeyed and soared over the rocky cliffs, dodging flashes of purple light.

"Did you get her?" Autumn asked breathlessly after they had gotten far enough away from Vyra's Lair.

"I think I just got her leg," Avery said.

"Where are Crystal and the others?" she asked, worried to hear the answer.

"They're all safe," Avery said giving Autumn the details of what happened in the clearing after she disappeared.

"And Cera?" she asked.

"Forrest brought her back with him," Avery said in a reserved voice.

The three of them were quiet for a moment. The pegasus soared over the Opacious Sea and Autumn let out a sigh of relief as she turned to see Vyra's Lair slowly shrinking behind them.

"I can't believe you got away from Vyra," Autumn said, thinking back on what Avery had told her. "She's so much worse than I imagined."

"She's batshit crazy, that's what she is," Luke said.

A large group of elves was waiting for them as they landed. The rest of the Initiates surrounded the pegasus and pulled Autumn, Luke, and Avery into relieved hugs as they climbed off. Crystal burst into tears when she saw them and wrapped Autumn in a bone-crushing hug, refusing to let go for quite a while. Looking past her mane of platinum hair, Autumn noticed all five of the silver roses lying forgotten in a heap on the black sand.

Atticus approached them, looking grave.

"Victor!" Autumn shouted to him, unable at first to form a coherent sentence. The others whipped around to look behind Atticus, thinking she'd seen him, and then turned back to look at Autumn with puzzled faces. "Victor is Vyra's brother. His name is Victor Vaun, not Lavigne."

Everyone looked at her with thunderstruck expressions. The blood drained from Atticus's face.

"How can that be?" Jastin said, the first to find his voice. "Vyra *killed* her brother."

"She didn't," Autumn explained. "She just told everyone she did. She needed someone to spy on the elves of Arbor Falls and decided that Victor would be the best to do this."

"And Victor went along with this? Why?" Charlotte said in disbelief.

Now, *this* Autumn didn't know. "Maybe he wanted to prove himself to her. She is his older sister, after all."

"You spoke to Vyra?" Atticus asked. Autumn nodded. "What else did she say?" he urged. Autumn screwed up her face in concentration, trying to relay as much of their conversation as she could remember, leaving out the part about Avabelle. Now was not the time.

"Why wouldn't she kill you right away?" Jastin asked.

"She's sort of crazy," Luke said. "Like off her rocker crazy."

"You talked to her too?" Atticus asked, turning to Luke.

"He more than talked to her," Avery said. "He struck her with lightning."

The others looked at Luke in awe.

"How did you all get away?" Charlotte asked in horror.

"We killed several Shadows and Atrums before we were able to get our pegasus up and flying," Avery answered.

"And Luke and Avery broke me out of that little prison tower," Autumn added.

"Vyra just left you alone in there?" Jastin asked in surprise.

"Victor was there," Autumn said and looked to Avery for permission to tell the rest. He nodded solemnly. "Avery shot him with an arrow."

There was a collective intake of breath and everyone looked at Avery in surprise. Avery was the only one who knew what Victor did to her. She looked at him wearily, hoping he wouldn't bring it up.

"I did what I had to do to get Autumn out of there," he said.

"So, Victor's dead?" Kyndel asked.

"I'm a good shot. Trust me. He's dead," Avery said.

Forrest glanced back at Cera's body, which was lying on a bed of leaves. "We should get back," he said sadly.

The Tetra Warriors that had been listening to their exchanges in sober silence suddenly came to life, getting the pegasi together and helping the now Quinn Warriors onto them.

Autumn and Avery climbed onto their pegasus, but this time he had her ride in front. She realized it was because he wanted to be able to hold her as he wrapped his arms tightly around her waist. She leaned back against him, the comforting and familiar magnetic pull soothing her nerves. Their pegasus took off and began the journey back to Arbor Falls.

Looking back at Alder Island, Autumn realized with a mixture of pride and regret that she was leaving her former innocence behind with it.

The Burial

CHAPTER FORTY-TWO

The Quinns' return to Arbor Falls was bittersweet. It was hard to feel like they had accomplished something when they had come back with two less elves than they left with. No one was all that concerned with the loss of Victor now that they all knew his true identity, but the loss of Cera had truly taken away any sense of victory they might have felt otherwise for making it through the Warrior Trial.

After all, they had broken their pact.

That night Atticus had the Quinns meet in the Warrior training tree and informed them that the two alternates next in line had begun their intensive training. They just stared up at him sadly, not at all cheered by this news. If anything, it made the situation that much more depressing. They didn't *want* any new Warriors. They had been a family. If anything, it felt like they were replacing Cera.

"I understand how difficult this is for all of you," Atticus began. "Trust me, it's difficult for me too, but we have to continue on. Death is part of being a Warrior. I'm sorry to say that she will not be the first loss you have to suffer through. I know the alternates can never replace her, but they are essential to the Quinns. Ember and Edric will be arriving shortly and I sincerely hope that you will welcome them with open arms. Think of how difficult it will be for them to come into this, knowing how you all feel about the situation."

Everyone nodded in unison, looking no happier than they had before his little speech. When the alternates arrived, the Quinns stood to greet them. Autumn didn't know about the others, but she was not getting the best vibe from these particular elves. She figured that being an alternate would cause them to feel slightly inferior to the actual Warriors who'd been through months of training and a grueling Warrior Trial, but these two looked exactly the opposite.

The girl, Ember Burns, scanned the Quinns with a raised eyebrow, as if to imply that she wasn't all that impressed. With flaming red hair that fell just past her shoulders and amber eyes that looked like two burning hot coals, she definitely lived up to her name. Atticus didn't even have to tell them what her Power was for Autumn to know that it was Fire. Crystal was already frowning at Ember in dislike.

The boy, Edric Ogden, had perfect, platinum blond hair that looked as if it took him all morning to style. His pale blue eyes were piercing and somewhat cold. His smile looked a little too forced and didn't quite reach his eyes. His Power was a Shield. He could erect a sort of invisible armor in front of himself or someone else, an offensive power that the Quinns could definitely benefit from.

They all politely introduced themselves to Ember and Edric. Kyndel's new partner would be Edric and Ember was now Forrest's partner. Atticus had the four of them leave for the training field to become more acquainted with each other. Autumn didn't envy them.

The next morning Autumn woke up with a feeling of dread resting like a stone in the pit of her stomach. It was the day of Cera's funeral. She squeezed her eyes tightly shut, trying to rid herself of the vision of Cera's vacant expression, her broken body, the sound of it hitting the forest floor. Autumn started when she heard a THUMP coming from her balcony. Avery.

She didn't feel like talking about how she felt, so she pulled the covers stubbornly over her head. Autumn heard Avery open her balcony doors and chuckle at the sight of her.

"I know you're awake," he said.

"Nope," Autumn replied, her voice muffled by her bedding.

Rather than ripping the bedding off of her, Avery lifted the covers and crawled underneath to lie beside her. The material surrounded them like a warm embrace. He pulled her close to him so that her face rested in the nape of his neck. Hot tears spilled out of her eyes.

"I knew you'd be blaming yourself for this," Avery said.

"If I would have been paying attention to everything instead of bickering with Kyndel—"

"Autumn, stop. It doesn't do any good to obsess over what you could have done. It won't change anything."

"I know, but—"

"Autumn."

"Fine," she sighed.

"Uh, are we interrupting something?" Luke said from somewhere within Autumn's room.

Autumn and Avery sat up quickly, pulling the covers down. Crystal and Luke stood at the foot of the bed with amused looks on their faces—well, Luke's expression was a little more disapproving and disgusted than amused. Autumn felt herself blush slightly and laughed when she saw that Avery's cheeks were flushed as well.

"May we join you?" Crystal asked. Autumn raised an eyebrow at her and Crystal let out a lilting laugh as she climbed onto the base of the bed to sit with her legs crossed. Luke frowned for a second, but then decided to join them.

"Do you think we're going to get along with those alternates?" Autumn asked.

Crystal made a sour face and said, "I don't really care for that Ember girl."

"Course you don't," Luke said with a laugh. "Her power is Fire. Haven't you heard fire and ice don't quite mix? That Edric Ogden just rubs me the wrong way. I don't think I care for him myself."

"Just because he's been with more girls at this school than *you* have," Avery said, receiving a glare from Luke. Autumn and Crystal laughed.

"It's going to be weird working with the Tetras now. It's just been the ten of us for so long," Crystal said.

"It's going to be weird doing something other than just

training," Autumn said. "We're actually going to be protecting Arbor Falls now, and fighting for real."

The others nodded with dazed looks as they took this in.

They changed into their Warrior uniforms for Cera's funeral as a sign of respect. Though Cera never made it through the Warrior Trial, she was still a Warrior to them.

The funeral was being held in the Warrior Burial Grounds, where all of the Warriors had been laid to rest over the history of the Underground. As they approached the burial grounds Autumn felt an overwhelming sense of peace emanating through the air. Forrest, Kyndel, Charlotte, and Jastin were already there waiting for them.

Autumn's head felt like it was in a fuzzy bubble as the funeral began. She couldn't quite process the fact that Cera was really gone. The Quinns watched with tears spilling down each of their cheeks as her small body was lowered gently into the ground. Autumn absentmindedly began to sing a slow, peaceful melody as her way of saying goodbye to Cera. She made sure to direct her song at Cera's grave so that no one was hypnotized. Forrest asked a few mockingbirds to join in. The birds and Autumn sang as each Warrior dropped a single, black rose into Cera's grave, an elf tradition.

Everyone began to leave and the Warriors squeezed closer together as they took in the sight of Cera's newly covered grave. Olympus was in attendance as well and used his Power to cover the new dirt in fine grass and beautiful, purple flowers. Rather than erecting a headstone, the elves cut down a tree, burning Cera's name into the stump, to represent her loss of life. The burial grounds looked like a land of deforestation.

Suddenly a Duo Warrior, who was supposed to be on guard duty, ran up to the group of Warriors. "There's been an attack on the elves of Willow Glen by Shadows, Atrums, and...Victor Vaun."

"Victor Vaun? But he's dead," Autumn said.

"No. It has been confirmed by their Head Elf. Victor Vaun is very much alive."

ASH

BOOK 2 TEASER

Olympus's Surprise

CHAPTER ONE

Autumn and the other Quinn Warriors crouched down behind an oversized rosebush, peering around the thorned flowers at the elf town in the immense valley below. The Atrums had managed to surround the elf inhabitants of Rose Valley with the help of a band of Shadows and their leader, Victor Vaun. This was Autumn's first time seeing him since watching Avery's arrow pierce through his heart only weeks ago. She had watched the blood spurt from his chest, watched him crumple to the ground. She had been sure he was dead, but there he stood, leading his evil followers into battle.

"Don't screw this up, Ogden," Luke warned Edric.

"Shut it, Oaken. I got this," Edric spit back.

"Now is not the time, lover boys," Forrest said. Luke and Edric both shot a glare his way.

"How much longer?" Kyndel complained.

"We're waiting for Willow's signal," Autumn snapped at her.

As if on cue they saw Willow, in the form of a white eagle, fly low over the valley.

"Now!" Avery shouted.

Autumn jumped out from her hiding place and belted out

a stream of Song as loud as she possibly could, aiming it at the Atrums, Shadows, and Victor. If she had only been aiming it at a couple of Atrums, it would have been a lot stronger, but the more creatures she covered in Song, the weaker her Power was. Rather than hypnotizing them, it simply slowed their reflexes. This was enough, though. The Tetras and Quinns had both opened attack on the Atrums and Shadows.

Edric used his Shield to erect a protective boundary around the Quinns, keeping them from harm. The Atrums in the valley quickly spotted them and sent dozens of flaming arrows their way, ricocheting off Edric's invisible Shield. Luke conjured up a fierce thunderstorm and the Atrums were pelted with rain, sleet, and hail. A tornado materialized from across the valley where the Tetras were stationed, sent by Jack, the small Tetra with enough force to take down fifty Shadows at once.

Meanwhile, Crystal took out ten Atrums with her jet of Ice as Ember did the same with her stream of Fire—the yin and yang of the Quinns. Forrest called for all the unicorns in the area to attack. Autumn watched as the sleek, black creatures galloped as if in slow motion into the valley, piercing any Atrum and Shadow they passed mercilessly through the chest with their deadly horns.

Jastin stunned a horde of Atrums with his Power of Mental Pain while Charlotte shot each one with a well-aimed arrow. Kyndel took down Shadow after Shadow with her own arrows, her Power of Invisibility enabling her to move around freely without being seen.

It became clear that the Atrums and Shadows had not been expecting an outside attack because they soon retreated on Victor's orders. He shot a murderous glare in the Quinns' direction before he and his followers disappeared into thin air, leaving their dead behind to litter the ground like forgotten trash. The Warriors let out cheers of triumph and the elves of Rose Valley came out of their tree homes to thank them for saving their town.

This was not the first time the Warriors had come to the aid of a neighboring elf town. Ever since the Warrior Trial a month before, the Atrums and Shadows had been attacking magical creatures all over the Underground on Vyra's orders. Atticus thought that they were trying to stir things up, hoping to start the second

Underground war. At the rate they were attacking, this seemed like a highly plausible explanation.

Much had happened since the Warrior Trial. Ember and Edric had both gone through their month of intensive training, nearly dying from exhaustion in the process. They also passed their own Warrior Trials, which Luke said shouldn't count because it was clearly not as difficult as the one the original Quinns had to endure. The two of them wouldn't say what it was they had to do, but everyone knew it didn't involve Alder Island.

"They probably had to fight petalsies or something," Luke had said. He had a minor problem with Edric Ogden, who had proven to be as much of a ladies' man as Luke himself.

"Or some fay fairies," Forrest had added.

For the past month the Quinns had been working with the Tetras much more frequently, especially when they were called to fight the Atrums and Shadows. Autumn got along with most of the Tetras, except for Candi, and this was mostly because she wore an ever-present frown and hated royals.

Autumn and the others still mourned the loss of Cera. She had been such a source of light and warmth to the Quinns. Visions of her death continuously haunted Autumn's nightmares. Atticus said that they were lucky they'd only lost one Warrior because of how dangerous the situation had been.

One of the only things that *hadn't* changed was that Autumn and Avery were still together—their red rose showcased in a glass case on Autumn's vanity, reminiscent of her favorite childhood fairytale. They had managed to keep their relationship a secret from everyone but Luke and Crystal. Dating a castle worker was still against Olympus's rules so they planned to keep it that way until after graduation in a few months when Avery would be receiving payment as a Warrior and would no longer work as a castle guard.

After accepting the praise and thanks of the inhabitants of Rose Valley, the Quinns and Tetras flew back to Arbor Falls. Autumn and Luke's winged horses, Thunder and Sundance, were finally old enough to ride. Sundance stayed true to her name, gliding over the setting sun as if she were dancing on the rays of sunlight. Luke flew next to Autumn on Thunder, who had definitely lived up to his name as well. His sleek, black body was easily the largest of all the other pegasi and he wasn't even full-grown yet.

Avery rode Knight on Autumn's other side and Crystal flew beside Luke upon her new pegasus, Pisces. Crystal was still uncomfortable with flying, but was slowly becoming used to it. Though, she didn't like doing the tricks Luke, Avery, and Autumn did, weaving and flipping between, above, and around one another.

"Could you guys just stay put? You're making me nervous," she called as Luke and Autumn coaxed Sundance and Thunder to do a barrel roll around each other.

"Sorry, Crys," Autumn said with a laugh, leveling Sundance out as Luke did the same with Thunder.

"We fight Atrums and Shadows every day," Luke said. "But *flying* makes you nervous."

"The flying doesn't make me nervous, but all of the flipping does."

"Don't worry, Crys," Luke said. "I'll teach you how."

Crystal frowned at this and Autumn and Avery exchanged an amused glance.

After they landed and put their pegasi back into their stables, they trudged up to the castle for dinner.

"Oh, I have your gown ready for your birthday ball," Crystal said, more animated now that they were on solid ground.

Autumn and Luke's eighteenth birthdays were coming up on March 7th, just a little over a week away. Olympus was having a grand ball in honor of their coming of age. Apparently it was a big deal or something. Avery laughed at Autumn's indifference.

"Turning 18 is extremely significant in the Underground, especially for royals," he'd said when she told him she didn't care about coming of age.

Autumn had simply shrugged. "It's just an age. It's not like I'll be any different or anything."

Avery shook his head in exasperation, smiling nonetheless.

When they entered Arbor Castle, Autumn and Luke were approached by a castle worker who informed them that they were to have dinner with Olympus that night. They said goodbye to Avery and Crystal and went up to their braches to change out of their Warrior gear and become presentable for dinner with their grandfather.

"Wonder what he wants to talk to us about," Autumn said to Luke as they traveled down the spiral staircase towards Olympus's living quarters.

"He probably just wants to congratulate us on saving Rose Valley from your ex-boyfriend and his stupid evil followers."

Autumn glared at him. She hated when he referred to Victor Vaun as her "ex-boyfriend." It brought back too many unpleasant memories.

When they approached the doors to Olympus's living quarters, the burly guards standing watch smiled at them and opened the double oak doors to allow them entry.

"Ah, children. You look more and more mature each time I see you. Must be your upcoming birthday." Olympus flashed them his white smile surrounded by a flaming red beard. His hazel eyes, a mirror image of the twins' own, twinkled brightly.

"Have a seat," he said, waving his hand at the two vacant chairs situated around the grand dinner table.

A waiter approached the table and Olympus ordered the dragon for the three of them. Autumn did like dragon, but she didn't quite enjoy being ordered for. She never told Olympus this, though. They exchanged light small talk until the food arrived, talking about the Warriors, the most recent attack, and the increased Atrum and Shadow attacks on all the magical creatures.

"Now, for the serious talk," Olympus said after the waiter had left them with steaming plates of dragon meat and mounds of fluffy whipped potatoes. Autumn and Luke glanced up from their food, listening intently. "When royal elves turn 18, a number of things come about. I won't list them off now so as not to overwhelm you. You'll learn everything in time. Tonight I wanted to address one particular change. Now, you may or may not know that on a royal elf's 18th birthday, it is generally announced that they will be the next elf ruler." Autumn and Luke's mouths dropped open and Olympus chuckled. "I suppose you did *not* know then. This is usually done with the oldest of the royal children."

Autumn glanced at Luke. Technically he was older by a couple minutes.

"However," Olympus continued, "because the two of you are twins, I see you as equal in age. You've lived the same amount of days and are equally wise." The twins listened to him with wide eyes. Autumn had to admit that she'd never given much thought to the matter of the next elf ruler. Judging by the look on Luke's face, she wasn't the only one.

"I refuse to choose between my grandchildren so I am giving *you* the job of deciding who will be the next ruler. It will be **your** decision. You have until your 18th birthday to decide."

At these words Autumn and Luke exchanged a quick glance.

"Perhaps I should first ask if both of you are interested in becoming the next ruler," Olympus said.

Autumn frowned at the table, thinking. Did she want to be a queen? It would be a huge responsibility. But then she thought of how many people she could help. How many lives she could change. Helping people had always been a passion of Autumn's—a dream.

Of course she wanted to be the next ruler, to have the power to make a real difference in the Underground. Then she had a thought. "If we were to become the next elf ruler, would we still be Warriors?"

Olympus considered this. "It wouldn't be advisable because of the dangers Warriors face, but I would say that it's up to you. If either of you want to continue being a Warrior in addition to ruling the elf world, then that's your choice."

Autumn and Luke were silent.

"So?" Olympus said. Autumn and Luke both nodded and then exchanged another glance. "Both of you?" Olympus asked. They nodded again. "Well, then, you will have to come to the decision together."

"But don't the men usually get the first pick?" Luke muttered.

Autumn shot him a glare. "Why should the *man* get to choose first? The woman is just as capable of ruling the elves, if not more so."

Luke rolled his eyes. "I highly doubt that. Like the *woman* could actually stand up to another magical creature ruler, since the woman feels the need to make everyone in the Underground happy."

"That is not true!" Autumn protested. "The woman can stand up to other rulers just fine. Besides, it's not like the *man* knows what is best for the elves or has any sense of compassion for anyone other than himself."

"The man has compassion, but he also knows that you can't please everyone."

"The woman never said that she had to please everyone."

"Well the woman sure acts like it."

"You are so stubborn!" Autumn shouted, standing up.

Luke stood as well. "You just can't admit that I would be a better ruler than you. People like me more."

"Ha! If you're talking about all of the girls you make out with then, yeah, I'm sure they do."

Luke turned slightly red. "You just want to use your power to help everyone and make them all happy. Well, that's impossible. You would go crazy trying to be the ruler because there will *always* be someone who's unhappy."

"You just want the power of being on top. *And* you probably think you can command all of the girls in Arbor Falls to bow down at your feet!"

Luke opened his mouth to reply when Olympus cleared his throat, silencing both of them.

"I think it would be best if you two slept on this," he said calmly. "I will send a castle worker up to your branches with some tea to calm you down. Perhaps you would do well to look at things from a different perspective."

Autumn and Luke left Olympus's dining quarters and traveled angrily up to their branches in silence. Luke entered his branch and Autumn traveled the short distance up to her own, slamming the door behind her. This was so typical of Luke, thinking he should be the next ruler just because he was the *man*. Well, if anything, Autumn thought that should count against him.

She plopped heavily down in her armchair by the fire, which had been lit by a castle worker sometime while she was away. Not long after she'd entered her branch, there was a knock on the door. Autumn hoped it was Luke, having come to beg for her forgiveness, but instead she found a castle worker with the tray of tea and cookies that Olympus told them he would send.

Thanking the worker, Autumn returned to her armchair, sipping her tea slowly. She was pleasantly overcome with a sense of calm serenity. Olympus must have asked them to put some sort of draught or something in the tea to calm them down.

As Autumn finished off the rest of her tea, she began to feel extremely drowsy. She moseyed into her bedroom and fell sleepily onto the bed, not even bothering to crawl under the covers.

A ray of sunlight falling across Autumn's face awakened her. It was Sunday morning and she had nowhere that she needed to be. She stretched and rubbed her eyes and then stopped suddenly. Something was wrong. Different. She looked down at her hands. But these weren't her hands. They were way too large, way too rough—like a man's.

Autumn hurriedly got up from her bed, knowing something was definitely not right because she was much taller than she had been last night. When she came to stand before her full-length mirror she let out a loud, bellowing scream. The sound that escaped her mouth was not high pitched like it should have been, but was instead a deep baritone.

She screamed because, looking back at her in the mirror with the same shade of hazel eyes as her own...was Luke.

About the Author

Melody lives in West Texas with her husband and two cats. When she isn't teaching English, she can be found in a cozy coffee shop with a latte and her laptop open to her latest novel, typing madly away with little awareness of the world around her. As a dreamer by nature with an overactive imagination—that is where she is happiest.

Melody can be found online at melodyrobinette.com

39899481R00202

Made in the USA
Lexington, KY
16 March 2015